CW01654549

For Fate's Sake

By Erica Kyles

For Fate's Sake

First published in 2024

ISBN: 978-1-3999-7848-4

TAUK Publishing

"Nobody can bring you peace but yourself."

Ralph Waldo Emerson

DEDICATION

For anyone trying to pick themselves up.

CHAPTER 1

Now

I am not a mother or a career woman. History once forced women to choose between being one or the other. Now, we are encouraged to be both. What does that say about me, a thirty-year-old woman with few prospects? There was a time when I had hope and aspirations about my future. Not anymore. I have become lost in a place I have always known. Devon's vast countryside and picturesque coastline no longer soothe my soul. I feel trapped. I cannot throw away fistfuls of sand and expect the beaches to disappear, so I have to go. As tides inevitably turned, my self-worth got swept away.

It all started with the least likely decision; I decided to wear period pants when it wasn't that time of the month. They weren't the eco-friendly style, but big and fading from black into washed-out grey. The reassuring kind that you don't mind accidentally bleeding onto and that make Bridget Jones's underwear look…sophisticated. If I hadn't worn them, I might not have fallen in love with Tobias. I know I would have remained focused on my career, been content with living in Devon forever and not fallen out with Daisy, my best friend. Maxwell Squire would not have been able to ruin all of those things that I cherished.

Then

I chose that underwear because of the skirt Daisy bought for me during the summer holidays. It was a 'thank-you' for being there after she broke up with her latest beau, but it felt more like a celebration. She was easily bored, but there was always a queue of admirers for her to choose from. She convinced me to wear it on our first day back at university—an admin day. It was the only chance I would have before being covered in fur, saliva and all kinds of animal mess during the second year of my Animal Welfare and Behaviour degree.

I loved the course. It was something I knew I would do from the age of seven, the same year I met Daisy, when my neighbour, Mr Wigglesworth, a retired school caretaker, and I saved a bee's life with sugary water. The bee looked dead as it lay motionless on the path beside a flowerbed of lavender. Mr Wigglesworth wafted the spoon in front of it, and after some encouragement, the bee started drinking the magic potion.

'Look, he poked his nose in the water,' I said.

Mr Wigglesworth laughed. 'That's not his nose, Alice. If you look closer, you'll see his tongue poking out.'

I leant in more. 'Wow!' I said as I watched its brown tongue flick the water like a messy puppy drinking from a water bowl. Its body rippled as it gulped. 'Its bum is wagging like my dog's tail when it's happy.'

'He is happy. We've just saved his life.'

I wish there was a human version of sugary water to help us get back up again. If it existed, I would have drunk litres of the stuff by now. Leaving Devon was never part of my plan. Thank goodness for my cousin Kate, offering me a chance to escape the last decade of my life. For that reason, London was the only option I had.

The bee's wings fluttered and stopped, fluttered again and stopped, then fluttered once more until they were buzzing like the sound of Om. The bee levitated until it was as high as Mr Wigglesworth's face. It danced around him as though curtseying in gratitude before zipping off towards the conifer trees at the rear of the garden. I ran after the bee, waving up at him.

'Bye,' I called out as he flew higher before disappearing. I then felt sad.

'What's wrong, Alice?' Mr Wigglesworth asked.

'I want the bee to come back.'

He placed his hand on my shoulder. 'He's flying home to tell his family that you've given him another chance at life.'

Mr Wigglesworth was right; I had done my bit. I found the bee and then waved him on his way. I pressed back my shoulders and held my head high—that was the moment I knew I wanted to work with animals when I grew up.

Thinking about my inevitable move to London, just like that bee, I wanted my old life to return. Unlike his vanishing act before my innocent eyes, my life faded away more subtly than that. It didn't feel like it, but somewhere deep inside of me, I hoped that it was now my turn to have another chance at living.

There was only one functioning cash machine on campus that morning.

'Alice,' Daisy groaned as she joined me in the queue. 'I can't believe we're back already. Not even my new hairstyle is making me feel any better.' She flicked her long, blonde locks over one shoulder.

'This is your final year, and then you're going travelling. You're almost there,' said Alice.

I worked full-time as a kennel assistant at a local animal rescue shelter to financially prepare for the year before starting university. That was all part of my plan—pre-the-unravelling-of-my-life. Working. My dream gap year would have been volunteering with sloths in Costa Rica, but I needed money, and even with a bursary in place, I couldn't afford the flight. Since then, I work part-time at the same rescue centre, varying my hours to fit around my studies. Daisy was studying Accounting and Finance, but, unlike me, she wasn't excited about her education. She chose her qualification because both of her parents were accountants, as were her two eldest brothers. She didn't know if she wanted to work in finance, but she loved the university's social life, so she stuck at it.

'Good to see you're wearing your gift.' Daisy smiled like a proud teacher. She looked down at my above-the-knee denim skirt.

'I should have worn jeans,' I said whilst smoothing and tugging my skirt lower. It was a breezy day. When I got dressed, I put on the skirt but changed into jeans before leaving the house. Then I felt guilty for not wearing it, so I rushed back upstairs and changed again.

'I've worn large period pants just in case I fall over or if a stupid boy tries to look up my skirt,' I whispered.

Daisy smirked. 'I would've worn red, frilly thongs.' She wasn't joking.

Daisy had four older brothers, and I was an only child, so we pretended to be sisters when we met new people, but no one ever believed us. Daisy was taller, slimmer and had blue eyes. Her hair was naturally curly, whereas mine was shoulder-length, straight and brown. She loved fashion, and I was happy wearing anything comfortable to muck in with animals. Daisy loved boys' attention, but my passion was animals and my career. I'd had a couple of boyfriends at college and university, but nothing serious. They got frustrated or jealous of the time and attention I gave to animals, or Daisy, over them. Yet, despite our differences, Daisy and I were close.

The queue grew longer, and I started panicking that I was going to be late for my first lecture. Getting dressed and undressed numerous times that morning meant that I left the house ten minutes late, so I missed my bus. I didn't have time to use the cash machine in Plymouth city centre next to the deli, which sold freshly squeezed orange juice, a rare treat to myself and where I often bought bird feed for my regular walks along the River Tavy.

The river carved its way amongst the fields near to where I lived with my parents, ten miles north of the city. Our house was on the end terrace of a small council estate on the edge of a village. We overlooked the countryside, and I often daydreamed that I lived in the property at the far end of one of the fields. It was quite a distance, but it was just possible to make out the yellowy-grey, bricked, detached building with adjoining stables. It was my dream home. I had never seen the property up close because it was hidden from the path on the walk to the river, but I just knew it would be mine one day.

We were nearing the front of the cash machine queue.

'You know I like to be early and prepared.' I sighed and looked back down at my skirt.

'He's cute,' Daisy whispered. Her gaze followed someone to the back of the queue.

'Who was that?'

She turned back to face me. 'Don't look now, but a couple of guys from the rugby team just joined the back of the queue.

The blond one smiled at me, you know, the one that everyone fancies. Does my hair look okay?'

'Of course, it does. You look lovely, as always.'

I didn't need to look at who she was talking about. I knew it was Niall, the most popular guy at university. Even Daisy didn't stand a chance with him.

When it was my turn to use the cash machine, I pulled my skirt tight and tucked it between my thighs to hold it in place. It was getting windier. Daisy stood to the side of the queue, trying to catch Niall's attention again.

'Hey,' a male voice shouted as I punched in my PIN. I looked over at Daisy. She was looking towards the rugby guys, twiddling her hair and smiling.

'Hi,' she purred back as I typed in the amount needed to pay for the first field trip of the term.

'You might want to give your friend a hand,' Niall shouted in his Geordie accent, and some in the queue cheered. Daisy ran over to me as my skirt had blown up at the back, exposing my underwear to the entire queue of people. She pulled it back down and held it there until I snatched the money and sped away. Daisy followed but struggled to keep up with me. It took until lunchtime before I saw the funny side of what happened.

'…and then I turned around, and all I could see were your humongous knickers!' Daisy retold her version of the story. We laughed so hard that we needed to hold onto each other to walk upright.

'I still can't believe that happened,' I said after we calmed down. We stared at each other for a few seconds before bursting into laughter again. My stomach and cheeks ached as I gasped for breath. Tears of hysteria blurred my vision. I wiped my eyes dry as I walked around the corner of the library and bumped into someone. 'I'm so sorry I couldn't see where I was going.'

'No, I'm sorry, that was my fault. I was looking at my phone.' The guy held up his phone to verify his words.

Without my eyes moving away from his, I absorbed all of him. He was tall, and his hair was the colour of wet sand slowly drying after being caressed by the turning tide. His skin looked as though he had been born from the sea, the heat of the sun colliding with the salt of the ocean, giving him a warm golden glow. His mouth was both shy and welcoming. The corners of his lips were bursting to reveal a smile. My mouth mirrored his.

'Hi, I'm Daisy, and this is Alice.' Daisy broke the silence.

'I'm…Tobias,' he said before pulling his gaze away from mine to acknowledge Daisy. 'It's my first day, and I was reading a message from my mate to figure out how to get to the canteen.'

'You're in your first year?' Daisy blurted. 'What are you studying, and where are you staying? Did you—'

I playfully cupped her mouth. 'Let him answer one question at a time!'

Tobias smiled at me before answering. 'I've moved back in with my parents, and this is my final year but my first and only year at this uni.' Daisy's body shifted forward to ask another question, but Tobias continued answering her initial barrage. 'I was studying at Loughborough but came back here to finish my Sport and Exercise Science degree because I'm hoping to become a semi-pro surfer.'

'That's interesting,' Daisy said. 'So, where do you go out drinking when—'

'Hang on,' Tobias interrupted Daisy, 'I thought I recognised you…Alice?' He smiled again. 'You're the girl that had *problems* at the cashpoint earlier.' My face burst into cherry blossom pink. 'Sorry, I didn't mean to embarrass you.' He placed his hand on my shoulder, and his thumb accidentally brushed against my jaw. A cool ripple passed down my spine before an explosion of heat spread across my entire body.

Daisy invited Tobias to walk with us to the canteen and then excused herself when we arrived because she 'remembered' she needed to make an important phone call.

'I love your skirt,' she shouted and winked as she walked away.

Life seemed great then. I was in love for the first time. Daisy and I were as close as we had always been, and I was studying towards my career and dreaming about my forever home. I was full of hope and yet oblivious to the devastation that had begun weaving its way towards me.

CHAPTER 2

Now

Ugly—that's what Daniel Smith said I would be when I got older. That was his response after he asked me out whilst queuing for the playground. I said no, and he pushed me over once we got outside. We were both ten years old. His comment didn't upset me back then, only my knees when they scraped on the tarmac floor. The scabs healed, but his words still haunted me now, twenty years later.

My life felt ugly, as did my surroundings, a concrete bus station oozing with dampness. The seagulls hovered above, scratching the silence with their screeches whilst fighting over scraps of food from the night before—soggy chips and half-eaten kebabs. The stillness of New Year's Day didn't offer the normal reflection on the year gone by or the wonder of hope for what was to come. January the first hadn't had that sentiment for a long while because I had been trapped in the past for long enough, and now I was uncertain of my imminent future. The numerous wrong decisions that I had made were dragging me further from where I thought my life would be. Perhaps my ten-year-old self had set me on the wrong path by saying no to Daniel and yes to Tobias.

I had considered leaving Devon only once before because I was chasing happiness, but what I was actually doing was clinging to something that distracted me from my painful reality. I wasn't sure if I was running away now or grabbing onto my only option out of desperation. Perhaps it was both of those things. London wasn't where I wanted to be, but it was my only chance to draw a line under what had happened and finally start over. The capital may be the big pond, but Devon was a smashed glass of spilt water with too many shards, and I didn't have the tools to clear that up.

A tannoy announcement confirmed my coach's departure in less than ten minutes. I fumbled in my handbag for my ticket but couldn't find it; I patted my coat pockets, jean pockets, and coat pockets again before looking back inside the bag. I let out a long sigh when I noticed it was caught within the wrapping paper of Daisy's present. With my ticket firmly in my hand, clothes carrier draped over my arm and my handbag slung over my shoulder, I dragged my holdall towards the coach.

'London Victoria?' the driver said. I nodded. I wondered if he checked with every passenger or just those that looked lost.

My coat flapped erratically in the wind, wrapping itself around my legs like a child clinging to its mother, begging her not to leave. 'You *can* get on,' he said as he took my holdall.

I made myself comfortable in a space behind the driver's seat, and as the remaining passengers boarded, I replayed the conversation with Mum when she dropped me off at the station.

'If I had been through all the things you had,' her voice broke, 'I would go somewhere different.' Mum's words were surprising. Not only had she lived in Devon her entire life, she had never driven outside of the county. She relied on Dad for that. Her only child was moving away. Was she proud that I was trying to help myself, or was it that she was relieved I was leaving? I hadn't been the easiest person to live with for a long time.

The coach passed familiar places as we made our way out of the city: the petrol station that sold the cheapest fuel, the university where I didn't finish my degree, the hotel where I recently quit working as a receptionist on a zero-hour contract, and the Brownies hut with the elephant in the outdoor play area. The trunk was a slide. It looked smaller than I remembered playing on it as a young girl with Daisy. It was weather-worn; its pink skin mottled with rust. I couldn't recite all of the Brownie Promise, but the part that I could remember I had failed on; I had not done my best or been true to myself.

The coach followed the main road out of Devon, running alongside the eastern fringe of Dartmoor. Haytor became visible in the distance. I was going to miss the views from up there overlooking the county's plaited countryside and the glittering sea visible on clear days. It was Daisy's favourite too. Tobias helped me arrange a surprise picnic party for her twenty-first birthday in the spring after he and I met. We played games and ate shop-bought food rather than homemade sandwiches or cakes, and Daisy and I drank too many homemade cocktails that one of our friends made. Everyone made it into Plymouth that night to celebrate her birthday, except for us two. Tobias had to drive us both home before the party finished on the tor. As a keepsake, and to remember the only part of her celebrations that either of us had that day, I bought us both a personalised key ring. It was a beautiful image of Tobias, Daisy and me hugging on top of Haytor. It was a sunny day, warm for late March. I chose that photo because our expressions are full of happiness, love, and we look invincible, like youth tricks you into believing. I threw that key ring away a few years later. I didn't want to look at the two people who I loved so deeply. I still loved Haytor, though.

When I was younger, Dad told me that the granite rocks at the very top of the tor were the teeth of an underground monster that had stalked an eagle. When the bird flew off, the monster forced the ground upwards like a mountain. The creature's teeth pierced the earth's crust to snatch its prey into its jaws, but before it could take a bite, lighting struck, freezing it into place forever. The eagle got away. The story made me smile. It was a kind lie, unlike the numerous mistruths I had been fooled by. I suppose I was the eagle, and Maxwell was the monster. Tobias was the strike that missed Maxwell and startled me, allowing Maxwell to take bite after bite until only a carcass remained. Daisy was the solid ground, even though I didn't always see that.

Once the surroundings became unfamiliar, I reached into my bag to retrieve Daisy's present. The stripy wrapping paper felt expensive, a luxury Daisy could afford as a chartered accountant. The label read:

Until you join the rest of us in the modern mobile world.
I already miss you xx

My old and battered mobile did everything I needed: phone calls, text messages and photos. I didn't need a phone with internet access to inform loose friendships on social media with updates on my life: *driving a second-hand car, minimal savings, being career-less, working on improving my self-worth.* My status was unchanged for five years, apart from my car—I recently sold that for extra money for my move. The torn wrapping paper revealed a pocket-sized street atlas of London. It was a thoughtful gift, but I would use it discreetly to avoid advertising myself as a non-local in a big city and putting myself at an even higher risk of mugging or worse.

I was going to miss Daisy even though we had only recently started talking again. She was going to be fine without me with her career, fiancé, the new home they were buying together, and renting her flat as extra income. At university, Daisy regularly joked that I was too serious about my career. 'Have more fun,' she said, and before meeting Tobias, 'you need to date more. Find out what you like.' We had somehow swapped roles; that worked out for her, but it ruined everything for me.

The underground map on the back page showed coloured lines crisscrossing each other like multi-coloured veins on the back of a decaying leaf. I studied it, trying to work out how to get to Bethnal Green, which wasn't necessary given that Kate was going to meet me at Victoria Coach Station and take me back to her flat. I was grateful she offered to do that because I had only visited London once before on a school trip to the Natural History Museum when I was twelve.

A hint of travel sickness stirred in my stomach from reading, so I placed the booklet back into my bag and focused on the horizon where bare farmers' fields were sprinkled with salt and pepper gulls and crows feasting on worms. I imagined shapes out of passing trees: a spindly one with long, straggly branches looked like a zombie, and a row of bare tree silhouettes on top of a hill looked like an x-ray of oral nerve endings. But I couldn't do that for long because the clouds cracked apart, allowing intermittent flickers of low-level winter sunlight through the window, which made me dizzy. I turned my gaze back inside the coach.

I plugged in my MP3 player earphones and reclined my seat so that my eye line was just lower than the sun's beam. Shortly after, the driver turned up the heating and dimmed the lights.

I instantly felt tired. But I didn't want to fall asleep on a coach full of strangers, so I sat back up. Outside, fluffy clouds dotted the sky back in the west like balls of pink candy floss—that was supposedly a sign that I shouldn't be going, according to a counsellor-cum-psychic whom I saw in the previous year, but I wasn't sure if I believed in signs or fate—and in the east where we were heading, it was gloomy. Low-level clouds scudded towards us as though they were running away from something, and headlights from oncoming vehicles guided them away from the darkness.

I caught my reflection in the window, and I stared at myself, wondering what I was doing. The coach rocked me into a hypnotic state. My eyes were heavy, my arms too, and it felt impossible to fight off sleep any longer. Soft music whispered in my ears like a lullaby, and I closed my eyes. A gentle song soon ended and was replaced by 'Surfin' U.S.A.' by The Beach Boys, Tobias's favourite song, and as he appeared in my mind, I smiled. It was six years to the day that I last saw him when he held me for the final time and gave me hope that everything was going to be okay, that I would have the courage to leave Maxwell. Tobias gave me hope that the end of my tough, difficult days was in sight, but it turned out that I was only part way through it all.

An ache gripped my throat as though someone in the row behind was trying to rip out my tonsils. I rested my forehead against the window and sobbed in silence until the rocking motion of the coach soothed me to sleep.

It felt as though I had been sleeping for a few seconds when I woke to a skidding sensation. I must have been asleep longer because it was snowing. An inch had already settled upon the central reservation. Traffic on the other side of the motorway had ground to a halt but their windscreen wipers remained on full speed.

The coach scrambled onwards. I looked ahead through the driver's window, and snowflakes shot from the darkness and onto the windscreen as though we were travelling through space at light speed. There were signposts for Heathrow Airport. We were getting near. I checked my phone for the time. Our estimated time of arrival was just over half an hour away. My mouth felt dry. Three text messages were listed on the screen: one from Daisy, one from Dad, and the last from Kate. The first two messages were reminders to let them know once I arrived safely at the flat. I assumed Kate's was to tell me she was on her way to meet me at Victoria Coach Station. But it wasn't.

Hey Cuz, can't wait to see you later. Sorry for the short notice but can you make your way to the flat? Landlord making last-minute visit. Call me when you get to BG Tube Station and I'll come down to meet you xx
P.S. Don't forget to buy an Oyster card at Victoria.

Oh, for goodness sake! How was I going to get to Bethnal Green on my own? How was I going to do it with all my stuff?

I knew Bethnal Green was in the East End, but how far east was the East End, exactly? I snatched Daisy's booklet from my bag and studied the underground properly to figure out where I had to go. The yellow or green line would take me to a station called Monument and then a red line to go to Bethnal Green. Deep breath: yellow or green to Monument and then red. Yellow or green to Monument and then red.

The coach passed through swamped rush hour junctions with cars, buses, lorries, scribbled road markings and crowds of people. There were more and more road signs. The driver made sharp turns down this road and that road as though taking us to the centre of a labyrinth before turning into Victoria Coach Station. By the time he announced our arrival, I decided I couldn't stay in London. It wasn't Kate's fault, but I felt let down once again. Why was it impossible for anyone to stick with their intentions?

The driver switched off the engine, and an abrupt stillness and silence filled the coach. I jumped up from my seat and was the first person to disembark and collect my baggage. Inside the terminal, I found the ticket desk and joined a short queue. A timetable hung on the wall adjacent to where I was standing and I could see the next coach for Plymouth was departing at six o'clock. That was less than an hour's wait before I could escape. But by the time I reached the ticket desk, the six o'clock coach was already full. Apparently, lots of people were making their way home after seeing in the New Year in the capital. The next available seat was on the overnight coach departing at eleven o'clock, which meant waiting around for the same amount of time as the coach journey itself.

I declined the ticket and sat down in a nearby waiting area to think. I started picking at the skin around my nails. I didn't want to wait in a coach station in the middle of London until late at night. I took a deep breath. I could go to Kate's for the weekend and return to Devon on Monday. As I made my decision, two police officers walked past, chatting and laughing. I noticed a couple sitting opposite snuggling, the woman resting her head against her husband's arm. A small group of teenage girls shared sweets amongst themselves whilst waiting in the ticket queue.

What did I have to return to? I was thirty years old and should have been settled into my chosen career, but it hadn't even begun. The starting line wasn't even visible. I had been staying with my parents since my last relationship ended. I no longer had a car or a job, and my well-being needed continued help. Arriving in London was daunting, but I needed to see this opportunity though. What other choice did I have? I couldn't allow anyone else to influence my decisions, not anymore.

CHAPTER 3

Then

Towards the end of my second year at university, Tobias drove me into Plymouth city centre for an interview. It was for a full-time summer job at a recruitment agency. He had finished his final exams and had lots of free time. He planned only to spend the summer surfing before finding a sports-related job until he had his big break. My plan was to reduce my dog shelter work to weekend mornings and then increase my hours back up when I returned to my studies after the summer. The recruitment job paid a lot more in comparison.

I was greeted by someone who introduced themselves as Dom, who led me into a stuffy meeting room. 'Sorry, it's hot in here. Maxwell was supposed to open the window, but he must have forgotten.' He opened the window.

My throat was dry, and I was relieved when he offered me a glass of water then left the room. Whilst on my own, I picked and pulled at my cuticles waiting for him to return. The job itself wasn't what I wanted to do—I never planned on doing admin work, and I certainly wasn't cut out for a sales environment—but it was a great opportunity to make contacts for when I graduated the following year.

The door behind me opened. I stopped picking at my cuticles and sat up straight.

'Apologies for taking so long.'

I turned around expecting Dom, but instead, an attractive man with thick, black hair walked into the room. He smiled as though he was in a toothpaste advert or a slow-mo Instagram reel. I didn't use social media, but Daisy updated me with trends because she often posted videos and photos. She convinced me to be in one of her videos, and we mimed a conversation about boys. It got lots of likes, apparently. I wasn't sure if I was flattered or embarrassed by that.

The guy wore fitted, charcoal-grey suit trousers which hugged his muscular thighs. His white shirt, which was somehow whiter than his teeth, squeezed around his biceps and pectorals. He smirked when he noticed me noticing the way his clothes fitted his body. He leant over for a handshake. I didn't have a chance to stand up from the chair. It may have been the awkward angle, but his grip was weaker than I expected. On closer inspection, his facial features weren't as neat as his style.

'I'm Maxwell, branch manager. I look after the senior roles across all three sectors: animal health, equestrian and agriculture.'

Dom returned with two glasses of water. 'Would you like a glass, Max?'

'I'd love a coffee, please, mate.' Dom left the room again. 'So, what car do you drive?' Maxwell caught me off-guard. Had the interview started? I hadn't prepared for this style of question.

'I borrow my mum's car,' I fidgeted in my seat. 'I'm still at university, so I can't afford my own at the moment.'

'I see.' He stared at me.

We sat in silence. My hands rested in my lap, and I started picking at my cuticles again. 'Mum's car is old but reliable, and I can normally use it when I need to, or my boyfriend gives me lifts. He'll drop me off most days—that's if I'm successful, of course.' I smiled at him and then looked down at my lap.

Shut up, Alice, I thought. *You sound like a cotton reel tumbling to the ground, unravelling and spinning out of control.*

'How did you find out about this position?' Maxwell asked.

I looked up. 'One of my lecturers told me about it.'

'Between you and me,' he leaned forward and lowered his voice, 'I think most people that look for work via recruitment agencies are lazy.' He leaned back in his chair and smiled. His voice now jovial. 'But it's easy money, so I'm not complaining.'

I nodded and smiled.

Dom returned with Maxwell's coffee, and they took turns asking questions whilst the other made notes of my answers. When they finished, and without conferring, Maxwell offered me the position. I accepted. My start date was the first Monday after the summer term ended, less than three weeks' time.

Tobias picked me up on my first day. He surprised me that morning with an early twenty-first birthday present. He had booked a cottage in St Porth, a quaint village in mid-Cornwall, for the coming weekend. I joked that he must have chosen Cornwall for the surf and not for me, but he said he wasn't taking his board. It was *our* time before things started changing now that he had completed his studies. I wish he and Daisy had taken gap years so that we were graduating at the same point in our lives. University was going to feel strange without them there when I returned after the summer.

My first week at work flew by. The team kept me busy with opening and distributing the post, taking phone calls and making drinks for them and their clients. On Friday morning, Maxwell suggested that our team of five go for a quick drink after work. I felt I should make the effort with my new colleagues but decided not to go because Tobias was picking me up from work to drive straight to Cornwall.

'You deserve a drink, Alice,' Maxwell said when I told him the reason why I couldn't go. 'You've done great this week. Come for one.'

I agreed to one drink. That was my first mistake with Maxwell.

It was a hot summer's evening driving to Cornwall. The windows were down and the music up as we drove towards the place where the sun sets. St Porth's roads were narrow, and as we reached the tiny village car park, Tobias's favourite song, 'Surfin' USA', played on the radio. We sat in the car singing and dancing until it finished. He switched off the radio and looked at me. I could see wildflowers dancing and could smell the scent of honeysuckle and lavender as I stepped into the green summer meadow of his eyes. He kissed me—passionately. It was the perfect start to our getaway.

We unloaded the car and made the short walk to our cottage, stopping on the way to look over the sea wall. Ripples of waves tickled the shoreline on the small, u-shaped, sandy beach below, and nesting gulls darted to and from the purple-speckled cliff face on the far side of the beach. The sea was calm within the harbour walls, but the distant ocean looked like patchwork denim roughly sewn together. With each crashing wave, the stitches were becoming weaker.

The orange hue of the sky tinted the gentle shoreline, and splashes of water from small, lapping waves glowed like lava. Tobias pulled me close and whispered that he loved me. We held each other as we watched the sun caress the sky; its warmth kissed my face as a gentle breeze played with my hair. As the sun dipped lower, long shadows spread across the harbour like fingers clinging onto the remains of the day. They didn't want to let go. I squeezed Tobias closer.

The period cottage was set back from the road. Tobias ducked through the front door and stepped into the narrow hallway. He banged his head as he carried our bags up the creaky stairs. We quickly unpacked before heading to the village pub for dinner and then returned to the cottage for an early romantic night.

The following morning, we visited Land's End for brunch, making sure we had the obligatory touristy photo shot in front of the famous signpost.

'New York is only three thousand, one hundred and forty-seven miles in that direction,' I read from the sign. 'I would love to go one day. Maybe we could after I've graduated and you're a surfing pro?' I joked.

Tobias hesitated before taking my hand and squeezing it. He didn't respond to my suggestion.

'Come on, it's time for a little surprise,' he said, and we left Land's End.

He had bought us tickets for a matinee ballet performance of Giselle at an open-air venue built into the side of a cliff face overlooking the Atlantic Ocean. Neither of us were ballet fans.

'I read it's one of the most romantic things to do in Cornwall,' he said as he laid a blanket over our granite seats. 'I hope it doesn't rain.' The sky in the distance was dark grey.

I sat down next to him. 'You're not going to propose, are you?' I laughed. He just smiled and placed another blanket on our laps.

We ate strawberries and shared a miniature bottle of champagne whilst waiting for the performance to start. A cruise ship sailed past, and then a low-flying helicopter. Tobias pulled out a pair of binoculars from his bag and held them up to his eyes.

'Where did you get those from?'

'They're Dad's.'

'We look like an old married couple sat like this.' I said. Tobias didn't acknowledge my comment, again. 'Can I have a go?' He handed me the binoculars, and I placed them to my eyes. 'I think they're broken; everything looks small.'

Tobias was rummaging in his bag for the flask of coffee. He looked up at me. 'They can't be, I've just used them.' He started laughing and then reached over to take them from me. He turned them around and placed them back in position in front of my eyes. 'You were looking through the wrong end.' We laughed loudly. Some of the older spectators gave us unimpressed looks. He wrapped his arm around my shoulders and kissed my cheek. 'That's just one of the many things I love about you, Alice.'

'There's a seal,' I squealed and pointed towards some rocks. I zoomed in. 'I think there are two; it looks like they're kissing.' I adjusted the lens again. 'Oh, no, that's not it.' I lowered the binoculars.

'What?' Tobias took the binoculars from me to look.

'There aren't two seals, there's only one, and it's caught a big fish.'

'The seal has to eat, Alice.' Tobias squeezed my knee.

'I know, but I can't bear the thought of the fish having its flesh torn from its body, its life being ripped away right now. Before you say it, I know that's nature.'

It took me a while to get into the performance. I wondered if the fish had looked to us humans, hoping that someone might dive into the sea and save it from the pain it was enduring, but no one did. We all remained seated, waiting to be entertained.

'I'm cold,' I said with ten minutes left of the performance. Dampness was rising from the stone seating and into my bones. I was ready to return to the cottage.

'I'm cooking dinner tonight, so you can have a nice hot bubble bath whilst I do that.'

I yawned and leaned my head on his shoulder. 'You're the best.'

Tobias cooked my favourite meal: vegetable moussaka. The scent of garlic and rosemary drifted upstairs as my skin gradually warmed in rose-scented bubbles. I left the lights off in the bathroom and the blind up to enjoy the view of the harbour from the roll-top bath. The sea was now stirring within the harbour walls; a storm was coming.

Dinner was ready by the time I was dressed. Tobias opened the kitchen door and called me downstairs. Jazz music followed the sound of his voice. He greeted me with a glass of red wine and a kiss. He was normally thoughtful, attentive, and calm, but something was different. He was nervous.

'Take a seat in the garden, and dinner will be served, Miss Berry.'

The tiny garden was sheltered from the harbour wind. The patio glowed with church candles dotted around the edges and tea lights perched on the table. The heat from a terracotta Chimenea soothed the space. The weekend had been perfect and romantic, I thought as I waited for Tobias—and then I realised what was happening. He was going to propose! The romantic gestures, ignoring my jokes about being old together. I gulped my drink and placed the empty glass on the table more forcefully than necessary. I was in love with Tobias, but I wasn't ready for that next big step. His parents were married with baby number two at our age. My priority was to graduate and establish the career I had dreamt about from a young age. Our relationship was great as it was. Nothing needed to change yet.

Tobias was quiet all through dinner. As was I.

'This is tasty,' I said to break the silence. He smiled with his mouth full. 'Shall I top up our glasses?' I asked.

He jumped out of his seat, swallowed his food and walked towards the kitchen. 'You stay there, I'll do it,' he shouted from inside.

After dinner, Tobias cleared the table. He knocked over my glass and dropped a knife on his way back to the kitchen and then remained there for a while. He didn't call out to say what was taking so long, and I didn't ask. When he came back outside, he placed our shared dessert in the middle of the table, and we sat in silence again. Tobias picked at the lemon tart, and I picked at it on my side. He smiled at me, and I smiled at him before both refocusing on the plate in front of us.

'It's turned out to be a pleasant evening,' he eventually spoke.

'It has.' We carried on picking.

Tobias rested his fork on the plate and sighed. 'There's something I want to speak to you about, but I've been waiting for the right moment.' He held my left hand into both of his. 'As well as finding love for each other, you are also my best friend.' He looked into my eyes. I nodded. 'I want it to always be this way.'

'Me too.' I dug my nails into the palm of his hand.

'What I'm trying to say is,' he squeezed my hand, and I squeezed back, willing him not to ask me to marry him. Not tonight, not this year or the next, but maybe in a few years' time. I took a sip of my wine, and his words tumbled from his mouth. 'I'm going to Hawaii.'

'What?' I almost choked on my wine.

'I've been offered a placement at a surf school to coach schoolchildren. They hold regular surf competitions, and talent spotters often hang out there. I may get lucky and get talent-spotted.'

I pulled my hand away from his. 'How long are you going for?'

'A year.'

'A year!' The feet on my chair scratched against the patio

as I stood up. 'Why didn't you tell me you had applied for a job in Hawaii?'

'I didn't think I stood a chance. There was no point worrying you over nothing.'

'Nothing? You think this is nothing?'

'That's not what I mean.' Tobias stood up and stepped towards me. 'This is a once-in-a-lifetime opportunity, Alice. It's only for a year. I'll be back by the time you graduate.'

'Why, when are you going?' He tried to cuddle me, but I shrugged him off. 'When, Tobias?'

'I fly the day after your birthday.'

'You're going a week tomorrow?' He nodded. 'How long have you known for?'

'I was initially told I didn't get a place, and they recommended I reapplied next year, but then someone dropped out at the last minute, and I got a call last week to see if I could fill the spot at short notice.'

'So you've known for a week, and you've only just decided to tell me.'

'I didn't want to spoil our weekend.'

My throat started burning. 'Well, it's too late for that.' I pushed past him, ran upstairs, slammed the bedroom door, threw myself onto the bed and sobbed until I fell asleep.

The following morning allowed a few seconds of ignorance before the reality of the previous night sunk in. Black mascara marks smudged onto the white pillowcase confirmed the truth. I rolled over, but Tobias wasn't there. His side of the bed was untouched. I crept downstairs and found him sleeping on the sofa, wrapped in his beach towel. There was a small gap between him and the back of the sofa, so I climbed up and squeezed in behind him. I hugged him tightly. I felt like the fish. I, too, had been swimming along blissfully unaware that my life as I knew it was going to be torn away, and there was nothing that I could do to change that.

CHAPTER 4

Now

Everything ached from the bitter cold when I left Victoria Coach Station. Even my thighs felt sore through my jeans and coat. A snowflake snuck in between my scarf and collar and pricked my neck. I pulled up my coat collar and tightened my scarf. Only a few people walked ahead along the hushed side street. A cab drove past and joined the end of a silent taxi rank. The sensation of snow crunched with each footstep whilst flakes covered walls and trees like white sheets draped over furniture in an abandoned manor house.

Around the corner, I was catapulted back into modern-day London as cars, buses and taxis whizzed along the main road, mutating the snow into brown slush. Horns honked, and bright lights shone down from lampposts and tall buildings like an interrogation demanding to know my reason for being there. I couldn't give them an answer. I kept my head down and joined a crowd of people waiting to cross at an intersection. A similar-sized group stood on the opposite side of the road, and when the lights changed from red to green, we charged towards each other in a desperate attempt to reach the other side before the lights changed back to red.

I weaved past loitering tourists, kissing couples, choking nicotine—there were so many smokers. I skirted around piles of rubbish balanced on the edge of pavements as I followed signs towards Victoria Train Station. When I reached the entrance, the stench of urine stung my nose.

Victoria Train Station was cavernous and just as cold inside. People darted here and there whilst pigeons waited patiently amongst loitering passengers. My hair was damp from the snow, and my ears were burning from the freezing temperature, so I bought a hat from a souvenir shop adjacent to public toilets. It cost twice as much as the same thing back in Devon, but I would have paid even more; it felt like a warm and soothing hug as soon as I put it on.

As I made my way towards the information centre, a pigeon clipped my new hat as it flew overhead. Then, a man accidentally kicked my holdall as he ran towards a departure gate. I shook my head because there was no apology, not even an acknowledgement. Why did men find it difficult to admit they had done something wrong, let alone apologise for it? I used my body to barge open the door to the information office and then dragged in my holdall. I picked up a leaflet and joined the back of a long queue, trying to cram in as much information about Oyster cards before reaching the front.

'Next,' someone shouted from behind the counter. 'Next!' I looked up. She was calling me already.

I smiled as I approached the counter, even though the woman didn't look at me. Her gaze remained fixed on her computer screen.

'Could I buy an Oyster card, please?'

'Pay as you go, or Travelcard?' the woman asked whilst punching at the keys.

'What do you think would be best?'

She stopped typing and looked at me over the top of her glasses like a stern headmistress. 'There's a long queue behind you, so I recommend you read that pamphlet and re-join the queue once you know what you need. Next!'

My body felt weak, and my feet ached from the cold. I still needed to reach Bethnal Green. The thought of the vegetarian lasagne Kate promised to have ready for my arrival, with homemade garlic bread and a glass of red wine, made my mouth water and my stomach rumble.

'Pay as you go,' I blurted. 'Please.'

'How much do you want?' She sighed. If I hadn't known that she was talking to me, I would have guessed that she was chatting to someone online.

'How much would you suggest?' She glared at me. I almost jumped at the shock of head movement and intense stare. I cleared my throat. 'Thirty pounds, please.' I had no idea if that was too much or only enough to get me halfway to the East End.

Somebody offered to help me with my holdall on the steps down to the underground station, but I politely refused their offer. Did they secretly plan to steal it? The entrance to the underground station was crammed with people standing in lines to pass through barriers, others coiled like a snake waiting impatiently for prey at the ticket desk, a group of teenagers hovered suspiciously by the cash points, Spanish tourists studied an underground map on the wall, a husband and wife bickered as their three children looked bored, and still, people continued trickling down the stairs.

I recapped my journey to Bethnal Green in my mind whilst discretely paying attention to the signs. I avoided making any eye contact as I made my way towards the fast-flowing queue for the barrier. People disappeared like water rushing towards a waterfall, filtering off to find the quickest route down. The current pulled me along as I tried to watch how the other passengers passed through the barriers. Each passenger summoned open a barrier before it snapped shut like the jaws of an angry crocodile. I looked down at my holdall and clothes carrier. It was going to be a tight squeeze.

'It'll be easier to use the wide barrier at the far end,' a man from Transport for London shouted over. I blushed and kept my head down as I squeezed out of the main queue and towards the end barrier. 'Don't forget to stand on the right,' he added after watching me struggle through the barrier.

I looked at him blankly. He smiled. 'When you get on the escalators.'

I smiled back and nodded a thank you.

A stream of people rushed down the left-hand side of the steep escalator whilst the rest of us waited patiently to be transported deeper underground. A woman's suitcase protruded onto the left side, but she quickly pulled it back after receiving a barrage of insults from the blockage of people trying to rush down. I clung tighter onto the handrail and my belongings.

It was easy following the signs for the green and yellow line, and as I neared the platform, a warm, metallic gust rushed past as a Tube train slowed to a firm stop. A loud, beeping noise sounded from the carriages, and the doors whooshed open. A man tried embarking before anyone got off the carriage. He received deathly stares. It wasn't necessary for someone from TfL to teach me that Tube etiquette.

The underground journey was overwhelming: so many people; dry heat; musty air; blacked-out tunnels; an itchy forehead from my new hat which I removed and stuffed into my handbag; a strong breeze blowing through the sash-style front carriage window carriage messing up my hair and slapping me across my face; a high pitched screech like nails on a chalkboard as the train slid along the tracks; no seating because all the seats were taken, and when one became available it was snatched up immediately; the juddering departure that caused me to stumble and fall into another passenger; that passenger's curse and irritated look; the harsh increase in speed as the carriage twisted and bounced along the track like a runaway train, stopping at unknown stations and others that I had heard of but had no bearing on my location; confusion on finding the red line at Monument because it was Bank Station that the Central line passed through and somehow the two stations were connected; forcing my way onto the fourth train at Bank because the first three were too full; the moment I realised I had been squashed too deeply into the carriage to disembark at Bethnal Green and having to continue to the next stop to escape; allowing a passenger to help me with my holdall to get off the Tube at Mile End and not caring if they ran off with it; and the weight of heaving that bag up the steps at Bethnal Green Station and back out to the world.

Ice-cold air shocked my lungs. The snow was heavier in East London, and my body temperature quickly dropped. I put my hat back on and tightened my scarf.

'Can you see the tall building to your right as you come out of the station?' Kate said when she answered the phone. 'It looks like a mini version of the HSBC Building in Canary Wharf.'

'What building?' I asked.

'It's got a pointed roof—we call it Canary Dwarf,' she laughed, but I didn't. I didn't understand the reference. 'I'm waving, can you see me? I'm on the tenth floor, third from the top.' The building was visible. It stood tall against four-storey blocks between it and the Tube station but too far away and too dark to see Kate. 'Walk towards the flat, and I'll come down and meet you.'

I put on my gloves and hauled my case along Roman Road. The snow was too deep for the wheels to turn.

'What took you so long?' Kate said as she wrapped her arms around me. I told her about my journey from Victoria. 'If I had known you were going to Mile End,' she smirked, 'I would have told you about the direct route on the *green line* from Victoria,' she laughed.

I wanted to cry. 'It's been a long day.'

'Don't worry, you'll get the hang of things soon enough,' Kate said. She linked her arm through mine, took my holdall, and we walked towards her flat.

She pressed the number forty on the entry system, and Fabrizio, her Italian boyfriend, answered straight away. 'Ciao,' he said, and the door buzzed open. The large foyer was filled only by a wooden counter covered in junk mail and two tall, fake plants, which added a splash of colour to the beige-tiled space.

'If the even-number lift breaks down,' Kate said, 'use the odd one to the eleventh floor and walk down a flight of stairs to the tenth.' She pressed the button for the even lift. 'They don't break down often and I've never known both to break down at the same time.'

When the door to the lift opened, I caught a glimpse of my appearance in the mirror. I looked how I felt—bedraggled. It was warm in the lift, so I removed my hat. My nose started running from the contrast in temperatures. Kate handed me a tissue, and I blew my nose.

'Don't worry,' she said, 'that's normal living here.'

I stared at the black smudge in the tissue. 'Are you sure?'

'Yes, especially when you've been on the Tube.'

The lift was clunky and wobbled as it travelled higher. I grabbed hold of the handrail. 'Is this safe?'

Kate laughed.

The lift juddered to a halt. I thought it had broken down, but we had reached the tenth floor. Four identical white doors were only distinguishable by a bronze number nailed to the centre of each one. Kate pushed open number forty.

'It's not locked,' I gasped. 'Shouldn't it be locked?'

Kate laughed again and walked inside. I followed her and locked the door behind us before letting out a long sigh as I leant back against the door.

Fabrizio took our coats, exchanging them for a glass of red wine. He kissed Kate on the top of her head, which, coupled with his kindness, brought tears to my eyes. I gulped down a large mouthful of wine and started a conversation to distract the yearning I felt for tenderness more than I had done in years. 'Dinner smells amazing.'

'It's ready; take a seat, and I'll bring it out,' Fabrizio said as he hung our coats.

We ate in the hallway-cum-diner and afterwards moved to the lounge, where I sunk into the corner sofa. It was too deep for my feet to reach the floor, and I felt like a little girl swinging my dangling legs. My eyes felt heavy, and I almost spilt the remainder of my wine when my head jolted back up.

'You should get an early night,' Kate said as she took my glass from my hand. I nodded, dragged myself off the sofa, and shuffled to their spare room. I crawled out of my clothes and changed into my pyjamas before going to the bathroom to use the toilet. I couldn't be bothered to clean my teeth.

Kate and Fabrizio's voices seeped underneath the lounge door into the dark hallway as I made my way from the bathroom.

'She seems better than your mum implied,' Fabrizio said.

'I think so too. Fingers crossed London helps her move forward once and for all.'

I waited a moment before clearing my throat. 'Goodnight, guys,' I shouted from the dark.

'Alice,' Kate called. I opened the lounge door and squinted from the light. 'Do you fancy going for a bimble tomorrow?' She looked excited, like a dog being told it was going for a walk after being stuck inside the house all day.

'Uh-huh,' I yawned. 'See you in the morning.'

'Don't set your alarm; we'll go when we're ready.'

I closed the door and stood in the darkness for a moment, picturing Kate and Fabrizio snuggled under a blanket on the sofa. Fabrizio's arm was tucked around Kate's shoulders. My stomach muscles tensed, snatching my breath. It had been so long since anyone made me feel safe and loved in that way. I desperately wanted to experience that again, even though the thought of it petrified me. But I was finally ready.

CHAPTER 5

Then

Returning to work after the weekend in Cornwall was difficult. I put on a brave face in front of my new colleagues and pretended that the weekend was amazing. Dom even joked that he thought I was going to come back engaged. I forced out a laugh before running to the toilet to cry. The toilets were on the middle floor of the Georgian building, and I made frequent trips throughout the day to compose myself. I made copious amounts of drinks for the team. I wanted to be on my own. I needed time to process what was happening. I wanted to be spending my last few days with Tobias, not constrained to a soulless computer screen, surrounded by strangers or losing my patience each time the office telephone screeched.

So much had changed since breaking up for summer, and yet only a week had passed. I couldn't wait to get back to university to focus on my career. I missed the soothing company of animals, and seeing them only at the weekend was going to be even harder now that Tobias was leaving. It took a lot of willpower not to walk out of my summer job. I needed the money to stay at university and to make contacts. My life had to keep moving forward in one area, at least. I glared at the screen, flinching the next time the phone rang.

I stared out of the window whilst on another drinks run. The kettle boiled as raindrops splattered against the window before sliding down the glass, bumping into each other as though elbowing one another out of the way. Others fell into puddles onto the flat roofing of the ground floor extension below, causing concentric ripples to spread across them. As the rain fell harder, the circles grew faster, overlapping each other like a psychedelic version of Spirograph.

'Alice!' Maxwell said as he appeared in the doorway. I gasped. My hand involuntarily covered my heart. 'I've got a candidate arriving in twenty minutes. Could you print off more registration forms? We're running low.'

'Sure, I'll do it as soon as I've made these drinks.'

Much to my annoyance, Maxwell stepped into the kitchen. It wasn't personal. I didn't want to talk to anyone, not him, nor the team, telephone enquiries or office visitors. The kettle started boiling, and steam began escaping. I wished I could convert from water to steam.

'The candidate is called Tom Apple-something-or-other.' Maxwell placed his mug on the side and spooned in coffee before leaning against the fridge. 'When he comes in, could you go through the forms with him and take a photocopy of his passport?'

'Yep,' I said whilst loading a tray with full mugs.

'Great, I thought it was about time that you got involved. You're more than capable of answering the phones and making drinks.' Maxwell stirred his coffee. 'Once you've done all of that, I'll take over from there and complete the registration process.' He picked up his mug and walked off.

I was relieved that he didn't offer to carry the tray because he had already invaded my time-out from the office. The kitchen was small, like a burrow to hide in, but with Maxwell in the same space, it felt like the walls were collapsing in. A predator was on the prowl.

There was a gentle knock on the office door before it opened.

'Hello, I'm here to see Maxwell Squire.' A man with a warm and friendly aura appeared at my desk. I naturally smiled back.

'Could I take your name, please?'

'Yes, of course, I'm Tom Appleshaw.' He shook my hand. His confident grip contradicted his polite manner.

'Maxwell is expecting you. But first of all, I'll run through the registration process.' I handed him the forms, and he followed me to the meeting room. I made him a coffee and returned to the room. His fingers brushed against mine as he took the mug from me. He apologised and blushed softly. That made me blush, too. I don't know why. I left him to complete the registration forms.

I returned ten minutes later to collect the completed forms. He looked into my eyes and smiled as he handed the paperwork back to me. I smiled back. I scanned the form, checking everything was completed and noticed that he had studied at the Royal Veterinary College in London.

'Do you still practise?' I asked. He was a qualified veterinary surgeon, but we didn't place those jobs at the agency.

'I do,' he said. I was tempted to tell him that we didn't cover that profession but decided that was Maxwell's responsibility. 'I've moved down from London to set up a veterinary practice,' he added, as though he read my mind. 'But that will take some time, so I'm looking for general temporary work alongside my locum work to help build up contacts in this area.'

He explained that he visited Devon with his parents every summer as a child and continued to visit every year as an adult, but not with his parents, he added and laughed. He loved the space the countryside offered, unlike London.

'There sure is plenty of space,' I said.

'I always knew I'd end up here.' His gaze caught mine again. There was something familiar about him, as though he was a long-lost friend, his vibe was calming and comfortable, and yet I had never met him before.

'I love Devon. I wouldn't want to live anywhere else.' I smiled at him. 'You've made a good choice.'

'I know.' His eyes smiled back at me.

'Right, I'll go and get Maxwell for you.' I walked towards the door but stopped before opening it. 'I almost forgot; do you have your passport with you?' Tom retrieved his passport from the inside pocket of his navy blazer and handed it to me. 'Thanks, I just need to take a copy of this.' I opened it. 'We've got the same birthday! You're seven years older than me. It's my twenty-first on Friday.' I don't know why I blurted out all of that. I closed the passport. 'I'll go and make a copy for our records, and then I'll bring this back to you.'

The photocopier took a moment to warm up, and as I waited for it to function, I thought about Tom. He was cute. His freckles made him look younger than twenty-seven. His strawberry-blonde hair was darker than Tobias's sun-kissed hair, and his ice-blue eyes were emphasised by his dark-framed glasses. The dusting of stubble across his face suited him but looked out of place, given his immaculate overall appearance. Tobias looked handsome in shorts and a t-shirt, but I thought how nice he would look dressed in what Tom was wearing: brown chinos and a light blue shirt. It was a shame Daisy had decided to go travelling soon, otherwise I would have been tempted to matchmake her and Tom.

'Alice,' Maxwell said as he passed the photocopier. He made me jump. 'Could you run an errand for me? I forgot my lunch. Would you pop out and grab me something? Charlie owes me lunch, so you can get the money from her.'

'Sure, is there anything you don't like?'

'I eat anything and everything.' He opened the door to the meeting room and stretched out Tom's name as though they were best mates. Maxwell had that charm about him. Before the door closed behind him, Maxwell pulled it back open. 'Just leave Tom's passport on your desk. He can pick it up once we're done. No need to disturb us again.' He closed the door.

Everyone, except Maxwell, had gone for lunch by the time I returned to the office. Tom's registration form was on my desk, ready to process.

'I thought Ben looked after the animal health sector?' I said. I was stuck on processing Tom's application.

Maxwell stood up and walked towards my desk. 'He does. Why's that?' He pulled a chair over and sat beside me.

'I wasn't sure who I should allocate Tom against because I thought you only dealt with senior-level roles, but that's not what he's looking for.'

Maxwell explained that Tom had plans to start and grow his business and that, in time, he would require staff at all levels: other vets, veterinary nurses, receptionists, kennel staff and cleaners. 'It's all about contacts,' Maxwell said. 'You have to sow seeds so clients remember you when they need future positions filling. That's how it's done in this industry.' He stood up and offered to make me a drink. He was the first person to do that since I started working there. I accepted. 'Put the effort in early so that the seed grows effortlessly; it's easy money from there.' He walked off to the kitchen.

The phone rang later that day. Ben, the recent graduate, answered it because I was already on another call. Charlie, the only other female in the team, was in the toilet, and Dom was registering a candidate. Maxwell never answered the phone. It was Tom Appleshaw, and I overheard Ben tell him that I was already on another call. I gestured to say my call was about to finish, but Maxwell stepped in, asking Ben to put the call through to him. Maxwell greeted the call with the same enthusiasm as when he first met Tom.

'No need to pop in to collect your passport, Tom. I'll get someone to drop it into you.' Maxwell waved at me whilst mouthing *passport*. He pointed to the phone. 'What time will you be home? Great, we finish around the same. No, it's fine. Someone can drop it off on their way home.'

I rummaged around my desk and found the passport in the in-tray. It was hidden under paperwork. I waved it at Maxwell as he carried on chatting to Tom, telling him about a role that Tom would be suitable for. He said Tom was his star candidate and that the company would love him—he bet his job on it.

'Alice, could you drop off Tom Appleshaw's passport on your way home? You'll pass by his road en route to the bus station,' Maxwell said as soon as he finished on the phone. I informed the team that Tobias wasn't picking me up from work this week, not that he wouldn't be picking me up from the office ever again. I insisted that I would get the bus to and from work this week to get into my new routine now that he was going away.

'Sure.'

'Great. And as a thank you, you can leave half an hour early.'

'Thank you, but didn't you tell Tom he will be getting home around the same time we finish?'

'That's fine, just post it through his letterbox. Oh, and one last thing,' Maxwell said, 'could you contact Mr Tucker and arrange an interview for Mr Appleshaw?'

'For the manual labour role?'

'Yes, it's on a farm, and they have animals.' Maxwell raised his eyebrows. 'Square pegs and round holes, and all that. We've got to look like we're being pro-active to our clients and candidates.'

I sighed under my breath. It seemed like a waste of time because that wasn't the type of job Tom was looking for. But Maxwell knew best, so I made the call.

On Friday morning, I was the first to arrive in the office, and I was welcomed by a decorated desk with twenty-first birthday balloons and banners. There was a birthday card, gift vouchers, a bottle of champagne, expensive-looking truffle chocolates and a triple chocolate cake from the team. A few minutes later, the door opened. It was a florist with a bouquet filled with candy floss delphinium flowers snuggled in between pastel pink peonies and a spray of white gypsophila. The accompanying message card read:

Happy 21st birthday.

Thanks for your help this week and for going the extra mile in returning the passport.

My new colleagues had spoilt me. I was grateful, but I didn't want a fuss because I was new and also because I couldn't handle the niceness with the upset of Tobias leaving in less than forty-eight hours.

Maxwell didn't come into the office that day, but he made the effort to meet the rest of us for celebratory drinks after work. Dom, Ben, Charlie and I already had drinks when he arrived, but Maxwell insisted on buying a bottle of bubbly. None of us had eaten anything substantial to line our stomachs. We only snacked on crisps and shared a large portion of chips, and we were all tipsy by eight o'clock. Dom left soon after that because he needed to go home to help put his children to bed, followed closely by Ben, who had to get up early for a wedding up-country, and then Charlie—she was running late to meet her husband in town for dinner.

Charlie hugged me before leaving. 'Happy birthday. Those flowers must have cost a small fortune, you lucky girl.'

That left Maxwell and me to finish off the rest of the champagne. He poured the remainder of it into our glasses and dashed off to the bar before returning with two shots of tequila.

'Max,' I hiccupped before licking salt from my hand and sucking on a lime, 'Can I ask you something?'

'Sure,' he said and downed his shot. I copied him.

'I've got a friend whose boyfriend recently told her he was moving to Hawaii for a year. What would you think if you had a girlfriend and she did that to you?'

'He clearly doesn't love her.' Maxwell took a big sip of champagne. 'That's for sure. If a girlfriend did that to me, then, well, let's just say that she wouldn't be my girlfriend anymore.'

'Do you honestly think he doesn't love her?' I said. I threw my head back, allowing the last of the champagne to slide down my throat.

He placed his hand on my arm. 'He's only thinking of himself, not your friend, and that's not love'.

'That's what Tobias is doing,' I sobbed. Alcohol and putting on a brave face all week had finally caught up with me. I was surprised that I confided in Maxwell, but he also had a way about him that seemed like he was my friend and not just my boss.

Maxwell placed his hand under my chin and raised my face to meet his. 'You're too good for him, Alice. If you were my girlfriend, I'd never leave you.' He stood up and pulled me up. 'He's an idiot.'

'Hang on,' I hiccupped. 'The flowers weren't from the team; they were from you, weren't they?' I swayed towards him, pointing my finger at his chest. Maxwell stared at me. 'You didn't need to send me flowers to thank me for the work I've done. It's my job. Plus, I got to finish early to drop off the passport.' I hiccupped again.

'It's the least I could do.' He placed his hand on the arch of my back and guided me out of the pub.

I stopped abruptly in the doorway. Maxwell bumped into me. I turned to face him. 'See, I am a bad person. I forgot to thank you for the flowers.' I started crying again. 'No wonder Tobias wants to get away from me.'

Outside, I stumbled along the road towards the taxi rank, singing something about waving my hands in the air and not caring about it. Someone shouted from the other side of the road. I stopped walking and stopped singing.

'Alice!'

'Tom!' I shrieked.

'Are you having a good night? he shouted.

'The birthday girl has had too much to drink,' Maxwell said. He put his arm around my shoulders. 'We're heading home now.'

I waved at Tom. 'Happy birthday!'

'Happy twenty-first birthday!' he called back. He went to say something else, but before he could, Maxwell gestured for us to move along the pavement.

'Goodbye, Tom.' I waved again.

Maxwell rode in the taxi with me to make sure I got home safely. Mum wasn't impressed that I hadn't eaten, but she was grateful that Maxwell had looked after me. She made me eat toast and drink a pint of water before going to bed.

My head hurt in the morning. I cancelled my morning plans with Tobias and stayed in bed until the afternoon. Luckily I didn't have to call in sick at the shelter; I had booked the day off for my birthday. I wasn't in the mood for my party, not because of my hangover but because it had also turned into Tobias's leaving do. I'm not sure how that had happened. He'd already had a family gathering the previous night. Why did he need another?

It was also Daisy's unofficial travelling celebrations even though she wasn't going away for another fortnight. What was there to celebrate? Daisy was going away for three months, but I needed her more than ever. I attempted a hair-of-the-dog for the first time in my life and drank half a bottle of wine before anyone arrived.

Daisy arrived first, followed shortly by Tobias and his close mates from Loughborough University, Tristan and Jonny. Tobias's twin brother, Owen, was visiting from Cardiff. Was anyone going to turn up for me? Daisy chatted to Mum and Dad downstairs, and I watched Tobias and his *crew* from my bedroom window. They all laughed whilst walking along the garden path. I wondered whether Tobias had told them about Hawaii before me. I took another sip of wine.

Other friends and my family members soon arrived, and the celebrations quickly got underway. Those who didn't know about Tobias's plan changed their congratulatory tone to one of sympathy when they spoke to me, even though they found his plans fascinating.

'How are you doing?' Daisy asked as I opened the door to the bathroom. It was the first opportunity that we had to speak on our own since she arrived.

'I'm fine. I'm going to be too busy with work and uni and the shelter to miss you two,' I shrugged. 'You never know, I might be too busy when Tobias returns.'

Daisy frowned. 'What do you mean? You're going to wait for him to return, aren't you?'

I shrugged again. 'Why should I wait around for him whilst he jet sets halfway around the world?'

'It's only a year. You could go and visit him.'

'Oh yeah, I'll just spend my hard-earned money chasing Tobias around the world. Not all of us have money we can throw away. Why don't you go visit him on your travels if you're so concerned about him?' I stormed off.

Tobias and I didn't get the chance to talk much either; we were both busy socialising, but I needed to speak to him. I waited until he was on his own in the shed, looking for extra blankets for people to sit on.

'I'll help,' I said before following inside the shed.

We rummaged around in the dark. The only light seeped in through the window from lanterns dotted around the garden. Tobias's hands gripped my waist, and he tried kissing me.

'Finally, some time alone.'

I pulled away from him. 'A year is such a long time, and we're both so young. Our lives will be on hold waiting for you to return.'

'It will fly by,' Tobias said before trying to kiss me again.

I pulled away. 'For you, perhaps.'

His voice lowered. 'What are you saying?'

'You're the one going on an adventure across the world, and I'm the one being left behind. I don't see how it will be fair on either of us if we stay together.'

'Please don't do this, Alice.'

'You're the one that's doing this, not me.'

Tobias rubbed his hands across his face and then moved close to hold me. He kissed the top of my head. 'I understand why you're saying this. I'm sorry for doing this to you—to us,' he whispered.

I squeezed him tight. 'It's the right thing for you, I get that. It's not the right thing for us.'

'But we'll remain friends?' He crouched down to my eye level. I nodded. 'And then I'll come back and win you over again.' He laughed. I didn't.

We hugged for what felt like the last time; we only broke apart when Tobias tried wiping tears from my face, but I pushed his hand away and left him alone in the shed.

The end of the party arrived too quickly, and each time somebody left, I wanted to dive over and grab hold of their leg to stop them from leaving. It was a step closer to the end of Tobias and me.

I didn't cry when Tobias left. He asked if he could pop around in the morning before going to the airport, but I didn't think it was a good idea, so we said goodbye then. We hugged again, but it felt more like a polite farewell rather than an I-love-you-so-much embrace. When we pulled apart, I noticed a long blonde hair stuck to his shoulder.

'I take it you hugged Daisy?' I said, pulling the hair off of him.

'The hair was probably already on you.'

'Perhaps I should keep it as a reminder of my best friend. It'll be the only thing left once you've both gone.'

'I'll be at the end of a phone. You can call me anytime.'

'We'll see,' I sighed.

Tobias's taxi arrived. I stepped back into the doorway and watched him walk along the garden path. He stopped at the gate before turning around to smile. The taxi pulled away, and Tobias blew me a kiss. And then he was gone.

'I don't know why you broke up with him, Alice.' Mum said when I closed the front door.

'Because he chose to go,' I shouted and ran up to my bedroom.

Sunday dragged. Tobias was already on his way to Heathrow Airport by the time I woke, and at midday, I pictured his plane taking off. I went to bed early that evening. A text from him woke me at two in the morning—he had safely landed in Los Angeles. His connection flight was on time. I replied, wishing him a safe flight. He replied instantly, saying that he already missed me.

I cried and didn't reply.

CHAPTER 6

Now

Kate knocked on the bedroom door at nine o'clock the following morning. She walked in with a screwed-up expression.

'You're going to need these.' She passed me a dressing gown and my new bobble hat. 'The heating has broken again. That's why the landlord came out yesterday—to save money by fixing it himself. There's no hot water either, so you'll need to boil a few kettles to take a shallow bath.'

'Has he called an engineer this time?'

'Yes, but only when I begged him, and now he's going to have to pay more for a weekend callout. Fabrizio's going to wait in for him, but we can still go out and explore the city.'

Kate boiled the kettle three times for a shallow bath. I tore off my pyjamas, hopped in, and washed as quickly as I could.

The wetter my body, the more painful my skin became. The boiling water cooled far too quickly. Stepping out of the bath, my body temperature cooled more to the chill of the room. I frantically dried off whilst thinking about the comforting warmth of my parents' home.

Kate was barricaded in the lounge. It was the only warm room in the flat. A plug-in heater worked tirelessly to hold off the discomfort that filled the rest of the space. The lounge looked bigger in the day as natural light shone in through two large windows, adding subtle tones of colour to the landlord's beige décor. Fabrizio's maroon saxophone case, an orange beanbag and a multicoloured stripy rug helped brighten the space a little.

I knelt on the corner sofa to look out of the window over a grey, dull London. Rooftops still gleamed white from un-melted snow, but the road below looked dirty. I shivered. Kate knelt beside me and draped a blanket around us both. She pointed out some of London's famous landmarks: the BT Tower in the far distance, Tower Bridge with its castle-turret tips semi-visible towards the south, and the Gherkin felt almost in touching distance in the heart of the city.

'What's that?' I pointed to a white haze. A mini snowstorm suddenly appeared, hiding everything in the direction towards Tower Bridge.

'That'll be a helicopter landing at the Royal London Hospital. They've got a helipad for emergencies.'

As the snow settled, it exposed a red helicopter and medical staff dressed in bright-orange uniforms running towards it whilst pushing a trolley bed. Kate climbed off the sofa, but I watched with curiosity and sadness as the bed was wheeled away from the helicopter, wondering what had happened that was so urgent and terrible that someone needed an air ambulance. Perhaps my life hadn't been too bad after all.

'We'll walk past the hospital,' Kate shouted from the kitchen, 'when we pass through Whitechapel.'

I jumped off the sofa. 'Whitechapel? As in Jack the Ripper's Whitechapel?' I said as I reached the kitchen. 'I didn't realise that was a real place.'

Kate laughed. 'Of course it is.'

We left the flat mid-morning, passing the hospital, just like Kate said we would. It looked taller than it seemed from the flat, and the helipad overlapped the roof like the palm of a hand waiting to catch a floating feather. We weaved our way along quiet residential side roads where modern multi-storey blocks sat opposite aged warehouses and yellow-bricked Georgian houses blackened from decades of pollution and exposure to the elements.

As Kate guided us through a labyrinth of East London streets, I wished there was a Kate-equivalent guide for life—someone who knew their destination and how to reach it. I hadn't known for a long time what I wanted to reach, so how on earth was I ever going to find where I was supposed to be? I hoped that this London opportunity would be like me being picked up from one of those grabber machines at the fair and plonked back at the start. Perhaps Kate was already guiding me in more ways than just not needing my A-Z map.

We reached a busy open space crisscrossed with lanes of traffic. Even if I had my map with me today, I'm not sure that I'd be able to work out where I was. Tall, modern buildings swamped the outer edges and tucked in the middle of it all was the Tower of London. It looked like a time-travelling Tardis that had landed smack bang in the middle of a modern city. I wondered if it could take me back in time and relive my life. I would be mentally prepared and able to handle things differently. My sense of self-worth would be stronger, and it would be easier to accept Tobias's decision to follow his dream. That's what I had been doing for so long, so why had I pushed him away hastily? Maxwell. It is so clear now what he was doing, love bombing, but I fell for it—stupidly. If there is one lesson that I have taken from him sneaking into my life, it is that I'll never allow anyone to treat me that way ever again.

'The Tower has an annual winter ice rink in the moat,' Kate said as we crossed over Tower Bridge. 'Do you want to go some point next week?'

I shook my head. In my mind's eye, I saw white, ghostly figures skating above the Tower and the image of Henry VIIII's beheaded wives skating with their heads tucked under their arms sliced through me. Those poor women, there had been one rule for him and another for them. They had been helpless in doing something about their destiny all because of their relationship with a man. How had things not changed in five hundred years? I still have my head physically, but it almost got chopped off mentally.

The temperature dropped even further as we passed over the River Thames. A few clouds smudged the pale blue sky as though frozen in place, and the grey river below flowed powerfully like a herd of angry hippos charging out of the city.

Once we reached the south side of the river, we headed west towards London Bridge, where we passed through Borough Market, Kate's favourite area of London. People were crammed around stalls whilst vendors called out to sell their wares, trying to attract more customers. A mix of fresh coffee, hot spicy cider, pungent cheeses and raw fish fought to fill the air, but they couldn't compete with the sizzling smoke from a Lebanese street food stall. The warmth from that stall brightened the day. I wanted to close my eyes and step into a warmer climate.

Trains rumbled and screeched along overhead train tracks, and dampness penetrated through the soles of my boots. It was an exciting space, and I was certain I would grow to like it in time, perhaps as much as Kate, but right now, I was ready for somewhere calmer and make do with indoor radiator heat.

We narrowly avoided being run over by a lively bunch of tourists on rented city bikes when we left the market and then dodged our way through an obstacle of people walking in the opposite direction. At times, I struggled to keep up with Kate, especially as we overtook pedestrians walking in the same direction as we headed parallel to the Thames.

'They're tourists,' she said as we passed by more people. 'Londoners walk fast.'

We squeezed past groups gathered around street performers on the Southbank: singers, mime artists, a male performer dressed as a cat but woofing like a dog, magicians and dancers. We crossed back over the Thames via Westminster Bridge and reached Big Ben and the Houses of Parliament. In less than twenty-four hours in London, my senses had been stimulated more than they had been in the last five years.

'I'm hungry,' I said. I was also tired from the previous day's journey. I didn't want to confess to Kate that all I wanted to do was return to the flat and curl up on the sofa because she was enjoying showing me the city. Kate had given me a lifeline by offering me the chance to stay at hers for free, and I didn't want to seem ungrateful. I reminded myself of this and plucked up some enthusiasm and energy to try and enjoy the rest of my London tour.

'We're not too far from the oldest wine bar in London. We can eat there.' Kate linked her arm through mine, and we continued walking.

En route to the pub, we added Downing Street and Horse Guards Parade to our sightseer's tick-list before reaching Trafalgar Square, where a small group of protesters had gathered, holding up banners and chanting.

'What are they protesting about?' I asked.

'I don't know. There is always some protest going on somewhere in London. I've even seen a naked bike ride pass through here.'

'Really?'

'Oh, yes. This is London,' Kate sang. 'Anything goes.'

The wine bar looked abandoned. The front door was shut, it was windowless and at a glance, it could have been mistaken as being boarded up.

'Perhaps we're too early,' I said, 'it's only midday, after all.'

'It's open,' Kate said and pulled me through a metal gate to the side of the building. I watched as she walked down some steps into what looked like the cellar door. I followed her into a dimly lit space.

'Are you sure it's open?' I whispered.

'Come on,' she beckoned.

The wine bar was a tight squeeze, with only a handful of tables tucked in here and there by the doorway and under the stairwell. They were all taken. I didn't want to stay if we couldn't sit down; my feet were aching. I followed Kate as she headed towards a dark archway and into a low vaulted ceiling space where electrical lighting gave way to candlelight.

'Have we walked around the whole of London, or back in time, or both?' I asked as we sat down. Kate laughed—she thought I was joking.

She went to the bar to order a cheese board and a bottle of wine, and when she returned, there was a faint rumbling sound and vibration underfoot. I stood up as she sat down.

'What's that noise?' I said whilst picking up my bag and coat.

'That's just the Tube,' Kate said. 'We're next door to Charing Cross Station.'

I re-hung my coat and flopped onto my chair.

When we left the comfort of the wine bar, I felt colder and even more tired. The wind had picked up, and the sky had clouded over. It felt cold enough to snow again.

'Where to next?' Kate asked.

I shrugged. 'I don't mind.' I did mind. *The flat,* please!

'Let's jump on a bus to Oxford Street.'

Borough Market was busy, but Oxford Circus was on another level. We barged our way through crowds of shoppers as we made our way underneath the Christmas lights. They were the only thing brightening up the afternoon.

The shops were cramped and hot, and I had little energy to remove my hat and gloves each time we entered a shop, only to reverse the process when leaving. It was a relief when Kate received a text from Fabrizio saying an engineer had fixed the heating.

'Are we going back to the flat?'

Kate looked surprised. 'We can do, if you want?' I nodded and pulled my hat tighter onto my head. 'Come on then,' Kate said and linked my arm again. 'It's best to come shopping during the week, anyway. It's slightly quieter in the evenings, too.'

Like a colony of ants returning to its underground nest, we made our way back underground and took the Tube back to Bethnal Green. We were home within twenty minutes. Kate and I changed into cosy fleece pyjamas and bootie slippers whilst Fabrizio made us hot chocolate. I fell asleep on the sofa before Fabrizio finished making them.

The following morning, the three of us decided to go out for brunch after Fabrizio's appointment—he was getting his tenth tattoo. We left the flat and walked west towards the hip area of Brick Lane, where walls were covered with trendy graffiti, and people meandered confidently decorated in their individual styles. Lots of them had piercings and tattoos, and most of the men had facial hair, either pristine beards or coiffed moustaches. Women wore unusual accessories: bowler hats, overly-long scarfs, braces, vampire-style sunglasses—it wasn't sunny—and headscarves. I felt plain and boring in my blue jeans and grey coat.

Kate accompanied Fabrizio to his appointment, but I decided to peruse the area until they were done. I browsed numerous vintage clothing stores and music shops until I found myself gazing at a tattoo parlour. I had considered getting a tattoo for a while, but I was never confident about what I wanted or where it should go on my body—forever. Even when I figured these things out, I still hadn't found the courage to go through with it. I let out a long sigh. From experience, I learnt that facing up to pain and pushing through to the other side of it was the only way to move forward. If I stayed on this side of my fear, I would never get a tattoo. I hesitated and then pushed open the parlour door.

A strong smell of sterile cleaning products stung the air, and it was so quiet in the parlour that my ears throbbed from the silence. The emptiness was soon pierced by a faint, intermittent buzzing sound coming from another room. I expected a scream or for someone to come running out with a madman chasing after them. But nothing happened.

Gruesome artwork covered the walls. An evil clown's face etched onto someone's shoulder glared down at me, a tattoo of a hammer claw ripping a calf muscle sent a shiver down my spine, and even a beautiful rose design made me feel queasy at the sight of blood oozing from the thorns. In comparison, skull and grim reaper tattoos looked mild, almost cartoon-like. With the mix of cleaning products, the buzzing and the images, I decided that it still wasn't the right time to get a tattoo. I walked back towards the door.

'Can I help ya?' a voice called.

I spun around to see a woman of a similar age standing behind the counter; she appeared from nowhere, like Dracula in his castle. Her body was covered in tattoos—even the palms of her hands were inked. My fingers curled into a ball at the thought. Her lips smacked as she chewed on gum whilst staring at me.

I cleared my throat, 'I'm not sure...'

She winked at me. 'Don't worry, I was a tattoo virgin once.' She pulled at the gum and twisted it around her finger. I forced a smile. How did everyone in London seem to know I was the new girl at everything? She wasn't even from London, judging by her Liverpudlian accent. 'Do you know what you're after?' she said. As she walked toward me, her gothic appearance suggested she would levitate any moment.

I took my phone from my bag to find a photo I had saved in there. She sniggered. 'Blimey, that's vintage.'

I blushed but continued looking for the grainy image on my phone. 'I saw this tattoo on someone on a night out ages ago. It means inner peace.'

She took my phone, studied it for a moment and then drew the tattoo in the air. I watched as her hand made a circular shape with her fingers, and then her wrist flicked as though drawing the swirl. Her hand froze in the air, and she seemed to go into a trance. 'It's not our normal style,' she said, still gazing.

'Well, thanks for your help,' I said, snatching my phone and yanking open the door.

'But I can do it now if you like,' she grabbed onto my arm. 'It won't take long…fifteen minutes, max.'

I met back up with Kate and Fabrizio half an hour later.

'What have you been up to?' Fabrizio asked as he showed me his clingfilm-covered forearm. It was tricky to make out the abstract guitar tattoo amongst the blurred blood and ink.

'Ta-dah!' I said and pulled up my coat and jumper, revealing a small clingfilmed patch taped over my lower spine.

'Does it mean something?' Kate asked.

I nodded. 'Inner peace.'

She squeezed my arm and smiled. I imagine it's what it feels like having a big sister care and protect their delicate younger sibling.

'You do realise they're addictive?' Fabrizio said. 'That'll be the first of many.'

'I think it will be my only one. It's a reminder to always know my mind.'

We headed for an eighties-themed café where we were seated near an upcycled wooden dresser and a large, duck-egg-blue American-style fridge. I sat facing Kate and Fabrizio and the fridge. A waitress quickly took our order. It was busy, and people were still queuing to be seated. Staff buzzed around the place, seating people, wiping tables, taking orders, and serving drinks and food. Whilst all of this was going on, I witnessed something that didn't seem real. I leant forward and whispered to Kate and Fabrizio.

'A woman has just climbed inside the fridge.'

Kate and Fabrizio turned around to look at the fridge and turned back to face me.

'There are a lot of crazies in London. You'll get used to them,' Fabrizio said.

'But she could die in there. She'll suffocate.'

Kate shrugged her shoulders. 'I'm sure she'll come out soon enough.'

My breathing felt shallow. I shuffled on my seat and glared at the fridge.

The waitress brought our drinks to the table. 'Can I get you anything else?'

'Brown sauce,' Fabrizio said.

'I'm fine, thanks,' Kate said.

I didn't want to cause the waitress more work; it looked like she needed the endurance of a marathon runner to work there, but I had to say something. When she returned with the condiments and cutlery, I whispered to her. 'There's someone in the fridge.' I nodded my head in that direction.

She placed the cutlery and napkins on the table. 'Are you sure?'

I stood up, walked to the fridge, and looked back at Kate and Fabrizio. 'I may be new to London, but I know what I saw, and we have to help.' I thought of my new tattoo.

The waitress joined me at the fridge and held onto its handle. 'Stand back.' I did as she said. She opened the door and gasped. I hurtled towards her and tugged on the door. I looked inside, then at the waitress, back in the fridge, and then at Fabrizio and Kate. They were clutching their stomachs with laughter. Inside the fridge were stairs and a sign with an arrow pointing to a downstairs bar. The waitress closed the fridge door. 'Welcome to London,' she grinned before walking off to seat more customers.

After brunch, we continued west, passing Liverpool Street Station and on towards The Barbican Centre, where it was first-come-first-serve for a free pre-performance viewing of the London Symphony Orchestra. It was something Fabrizio liked to do at least once a month, being a musician. It wasn't something I would have chosen to do, but my admiration for his passion for filling his life with his interests swept me along.

The building looked like a multi-levelled concrete maze. At first, I assumed it was a council estate, but Fabrizio said it was famous and that some of the brutalist architectural apartments were worth over a million pounds each. I found that difficult to believe, a bit like when someone makes out something they are not, a trait I particularly dislike in humans. Why couldn't people just be more honest with each other, and that would help us be more honest with ourselves?

We walked along indoor corridors and outdoor corridors and climbed staircases inside and out until we reached an intimate concert hall. The seating was curved as though hugging the stage, and we luckily found some seats in the back row. As soon as we were seated, the room darkened, and the orchestra was lit up brightly by overhead lighting. The heat from the spotlights quickly warmed the room, and a couple of older audience members nodded off in the front row.

It was cosy in there, and I could have easily fallen asleep, but I was mesmerised by the conductor's control of the orchestra with his baton. It was such a different experience from what I would have normally been doing on a Sunday afternoon back in Devon. The nearest thing to it was waving the remote control in front of the television, flicking through channels before falling asleep for an afternoon snooze.

We arrived back at the flat just before tea time. I decided

to get an early night because I wanted to give Kate and Fabrizio some space and because I needed it, too. A lot had happened since Friday morning at the coach station. The weekend passed quickly, and it was a safe way to break into the London lifestyle with Kate's full support, but from tomorrow, I needed to focus and find my way and life in the city.

I crawled into the single bed, kicked the duvet up and caught it under my feet to trap the heat from my breath under the duvet. A draft rippled underneath the beige-flecked curtain. It was thick enough to block out light, but it didn't stop noise creeping up from ground level. Emergency sirens pierced the window, as did car horns and a rowdy group of people that cheered after the sound of glass shattering. I closed my eyes, took some deep breaths and consciously relaxed my shoulders back onto the bed. Meditation helped for a while to block out the noise until a female voice startled me. She sounded emotional and angry. I knelt up and pulled the duvet around my shoulders before peering between the curtains.

The sky was clearer, and moonlight shone brightly over the snow-covered roofs. A passing cloud covered the moon like a spider's egg sac within a dense web. The city was lit up even brighter by man-made light. It looked full of life, and I wondered if I was the only person all alone in London. The wind whistled through the window, and I pulled to the duvet tighter.

The girl caught my attention once again. The single-paned glass didn't allow her any privacy. It felt intrusive listening to her conversation, even though she was speaking loudly enough for the entire neighbourhood to hear. She was talking on her mobile phone. Judging by her accusations of somebody cheating, I guessed she was arguing with her boyfriend. A shiver sliced down my spine when her words changed, and she started apologising to him. I thought of Maxwell and how I wished, not that I hadn't met him, but I had not fallen for him. I wanted to open the window and shout down to her to stop what she was saying. It was a trap.

CHAPTER 7

Then

Tobias sent an email a few days after arriving in Hawaii inviting me to a Skype session at the weekend. Curiosity got the better of me, so I agreed.

'What have you been up to?' He asked after panning his laptop around his sun-filled condo. He was wearing my favourite green t-shirt; it made his green eyes greener and his pupils sharper as though they could x-ray my thoughts. He perched on the end of his bed in front of a glowing window. Outside, two palm trees were stretching in the morning breeze, and then they began waving at me—his old life back in boring Devon. I was tucked up in bed wearing scruffy pyjamas with my hair tied up in a loose bun. The ten-hour difference made him seem so far away.

'The same old things: work, the shelter, catching up with

Daisy as much as we can before she goes travelling.'

Tobias said it took a few days to get over jetlag, and he struggled on his introduction day at the surf school. Since then, he had surfed daily and went on a night out in Honolulu with his new colleagues. Three of them were going on a volcano tour that morning.

He squinted from the sunlight. 'The surf is incredible. There's so much wildlife, you would love it here.' The excitement of his new adventure was clear in his expression. His smile reminded me of the first time I told him that I was in love with him. I pinched the inside of my leg to focus on physical pain instead of the longing I had to go back to that time.

'What time is it there?' I asked.

'It's just coming up to ten, which means we've been chatting for an hour.'

'That's gone quick.'

Tobias raised his eyebrows. 'Too quick.'

There was a knock at the door. 'Hey Tobias, you ready? We're gonna shoot in a mo.'

'Who's that?' I asked.

'Just Flick.'

'Who?'

'Sorry, I mean Felicity. She's one of my housemates.' There was an uncomfortable pause.

'Hurry up, T, we're going!' Felicity shouted again.

'T?' I raised my eyebrows.

'That's what they all call me here.' He stood up. 'Yeah, just coming,' he called out to her. I wanted to ask if he calls her 'F' but thought better of it. 'I've gotta go. They're waiting for me in the Jeep.'

'Have a nice time.' *But not with Flick*, I thought, forcing a smile.

'Thanks—I've really got to go. Speak soon, bye.'

I stared at the blank screen. 'Bye.'

Daisy had her official going-away drinks the following weekend. She was travelling around Europe before returning in September to start her graduate accountant job. It was only three months, but I was going to miss her a lot. I drove into Plymouth that evening and didn't drink because I needed to get back for a ten o'clock Skype session with Tobias.

On the drive home, a text message pinged through. I guessed it was Tobias telling me he was ready to chat. I was running late due to getting stuck behind a tractor for the last two miles of the journey, and I started panicking that I wouldn't make it in time. I parked the car and hurried along the garden path to the front door whilst trying to read the locked screen on my mobile. Tobias was ready. He sent that message ten minutes ago. I rushed upstairs and switched on my laptop. Why was it taking so long to start up! I unlocked my phone to read the rest of his message and to let him know that I would be jumping on the call any minute, but I was too late. Tobias had been ready for the call, but he was struggling to get a good internet connection. He apologised and asked to rearrange our catch-up for the following week. I slammed the laptop before it had fully booted up.

I went back to my car, texted Daisy to tell her I was on my way back and downed the shot of tequila she had waiting for me on arrival. It ended up being a messy and late night, and the following morning, I called in sick at the animal shelter.

Dom tried arranging a team-building bowling session one evening after work. Everyone was able to make it until the morning we were going. Charlie cancelled because of a last-minute meeting with a client that she had been trying to work with for a long time; Ben's wife was unwell, so he needed to leave early to go home and help her with their baby. That left Dom, Maxwell and me. Dom suggested postponing bowling to the following week so that we could all go. I was disappointed we weren't going because I wanted to be able to tell Tobias about doing something different the next time we spoke.

'Damn it,' Maxwell said, 'that was my excuse to get out of the networking event that Tom Appleshaw invited me to this evening.'

'Surely that's a good opportunity to get more clients on the books?' I asked.

'Yes, normally, but it's such a small event it's not worth my time. Besides, you should be thanking me for saving you too because he invited you also. I told him you were busy.'

'Thanks, I suppose.'

The phone rang, and Maxwell answered. 'Hi Diane, how

are you?' Maxwell took a sip of his coffee and pulled a disgusted expression. He held his mug towards me and mouthed, 'Cold'. I walked over to his desk and collected his mug, and he carried on his telephone conversation.

I was in a daydream in the kitchen when Maxwell walked in.

'Haven't you made those drinks yet?' he joked. He picked up his mug and poured the coffee granules into the bin. 'I fancy tea.'

'Okay, I'll bring it to you in a second.'

'It's okay, I'll wait. I need a break from my screen,' he said and sat down at the small table tucked into the corner of the room. 'It's a shame about tonight. I was looking forward to a pint.'

'Me too,' I said, 'the bowling, I mean, not a pint.' Maxwell laughed. 'It's such a lovely day; it seems a waste to go straight home.'

'We could still go out?' Maxwell stood up. 'We could go for a drink or two.'

I pictured a cold glass of white wine whilst sitting in a pub garden soaking up the evening sun. Tobias was in Hawaii, Daisy was somewhere in Europe, and I didn't have anything better to do. 'That sounds like a nice idea.'

'Great, but let's not mention it to anyone else,' he whispered, 'Dom might think we're undermining his plans.'

Maxwell and I stayed out for a few drinks, and afterwards, he insisted on walking me to the bus station. He asked how Tobias was, and then he told me about his ex-girlfriend.

'We were together five years, but we broke up because she wanted to get married and I didn't. Well, not to her, anyway.'

'I'm sure that hurt her, but it sounds like it was the right thing to do for both of you.'

Maxwell stopped walking and looked at me. 'My ex wasn't the one for me forever, but I loved her, and I wouldn't have left her behind to move to the other side of the world.'

I carried on walking. 'I don't think Tobias asked me because I'm studying. He probably didn't want to interfere with that.' I stared at the ground. I had softened a little with his decision to go. I was enjoying our catch-ups, and it was already less than a year until he returned.

'You could have done another gap year. He would have known that. I think Tobias is an idiot for leaving you behind.'

'Thank you.'

Maxwell held my arm. 'I mean it.'

I smiled at him. 'Thank you for being a supportive friend; it means a lot.'

Maxwell linked his arm to mine, and we started skipping. He pulled me along, and we laughed until I was out of breath.

'It's funny how guys move on faster than women,' he said.

'Why is that?' I managed to say whilst trying to catch my breath.

'I wouldn't be surprised if he's moved on with that *Flick* girl you mentioned.'

I stopped walking, and my stomach knotted as though a thread had caught on a thorn bush.

'Do you think he has?'

Maxwell turned and faced me. 'Of course he has, he's a guy.'

'I wish you hadn't said that.'

'Sorry, I only told you that to protect you.'

'What do you mean?'

'You need to be prepared for when he tells you something like that. He's not going to wait around for you forever. You broke up with him, remember.'

'You're right,' I sighed.

He playfully nudged me, but I didn't laugh. 'I've got an idea…so you move on just as fast.' He held onto my shoulders and looked into my eyes, 'Let me kiss you.'

'No, we can't do that,' I tried to wriggle free from his hold, but he held on.

'Just think of it as a friend helping out a friend. It's only a kiss.'

Maxwell was right—it was just a kiss. I nodded, and he leaned in and kissed me.

Maxwell acted normally at work the following day as though nothing had happened between us. I was unsure if that was a good thing or not. I tried to act normally, too, but it didn't come as naturally to me, and by the end of the day, I was exhausted. As soon as work finished, I rushed out of the office, but before I reached the end of the road, Maxwell called out my name. He caught up with me and then told me how much he enjoyed our kiss and asked me out to dinner. I said yes. Why should Tobias and Daisy be having all the fun?

We went out Saturday night, but I only agreed to go then because he promised he could drop me home in time for Tobias's call. When I spoke to Tobias, I told him I had been out for dinner but omitted the part about it being with Maxwell.

Maxwell insisted on paying for everything. We went to the cinema the following week and had dinner out a few nights later. He asked me back to his place after dinner, but I declined; I wasn't ready to take the next step and he respected my decision. But I *was* ready after a handful of dates later and stayed over at his after he cooked us a meal.

I started dressing the following morning when Maxwell got up to use the bathroom.

'What are you doing?' he said on his return.

'I need to go home and get ready to go to the dog shelter.'

He started tickling me. 'But I was going to make us breakfast in bed.' He undressed me, and I climbed back under the covers.

We became an official couple within a few weeks, and Maxwell was excited about telling our colleagues we were together. We became inseparable to the extent that I hardly noticed Daisy's absence. I couldn't help but get swept up by

Maxwell's attention and generosity, and after a while, my calls with Tobias faded away.

Maxwell and I went out for dinner most nights, and I stayed at his most of the time. He lived alone, and I lived with my parents, so it made sense to stay at his to get some privacy. But every now and then, I liked to stay at home to spend quality time with my parents.

'I've got a surprise for you tonight,' Maxwell said as soon as I arrived at work after staying with Mum and Dad. I wanted to see them before they went away for a long weekend in Wales.

'I've got a surprise for you too. I was going to ask if you wanted to come over to mine tonight,' I said. 'I've got the place to myself, so I'll make us dinner, and then we can watch a movie.' I thought it would be nice to return the favour and do something for him because he was always spoiling me. Plus, I was craving home-cooked food, and the novelty of eating out so frequently was starting to wear off. I also liked the idea of not having to get dressed up either.

'Alice, you've spoiled my surprise. I've reserved a table at that new fancy seafood restaurant, the one overlooking the harbour, and afterwards we're going on a bar cruise.

I wasn't too fussed about going there, especially being a flexitarian. I mostly opted for the vegetarian option when eating out for inspiration for home cooking. But I agreed to go because I could tell how excited Maxwell was.

'How did you manage to get a table for the restaurant? They're supposed to be fully booked for weeks.'

He slapped my bottom, 'Anything for you.' I screeched, and he pulled me in for a quick kiss before anyone else arrived at work.

Maxwell enjoyed his lobster meal, but my spinach gnocchi was sickly after watching the waiter retrieve the live lobster from the tank after taking Maxwell's order. I didn't remember telling Maxwell that I wanted to try this restaurant. I didn't generally eat seafood, and I certainly wouldn't have come knowing there was live 'food'. But I didn't say anything to Maxwell because I didn't want to sound ungrateful.

The wind picked up that evening, and once the boat left the comfort of the harbour, it started swaying from side to side. It was too cold to stand on the open-top deck, so we stayed inside, but I started feeling queasy.

'Come outside,' Maxwell said.

I sat on the edge of a seat with my hand over my mouth. 'I can't move.'

'Come on, you'll feel better for it,' he stood up. I shook my head. 'You need to look at the horizon so that your eyes and ears understand each other.' He tucked his arm underneath mine and helped me up. We stumbled with each footstep as the boat rocked. Outside, waves smacked into the side of the boat, throwing up sea spray into our faces each time the boat dipped towards the sea. I was cold and wet, but the sick feeling slowly eased off. I clung onto the railings until we returned to the harbour. Maxwell stayed by my side.

Maxwell had lots of life experience, and he enjoyed introducing me to new things. He was a confident driver and often drove us to the countryside for weekend adventures, and if we ever got lost, he knew how to find his way again. He encouraged me to try new foods like Lebanese street food and took me to unusual venues. We even dined at a rooftop bar in Exeter one sunny evening. In his spare time, he liked to keep active. He enjoyed hill walking, which I quickly took to, and he also wanted me to try new activities like indoor rock climbing and kayaking.

Everything felt as though it would be okay with Maxwell around, and I found his confidence and knowledge intoxicatingly attractive. He was only a few years older than Tobias, but he was so much more manly.

To make up for the seasickness episode and to create new memories, Maxwell booked us back into the fancy seafood restaurant. The meal was better than the first time we ate there, probably because the lobster tank was empty, and we weren't going on a booze cruise afterwards. It was a great idea to rewrite our experience there.

The waiter brought over the bill, along with complimentary mints.

'I'm tired tonight,' I said and reached under the table for my bag. 'Do you mind dropping me home afterwards?'

Maxwell handed me a mint. 'Are you sure I can't tempt you to stay at mine?'

I unwrapped the foil packaging from the mint. 'Not tonight, and besides, I've got to get up early to work at the shelter. I'm doing an extra shift because two people are on holiday.' I went to place the hard-boiled mint into my mouth, but something stopped me.

'What's that?' There was a red blob on the mint.

Maxwell was smiling. He had hidden a chilli flake from the condiments within the wrapping. We both laughed. I removed the chilli flake and ate the mint. We chatted whilst waiting for the waiter to return to take payment. Maxwell was still trying to tempt me to stay over at his.

'Lean forward,' I said, 'you've got something on the corner of your mouth.' We leaned over the table towards each other, and I wiped my finger on the corner of his mouth.

'Has it gone?' he asked.

'No, it's still there. Try licking it.' I demonstrated with my tongue, and he mirrored me. 'That's it, you've got it.'

'Yuk, what is that?' Maxwell said and gulped down the remainder of his water. 'My mouth's on fire.' The waiter walked over. I clapped and laughed.

'Yes! I did it.' Maxwell stared at me. 'You didn't have anything on your lip. I put the chilli flake there when I pretended to wipe something off.' I giggled again.

The waiter stifled a laugh. Maxwell glared at him before looking back at me. 'For goodness sake, Alice, I wouldn't have allowed you to eat the chilli flake.'

'Sorry, it was just a joke.'

'Well, you took it a bit too far.'

Maxwell made the payment, and the waiter didn't make eye contact with either of us again. We sat in silence for the majority of the drive back to mine, but I eventually broke the silence.

'I'm sorry for taking the joke too far.'

'It's okay,' Maxwell said, 'I'm tired too, so I think it's a good idea that you stay at your parents tonight.' We pulled up outside the house, and he kissed me on the cheek before I got out of the car. He wound down the window. 'I'll miss you tonight,' he blew me a kiss and drove away.

I felt guilty for taking the joke too far and was still annoyed with myself the following day. I sent him a text from the animal shelter and asked to see him that evening. I suggested staying in with a takeaway and a movie. He replied straight away, saying he couldn't wait.

September soon arrived, and Daisy returned from her travels. It was great fun catching up at the beach and hearing all about her European travels: wine tasting in Italy, water-skiing in the South of France, a city tour around Barcelona and the handsome travellers she met along the way.

'How are things going with Maxwell?'

'Good,' I said and told her about all the meals he had taken me on and our weekends away.

'Wow, it sounds like it's getting serious,' she teased.

'Hardly; we're just having lots of fun.'

'I hope you're still going to have time for me.'

'Of course, I will. A man will never come between us, ever.' I hugged her. 'It's so good to have you back.'

After spending a few hours at the beach with Daisy, I drove to Maxwell's.

'How's Daisy?' he asked as he poured me a glass of red wine.

'She had an amazing time.' I repeated some of her stories.

'It sounds like she had a great time. I hope she's not too depressed about being back.'

'She's fine. But she did say she hoped I still had time for her now that we're dating.'

'I didn't put her down as the jealous type.' Maxwell placed his arm around my shoulder.

I laughed. 'She was only joking.' I changed the subject to his day rock climbing.

A few days later, Maxwell and I were watching television. He was flicking through the channels, trying to find something to watch after dinner.

'Stop!' I shouted, 'go back.' Maxwell flicked back to a travel programme. They were in New York City.

'That's Battery Park,' Maxwell said as the camera panned around to a fortress overlooking the water.

'I didn't know you had been to New York.

He nodded. 'The park overlooks the Statue of Liberty.'

'I would love to go there.'

'We should think about going on holiday somewhere.' He crossed his arms behind his head as though lying on a poolside sun lounger, 'Definitely a beach holiday.'

'You'll have to go on holiday without me. I can't afford to go on holiday at the moment. I'm saving most of my money for when I go back to university soon. I don't think I could take any time off from the rescue centre; they need a good amount of notice to reshuffle their rotas.

Maxwell sat up. 'I've been meaning to talk to you about that.' He held my hands and pulled me towards him so that I was sitting on his lap. He rested his hands on my hips. 'I want to start my own recruitment agency. No, let me rephrase that: I *am* going to start up my own recruitment agency.'

'That's amazing.' I kissed him, 'I'm so excited for you.'

He kissed me back. 'I'm going to quit my job and start working from home. It's something I've been planning for a long time, and I've been waiting for the right moment to go for it.'

'You should, you'll be amazing.' I interlaced my fingers into his. 'You'll have staff and an office in no time.'

'I hope to have a member of staff working with me straight away.' He looked into my eyes. 'Come and work with me, Alice.'

Maxwell had it all planned out: I would take a gap year to help him get things started; neither of us would take a salary, but we would share the commission he made. He had plenty of money saved up to cover his mortgage and bills, and because we would be working long days, he asked me to move in with him rent-free. It was only for a year, and I could save more money over the year, based on Maxwell's commission estimates, than I had during my first two years at university.

Maxwell handed in his notice the following week and was put on gardening leave immediately, and whilst he worked on the initial setup, I stayed at the recruitment agency for a few more weeks until my contract ended. Working with Maxwell also meant the dog shelter had to be put on hold too, but I promised the manager, Nita, that I would return. She said I was welcome back anytime.

CHAPTER 8

Now

My alarm clock woke me to the dark. By the time Kate and I arrived at the coffee shop, less than five hundred meters away, it was still dark. As a thank you for allowing me to stay rent-free, I volunteered to work at Kate's café even though she insisted there was no need for me to do that. She wanted to help me, but I also wanted to help her. Kate had given me a lifeline I would forever be grateful for. Besides, it was good to integrate myself into the city instead of hiding away in the flat—I had hidden from life for long enough.

The café opened at half-past six, and by seven, it was steadily busy with customers mainly ordering takeaway coffee in reusable cups. As an avid tea drinker, it was a steep coffee learning curve understanding the difference between a single shot espresso and a babyccino.

'People can't function before their morning coffee fix,' Kate said after the morning rush.

I wiped my brow with the back of my wrist. It had been frantic, but I could see why Kate enjoyed working at the cafe: the scent of freshly baked pastries and coffee danced with jazz music and the bright yellow walls and azure blue furniture added some spice to a winter's morning. To my surprise, there were regulars. They asked Kate and her staff about their weekend and vice versa. I presumed London was too big and too fast for routine and familiarity, but I liked that it wasn't always like that.

After the other team members finished their morning break, Kate made our drinks. I sat at a window bench, watching Kate in the kitchen. I thought how lucky she was to have carved out her passion into her career, which also allowed her the opportunity to meet her lovely boyfriend, Fabrizio. He performed with his band one evening when the café held a jazz evening two years ago. I was envious of Kate and her life. I felt a nudge of regret. Not seeing through my passion for working with animals was something I felt embarrassed about. Yes, I fell foolishly in love; perhaps it will be fourth time lucky, and I can't help how people acted, but I did have a choice over what I did. Not completing my degree is something that I will regret forever.

I needed to look for employment, but the thought of my life slipping past working Monday to Friday in an unfulfilling office every week for the rest of my working life didn't fill me with excitement. I missed the old me who knew what she wanted and had the drive and determination to make things happen. Me now and in recent years was simply clinging onto existence, going with whatever got me through one day to the next.

Kate handed me my drink. 'Try this.'

I smelt it. 'What is it?'

'I know you don't drink coffee, but you may like it. It's a gingerbread latte.'

I took a sip and smiled. 'It tastes like Christmas in a mug.' Perhaps coffee was the beginning of the new me.

One of the recruitment agencies I contacted before moving up to London left a voice message on my phone that morning, and I listened to it whilst on a toilet break.

'Hi, this is a message for Alice Berry; this is Clare at City Recruitment. I have a vacancy that has just come in that I think you are perfect for—you have the right skills and experience that they require. But you'll need to come into our offices to register before we can send you for an interview. We have a two p.m. slot available tomorrow, so I'll book you in for then. See you tomorrow. Oh, and don't forget to bring some I.D. with you.'

I wasn't excited about the role and working with Maxwell. I knew recruitment agents had the gift of telling you what you wanted to hear rather than the facts, a skill that seeped into his personal life. But I was pleased for the opportunity to take another step forward.

After the mad lunchtime rush the following day, I returned to the flat to change out of my jeans and sweatshirt and into something more office-appropriate: black trousers and a blouse. To test myself and to begin the severance process of relying on Kate, I planned my journey using Daisy's A to Z booklet before leaving the flat. I studied the Tube and street map to familiarise myself with the journey to the recruitment office near Moorgate Tube Station. I noted down a basic itinerary on a scrap piece of paper: *red to Liverpool St, change for the yellow, pink or purple line to Moorgate, left out of the station onto the main road, first left into Circus Place.*

It was strange being on the Tube on my own again, but I felt different compared to whom I was just four days earlier. It almost seemed normal being on the underground; I even managed to sit down. The Tube screeched to a halt at Liverpool Street. I took a sneaky peek at my notes to remind myself of the rest of the journey before disembarking. I arrived easily at Moorgate as planned, but when I exited the station, I was stumped. From memory, my notes were to turn left from the station, but there was another station exit on the opposite side of the road, like a mirror image. Which way was the correct left, left from here or left from over there?

Tall, concrete buildings barricaded the long road in both directions, and it seemed impossible to work out which left was towards Circus Place. My breathing quickened. It was less than fifteen minutes until my appointment. The stress of being lost and late was stronger than my fear of being mugged, so I reached inside my handbag for Daisy's street map, but it wasn't there. I must have forgotten to pick it up before leaving the flat. I crept forward to the edge of the pavement and looked up and down the road to see if there was anything that would make it clear which way I needed to go, but there wasn't.

A short, sharp downpour forced me to take shelter at a nearby bus stop. I cursed under my breath, not wanting to draw attention to my frustration from the silent rain-dodgers who were also taking cover. Time was dripping away, and I still didn't know which way to go. I held back the tears of frustration brimming inside.

The rain eased off as quickly as it arrived, and I patiently waited for it to stop completely before making a move, whatever that may be. I held out my hand to check the lightness and looked up to see if it was clear enough to leave the shelter. Above, I noticed the bus stop sign: *buses towards Old Street.* I remembered on the map that Old Street Station was north of Moorgate, and the recruitment office was south, which meant I was on the wrong side of the road to turn left. I darted from the shelter and crossed the road like a skier zigzagging their way around traffic in a slalom race. I made it to the appointment with two minutes to spare.

'We've arranged an interview for you. It's a temporary admin support role with a stationery company based in Clapham North,' the recruitment consultant said after taking my details and checking my I.D. Where was Clapham North? I'd heard of Clapham Common, but where was that? 'I see that you have years of sales admin experience, so the job will be straightforward for you.'

'Great, when is it?'

She looked at her watch. 'In just under an hour.' She stood up and walked towards the door. I followed. 'If you jump on the Northern line to Clapham North, you'll be there within twenty minutes. The office is beside a grey-fronted coffee shop opposite the station. You can't miss it.'

'Who do I ask for?'

'I'll email you the details so you've got them when you get off the Tube. You can read them over a coffee before you go in.'

'Would you be able to print the details off for me, please? I can't get emails on my phone.'

'Sure, my phone broke last week, and I couldn't get emails for twenty-four hours—it was bliss.'

I just smiled at her and nodded the truth that my phone wasn't modern enough to receive emails.

The interview took place with the human resources consultant because the departmental manager was off sick that day. She wasn't a friendly H.R. representative and wasn't enthused as we powerwalked around the open-plan office. I was shown the kitchen, toilets, introduced to the sales team—the department that required the admin support—and then we sat in the meeting room. She wouldn't be my manager, so I overlooked the uncertainty I felt about her and the role.

'The recruitment agency can confirm the rate of pay and holidays etc. Any other questions?' she asked during our brief chat. It was all so quick that I couldn't think of anything that she hadn't covered. I shook my head. 'Great, we'll see you tomorrow. It's a nine-thirty start and six-thirty finish, with half an hour lunch break.'

The dress code was smart-casual, and I needed more outfits than I had brought to London. I assumed there would be more time to go shopping before starting work, so I had to return to Oxford Street, now. I would make a return trip to the red line at Liverpool Street and reverse Saturday's Tube journey to Oxford Circus Station. I didn't need my A-Z to work that out.

I waited outside the office to cross over the road to head back to the Tube station, but I changed my mind when I saw a bus heading towards Oxford Street. I decided to take that instead. I swiped my Oyster card and took a seat on the top deck. I was feeling pleased with myself: I had successfully used the Tube on my own, received a job offer and was now travelling on a London bus all on my own. London life was becoming easier by the hour.

The bus made a handful of stops in South London before a pre-recorded message played informing passengers that the destination of the bus had changed, and within seconds, another announcement informed us that the bus was terminating. It pulled into a bus stop, cut the engine, the lights went out, and most passengers disembarked peacefully. A few huddled around the driver to find out what was happening, but he didn't know.

The rest of us waited patiently at the bus stop. The next bus was only a minute away, according to the amber text on the digital notice board, but before that bus arrived, the information on the screen disappeared and was replaced by a solid amber line. The bus network had flatlined. People started tutting and cussing and some stormed off.

'Let's walk to Lambeth North to see if we can get a bus from there,' an elderly woman said to another lady of a similar age. I didn't know where I was, when the next bus would arrive or where Lambeth North was. My only option was to discreetly follow the elderly ladies to Lambeth North.

'That's odd,' the taller lady said as they walked ahead along a curved road.

'Yes, it is,' the other agreed.

I didn't know what was going on, but judging by their reaction, something unusual was happening, which oddly made me feel a bit better that it wasn't just me struggling to reach my destination. A huge crowd was gathered around a row of bus stops. From what I had seen so far during my short time in the city, London flowed. It wasn't stagnant like it seemed to be right now. Double-decker buses were parked up one behind the other, following the curve of the road like a red bus-train which grew longer and longer each time another one joined. Voices from the crowd, agitated and frustrated, got louder. I joined the impatient gathering along with the two ladies, and the chaos quickly absorbed us, sucking us deeper into the mass. I lost sight of the women.

A middle-aged guy climbed up from the crowd and stood on a seat in one of the bus shelters. He called out to get people's attention, and with his eyes fixed on the screen, he read aloud from his mobile phone. 'There's a student protest taking place at Parliament Square…buses have been stopped from crossing over Westminster Bridge.' Loud moans and groans spread across the crowd. 'Tubes aren't stopping at Westminster Station either.' People quickly dispersed as though they were on a treasure hunt with a grand prize at the end: an operational bus. The crowd drained away, leaving just a few of us with the bus-train. Even the drivers disappeared. The empty and darkened buses made me feel uneasy. I wanted to cry again.

The abandoned buses reminded me of the loneliness I had felt numerous times over recent years. Tobias leaving was a struggle and I didn't cope any better the second time someone rejected me. Oh, how I hated being the one left behind. I needed to get away from these buses, fast.

I walked in the opposite direction from where I had arrived; it was the only logic I had to find a way forward. A shimmer of burgundy tiles caught my eye. It wasn't obvious at first that it was the front of Lambeth North Tube Station. It was nestled at the end of a building block. Luckily, the red circular Tube sign gave it away; otherwise, I would have walked straight past. Relief coursed through me as I hurried across the busy junction, but as I approached, black-punched shutters protected the station from the outside world and from me getting in. It was locked shut. A piece of paper taped onto the shutters flapped in the breeze. The handwritten note suggested travellers should use Waterloo Station as an alternative. I didn't know where Waterloo was either, so I carried along the main road, walking away from the bus-train. It was getting dark, and up ahead was an even darker underpass.

There was a road sign just before the dark tunnel informing those who dared to pass under the bridge would find a roundabout on the other side. Waterloo Station was to the right of that. I headed into the gloom where the only light was from passing traffic. My pace quickened until I reached the other side. The roundabout wasn't like any I had seen before. Six lanes of traffic swamped the roundabout, and the exits weren't visible because they were hidden by tall buildings on and around the roundabout. The earlier road sign had been an exaggeration. This was a metropolis island, not a roundabout. I couldn't see Waterloo Station or the exit for it. I suddenly felt small and lost once again. It was getting darker, and I hadn't seen a pedestrian since the bus-train.

A woman appeared from a dark alleyway beside the underpass. She was wearing a green-grey uniform that I didn't recognise, but it made me feel safe enough to ask her for directions—my luck of blending in as a local had run out. She laughed when I asked her where Waterloo Station was. I forced a fake one back.

'Look up,' she said. I looked up at the bridge I had walked under. 'Those are Waterloo's railway tracks. Follow the alleyway underneath the tracks and walk alongside the taxi rank. Turn left at the main road and you will reach your destination.' She laughed again as she walked away.

The alleyway was narrow and darker than the tunnel. I resisted the urge to run until I made it safely to the taxi rank. Flashes of red passed by at the end of the road. Buses were still operating in this area. When I reached the main road, a bus shot past and pulled up at a stop less than twenty meters away. I ran to join the queue because I caught a glimpse of its sign; it was heading towards Tottenham. I knew Tottenham Court Road was right next to Oxford Street. I was back on track. London was easier than my love life. It has taken me years to find a way forward after being stuck for so long. If today is anything to go by, I am full of hope that my life in London will be easier to navigate than it has over the past decade.

A passing stranger asked someone in the long queue which bus they needed to get to London Bridge, and somebody in the queue asked the person behind them why it was busy. Things must be bad for Londoners to make conversation with one another, Kate said no one makes eye contact on public transport, but this camaraderie made me feel comfortable to double-check with the guy in front of me in the queue. He looked sensible, wearing a red sports jacket. He nodded when I asked if the bus was going to Tottenham Court Road. I let out a sigh of relief.

We were twenty minutes into the journey when I realised something didn't seem right. I guessed the bus would have arrived at Tottenham Court Road by now. Central London was bright and touristy, but the area outside was a mix of industrial and residential buildings. The streets weren't jam-packed either as they had been on Saturday. Kate did say it would be a bit quieter during the week, but surely not to this extreme.

I needed help again, and with no other choice, I approached the driver.

'Excuse me, how long until we reach Tottenham Court Road?' The driver shook his head and didn't answer until he pulled over at the next stop. Another commuter rule: don't speak to the bus driver unless the bus is stationary.

'This bus is going to Tottenham, as in North London Tottenham, not Tottenham Court Road,' he said.

The sports jacket guy was still on the bus. He sat at the back on his own. His reflection was in the driver's rear-view mirror. He swigged from a bottle wrapped up in a scarf, and then he hiccupped. A lesson to myself: don't take travel advice from an intoxicated person. The driver kindly gave me brief instructions on how to get to Tottenham Court Road. I disembarked, crossed over the road and waited for the correct bus to take me to my intended destination.

Oxford Street was as busy as it had been on Saturday, so I nipped into a department store to avoid having to dart in and out of shops, and without trying anything on, I picked up clothes in my size that had a good chance of fitting: a pair of black trousers; three blouses, two plain A-lined dresses, and a charcoal-grey blazer. I needed a capsule wardrobe to mix and match to help keep the cost down and to keep my belongings to a minimum for when I could afford to move out of Kate's place. Before heading back to the flat, I surrendered and signed up for a smartphone—it was clearly a necessity in this city.

Both lifts were out of service back at the flat, and I climbed flight after flight of stairs to reach the flat. Kate apologised for both lifts being broken, assuring me that it had never happened before. She said it would have been quicker to walk from Liverpool Street to the recruitment agency's office rather than getting the Tube to Moorgate. Apparently, we passed nearby the office on Sunday afternoon. I let out a long sigh. I could see why so many people drank coffee in London; they needed the boost to get them through the day.

CHAPTER 9

Then

Postponing my degree didn't go down well with my parents. One night, I overheard them discussing Maxwell; Dad was angry with him for asking me to give up my dreams for the sake of his own. Mum tried soothing him by saying I would realise my mistake soon enough. *It was only a year, not the rest of my life*, I thought. *What was their issue?* Maxwell was going to support me when I returned for my final year at university. At least he wanted me to be part of his life, unlike Tobias. He didn't ask me to go to Hawaii with him for just a year.

I only needed my essentials when I moved in with Maxwell because he already had everything in his home. He was at a networking event that day, and because I only had a holdall and a couple of boxes of stuff, I didn't need help. He left a key under the doormat, and it felt strange walking into his house on my own. His space was normally immaculate, but today it was untidy: the curtains were half drawn, an empty pizza box was sprawled across the coffee table, a pile of washing up sat slumped in a pile in the sink, wet washing was trapped in the washing machine, and his bed wasn't made. He must have got up late after a late night with his golfing mates.

Before unpacking, I tidied up. I pulled the curtains and opened a couple of windows to allow in fresh air, washed and dried up, emptied the washing machine and put the items in the tumble dryer. Maxwell didn't have a washing line in the garden, which was one thing I wanted to change because it was wasteful to use electricity on a sunny day. It was both unkind to the environment and the pocket, and I loved the smell of clean washing mixed with fresh air.

The last room to tidy was his bedroom. I straightened the bottom sheet, plumped up the pillows and shook out the scrunched-up pale blue duvet. I smoothed my hand over the duvet, pulled it tight at the corners and then stood back to admire the neatness of my work. Sunlight filtered in and sparkled on something under the bed; I crouched down to pick it up. It was a butterfly back from a silver earring. I sat on the bed and stared at it in the palm of my hand. Was it mine?

I messaged Maxwell to ask him. He called me back immediately.

'No, it's not yours. Mum popped over the other day to clean the house because I've been so busy. She texted me yesterday to say she lost her earring and wondered if it had fallen off at mine.'

'It's only the back, not the earring itself.'

'That's a shame.'

'I'll have a look for the front. Shall I call her to let her know?'

'No,' he said, 'I'll do that and thanks for finding her earring. I love you.'

Maxwell came home with a dozen red roses that evening. 'What are these for?' I asked.

'They're a "welcome to your new home" present.' He retrieved two wine glasses from the cupboard and a bottle of red from the wine rack.

'You didn't need to do that.' I kissed him on the cheek. 'Are you sure they're not really for your mystery woman?'

He stopped pouring. 'What?'

'The back of the earring I found under the bed…'

'I told you, it's Mum's.' He carried on pouring the wine.

'I'm teasing you, silly.' I playfully hit him on the arm.

He insisted I put my feet up on the sofa with my glass of wine while he made dinner.

The following morning, he made breakfast. There was a jug of orange juice and a pot of tea on the table, and he made my favourite breakfast of smashed avocado on toast sprinkled with sea salt and chilli flakes. He made himself a sausage sandwich.

'Do you think we could get a washing line for the garden?' I asked.

Maxwell spoke with his mouth full. 'Calm down, Alice,' he sniggered, 'you've only just moved in.' He swallowed hard, winked at me and took another big bite of his sandwich.

'It'll help save on electricity.'

He placed his sandwich on his plate and rested his arms on the table. 'We've got lots going on with the business, and that's our priority at the moment. It's an unnecessary expense.'

'But I thought…'

'One thing at a time, hey?' He picked up his sandwich and carried on eating.

I worried for the rest of the morning that he thought I was nagging him in his home, and I was annoyed with myself for going on about it. He was right. There were other priorities. It was only a washing line, for goodness sake. It may save money in the long run, but we couldn't afford extras like that, not until the business was established. What was I thinking?

Maxwell placed his first candidate within a few weeks of me moving in, and to celebrate, he took us out for dinner in Plymouth. Whilst waiting at the bar to be seated, we bumped into one of his university friends who he hadn't seen since they left six years previous. His friend, Nathan, and his fiancée, Holly, asked us to join them for dinner. Nathan was charming and funny, and Holly and I enjoyed listening to him and Maxwell reminiscing about their partying days at university. It was a pleasant evening, and afterwards, Nathan and Maxwell swapped numbers to stay in touch.

On the drive home, Maxwell placed his hand on my knee. 'When you and Holly went to the toilet, Nathan said he was impressed I had such a pretty girlfriend.'

'Did he?' I was unsure of what else to say.

'He sounded surprised, which annoyed me. He joked that I'm punching above my weight.'

'Of course, you're not. What a stupid thing to say.'

'I reckon he fancied you.'

'I doubt it,' I laughed. I rested my hand on his. 'His fiancée is stunning.'

'She's got nothing on you.' He smiled at me. 'Perhaps she's a bit slimmer, but that's it.'

Maxwell was right; she was tiny. The top of her leg was the size of my arm. She picked at her dinner and ate slowly, but I ate all of mine. Perhaps I should have left some?

Nathan and Holly invited us to their New Year's Eve party, but Maxwell wanted to stay in. He told them he wanted to spend a romantic night in with just the two of us, but the truth was, he said, we couldn't afford to go out. Maxwell planned a three-course meal for us, but I started to feel unwell on New Year's Eve morning and got progressively worse with flu-like symptoms as the day went on. He still cooked dinner, even though I had no appetite. I lay wrapped up in a blanket on the sofa.

'Shall I open the bottle of champagne your parents bought us as your moving-in present?' Maxwell shouted from the kitchen.

I was shivering, my eyes hurt whenever they moved, and the surrounding muscles felt bruised. 'Can we leave it for another night when I feel better?'

Pop! The cork shot out of the bottle. 'Too late.'

I ate a few mouthfuls of food but didn't touch the glass of champagne on the floor beside me. Maxwell drank it because he didn't want it to go to waste. He was bored and finished the rest of the bottle whilst watching an action thriller movie. I was too tired to keep my eyes open, and I flitted in and out of sleep during the movie. I woke to a loud noise. A car had crashed in the film on a New York street, and the driver had scrambled from the wreckage and was running through a park.

I murmured, 'Is that the park you went to?' and closed my eyes again.

'I've never been to New York.' Maxwell said. I was certain he said he had been, but I felt too poorly to ask, and I fell back to sleep.

Maxwell worked on New Year's Day, but it was a few days until I started to feel well enough to work all day. I only managed the mornings, at first, before my energy dipped, and then I would lay on the sofa under a blanket whilst he worked.

'Do you remember a while back you suggested going on a beach holiday?'

Maxwell was focused on his screen. 'Uh-huh.'

'Can we go somewhere? I need a rest and some heat. The Canaries are supposed to be warm this time of year.'

'We can't afford to yet.'

'How about I use some of the money I saved up for Uni?'

'We might need that to contribute towards the bills.' He walked over, kissed my forehead and then went to the bathroom. 'So don't go spending it,' he shouted as he was going to the toilet.

Later that day, Maxwell received a text from Nathan. It was an invite to his stag do in April before the wedding in June. He wanted to book a villa in Spain for a long weekend and needed numbers before he could book something. Maxwell confirmed he was going and transferred his deposit straight away.

'But I thought—' I started saying.

'Before you say anything,' Maxwell interrupted, 'I've known Nathan for a long time, and it's not every day one of your friends gets married. We'll go on plenty of holidays soon enough. Besides, I can offset some of the costs against the business as I'll be networking with his mates, and I'll still be taking calls and checking my emails, so it's not going to cost anything near as us going on holiday.'

He was right about marriage, and I was sure that as soon as I was over the flu, I wouldn't feel the need for a holiday. Besides, the winter sun was shining through the window and with the heating on, I closed my eyes and pretended to be on a sun lounger on a tropical island. It felt real until I opened my eyes, expecting to see a swimming pool in front of me and not the kitchen sink.

Maxwell wanted a good suit for the wedding to impress the guys he went to university with. Apart from Nathan, he hadn't seen any of them since graduating. After an unsuccessful shopping trip to Plymouth, we visited Exeter to catch the end of the January sales. It made sense to get one in the sales, especially because the type of suit Maxwell wanted to get, which he said would last him years, cost the same price as a cheap winter package holiday.

We worked long days and lots of weekends, too, but it was worth it because things soon picked up after only six months in business. Maxwell was good at his job, and as word-of-mouth spread from him attending meetings and networking events, our candidate and client base increased. By the time the stag do arrived, Maxwell was bringing in commission most weeks. The risk we had both taken was starting to pay off. He was able to go away and not worry about money.

Maxwell brought me back a selection of gifts from the stag do: my favourite perfume, Channel No. 5. I had never owned a bottle of it. I sprayed it in the store whenever I went shopping. He also bought me a keyring with 'I Heart Spain' written on it and an expensive straw hat that *apparently* everyone was wearing out there.

'You can wear it when we eventually go to Tenerife,' he said as I modelled it. 'With the business starting to do well financially, we should go on a holiday soon.'

He showered after unpacking and walked into our bedroom with his towel wrapped around his waist.

'What's that on your back?' I held onto his shoulder and pulled myself around to take a closer look. 'Are those scratches?'

'Oh, those.' He untied his towel and dried his back.

'How did you get them?'

'Nathan got called onto a stage at a stripper's joint, but he didn't want to go up and begged me to go up in his place. All the lads egged me on.'

'Why you? Surely one of the single guys could have gone on stage?'

'Don't be angry with me, Alice. It was the uni lads that wanted me to go up. That's what we used to be like back in the day, daring each other. So I took one for the team.'

I remained silent and walked over to the pile of clothes he had thrown on the floor before showering. I picked them up and threw them in the washing bin in the bathroom. Maxwell crept up behind me and hugged my waist from behind. He started tickling me. I laughed, and he tickled more. I pulled away from him and ran into the bedroom, screaming and laughing. He caught up with me and tickled me again until we both fell onto the bed into a mess of laughter.

We went shopping in Bristol the following weekend so that I could buy an outfit for the wedding. It was Maxwell's suggestion to have a nice day out. Before we left, he surprised me with a gift of one hundred pounds to buy an outfit, but I told him it was too much money—I had black shoes and a handbag that went with everything, so I just needed a new dress. But he insisted I take the money, and after convincing me to keep it, I got excited at the thought of buying a nice dress with matching accessories. It had been a long time since I had bought anything new. It had also been a long time since getting dressed up for an occasion. Maxwell and I worked at home and ate in most nights, so my normal attire was jeans, a jumper, hair up in a ponytail and a dash of mascara.

We arrived in Bristol just before midday, and Maxwell was hungry. We decided to eat first to avoid the lunch rush and found a harbourside restaurant with al fresco dining. The late April sun was unseasonably warm.

'It's too nice to go shopping,' Maxwell said, sipping his second pint.

I looked up at the sunny sky. 'I know.'

'Why don't you have another alcoholic drink?'

'I won't be able to drive the car back.'

Maxwell shuffled his chair closer to mine and placed an arm around my shoulders. 'Let's get a hotel and stay the night. We can go shopping in the morning before heading home. It's been too long since we treated ourselves.'

'But we haven't brought a change of clothes or anything else with us.'

'We can buy toothbrushes and underwear later on. Wearing the same clothes tomorrow won't kill us. Besides, no one knows us here, so who cares. Come on, let's be spontaneous. We deserve it with all the hard work we have both been putting in.'

'You're right.'

Maxwell called the waiter over to order more drinks.

It rained the following morning, and we both felt delicate from drinking late into the evening. Maxwell was sick before we checked out. He soon perked up after trying on numerous pairs of shoes to go with his January sale suit, and after narrowing his choice down to the most expensive pair of brown shoes, he decided he needed a new shirt as well. It was to complete the look.

I thought purchasing a white shirt would be easy, but Maxwell tried on one in a shop but didn't like the way the collar sat; he wasn't impressed by the quality at another shop and thought a cheaper shop's shirt looked more off-white than white. We returned to the first shop. Maxwell tried on the first shirt again, and this time he liked it. He blamed his hangover on his earlier poor judgement.

'It looks pretty cool. I look pretty cool!' he said, admiring himself in the mirror.

'Yes, you do, sir,' the sales assistant said. 'Would you like me to put it behind the counter for you?'

'Not yet. Could you bring me a handful of green ties to try on with it?' Maxwell continued looking in the mirror.

I stood up. 'Our parking is going to run out in an hour and a half. Shall I head off to look at dresses, and you can find me once you're done?'

'But I need your opinion on the ties. It won't take long,' he said. I sat back down.

After choosing a tie, and with only an hour remaining on our parking, we rushed around women's shops. Only five dresses out of as many shops looked suitable but none of them looked as nice on. Each time I tried one, I got hotter, and my hair became more and more static. We squeezed in one last shop before having to get back to the car and found three suitable dresses, but after trying on two and feeling unattractive in them both, I didn't bother with the third and gave up.

The following weekend, the weekend before the wedding, Maxwell played golf, and I went shopping in Plymouth. I could have walked to the shops from Maxwell's house; it was only a twenty-minute walk into town, but he insisted on dropping me off. It was the least he could do to make up for him hogging the shopping time in Bristol. That meant I arrived twenty minutes before the shops opened, so I treated myself to tea and a croissant in a café whilst waiting for the shops to open.

There were plenty of shops with nice dresses, but I was feeling under pressure to get something, and nothing felt right. I wanted to make a good impression on Maxwell's university friends because I knew that meant a lot to him. With little time left until the shops closed, I hurried along Royal Parade and nipped into any shop that sold dresses. It didn't matter what the store's target market was; I needed to get something.

Daisy called as I dodged my way around dawdling shoppers. 'What are you up to next weekend?'

'We're at Maxwell's friend's wedding, remember?' I managed to say breathlessly.

'Tobias returns from Hawaii on Friday and has asked Tristan to arrange a get-together before he flies up to Scotland.'

Tobias's plans were cut short in Hawaii by two months, at short notice, just like when he went. He hadn't been scouted during his time out there as he had hoped. He fell out with the owner because Tobias's enthusiasm had dwindled over time. He was homesick, but instead of moving back to Devon, he decided to move to Scotland to work with a friend to set up a surf school on the north coast. His decisions still made no sense to me.

I stopped outside a clothing store and stared through the window like a magpie looking for scraps. 'When's he going to Scotland?'

'Remember I told you that he'd only be in Devon for a week before he goes?'

'No, I don't remember that.' I carried on walking along the parade.

'I told you that last month when I found out he was returning from Hawaii.'

'I remember you said he was coming back but you didn't say when.'

'That's because he didn't know until his flight was booked. So are you able to come for at least one drink on Friday night?'

'I won't have time. Maxwell wants to leave before rush hour.'

'Surely you could squeeze in a quick drink before you go?'

I interrupted Daisy when I saw the perfect dress in a charity shop window. It was a designer make, too. Thirty pounds seemed expensive for a second-hand dress, but it was in my size, and I loved it. I looked at my watch. 'I've got to go.' The shop was closing in twenty-five minutes, and if the dress fit, there was enough time and money to buy new shoes and a handbag. 'I've found a dress.'

'Do you want me to pass on a message for you?

'Tell Tobias I said hi and that I'll catch up with him next time he's home. Thanks, Daisy.' I hung up and walked into the shop.

The lady in the shop undressed the mannequin and handed the dress to me. It fell to the floor as the soft satin slipped from my hand. I scooped it up, hurried over to the changing room and quickly undressed. I slid my arms and head into the dress allowing it to cascade down my body and into place. I tied the thin waistband and halter neck straps and admired my reflection in the mirror. Pale yellow and grey swirls exaggerate my late spring suntan. It was the one.

A discounted designer shop a few doors along had an array of handbags and shoes, and I quickly found a pair of grey peep-toe heels and a slightly darker shade of grey handbag that was in the sale because the metallic chain had snapped off one side. Dad could remove the other side, and I would use it as a clutch handbag. With ten pounds left from the money Maxwell gave to me, I purchased a candy floss pink lip-gloss and matching nail varnish set to compliment the look, also from the bargain bin. The cardboard box was damaged, but the goods inside looked in perfect condition.

There wasn't a queue at the counter, so I walked straight over to a cashier and placed everything on the counter. The lipstick and nail varnish set fell onto the floor. The lipstick somehow managed to escape the broken packaging and rolled towards the short queue that had formed in my brief time at the counter.

The person at the front picked it up. 'Here you go,' the man said as he handed it to me.

'Thanks,' I said, and his hand placed it into mine. I recognised his voice and looked up.

'It's Tom, isn't it?'

'Yes.'

'I'm Alice from—'

'The recruitment agency,' we said at the same time. He smiled, and we both stood in awkward silence.

'I'd best get back to the checkout.'

I paid for my items and when I walked away, I looked back at Tom. We smiled at each other again. I was tempted to ask for his number for Daisy, but I thought better of it as the moment had passed.

Maxwell ended up working later on Friday, so I could have gone out for a drink with Tobias after all, but it would have been too much hassle for me to go into town for one drink and then for Maxwell to find me and pick me up. I painted my nails instead and waited until Maxwell was ready to leave for The Cotswolds.

Our hotel was a ten-minute drive from the venue and a third of the price of a room at the fifteenth-century manor house. Maxwell said it was still cheaper to drive there and get a taxi back to the hotel than to stay overnight at the wedding. The following morning, we started getting ready. I got dressed in the bathroom because I wanted to surprise Maxwell with my new outfit.

'Ta-dah,' I said as I opened the bathroom door. 'What do you think?' My hair was still wet, and I still needed to apply my make-up, but I already felt nice in my dress and shoes.

'The dress is nice,' Maxwell said and continued styling his hair in the mirror.

I walked over to Maxwell and kissed him on his cheek. 'You look very handsome yourself, Mr Squire.' He winked at me.

Maxwell was ready before me and left the room to wait at the bar. I roughly dried my hair before styling it into a messy updo with intentional loose bits dangling. I had never taken the time to perfect a neat hairstyle. I was still more of a wash-and-go girl, but my hairstyle turned out to look much more chic than I was consciously able to pull off. I applied natural tones of makeup and added a dash of colour and shimmer from my new lipstick. It had been so long since I felt this nice. Maxwell often dressed in suits for meetings and networking, but my role was entirely home-based. My new heels felt like magic slippers.

I stood in front of the mirror, swooshing my dress from side to side to make sure everything looked okay. I felt comfortable and I felt good and hoped Maxwell was going to feel proud of being with me in front of his old friends.

I walked into the bar, and Maxwell watched as I made my way over to him.

'Well?' I smiled. I was excited to hear his response.

He downed the rest of his pint. 'You look pretty. Are you ready to go?'

Maxwell drove us to the venue. He parked up, and he handed me the keys to keep in my clutch bag. We walked across the gravel car park towards the building. Two male waiters were outside on a smoke break. One of them wolf-whistled which made me look. One smiled at me, and the other winked. I blushed, squeezed Maxwell's hand tighter and looked away.

'Did you hear that?' Maxwell said.

'What?'

'One of them just said "I wish I was that man" as we walked past.'

'Did they?'

'They obviously thought I looked cool-as in my suit.'

I smiled at him. 'You do look extremely handsome.' I felt foolish for blushing. I now understood that they were making those gestures to me because I was lucky to be with someone like Maxwell. I suddenly felt disappointed because I wanted Maxwell to feel that way about being with me. I wished those guys had whistled at me and that Maxwell had heard and that he would be proud of me. I thought I looked the nicest I ever had since being with him but that can't have been the case because Maxwell didn't make a fuss about what I looked like. I felt annoyed with myself for not making more of an effort.

Some of Maxwell's university friends were already in the bar when we arrived, plus a few guys from the stag do. Some were with wives or girlfriends, and a handful of them were single. Everyone introduced themselves, including a famous single rugby player. He kissed me on the cheek, just as all the men had when he introduced himself. Maxwell and I moved along the bar to order drinks. He whispered in my ear, 'You can say you've been kissed by a rugby player now.' I smiled; I was unsure of what to say, again. 'He's always loved himself. He thought all the girls at uni were after him.'

'I'm not after him; I'm with you.'

'Yeah, but he'll think that you will be.'

We re-joined the group who were taking turns telling funny stories from the stag do: who got drunk first, who wore the funniest fancy-dress costume and who kissed the most girls out of the single friends.

'I'm surprised one of you didn't volunteer to get up on stage with the stripper instead of Maxwell,' I said to two of the single guys and the rugby player.

It went quiet, and I blushed again. Did they all think I was trying to be one of the lads? I hoped I hadn't embarrassed Maxwell.

'Maxwell certainly took one for the team,' the rugby player eventually said. He raised his glass and took a sip of his pint. 'You didn't mention you had a lovely girlfriend.' The rugby player looked at me, and I looked at the ground. 'Where did you meet her?'

'Oh, you know,' Maxwell laughed, 'she hounded me at work, and I eventually agreed to go for a drink, and the rest is history.' There were a few awkward laughs, and then somebody changed the subject by observing how posh the venue was.

'Ladies and gentlemen, can I get everyone's attention, please?' The Master of Ceremonies called. 'Before you all get excited, the bride isn't here yet. The receptionist has asked if anyone here has a silver car. I looked at Maxwell. 'It looks as though the handbrake wasn't put on properly, and it's rolled into a hedge in the car park.' Everyone laughed, including Maxwell, but he stopped when he called out the registration.

'You idiot, you left off the handbrake,' Maxwell hissed at me. 'Give me the keys, and I'll go and sort it out.' Maxwell stormed off to the car park. I don't know why he said that. It was accidental, and no other cars were damaged. I didn't want to remind him in front of others that he had driven. I didn't want to embarrass him further in front of everyone.

One of the wives whispered to another. 'How embarrassing.' I looked at them, and they sniggered before looking away.

'Female drivers,' Maxwell joked when he returned. He downed his pint, linked my arm and pulled me to find a seat ready for the ceremony.

After the ceremony and the photos, we were seated on round tables in a marquee. We were seated with the sniggering wives.

'Are you vegan?' The wife sitting on the other side of Maxwell asked me when my meal was placed in front of me. 'If so, you shouldn't be drinking the wine—it's not vegan.' There was lamb shank or a vegan option for the wedding breakfast. I opted for the tofu steak with coriander and vegan cream. 'Do you know they use egg whites, milk protein and sometimes something to do with fish in the fining agents?' She pulled an expression of disgust. I wasn't sure if that was the thought of the fish ingredient or me.

'I'm a flexitarian, so it's fine.' I said. Although it wasn't fine, I didn't know any of that about wine.

'What's a flexitarian? I've never heard of one of those before.'

Before I could explain that I did eat meat but very little of it for the sake of the planet and animal welfare, Maxwell jumped in on the conversation. 'It's a current trend that she's following. I don't get it that she eats meat-free sausages or burgers. You either eat meat, or you don't, in my mind.'

The sniggering wife placed her hand on Maxwell's arm and laughed.

The other unkind wife sat opposite us joined in. 'I love your dress. Where is it from?' The respective husbands of these two were in deep conversation about investment, and I was pleased that the rugby player and his friend were talking about rugby. At least not all attention was on me.

Maxwell answered for me. 'I bought it for her as a thank you for all the hard work she's been doing lately for my business.'

'That's so sweet,' she gushed.

'But I'm not going to tell you where it's from because I don't want anyone copying my beautiful girlfriend.' He winked at her.

'You tease,' she laughed. I took a large gulp of my fish-infused wine.

'I agree with Maxwell,' the rugby player surprised us all by joining in on the conversation, 'you do look beautiful.' He smiled at me and then at Maxwell and then stood up. 'Would anyone like a drink? I can't drink any more of this wine. I'm going to the bar.'

Maxwell offered to help him with the drinks.

'Could you just tighten my straps before you go?' I asked Maxwell before he got up from the table. My dress felt slightly loose, and I felt self-conscious in it. Maxwell untied it from around my neck and made a short, sharp pull before tying it back up. It was too tight to sit up straight properly, but I didn't say anything. I didn't want to make a fuss in front of everyone. It would loosen off again soon enough.

The wedding party became raucous after the speeches; the constant flow of wine contributed to the lively atmosphere, and soon, the day's events turned into the evening party. Additional guests arrived, and the dance floor was busy with people dancing to typical wedding songs like 'The Time Warp' and 'Don't Stop Me Now'.

Maxwell eventually decided to dance when 'Livin' on a Prayer' came on. He pulled me up to join him. I followed him onto the busy dance floor, where the music was even louder. It was difficult to see anyone from the smoke and flashing lights darting around the busy space. I lost sight of Maxwell, but then someone took hold of my hand and guided me through a group of people deep within the dance floor. He pulled me into a slow dance embrace. I looked up, it wasn't Maxwell—it was the rugby player.

I pulled away and looked around for Maxwell through the smoke. The rugby player stepped towards me and spoke in my ear. 'You're too good for him.'

'What do you mean?'

Before he could answer, Maxwell found us.

'May I have the pleasure of dancing with my girlfriend?' Maxwell asked, and the rugby player smiled at me and walked away.

'Why didn't they know you had a girlfriend?' I asked Maxwell as we danced.

'Most of the blokes were banging on about their nagging wives and girlfriends, and I didn't want them to think I was showing off by talking about you and how you're nothing like that, so I kept quiet.'

We danced in silence for a moment. 'Why would the rugby player say I'm too good for you?'

'Because you are! Look how stunning you are. All of those guys would kill to have you as their girlfriend.'

'It didn't come across that way. It sounded like a warning.'

Maxwell stopped dancing. 'What are you trying to imply?'

'Nothing, I'm trying to make sense of what he was saying.'

'Do you think I cheated on you? Is that it?'

'No, of course not. I just don't understand why he said what he did.'

'I love you and I only have eyes for you. Ignore what he said, and don't let him ruin our night. I told you; he still thinks he can get anyone. He's trying it on with you; it's what he does.' Maxwell pulled me tighter to him, and we carried on with the dance.

CHAPTER 10

Now

On the first morning in my new job, I planned and double-checked my commute before leaving the flat, checking my pocketbook, an app on my new phone, and with Kate. If I had to, I felt comfortable using my phone in public. Everyone was doing it even though there were Metropolitan Police posters plastered around stations warning people to be vigilant about mobile phone muggings. At least I would look like a local using my mobile rather than browsing Daisy's booklet.

My line manager, who was off sick the previous day, met me in reception.

'Good morning, Alice, I'm Mr Richards, Head of Sales and Office Management.' His voice bellowed as he shook my hand. 'But you can call me Sean.' He winked at me. He loomed above, but I didn't feel threatened. My past almost defeated me, but I was battle-hardened with scars and internal armour. The downside to it was that it had protected me too well in recent years by not allowing anyone close. They had been kept at sword's length and seen as a foe and not a friend. But I was ready to let down that guard for the right person.

I had the type of face that showed my thoughts even when I didn't realise it was happening, so I forced a professional smile because I knew my eyes were showing my instant dislike of this man. His inappropriate greeting, his greying, unkempt beard, his middle-aged paunch and the smell of fast food and stale nicotine were contributing to this factor. He suggested we take the lift instead of walking up one flight of stairs. His voice was louder in the enclosed space, and I cringed when he over-enthusiastically told me how much he loved his job.

'Are you ready to go for a bimble to meet everyone?' he asked as the doors to the lift opened. I nodded. It was going to be a long four-week contract working with him.

Things improved once I met the rest of the small team. There were three guys and one girl, all in their late twenties and early thirties. The girl, Teagan, was given the task of carrying out my training. We hit it off immediately, bonding over past relationships and our love of animals. She showed me the best places to buy lunch along the high street at lunchtime and invited me along to the staff drinks the following evening.

'So, how was your first day?' Teagan asked as we left the office together later.

'*Most* people are nice.' We were still new to one another, so I needed to be careful with how much I said.

'Between you and me,' she spoke softly, 'everyone thinks *he's* an idiot.' She looked over to Sean's office. We looked at each other, pausing to check we were on the same wavelength and giggled. I had made my first London friend.

I arrived at work earlier than Teagan the following morning. I sat at her desk, waiting for her to arrive and wished I hadn't been punctual. Sean approached the desk and made small talk about my first day whilst two guys walked past our section, chatting and laughing. The handsome one of the two smiled as they neared, and even after they passed by, the sound of their cheery voices floated around the open-plan office.

'Sorry about that,' Sean said.

'Pardon?' I said.

'I'll have to have a word with their manager about their swearing.'

'I didn't hear any swear words.' I was relieved to see Teagan appear at the far end of the office.

'I'm glad you've settled in.' Sean walked off towards his office before Teagan reached her desk.

We had a quick catch-up, and I offered to make Teagan a drink whilst she popped to the toilet. Sean's office was en route to the kitchen; his door was slightly ajar.

'No, I'm at bloody work,' his raucous voice seeped from his room. I caught a glimpse of him as I passed by. He was talking on his mobile whilst his feet rested on his desk, and his free arm was tucked behind his head. His words were followed by a tinny smoker's laugh. He stood up when he saw me and walked around his desk. I sped up to get away from his office. 'I can't believe you're on the lash already, I'm at effing work.' His door slammed shut.

Teagan had a dental appointment at midday, so I took an early lunch and ventured out on my own to buy something to eat. On the way out, I bumped into the handsome guy from the morning, and he held the door open for me.

'Thanks,' I said as I passed through.

'You're Alice, the new girl, right?' I nodded. 'I'm Josh, from I.T.'

Josh was charismatic and easy to talk to. He laughed when I told him he reminded me of a dark-haired version of Niall from One Direction—he'd been told that before. He asked lots of questions as we continued our conversation outside the office. He was heading to London Bridge to do a quick errand and to pick up some lunch and asked me to join him. We jumped on the Tube and chatted the entire way, there and back. He was from Surrey, and I told him I was from a village northwest of Plymouth. He visited Devon for the first time two years ago and tried surfing. He wasn't keen on it; he preferred football. He was a year younger than me and had lived in London since studying at university.

I was pleased when he mentioned the staff drinks. I suddenly felt excited and nervous about going along. It had been a long time since anyone made me feel that way, but I liked it. I was ready to feel that way again. I had been single for five years, partly through choice and partly because I felt I had nothing to give. I dabbled with online dating a few times, but my patience quickly ran out, and I deleted my account after becoming disheartened from the lack of progress in building genuine rapport. One guy, after initially coming across as normal, told me on the second day of messaging that he had a high sex drive and was circumcised. There was another guy who ghosted me after a civilised conversation about films. I thought online dating was going to be like online shopping: log on, pick what you wanted and checkout. But I never found what I was looking for and gave up.

Later that afternoon, during the three o'clock slump, a voice startled me in the kitchen. It was Josh. He picked a mug from the cupboard and joined me by the kettle. He stood close as we waited for the kettle to boil.

'I enjoyed talking to you earlier,' he said whilst focusing on the boiling water as he poured the kettle. I giggled. He smiled. We were interrupted by the company accountant. He was looking for Josh because his computer had crashed, and they both dashed off. I waited with an uncontrollable smile for my tea to brew.

'Be a sweetheart,' Sean said to Teagan ten minutes before we were due to finish work, 'take the petty cash tin to the finance department to get it topped up.' He handed her the tin. 'We've been raped of all the money.' I rolled my eyes. I hated this man.

Teagan left straight away.

'The accountant will drop anything for her; she just needs to flutter her eyelashes,' Sean said. I looked at him. My expression must have shown that I thought it was disgraceful. 'It was a joke! There's no need to be so serious.' He walked back to his office.

A group of us made our way to a wine bar in Clapham Common straight after work. I was excited to experience my first proper night out in London. We were the first department to arrive; the others followed sporadically. The venue was dimly lit, and the long, narrow bar quickly filled up. Josh headed straight to the reserved area as soon as he arrived. He didn't see me, which I was pleased about—I needed another drink to calm my nerves. It was so long since I entertained male attention. I had convinced myself it was because I needed more *me*-time or that there wasn't anyone good enough to tempt me into a relationship, but the truth was that I was scared to get close to anyone because it was me who didn't feel good enough. I lost the courage to be vulnerable again. I built a wall so high and thick and remained safely behind it for too long. It was time to be brave again.

We were given a strip of raffle tickets to use as drink tokens and once they were spent, we had to buy our drinks. The accountant was in charge of the raffle book, but he could only stay for one drink, and he gave Teagan his remaining raffle tickets as he left. I thought Sean was right; the accountant did have a soft spot for Teagan, but that wasn't the case—they were good friends. Teagan told me that he dashed off to meet his boyfriend's parents for the first time. Sean was wrong. I smiled at the small triumph of knowing that.

The evening quickly livened up, and people became louder and chattier. Josh moved away from a group of people I didn't recognise and joined the group I was in. I was pleased he did that because I didn't have the confidence to approach him. I was still adjusting to the feeling of liking someone, and the idea of Josh knowing that made me uncomfortable, as though that would give some control over me, but I reminded myself it was one of the most natural things in the world for a human being to be attracted to another. It was normal.

Josh joined in the small talk about work. People left the group, others joined, and eventually, he found his way beside me.

He nudged my arm. 'How's your evening going?'

'Good.' I took a sip of my drink.

'I hardly recognised you tonight.' He leant in closer. The music had increased, competing with people's voices. I took another sip of my drink. He spoke close to my ear, 'That lipstick suits you.' I blushed. 'You look equally as beautiful with or without it.'

My heart raced. I had never known anyone to be so direct—life in London was faster in many ways. I had noticed things about him: how his positive presence brightened the room, his deep, soothing voice and his manners. But I wasn't going to express my thoughts to him so soon.

'Aren't you going to introduce me?' An older, shorter guy interrupted us as he joined our group.

'This is Alice,' Josh said. 'Alice, this is Malcolm, Head of I.T.' Malcolm shook my hand. Josh continued, 'Alice is new. She's supporting the sales team and has recently moved to London from a village in Devon.'

'It's good to meet you, Alice,' Malcolm said. He asked to speak to Josh outside. That was the last I saw of Josh that evening, which was probably a good thing because I was feeling exhausted from the connection we had. His attention towards me was a lot to process. I could now enjoy the night getting to know other colleagues with a sprinkle of excitement that Josh may be attracted to me.

The bustling bar made it easy to avoid Sean. I saw him early on sitting in the reserved area on his own with his feet up on the table. My luck ran out. He approached me as I made my way towards the bar.

'Where have you been all night?' he said.

'Here.'

'Have you used up all your raffle tickets?'

'I'm just about to spend my last one.'

He placed his hand near his hip. 'I've got something in my pocket that will make you happy.' Sean looked me up and down. The accountant had given the raffle book to Sean when he left.

I paused before responding. 'Do you know where the toilets are?'

He pointed behind him, 'Yes, over in that corner.'

I thanked him, turned around, and walked away in the opposite direction.

I didn't bother buying another drink. I felt deflated, bumping into Sean. Since Josh had left, the small talk had become hard work in the loud music. I checked the time; it was nearly midnight, so I dashed to catch the Tube before it closed for the night. I stepped outside, and the fresh air hit me. It made me feel tipsier and angrier about Sean. I stormed towards the station. I was going to call the recruitment agency in the morning to make a complaint.

'Swit swoo, look at you,' a guy shouted from a group of middle-aged men. They all laughed. I glared at them as I entered the station.

'Cheer up, love,' another shouted, and they all laughed again. I was tempted to tell them they were idiots but decided it was safer not to.

My head was muzzy the following morning. Kate kindly made me a cup of tea and brought it to me. She perched on the end of my bed to listen to the previous night's events.

'I've just thought of a new name for him,' Kate looked at me with a serious expression. 'Dick is short for Richard, right?'

'Yes.' My brain was struggling to keep up with Kate.

'If you move the comma, you come up with a brand-new name and title for him: instead of Mr Richard, Head of Sales, you have Mr Dick Head, of Sales.' I laughed. 'Think of that today when he makes you angry.'

'Thanks, I'll try it.'

When I exited Clapham North Tube Station, just before reaching the office, there was a voicemail from the recruitment agency. My four-week contract had been cut short and was now terminating at the end of the day with no explanation why. There wasn't time to call them back before starting work.

Sean's voice ricocheted from his office. He was on the phone as I arrived at the office. 'Do you need your chest rubbing better?'

I shook my head. Not even the thought of Kate's new title for Sean helped. He walked out of his office and told us Teagan had called in sick. *Poor Teagan for being ill*, I thought, *but poor Teagan for receiving a comment like that.* Luckily, I had Teagan's number to stay in touch. She was the best thing to come from the job.

'That means we'll have to run through some bits together,' Sean said to me before walking back into his office. He returned to my desk, wheeling his chair and balancing a cup of coffee and a packet of biscuits in his other hand. He dunked a biscuit before stuffing the entire thing in his mouth—he repeated this whilst showing me the reports he wanted me to run from the database. It was going to be a long day.

He picked at his teeth with his finger and afterwards placed the same hand on my mouse. A soggy, chewed-up bit of biscuit was resting on the end of his finger. My stomach churned. I already felt delicate from the night before, and it took all my strength not to run off to the toilet to be sick. When Sean finished the training, he went for a smoke. I wiped the mouse, keyboard and desk with antibacterial gel from my handbag.

He returned to my desk after his cigarette break. 'I hope you haven't eaten all of my biscuits,' he laughed, 'otherwise, I'll have to smack your bum...I mean wrists.' He picked up the remaining biscuits and wheeled his chair back into his office.

A flash fire raged in my stomach, and the intensity forced me to stand up and march over to his office.

My voice didn't sound as strong as the flames felt when I spoke. 'Could I have a word, please?'

'Sure,' Sean said. 'Take a seat.'

'I don't feel comfortable with some of the comments you make.' I listed some examples. 'I find them inappropriate and unprofessional.'

'Thank you for bringing this to my attention, Alice,' he sounded sincere. 'I will try my hardest not to make those types of comments anymore.' I thanked him and stood up to leave. 'But,' he said as I reached the door, 'you should know that I worked in the construction industry before here, and I was one of the milder ones.' I stopped and looked back to look at him. He remained seated with his elbows on the desk and hands clasped. He faced forward, but his eyes stabbed up at me. 'Sorry we had to cut your contact short,' he smirked. 'It's been short and sweet. It's a shame you take everything too seriously.'

I left the room.

I returned the recruitment agency's call on my lunch break, and after informing them of my complaint about Sean's behaviour, they told me they had a much better role. It was an immediate start as a receptionist for a corporate bank in the heart of the city. I wanted to finish at the stationery company right then, but the recruitment consultant sweet-talked me into working the afternoon, promising to make me a priority for finding something long-term or permanent.

My final day was miserable: I had been sacked, bullied, and harassed. I was hungover, friendless without Teagan and I hadn't seen Josh. Every time somebody passed through the office, I looked up to see if it was him. With the confidence of knowing I may not see him again, I decided to email him.

Hi Josh,
Are you catching the Tube after work? If so, I'll meet you outside the office if you want to join me…
Alice

I pressed send and went to the kitchen to make my final drink. Whilst stirring my tea, I fantasised about how our Tube journey would go: Josh and I chat about our weekend plans, he asks if I fancy grabbing a quick drink at Liverpool Street before heading home, we end up staying out later than *just* one, he wishes me a good weekend and tells me he's looking forward to seeing me on Monday, I explain about work and he asks for my number, we hug, he texts me on the train home and asks me out for dinner to celebrate my new job…

I returned to my desk and shook the mouse to wake up the screen. My stomach flipped over when I saw there was a new message in my inbox. I silently squealed before opening his email, but my heart slid out of my chest when I read the words of an automated response.

Thanks for your email.
I am out of the office today to celebrate my first-year anniversary. See you on Monday.
If you have anything urgent today, please email Malcolm or contact him at ext. 2472.
Josh

He was married! He didn't wear a ring. He never mentioned his relationship status. He told me I was beautiful. He said he enjoyed talking to me. He remembered what I'd said. I didn't understand. I knew I was out of practice when it came to flirting and romance, but I didn't realise I was as bad as this. I was disappointed, shocked, and angry, but I had wasted too much time over men in the past, and I wasn't going to allow that to happen now. He wasn't who I thought he was, and that made it easier to draw a line under it. I had overcome much worse behaviour and had learnt the hard way it was better to be alone than lonely with the wrong person.

Sean didn't mention to anyone that it was my last day, and neither did I. I didn't want a fuss or any questions, and I left the office wishing my ex-colleagues a good weekend. A bus heading for Liverpool Street was at the bus stop as I stepped out of the building. I ran to catch it, and as I reached the back of the bus, I dropped my handbag and almost tripped over it. I bent down to pick it up, and as I stood back up, the bus pulled away. I let out a long sigh. London was tough, but I wasn't giving up.

CHAPTER 11

Then

My twenty-second birthday came and went. Soon after was Maxwell's and my first anniversary. As a surprise, he booked us a last-minute holiday to Spain. I spent the week lounging by the pool, but he still answered emails and took phone calls from his sun lounger. He insisted I took the week off because the business was getting busier, and until he could afford to hire staff, he couldn't see another window for a holiday for a long time. I decided to postpone my studies for one more year to continue working for Maxwell and help him achieve that milestone sooner. What was one more year for the rest of my working life? I was only twenty-two with forever in front of me.

The weather was just as hot when we returned home; buying ice-lollies from the local shop became part of my daily routine. It was the only time of the day that I took a proper break from my desk. One day, I walked halfway towards the shop before realising that I had picked up my holiday purse with leftover euros instead of my everyday one, so I returned home. Maxwell was going to have a cold shower to cool down whilst I was at the shop, so I crept indoors to avoid startling him, but when I opened the front door, his voice travelled down the stairs. He must have taken a last-minute phone call. I still didn't want to disturb him, so I crept along the hallway. His phone was on speaker, and the female voice on the other end of the phone became clearer as I reached the bottom of the stairs. The conversation didn't sound work-related, so I tiptoed upstairs to listen to her talk.

'After the networking event, I'll show you that my mouth isn't only good at negotiating deals,' she said.

I shoved open the bedroom door and stared at Maxwell. He stared back.

'Maxwell, are you still there?' the woman's voice pierced the phone. 'Is she back?'

'I've got to go.' He ended the call.

I crossed my arms. 'Who was that?'

'That's Sara-Ann. She attends a lot of the same networking events.'

'Did she just say what I thought I heard about her mouth?'

I was shocked by his delayed yet honest response. 'Yes.'

'Give me your phone.' I tried snatching it from his hand, but he hid his arm behind his back.

'Why?' he said. 'She was only flirting.'

My body shook with anger. 'Just give it to me!' I pointed at him.

'Don't you dare point your finger at me,' he shouted, 'otherwise I'll break it!' I felt winded, as though he had punched me in the stomach. My head was spinning, and I was unable to process what was going on. 'I don't know what's happened to you,' he spat, 'You've become so possessive and jealous, it's pathetic!'

I ran downstairs and into the living room and punched the sofa as I threw myself onto it. I screamed into the cushion so loudly that it hurt my throat. Maxwell stayed upstairs. I started crying. I couldn't stay here with him. I bolted from the sofa and pulled the front door open with such force that it slammed back against the wall. I ran off. I had no idea where I was going, but I ended up calling my parents to pick me up.

Dad made me a cup of tea in bed the following morning. Before he said anything, I told him that I had made a mistake. There were fifteen missed calls on my mobile from Maxwell and a single voice message begging me to go back. He sounded emotional, desperate. I was exhausted and embarrassed that I'd overreacted so much. Maxwell wasn't the one who said the words; it was Sara-Ann. It was clear she was flirting with him, and he could have easily agreed to her proposition, but he didn't. So why did I get so angry with him? I called him and apologised for my behaviour. He picked me up later that afternoon, and neither of us mentioned it again.

Daisy asked to meet up the following weekend. I invited her around to ours, but she insisted we should meet up for a walk. It had been too long since we did anything together. She suggested taking a picnic on Haytor. We hadn't seen each other since before the wedding back in the summer.

'Can you believe Tobias has been in Scotland for almost four months?' she said and then bit into her sandwich.

'I know, time goes so quickly, especially when you're building up a new business.'

'At least you're going back to uni soon. That will be good for you to carry on with the career that you've always wanted.'

'Oh, I'm not.' I said whilst picking blades of grass from around the edge of our picnic blanket. 'I'm postponing it for one more year because the business is growing more rapidly than Maxwell predicted.

'Did Maxwell ask you to do it?'

'No,' I snapped. 'It was my decision.'

Daisy took a sip of her coffee and then reached inside her handbag, 'Here, I brought you some magazines. I've read them and thought you might like to read them instead of me throwing them away.'

'Thanks,' I said and flicked through the small mix of lifestyle and celebrity magazines.

Daisy held my arm, 'I thought this one may be of particular interest to you.' It was a lifestyle magazine and the month's theme was relationships. She pointed to the special feature: *Are You in a Mentally Abusive Relationship?*

'Why would that be of any interest to me?' I said and placed the magazines in my bag. 'I don't have time to read magazines. I'm too busy with work, but I'll pass them on to Mum—she has time to read.'

'Alice, you know you can talk to me about anything at any time.'

'I know, and the same goes for you. Anyway, we'd best be heading back. Maxwell's taking me out for dinner tonight.'

'That's nice.'

'I know, he only told me this morning just before you picked me up. He said it's a treat before work gets madder after the summer holiday.'

Maxwell and I continued our routine of working long days, and early Autumn soon turned into winter, and spring quickly arrived. The business was doing well but not as well as predicted, and this time, Maxwell asked me to postpone university for a third year just to make sure the business had strong foundations before I stepped away. I agreed to it. The year had passed by so quickly that one more year wasn't a concern. Daisy once told me that most start-ups normally take up to three years to make a profit; it was something she learnt in her accountancy training. Maxwell was making a profit, but he wanted to expand, rent office space and employ staff. It seemed obvious that I should see through my commitment to him and his business—he was almost there. He said he would support me financially when I returned to my studies, so there was a lot for us both to look forward to. It felt reassuring to have joint plans for the future, unlike Tobias, who thought of himself by disappearing at short notice to pursue his.

It was my mum's fiftieth birthday that October. I called her early to wish her a happy birthday.

'You're catching me up,' she said.

'What do you mean, I'm in my mid-twenties?'

'You're only three years younger than I was when I gave birth to you. You still have one year to go before you start the final year of your degree.'

I sighed, 'Relax, Mum, by the time I qualify, I'll still be a year younger than you when you had me.'

Maxwell was annoyed with mum's comment after listening in on my conversation. We got into an argument as soon as I got off the phone. It was our second argument of the morning. He had returned home in the early hours after a drinking session with his new golfing buddies. It was a hobby he had resumed from before I knew him to help destress from work and also to network. I stirred when he staggered into the bathroom door. He filled the sink and washed before coming to bed. I asked him why he did that, and he said he was sweaty from running home—he ran out of money, so the taxi dropped him off a mile down the road. He got angry because of all my questions. I was trying to make sense of why someone would wash after a night out.

I wasn't frustrated at his lateness, but it made me feel lonely. I had stood at our bedroom window until midnight, waiting for him to come home—he said he was only having a few drinks after golf, so I was expecting him back no later than nine o'clock. He didn't answer any of my calls or read any messages I sent, wondering where he was. Whilst standing at the window, I had an almost out-of-body experience. It was like I was watching myself through the bedroom window from up above. It was more like a movie than something spiritual, but whatever it was, it looked sad. Was he with Sara-Ann? Something wasn't right with my life, but I couldn't work out what.

Maxwell was hungover, and combined with our second argument, he declined to go to Mum's party. He offered to drop me off and pick me up so that I could have a drink. When we arrived at my parents' house, I tried to convince him to come in for one drink, but he snapped at me and told me to hurry up and get out of the car because he needed to get home to do some work. He sped off, disturbing a pile of autumnal leaves like an angry swarm of wasps.

The party went well, but Mum felt sad that Maxwell wasn't celebrating with us. I overheard her moaning about him to one of her friends, and that upset me. I wanted to be with Maxwell and for him to hold me and tell me everything was going to be okay. I needed his reassurance. I asked him to pick me up earlier, but he refused, insisting I stayed longer for Mum's sake. But I just wanted to be with him.

'How was the party?' he asked when he picked me up at the original agreed time of midnight. The party finished at eleven, but he said I should stay and help tidy up.

I hiccupped. 'It was okay, but I missed you.'

I held his hand and kissed the back of it. He pulled his hand away from my mouth and started up the car. 'You're drunk.'

'Did you get everything done that you needed to?' I said and hiccupped again.

Maxwell didn't answer. He turned on the radio and drove fast. At junctions, he slammed on the brakes, pulled away quickly and swerved across lanes on the one-way system. 'Can you slow down, Maxwell,' I took a deep breath, 'I don't feel too good.' He didn't listen. 'You need to pull over,' I said, but it was too late. I unwound the window and was sick as he drove around a roundabout. A lot of it stuck to my hair, and the rest slid down the outside of the car door.

His eyes stayed fixed on the road. 'You are disgusting.'

My head slumped against the door, and I fell asleep.

Maxwell ran upstairs when we got home and turned on the shower whilst I tried undressing in the hallway. I was tired and drunk that I curled up on the hallway floor and fell asleep almost naked. I woke to Maxwell tugging off my jeans and underwear before picking me up and carrying me to the bathroom.

'Get in the shower,' he demanded. I did as he said but struggled to climb into the bath. One leg managed to get inside, but it felt too heavy to move and my balance didn't feel great. Maxwell shoved me, and I fell into the bath. The warm water poured onto me, wetting my hair. He left me there to clean myself, but I was sick again, and it blocked the plughole. Water started filling up the bath. I clumsily poked chunks of sick through the holes in the plughole to help unblock it.

'Get out,' he shouted when he returned. I stayed in the bath, my head swaying back and forth and side to side. 'Right,' he said and switched the shower onto cold. I started shivering and was still unable to move. He left me there until a point I couldn't recall what was happening.

The next thing I knew, it was daylight, and I was in bed. My hair was still damp. I rolled onto my side, and I winced in pain. I pulled the duvet and saw a huge purple-grey bruise on my hipbone.

'What happened,' I whispered. My forehead clenched from the discomfort of my hip and my hangover.

'I threw you in the bath last night because you were a state,' Maxwell said whilst yanking on his running gear. I pulled the duvet over my head and closed my eyes, and Maxwell left the house without saying another word.

Another Christmas came and went, and life remained full of long working days. Maxwell's networking started seeping into his social life, and he started going out frequently, staying out later and later. At first, it felt healthy to have some space from one another. For two and a half years, we had lived and worked together. I rarely saw Daisy or my parents because we were working hard. When he did go out, I initially started enjoying some me time. But as the frequency and duration increased, I didn't want to confess to anyone that I was starting to have doubts about my happiness.

I often waited up for Maxwell at the bedroom window, and when I saw taxi headlights, I jumped into bed pretending to be asleep. By the morning, everything felt back to normal when he rolled over for a cuddle despite the smell of alcohol on his clammy stubble. After a while, the odour started to repulse me.

On the rare nights that I went out, Maxwell pleaded with me to change my mind and stay in with him because he missed me. I often changed my outfit of choice because he said I looked better in this outfit or that one. I often stuck with my plans when he wanted me to stay with him, but I compromised by cutting the time I came home. But I did cancel sometimes when he got moody, and it was too much hassle going out. Why would he want me to stay with him if he was having an affair with Sara-Ann?

One evening, he was out with his golfing buddies, none of whom I had met, and I was out with Daisy and a couple of her friends from work. We ended up bumping into each other in the largest nightclub in Plymouth. It was three stories high, with numerous rooms on each floor, all playing different genres of music. Maxwell and I spoke briefly, but he insisted I go back over to the girls and continue enjoying my night out.

As the evening drew to an end, I left Daisy and her friends to find Maxwell to get a taxi home together. It took a while to find him, but when I did, he was no longer with his friends. He was talking to a girl. I watched them from a distance because they were close— closer than I could believe. Her arms were draped around his neck, and he was talking into her ear.

Watching them together felt like I was crying out in a dream, but nobody could hear me.

The final song finished, and I walked towards them and called his name before getting too near. He pulled away from her when he saw me, and she walked away and joined a group of girls. My coat was in the cloakroom, so Maxwell and I waited in the queue. The girl and her friends had to walk past the cloakroom to leave the building. She stopped to say goodnight to Maxwell, kissed him on the cheek, and then hugged him. She didn't acknowledge me. I don't know why I did it, but after she left, I sarcastically repeated her words and actions, and when I pulled back from the embrace, I punched Maxwell in the arm.

He laughed at me.

Maxwell could still be caring from time to time. I tripped and fell awkwardly onto the settee one morning and bent back my middle finger. A lump on the joint appeared the following day. I wasn't concerned about it and assumed it was a delayed reaction to the injury, but Maxwell was worried it may have been a cancerous lump and begged for me to get it checked out, which I did, and it was fine. It was a painful ganglion, and it was reassuring to have the peace of mind that it wasn't anything serious.

When I started to think that I was unhappy with Maxwell, he would surprise me and take me out for dinner or a weekend away in the countryside, and the doubt disappeared. One evening, Maxwell was at another networking event, and Mum invited me around for dinner, but I declined. I wasn't in the mood for socialising. Instead, I sat alone in the darkness, contemplating my future and my return to university after the summer. I just hoped that Maxwell and his business were ready for me to do that.

As time passed by and Maxwell was on another night out, I thought more about our relationship and how it was different from when we first started dating. Perhaps we had spent too much time with each other, and working long hours together would be tough for most couples. He seemed to get frustrated a lot, but I put that down to the responsibility of running his own business. But I still loved him. Maxwell had allowed me to live rent-free in his home for almost three years, given me work, treated me to meals, and often cooked. I felt ungrateful for all he had done for me. But I was unhappy.

One evening, whilst he was at a networking evening, I thought about things to try and figure out why I was feeling the way I did. But it was hard. I had reached a point where I didn't care if Sara-Ann was there that evening. I came up with an idea—I pretended to be a friend telling me my story as if it were hers. It felt crazy at first talking to myself, but when I told myself about the time "*her*" boyfriend came home from a stag do with scratches on his back, when he humiliated her at a wedding, that he threatened to break her finger after she overheard him having a flirtatious conversation with a woman, that he chucked her into a bath and ran freezing water on her, that she found the back of an earring underneath his bed the day she moved into his place, I started crying. Even the reaction to the chilli flake at the very beginning was a red flag that I ignored.

My dad would never treat me this way, so why had I allowed Maxwell to do it? I had to leave, but it wasn't going to be easy; I was financially dependent on him, and I still loved him even though I started to dislike him. I could see why some people had affairs—I wanted someone to come along on a white horse to rescue me, but nobody had, so I needed to find a way to rescue myself.

The UCAS closing date came and went, and I still hadn't found the courage to leave. He had been nicer to me since my epiphany; perhaps he sensed a change in me. It was the nicest he had been in a long time, but that changed when Daisy called me about Scotland.

'What are you doing for New Year's Eve?' she asked.

'We haven't made any plans yet.'

'There's a group of us going up to Scotland to see Tobias. You should come.'

'Thanks for the invite, but I can't afford it.' I hadn't told anyone how I was feeling or what I wanted to do, not even Daisy. I needed all of my money for the day I finally found the courage to leave Maxwell.

'You have to come—it won't be the same without you. I'll buy your flight ticket.'

'That's kind, but I doubt I'll be able to pay you back at the moment.'

'You don't have to, Alice. Come. Please.'

I let out a long sigh. 'Let me speak to Maxwell first about it.'

Daisy didn't question why I needed to ask Maxwell's permission to go.

Maxwell returned from his meeting a few hours after Daisy's phone call. He was in a good mood. He had secured a contract with a big organisation, and to celebrate, he wanted to go out for dinner. He was in the shower when I finally built up the courage to ask him.

'No, you can't go. You can't afford it.'

I cleared my throat, 'I know, but Daisy has offered to pay for my flights.'

'How dare she put you in this position?' He switched off the shower. 'If she was here now, I would strangle that girl.'

'She's only trying to help.'

'How many times do I have to tell you that she is trying to come between us?' His voice rose. 'She's jealous, Alice.'

'But—'

'I refuse to talk about this anymore,' he said, frantically drying himself.

The following week, Maxwell came back from a business training session, something Sara-Ann had organised. He was in a good mood and jumped straight into the shower— again.

'Alice,' he called me upstairs. 'I've been thinking today,' he said, scrubbing his hair and body clean. 'If you want to go to Scotland, then you should.'

'Really? Are you sure?'

'I want us to invest further into the business next year, and I don't want you throwing that back in my face telling me you couldn't afford to go to Scotland.'

'I wouldn't do that but thank you.' I ran downstairs before he could change his mind and called Daisy to book my flight.

Maxwell and I stayed in on Saturday night with a takeaway, watching Saturday-night television. We were snuggled on the sofa when a competition to win a trip to celebrate Hogmanay flashed up on the screen.

'Look, that's Scotland,' I said, pointing at the screen.

'Aaaaah,' Maxwell said and switched channels.

I sat up. 'What do you mean, "aaaaah"?'

'It's a shame you can't go to Scotland for the New Year.'

'But you said I could go?'

'No, I didn't!'

'Yes, you did!'

He sat up. 'When exactly did I say that?'

'In the shower the other day,' I spoke softly. 'You said I could go because you want us to invest in the business next year and—'

He spoke over me. 'I have never said anything about you investing in the business.' He stood up and threw the remote control onto the sofa. 'I'll tell you what, I'll lend you the money to go to Scotland, and I'll tell you exactly how and when you'll pay me back.' He stormed upstairs.

I didn't need his money to go because Daisy had already paid for the flight, but I didn't reiterate that. I was going. It was paid for. I wanted to go.

He returned downstairs a couple of hours later. 'We need to talk.' He sat down beside me on the sofa. 'I've been thinking, Alice,' he took both my hands into his. 'I think our relationship is ready to move up to the next level. How do you feel about starting a family?'

CHAPTER 12

Now

Teagan and I met for Sunday brunch in Hyde Park. It was a clear and chilly morning. Sunlight danced on The Serpentine like shimmering stars. It was the type of morning where tiny clouds of breath appeared in front of your face, but the heat from the sun was strong enough to warm which ever part of the body it touched. I choked on my tea from laughter when Teagan confessed that she was hungover on Friday, the real reason why she was off sick. I wanted to confess to her about Josh but decided against it; he wasn't worth another thought. I did tell her about Sean, and I was glad that I did.

'I contacted the external HR consultant about six months ago to raise my concerns over his behaviour,' Teagan said.

'What happened? What did they say?'

'She didn't reply to my email. I waited a week and had to

chase her up to check that she'd received my email.'

'And?'

'She said she had spoken to him, and that was it.'

'Did she offer you any support or that you could speak to her anytime?'

Teagan raised her eyebrows. 'Nope.'

'As a fellow woman, she should have been more proactive about the situation.'

'I did feel let down by her. She's scary, not the impartial HR representative that I hoped for.'

'Her income from the company sounds more important than doing the right thing,' I said. 'Were you tempted to leave?'

'I couldn't afford to. I needed the money.' Teagan looked sad. 'I had only been with the company for four months when that happened, and there was no way another employer would have considered me with less than a year's experience on my C.V.'

'Of course they would, especially if you explained why.'

'I was lucky to get the job in the first place. Mum had been sick for a long time, and I had taken off a year to look after her. Anyway, I've almost been there a year now, so not long until I can escape him.'

Teagan suggested going for a walk around Hyde Park. It was bigger than I imagined, and I lost my bearings until we exited the park near Buckingham Palace. I took a selfie with the palace behind us and sent it to Mum and Dad, and Daisy. Just before we left, a rush of excitement washed over loitering tourists near the entrance—a car was driving away from the palace and towards the gates. We hurried over to the crowd and caught a glimpse of Prince Edward. I had only ever seen him on TV. I wanted to take a photo to show Mum, but the car came and went before I had the chance. London was full of surprises, good and bad.

We made the short walk from the palace to Victoria Station. The station looked smaller than it did on the day I arrived in London. Teagan and I went our separate ways, and I made the journey back to Bethnal Green with ease.

On Monday morning, I made my way to the City of London. It felt like the real working world of London. Old Broad Street was busy with takeaway coffee-carrying, mobile chatting, suited, super-fast-walking zombies—these pedestrians walked faster than the traffic. They chatted without pausing for breath and carried their drinks like fashion accessories.

Building number one hundred and twenty-five was the tallest building on the road. I counted the floors twice, and each time, I came up with a different number: twenty-four and then twenty-seven. Either way, it was high. Grey clouds reflected off the glass exterior, camouflaging the building against the sky. Three revolving glass doors stood guarding the entrance, and as I neared them, I held out my hand to push one of them, but I stumbled as I lost my balance when it automatically moved.

Inside, a high ceiling emphasised the silent echoes from the matching marble floor and walls. There were twice as many reception desks as there were revolving doors, and the receptionists were dressed identically in fuchsia uniforms. They looked more like air stewardesses than receptionists.

'You can look away now,' the receptionist politely said after taking my photo. She smiled like a celebrity smiling on demand. She made a discreet phone call to advise someone of my arrival. 'Please swipe your badge through the security barrier and then take the lifts on the right-hand side to the twentieth floor.'

There should have been a warning sign alerting riders to the fact that the speed of the lift would flip your stomach and pop your ears before smoothly reaching the twentieth floor within seconds. The doors opened to a stunning view across South London. Windows ran from the floor to the ceiling, and the sight was so distracting that I forgot to introduce myself to the receptionist.

'Hello, Alice?' A voice brought me out of my distraction. I blushed at my unprofessional behaviour. The receptionist laughed, 'Don't worry, that view hypnotises everyone the first time they see it.'

'I'm glad I'm not the only one.' I was grateful for the woman's kindness.

'I'm Sholina, the office manager here at the bank.' She walked around the reception desk to shake my hand. 'I'll be showing you the ropes today.' We walked into a meeting room where the view was even better. I was left to admire it whilst she made our drinks.

Secret rooftop gardens added colour to the sepia landscape; London was whispering a secret that only a chosen few had the privilege of knowing, and I was one of them. It beckoned me to the window. The front of my shoes pressed up against the window as I looked down—a long way down. The city flowed peacefully without the sound of traffic, heavy machinery digging up roads or laying foundations, conversations of countless inhabitants, police helicopters and aeroplanes, or emergency service sirens. The commuters looked less zombie-like and more like a starling murmuration gliding and dancing their way around the city.

Sholina walked back into the meeting room. 'Thank you for helping us out at such short notice—our receptionist starts jury service today, and the temp we had lined up called on Friday afternoon to say they had found a permanent role.'

All that was required of me was to welcome visitors, answer the phone, open and distribute incoming post and frank the outgoing post whilst admiring the view. I hoped the jury service would last longer than two weeks.

Thursday was the new Friday in London, and that week, Sholina invited me to the company's belated Christmas do. We headed north of the city to what looked like a disused building in The Angel. Before we entered the building, Sholina let us all into the secret about the evening's events: we were there for an immersive play. We would be participating in it. I disliked talking in big groups and disliked role play even more. I wanted to leave. Sholina must have seen the fear on my face because she reassured me that I just needed to go along with the flow and could join in as much or as little as I felt comfortable with.

Other staff parties were at the venue, but it was impossible to work out who was part of the audience and who was a paid actor for the pretend company, Poker Face Production. We were split into groups, known as departments, and fortunately I was in the same team as Sholina and her close colleague, Nikki. We were part of the 'marketing team'. The head of marketing, who was definitely an actress, but at times I was convinced that she wasn't, showed us around the building. We visited offices where some staff members were working late, and a few of them moaned about doing the late shift and not being able to come to the Christmas party. It was easy to forget they were actors and that the Christmas party wasn't a real Christmas party. We played games in the staff canteen, and then we were led to a large hall where all of the departments congregated.

There was a bar, and Christmas songs played whilst some people danced, others played more party games, and the rest sat or stood around chatting or watching what was going on. The music stopped, and we all gathered on the dance floor to listen to the pretend C.E.O. give a speech from a balcony about the company and how well it had done that year. He thanked everyone for their hard work—he couldn't have done it without us. His speech was interrupted by a large guy in the crowd who threw up in the middle of the dance floor. Everyone swiftly moved away from him, but he remained wilted on the dance floor. It spoilt the night, and people were moaning about him. The lights came on, and somebody ran towards him with a mop and bucket, but just before they started cleaning up the mess, the large guy bolted upright and burst into an operatic song. He was part of the play.

'This is one of the most surreal experiences ever,' I said to Nikki, 'but I love it. I'm grateful Sholina invited me.'

'Me too,' she said. 'You've fitted in so well this week, Alice. It's like you've always been there.' My heart swelled at the compliment. I felt the same way. 'What are you up to Tuesday night next week? My friend Priya and I are going speed dating—you should come!'

'Thanks, I'd love to.' I agreed to go for the opportunity to experience what London had to offer and not just for the opportunity to meet someone.

The recruitment agency called Monday morning to tell me about a nine-month maternity cover position at the Inner Temple, the city's legal district. They wanted me to go for an interview the following day, which was perfect timing because Sholina had just informed me that the receptionist's jury service had concluded, so I only had one more day's work.

Sholina allowed me to finish at two p.m. but still claim the hours until the end of the day. It was a thank you for my hard work. I had plenty of time to get to my interview at the Inner Temple, so I decided to take a bus instead of the Tube to take in the view because I hadn't seen much of the business district of London.

Halfway into the journey, the bus pulled up at a stop opposite St Paul's Cathedral. It was the largest building I had ever seen. I felt as though I had shrunk down to the size of the pigeons busying themselves amongst the tourists. The front door and pillars were ten times the height of the people gathered on the steps in front of it. A woman sat on the steps as pigeons strutted around her as she fed them, like the bird lady in one of my favourite childhood movies, *Mary Poppins*. The song about feeding the birds for a tuppence whirled in my mind. I smiled. London was starting to feel magical.

The bus continued, and the magical song played on repeat in my mind, but the tune came to an abrupt stop when something on the bus caught my attention. I faced forward, but my eyes looked down sharply at the man sitting on the seat opposite. It took a few seconds to register what was happening, but when I realised that his coat was laid over his lap and the movement from underneath was his hand, I jumped up and shot forward to a seat by the door. I didn't know what else to do. Should I say something or ignore him?

Before my mind could process how to deal with the situation, an announcement sounded over the bus speakers—like a helping hand from a stranger pulling you up after a fall—the next bus stop was for The Royal Courts of Justice. I sat still, not wanting to give anything away that I was about to escape. I waited for a few seconds after the door opened before jumping off, and I made it through just before they closed.

The bus pulled away with the man still on board. I watched as he passed by and into the distance. He didn't look. As soon as the bus was out of view, anger set in. *I should have said something. No—his behaviour was so obvious that the attention was probably the kick he was after. Should I have said something to the driver? I could call the police, but what could I tell them? There's a man on a red bus in Central London with a coat on his lap.*

I started to feel weak as my adrenaline eased, so I decided to get an espresso at a nearby coffee shop. People in the city aimed to get from A to B as quickly as possible with minimal eye contact or interaction, but, like an angel, a woman chatted to me in the queue. She looked assertive in her sharp, navy skirt suit, but her smile softened her appearance. I guessed she was about the same age as my mum. I was grateful for her interaction because it made me feel safer. Surprisingly, I didn't feel homesick or scared. I was sticking to the promise that I made to myself the night I arrived in London. No one was going to throw me off my path ever again.

The conversation about the weather came to a natural end, and after a few seconds' pause, she asked if I was okay. She said I looked as though I had a lot on my mind. I told her what happened on the bus.

'That's awful,' she said.

'I'm fine,' I said. I was okay but felt tired from the shock. 'I guess this type of thing happens all the time in London.' I shrugged.

'Oh no, sweetie, I've lived in London my entire life,' she placed her hand on my arm, 'and that's never happened to me or anyone I know.' She insisted on buying my drink.

Before leaving the coffee shop, I reread the directions the recruitment consultant had given me to find the office as it was tricky to find. The starting point was at a place called Prince Henry's Room on Fleet Street, opposite Chancery Lane, which she said was the easy bit. It was. I could see the Tudor timber-framed architecture across from where I was sitting and the gate I needed to pass through. I made my way over.

The gate led into an archway and onto a pedestrianised area. It swung shut behind me, blocking out the traffic noise from Fleet Street like a portal to the past. I was now standing on a cobbled walkway lined with cast-iron lampposts. There weren't any vehicles, nor was anybody else around. I looked behind at the closed gate and hesitated before taking small, soft steps forward.

The recruitment consultant had informed me that the Inner Temple was the home of barristers. Their offices, known as chambers, looked similarly lifeless. Only a few lights were on in the vast number of offices. It was as though there had been an emergency, and everyone had abandoned what they were doing. Either that or barristers were generally messy, judging by the piles of string-bound files smothering desks, ties flung over the backs of chairs and shelves overflowing with books.

A casually dressed man exited the building where I thought my interview was being held. I asked him if I was in the right place. He nodded and held the door for me. I turned around to thank him, but he had disappeared.

The interview went well but they had two more candidates booked in for the following day. I wanted the job. It was good pay, easy to get to, it would give me the financial freedom to rent somewhere, and the contract was long enough to settle into the job. However, I was mainly excited about being involved with arranging the annual dog show that was taking place on the May Day Bank Holiday.

Straight after the interview, I needed to find Blackfriars station to meet up with Nikki at King's Cross. It looked easy enough to find, judging by the map on my phone, I just needed to head east out of the Inner Temple. I dropped my phone back into my bag and followed a route past a locked garden and into an open area full of expensive-looking vehicles: sports cars, classic cars, and four-by-four types. They weren't the typical family vehicles in supermarket car parks back in Plymouth. I knew very little about cars, but it was clear they were pricey.

Apart from the interview, I still hadn't seen anyone wandering around the Inner Temple. There was so much material evidence of life but nobody to show for it. Tudor Road wasn't as easy as I thought it would be to find from the expensive car park. I needed to check my phone again. Before I reached into my bag, I noticed a delivery man again. He was unloading boxes from a white van but wasn't wearing a uniform as such, just a pair of jeans, a navy sweatshirt and smart, brown shoes. Perhaps manual workers were required to dress smartly around here, shorts and boots being a no-no.

'Excuse me,' I called, but he didn't hear. I shouted louder, but he still didn't hear me.

'Can I help you?' The question came from behind. I turned around to see a man dressed in a pinstripe suit and shoes polished with so much effort that I could see my reflection in them.

'I'm trying to get to Blackfriars Station.'

'You're not far away,' he said, pointing with his black umbrella. 'Head over there, towards the security barrier, and Tudor Road will bring you out at Blackfriars.' He bowed his head and walked away.

Before setting off in the direction of Blackfriars Station, the delivery man caught my attention again. He was standing in the doorway of the brightest-red-bricked building in the square. It looked like a castle with its turreted roof. He was staring in my direction. I looked behind me, but there wasn't anyone this time, and when I turned back, he had disappeared. He was handsome but unfriendly. Perhaps he was behind on his delivery schedule. I quickly forgot about him as I walked along Tudor Street with the hope that the men at speed dating would be friendlier.

CHAPTER 13

Then

Maxwell's proposition of having children was bait. I knew he could sense me pulling away because I was. We had various conversations during our relationship about the future, but they were mainly career-focused. Having children was not on my radar. On the rare occasion when Maxwell mentioned having children, his views on parenting concerned me: no elbows on the dinner table, no cakes or biscuits in the house, and they would go to boarding school. Maxwell and I rarely ate dinner at the table; he had a sweet tooth, and neither of us went to boarding school.

A regular conversation at the beginning of our relationship was that we both shared the same morals when it came to relationships and being faithful. He told me he would leave someone rather than cheat, but that no longer seemed true. I was certain he and Sara-Ann were up to something, but I was too numb to feel anything about that anymore. It was difficult to know what was real these days. One thing I was certain of is that I was relieved that the idea of having children to improve our relationship was not for me. Our relationship was a mess. I was a mess. The planet was in a mess. I needed to protect an uncreated child from it all.

I still loved Maxwell but no longer wanted to be with him. The hardest part was that I was emotionally dependent on him. I could see that now. He made me happy, but he also had the power to knock me back down and yet only he was able to pick me back up again. A cycle of highs and lows, doubt and confusion, spun around my head like a washing machine stuck on a fast spin. I could no longer tell what was up and what was down. But I knew I had to figure a way out. I just didn't know how or when.

Maxwell didn't dispute the Scottish trip again. He started making me breakfast in bed—something he hadn't done in a long time, bought me flowers for no reason, became more affectionate, and we didn't have any arguments before I went away. We even spent Christmas Day with my family for the first time in our relationship, and that was his suggestion. Since we had been together, we normally spent it on our own with a quick present pit stop with my parents. But we kept to our other Christmas traditions of popping to his dad's on Christmas Eve and his mum's for Boxing Day lunch.

Daisy drove us to Exeter Airport on the morning of our flight, where we met Jonny; Tristan and his girlfriend; Tobias's twin brother, Owen, and his new girlfriend Naomi; and Patrick, Tobias's best mate apparently from primary school—I had never heard of him before. The last time I saw Jonny, Tristan and Owen was at Tobias's leaving do, I mean my birthday. So much had changed since that night.

Perhaps Maxwell was right, I thought, sitting at the back of the minibus with everyone's luggage piled up around me. *I shouldn't have come.* Everyone was chatting and laughing, but I felt tired and unsociable, so I pretended I needed to rest whilst staring out at the Scottish landscape. I wasn't sure what was worse: feeling out of place in a group or being alone at home. Maxwell had booked a last-minute skiing trip with some of his golf buddies. He was probably with Sara-Ann.

The scenery changed with every twist and turn on the coastal road. We crossed over a long bridge, passed through tiny villages, spotted oil platforms dotted out at sea like surfers waiting to catch a wave, and crossed a river where the water punctured the land to the far west and distant mountains. We passed hardly any traffic on our five-hour journey north of Aberdeen airport.

'Wick, ten miles!' Jonny shouted from the driver's seat. A wave of nerves travelled from my heart via my stomach and tingled through my legs.

'Hide behind the minibus,' Daisy said on arrival at Tobias's flat.

Owen laughed. 'His face will be a picture when he sees you.'

I did as they suggested.

'It's so good to see you guys,' Tobias shouted as he opened the front door. The sound of his footsteps ran towards the minibus. He was greeted with hugs and happiness. I felt foolish for hiding but more so for coming. As each of them collected their bags, one by one, they smiled at me with excitement. I wished I felt the same way.

'It's been too long,' Daisy said. 'I wish you stayed in Devon when you returned from Hawaii, but I can see why you came here; it's stunning.'

The tone of his voice changed. 'There wasn't anything to stay for.'

'How dare you? Devon has the best clotted cream on the planet.'

Daisy must have playfully hit Tobias because he laughed after a mocked, 'Ouch.'

'You know what I mean.' Tobias cleared his throat. 'How are you? How's Alice?'

Tobias's voice sounded familiar, even with the faint American-cum-Scottish twang. It transported me back, and for a moment, it felt like we were still boyfriend and girlfriend. I wanted to run from behind the minibus and into his arms, but the stupidity of the thought paralysed me. Would Tobias even want me here?

'I'm good, thanks,' Daisy said, 'and Alice is too.'

There was a short pause before he spoke. 'Does she know you're all here?'

'Yes, she said to say "hi".' There was a longer pause. 'Come on,' Daisy said, 'we're here to party. Would you grab my bag from the back of the minibus?' I held my breath.

Tobias joked, 'I see you're still as bossy as ever.'

'Some things never change,' she said. 'I'll go inside with the others. Hurry up.'

'Yes, your majesty. Stick the kettle on, and I'll be with you in a second for the grand tour,' he laughed as the sound of his footprints moved closer to the van.

'Does that include me in the grand tour?' I said as he reached the back of the vehicle.

'Alice!' Tobias scooped me up into his arms. 'I can't believe you're here!' He lowered me back down and stared at me before scooping me up again. 'I'm so happy you're here.' I closed my eyes and, for a moment, melted into him and back into the comfort of happiness.

After the grand tour of the flat, we all squeezed into the lounge and listened to Tobias's stories about his time in Hawaii. He showed us photos, too. A stab of jealousy niggled in my heart when he showed us a picture of him and Felicity on a white, sandy beach. Her arm was draped softly around his shoulder as though they were in a playful headlock. Both of them were laughing. Her perfect Californian smile snarled at me.

'And there's me thinking Felicity would have followed you to Scotland,' Tristan said.

'No, she loves the sun too much,' Tobias said whilst looking at me. 'We were good friends, but we haven't been in touch much since I left.'

Daisy discretely squeezed my arm. 'So, how's surfing in Scotland compared to Hawaii?' she asked.

'Colder,' Tobias said, and everyone laughed. 'On a serious note, there's something spiritual about it, and I'm grateful to my mate Scott for this opportunity.'

Later that afternoon, Tobias showed us around the quaint town. We passed Ebenezer Place—the shortest street in the world according to Tobias and the Guinness Book of Records—and then crossed over a river to the cobbled high street and onwards to the harbour. After that, Jonny and Tristan suggested a pub crawl to see the rest of the town. Everyone thought that was a good idea.

The afternoon swirled into the evening, and it became livelier with each drink. None of us had eaten since we arrived, and luckily, Tobias still had the sense to suggest takeaway pizza back at his flat. He gave Daisy his front door key, told everyone to head back to the flat and asked me to stay with him to help carry back the boxes.

We laughed as we reminisced about university whilst waiting for the pizzas to be cooked. 'Do you remember when you bumped into me?' he said, nudging me too hard that I lost my balance. He caught my arm.

I nudged him back. 'You bumped into me.'

'Perhaps we bumped into each other.' He smiled at me.

I looked down at the floor. 'Perhaps.' He giggled and giggled again until he was laughing so much he couldn't speak. 'What are you laughing at?' I asked and started laughing.

'That time you looked through the binoculars the wrong way!' Tobias's laugh was infectious. Even the guys behind the pizza counter started smiling at us.

'How are you, really?' he asked after his laugh subsided.

'I'm good.'

'How are things with Maxwell?'

'Fine.'

'Honestly?' he nudged me again. 'I know you, Alice.'

I snapped, 'No, you don't. You haven't known me for years. I haven't known you since the day you told me you were going to Hawaii.' I stood up and walked out of the shop, instantly regretting what I said.

Tobias followed. 'I'm sorry,' he said and pulled me close to him. His arms felt familiar and mixed with his scent, and once again, I was transported back to a time before my life started unravelling. To a girl full of dreams for the future. To hope and love. That person was a stranger to me now. I started sobbing in his arms. I was the same snotty mess as the night in Cornwall when he told me he was leaving.

'I don't know who I am anymore,' I said and held on to him tighter. 'I'm anxious when I'm with him and anxious when I'm not.'

Tobias rocked us gently side to side. 'I shouldn't have left you.'

'It's not your fault.' I looked up at him. 'I knew from the start that some things didn't add up with Maxwell, but I ignored them; I didn't want to see them. I just wanted to be happy again like I was with you.' I leaned into him again, and we hugged in silence. 'I'm going to leave him,' I whispered. 'I just need to find the strength to do it.'

'You're stronger than you know.'

'Am I?' I pulled away from him and walked back into the shop. 'Can we talk about something happier?

A pile of six pizza boxes stood to attention on the counter.

'As you're so strong, Alice…you can carry all the pizzas home,' Tobias said and pretended to run out of the shop. He winked at me and walked back to the counter. He placed three of the boxes in his arms and asked me to add one more. I did that, but that unbalanced him and the box slid off along with one other. Before placing both boxes firmly back into his arms, I noticed smudged mascara on his jacket.

'I need to get out of the habit of leaving makeup marks whenever you're around,' I said.

'At least I didn't cause them this time,' Tobias said. I stared at him. 'Sorry, that was meant to be a joke.'

'I'm glad you went to Hawaii,' I said and stormed off with the other two pizza boxes. Tobias ran after me.

'That was a joke, too,' I teased him when he caught up. We laughed and chatted all the way back to the flat. The remainder of the evening was full of fun and ease. I wanted to rewind time and go back to university.

The following day, a few of us drove to John O' Groats whilst the others stayed in bed with hangovers. We didn't stay long because the weather turned wet and windy, but we did manage a group photo under the famous sign.

'Alice, New York is on this sign too,' Tobias said.

I remembered New York City was three thousand, one hundred and forty-seven miles away from Land's End. 'New York is over eighty more miles away from here. It seems to be getting further away.' I shouted as the wind forcefully swept from the west.

That evening, everyone was surprised when the landline rang.

'That's odd,' Tobias said, 'hardly anyone calls the landline.' He answered. 'It's for you, Alice,' he said, holding the phone in my direction.

It was Maxwell. 'Happy New Year!' he shouted down the phone over loud music thumping in the background. He was drunk. 'It's almost midnight here in Andorra.'

'How did you get this number?'

'I rang around letting agents earlier but with no success, so I googled his surf school, and someone there passed on his details. I told them I was trying to get hold of my girlfriend.'

I turned and faced the wall and away from the lounge where everyone was. 'Why didn't you call my mobile?'

'I think I lost my mobile last night, and I don't know your number off by heart, Alice.'

'Happy New Year, Maxwell.'

'Happy New Year,' he shouted again. 'I've got to dash, Phil's got the shots in. Love you. Oh, and tell Tobias to keep his hands off my girl.' The phone went dead.

At midnight, a handful of New Year messages came through on my phone, and whilst I was reading them, I checked to see when Maxwell was last on WhatsApp. It was less than an hour earlier. Either he found his phone, or he never lost it in the first place.

The following morning, I woke up with a headache. I didn't drink much the night before and went to bed early for Hogmanay celebrations. It was a tension headache from the thought of returning to Devon and Maxwell and slotting back into a life that was making me anxious. The only blessing was that Maxwell wasn't due back from his ski trip for a couple of days, so that gave me forty-eight hours to mentally prepare to leave him. Being with Tobias and Daisy reminded me how it felt to be happy and relaxed, and that was enough incentive to give me the courage I needed.

A week passed after Maxwell's return from his ski trip, and the right time still hadn't arrived to leave him. He was overly nice to me, and that weakened my decision to go. I didn't want to hurt him, even after everything he had said and done, because there was a part of me that still cared for him, and I felt sorry for him, knowing that he was going to be left behind. I knew how that felt.

A few weeks later, Maxwell woke me by twiddling my hair, and I pretended to stay asleep because that was his way of trying it on. As soon as he rolled away, I rolled out of bed, put on my dressing gown and went downstairs to make breakfast. Ten minutes later, Maxwell shouted from the hallway that he was going for a run. The front door slammed behind him. Today was going to be the day that I was going to leave.

I was staring out to the garden whilst waiting for my tea to brew when a text message came through from Daisy. We were supposed to be going to the cinema that evening, but I wasn't sure if I was going to make it; that was dependent on how it went with Maxwell. I hadn't told Daisy or my parents what I was planning; only Tobias knew. I read Daisy's message, she wasn't feeling great, but she still wanted to go to the cinema and asked if I could make the earlier viewing. I didn't reply because I didn't know how my day was going to go.

My phone beeped again. This time, it was Tobias:

Berry, not heard from you since your trip to Bonnie Scotland. Hope all is OK. T xx

I replied straight away.

Today is the day! He has gone for a run, but the deed will be done. Wish me luck xx

My phone rang. It was Tobias. He was in a convoy of surfers heading down the west coast of Scotland for a weekend. He called to reassure me that everything would be fine and that I needed to stay strong and focused for the sake of the rest of my life.

'What would I do without you?' I joked.

'That's a very good question.' I could hear Tobias smile down the phone.

'I should go, in case he comes back.'

The line started breaking up. 'The signal's not…here anyway.'

'Thanks for calling!' I shouted.

'I'll call…next...'

'Speak to you soon,' I said, staring at my phone, unsure if he had heard me.

'Alice?'

'Yes?' I said and pulled the phone back to my ear. 'Tobias?' The line went dead.

I jumped in the shower instead of calling Tobias back. I wanted to be dressed when I had the conversation with Maxwell just in case I needed to leave the house then and there. After dressing, I dried my hair and, part way through, felt a hand on my shoulder. I jumped and threw the hairdryer down onto the bed.

'It's only me,' Maxwell laughed. He undressed out of his running gear and jumped in the shower. 'I hope you've left me some hot water,' he shouted from the bathroom. I pretended not to hear and finished drying my hair before going downstairs to practise what to say to him. My mouth was dry, and my hands clammy. *When should I say it? How should I start it?* I thought as I wiped the kitchen sides over and over.

Maxwell's phone rang before he came downstairs, and he ended up staying in the bedroom for half an hour.

'Who was it?' I asked after he finally made an appearance.

'Something to do with work,' Max said and slapped my bottom.

'On a Saturday?' I said, polishing the coffee table in the lounge.

'You know how it is when you own your own business,' Max said. 'I'm going to pop to the shop to get some lunch; I fancy some soup.'

'We've got soup,' I shouted, but he had already walked out.

I sat cross-legged on the sofa, waiting for him to return. My foot twitched involuntarily; I couldn't stop it. My mobile rang. It frightened me so much that it hurt my heart. I didn't look to see who was calling and let it ring off. The phone rang again straight away so I checked it. It was Daisy. I left it. The cinema would have to wait. But when she called a third time, I answered.

'Alice,' she said before I even said hello.

'Are you all right?'

Daisy paused. 'I've got some bad news.'

Daisy's call irritated me. It wasn't her fault she was feeling unwell, but she would have seen that I read her message earlier and that I would respond eventually. I suspected her bad news was that she wouldn't be going to the cinema…

'Don't worry if you can't make it to the cinema later, I can't make it anyway.' There wasn't time to explain what was happening.

'It's not that,' Daisy interrupted.

I snapped, 'Daisy, I can't talk at the moment.'

She started crying. I wanted to cry with frustration.

'I'm sorry,' Daisy managed to say through her blubbing.

I rubbed my eyes. I was already exhausted from the day. 'There's no need to apologise. I'll call you later. I promise.'

Daisy was still crying. 'It's not me, it's Tobias… he's been involved in a car accident.'

'Is he all right?' I asked. There was no reply. 'He's okay?' I shouted.

Daisy sobbed. 'He didn't make it.'

'But I spoke to him earlier.'

It was windy on the drive, and the guys travelling in the van in front of Tobias hadn't tied their surfboards down properly. One of the surfboards caught a gust of wind, ripping it from the roof rack and straight through the windscreen of the van behind. The driver swerved and hit a tree. They both died instantly.

'Look, Daisy, I can't talk now,' I took in a deep breath. 'I'll call you later.' And before Daisy had the chance to reply, I hung up.

CHAPTER 14

Now

By the time I arrived at King's Cross for speed dating, Nikki and her friend, Priya, were already at the venue. The long, narrow bar was tucked down a side street around the corner from the station and inside it was busy and comfortingly dimly lit.

'It's two for one.' Priya waved two cocktails as Nikki introduced us. One of her drinks was bright orange with a twisted strip of orange peel hooked to the side of a saucer-shaped glass. The other drink was in a tall cocktail glass; it looked more like an electric blue slush puppy than an alcoholic drink with an assortment of jelly sweets sprinkled on top. Priya took a sip of the blue drink, and it turned her tongue the same colour.

I went to the bar and bought Daiquiri cocktails on the same

deal, and before I managed to squeeze my way back to Nikki and Priya, I finished one of the drinks and placed the empty glass back on a random table.

'Why didn't you get two?' Nikki asked.

'I did,' I smiled at her.

'You've overtaken us,' Priya said.

'These martini glasses are small; one long sip and it's gone.' I smiled.

'Don't get drunk before the event,' Nikki laughed.

A young woman rang a handbell before announcing the speed dating event was due to commence in fifteen minutes. She asked those who were attending from the bar to register upstairs. Unlike the rowdy atmosphere downstairs, upstairs was as quiet as a museum. We were all issued name stickers, and then women were asked to sit at a table, and the men were asked to join one of us. Each date lasted for three minutes before the handbell rang, prompting the men to move clockwise to the next table.

The guys were pleasant enough, but they all blurred into one: professional, in their thirties, chatty with an air of forced confidence, not unattractive but not attractive either, and most had come along with a female friend. There wasn't a natural spark with any of them. The tenth and final guy to sit at my table before the interval made me realise that I was ready for another cocktail. Chris confessed to breaking the rules because he was only twenty-nine—the event was for people in their thirties. He had come along on his own.

'I like fast cars,' he said without being prompted by a question.

'What's the fastest car you've driven?' I asked whilst trying to mask a yawn.

'I did over a hundred once on the M6 in an Astra,' he said and took a sip of his drink.

I forced a smile and resisted the urge to be sarcastically impressed.

'So, have you been speed dating before?' I didn't know what else to ask.

'This is my fifth time because I haven't found a connection with anyone yet, but I'm hoping tonight's the night. You've got to take the positives from the negatives,' he said just as the bell rang. That was my positive.

It was tiring chatting with one stranger after another under controlled conditions. During the interval, I decided I needed water to perk me up. Nikki and Priya bought more cocktails. Nikki sat on the table to my right, which meant she met each man three minutes before me.

'You're in for a treat,' she said during the break, 'the guy you're chatting to next told me I was the most beautiful girl in here, but he said the same thing to Priya beforehand.' They both laughed. I was tempted to leave—ten guys was enough for one night, but I didn't want to look ungrateful to Nikki, so I stayed.

The session resumed fifteen minutes later, and I hoped the second half was going to go faster than the first. It had been a different experience, but I could sense that I wasn't going to meet the man of my dreams tonight. I thought about my bed and how much I wanted to be curled up underneath the duvet instead.

The guy Nikki mentioned shook my hand before he sat down. He was easy to talk to and handsome too. I guessed he was Italian, but he was Greek and had lived in London for two years. He didn't say what Nikki told me. Was that a positive or a negative? He seemed nice. The bell rang, and he stood up. I thought he was going to shake my hand again, but he kissed it instead, and *then* he told me I was the most beautiful woman in the room. Next!

The penultimate guy to sit at my table that evening was a junior doctor called David. He was by far the best-looking guy at the event; he was funny and spoke well. He was on a placement at The Royal London Hospital and worked in the emergency department that receives patients by helicopter. I wondered if he was working that time I saw a helicopter land at the hospital. There wasn't anything not to like about him. I no longer felt tired.

My life in Devon for the past few years had felt like the grey man. I had played it safe, but it was boring, and London was already giving me the confidence to push forward. I was ready to feel excited about love again, to be *in* love again. Loving Maxwell scared me for a long time, and I knew he no longer had power over me; I just needed to believe it. The trail of destruction from being sucked into that relationship and then being spat out the other side shipwrecked my life. I sank to the bottom of the ocean, entangled in ghost nets. I almost drowned. Yet the desperation for a last breath of air helped me to scramble to the surface. I never wanted to feel that way again, so I remained in shallow water, staying safe and in control. But nothing happened there, and I needed to push myself and swim out of my depth once again. The encounter with Josh highlighted my lack of recent dating experience, but it didn't scare me to swim back to shore. Instead, I trod water for a moment, stabilised my breathing and pushed on because I knew my inner strength. Now, David was enticing me to swim out even deeper. His presence was like calm water.

The bell rang.

'It's lovely to meet you, Alice. I've enjoyed your company.' His words whispered in my ear like the enchanting sound of the sea from a conch shell. I wondered if David would be the one to break my dating patterns. I was ready to get it right. But the words that left his lips next hit me like a freak wave. 'I could carry on talking to you,' he smiled, 'I can't believe how well we've clicked, considering I'm superior to you.'

'Excuse me?' I stood up. My chair scratched the floor like nails down a chalkboard.

'Sorry, I didn't mean it like that. It's just that I hadn't expected to hit it off with someone so easily tonight.'

'With someone like me, you mean, who didn't finish uni, hasn't got a career, and doesn't speak as well as you?'

'Yes. I mean no.' My face blushed. 'I'm sorry, I didn't mean to make you blush.'

'You didn't. I'm on my period, and I blush easily when something irritates me.' I hissed at him. I wasn't on my period, but he had irritated a deep and painful wound, and like a wounded wild animal, I was lashing out with no concern for the pain I may cause. I just needed to protect myself. People were looking.

His face turned red. 'Look, can we start again?'

'I don't think so. Good luck in your search for love, David. You're going to need it if you're looking for someone as superior as you.'

The flat was oddly quiet the following morning after Kate and Fabrizio left for work. It was my first time alone in the flat since being in London, and having nowhere to go, the calmness was unnerving. I liked being swept up in the noise and rush of London; I found it comforting. I didn't like not having somewhere to be in London. I wanted to get out there and live in it.

It was a relief when the recruitment agency called later that morning, offering me the job at the Inner Temple—a nine-month maternity contract in London meant I was able to commit to a house share. I began online house hunting. The process in London was fast, and rooms went faster, so I needed to make the most of my short free time to find somewhere before starting my job the following week. An estate agent arranged to meet me that afternoon in Clapham on a long residential street. Most of the Victorian three-storey houses looked as though they had been converted into flats judging by the communal entry systems, but they looked spacious, so I was looking forward to viewing a six-bedroom flat share. It was one of the cheapest rates I found online, and it would only cost forty per cent of my salary.

We met outside a shop parade. I assumed the agent suggested there because it was an obvious place along the road, but it was because the six-bedroom flat was perched above the convenience shop. I followed him down a narrow alleyway alongside the building and climbed up a metal staircase to reach the front door. The fifth and sixth bedrooms were converted from the lounge and dining room, and apart from the kitchen and bathroom, there wasn't any shared space—not even a garden.

None of the housemates were in, but evidence of their existence was dotted all around the place: a pile of washing up was left in the sink, crumbs scattered across the sideboard, a rugby scrum of coats hung in the hallway, a clothes-horse with a single sock on it sat on the landing, and a collection of toothbrushes and toothpaste occupied the sink space in the bathroom. Each bedroom had a combination lock on it. The place didn't feel like home. It felt like a prison.

The following morning, I viewed a room in a large house in Wimbledon on a respectable-looking street. The estate agent was keen to inform me that a dentist and social worker rented rooms from the live-in landlord. The estate agent couldn't make the viewing, so the landlord greeted me instead. He was tall and wore thick-rimmed glasses. He was friendly, but I felt uncomfortable—he reminded me of the unassuming head vampire in *The Lost Boys*. I stepped into a grand entrance hall.

Nobody else was in, but the television was on, which made it feel homely, and the false sense of security of daytime television led me to follow him upstairs. The stairwell crept up to a four-sided landing. I counted twelve doors, three on each walkway. All but one door was closed. The landlord walked into the open-doored room and straight over to the window. The view was great, overlooking Wimbledon Park. Green grass and trees stretched into the distance towards a lake.

'In the summer, you can hear the crowds cheer from Wimbledon itself,' he said. I turned back to look at him.

'It's a great room.' I admired the oversized furniture.

'Thank you,' he smiled, 'I shipped the furniture from the States.'

The house was grand and in an affluent neighbourhood. It was somewhere I could never afford to live on my own. If the landlord wasn't so creepy, it was tempting to say yes, but my mind was made up when I noticed the red satin sheets on the king-size bed with an old teddy bear sat on top. I freaked out but needed to look calm—that's what people do in scary movies, not to agitate the bad guy.

'I'd love to see the garden,' I said and walked towards the door. 'I bet it's lovely.'

He followed me out of the room and down the stairs and

showed me the garden. It wrapped around the house, so I was able to make a seamless escape when he invited me back in for a cup of tea.

With little success and experience in how to find a nice place to live, Teagan kindly offered to come with me to the two viewings I had arranged for Saturday morning. We met outside Brixton Tube Station, where red buses crisscrossed along the road, music burst out from shop doorways, and the scent of Caribbean food drifted in the air. We passed a religious group handing out leaflets outside a fast-food restaurant as we weaved our way across a busy junction to a quieter road for the first viewing.

The ground floor flat was tucked behind a main row of houses that sat along Baytree Road. The road was quiet, which was a contrast to the hustle and bustle going on down the road. Ella greeted us at the door, and on first impression, she seemed nice. She offered us a drink, and we sat down for a chat. She worked as a part-time dental nurse and as an events manager at a human rights charity. She had rented the flat for a few years, which helped to keep the rent down because the landlord knew he had a reliable tenant. The only reason the other flatmate was moving out was that she was moving in with her boyfriend. It all sounded ideal.

My period came whilst we were chatting, and luckily, I had come prepared with sanitary towels. The dull ache from when I woke indicated that 'she' would be arriving any time today. I asked to use Ella's toilet. Cramps clawed at my stomach, but I forgot to bring pain relief—I wasn't as prepared as I thought. My period was heavy and painful. I took a few slow, deep breaths whilst sitting on the toilet, but that didn't help. I stuck my war wound dressing into my underwear, zipped up my jeans and flushed the toilet. But it didn't work properly. It stirred weakly, and instead of the water going down, it crept up a little. I flushed the chain a second time. The water rose even higher; it was just below the rim. Red mushed-up toilet paper swirled on the surface. I didn't dare pull the chain again. Only a plumber could fix the problem. Tears of embarrassment, frustration and hormonal fluctuations stirred inside.

I opened the door. 'Ella, I think you need to call a plumber. The toilet isn't flushing.'

'Pardon?' she shouted from the lounge before appearing in the hallway.

'I said,' I shouted and then lowered my voice to adjust to her presence, 'you need to call a plumber.'

'Is the toilet blocked?' She barged into the bathroom. 'That happens sometimes. You just need to use the toilet brush as a plunger.' Before I was able to compute her instructions, she picked up the toilet brush and started plunging away.

'I'm on my period,' I whispered.

'It's not a problem,' she said, thrashing the brush up and down. 'I'm a dental nurse and see blood all the time.' And with an extra plunge, she flushed the toilet, and all was resolved.

Teagan and I made our excuse to leave soon afterwards.

'I feel violated,' I said.

'I'm not surprised,' Teagan linked her arm to mine. 'I take it you're not going to live with the period poker?' She looked at me with a serious expression before bursting into laughter. Surprisingly, I was able to laugh too.

We walked back to the busy junction and jumped onto the number thirty-seven bus to East Dulwich for the next and final viewing of the day. It was only a twenty-minute ride away, but it felt as though we had been transported outside of London and into a village as the bus passed green spaces. East Dulwich felt calm and safe with people and buses passing up and down the busy high street. It was lined with delis, bars, estate agents, a mini department store, a few antique shops, restaurants, clothes shops and more. I liked it.

We disembarked near a busy junction opposite Peckham Rye Common and followed a tree-lined road. The yellow-green common across the road spread out into the distance; it wasn't possible to see where it ended. It was the only colour against the grey sky and bare brown trees until a green blob landed on a branch of a nearby tree.

'It's a parrot,' I said, pointing to the tree. 'Someone's lost their pet!' Then another parrot landed on the tree, followed by another, and another. They looked like mini toy dragons but sounded like squealing monkeys.

'They're not pets,' Teagan laughed, 'they're feral.'

'They're wild? Are you sure?'

'Yes, they're all over South London.'

Life in London was a constant learning curve. Even the wildlife was different.

We found the flat. The building wasn't as grand-looking as some of the other impressive-looking houses on the street, but it stood proud, proving it belonged there as much as the rest in the neighbourhood. It was narrow in comparison too and had probably been squeezed in at the end of the terrace as an afterthought.

It, too, was four storeys high. The curtains and blinds on the other floors were still closed, blocking out the world even though it was ten in the morning. The top floor looked much more welcoming as a hint of an amber glow shone through wooden-slatted blinds. In front of the windows sat stainless steel window ledge planters, each with a sprinkle of colour peering over the top. I had a good feeling that was the flat we had come to see.

Teagan pushed the gate open, and we walked through the garden and up a short flight of stairs, where we found a keypad and pressed the buzzer for flat D.

'Hello?' A girl answered.

'Hi, it's Alice Berry. I've got a viewing at ten.'

'Hi Alice, come on up. We're on the top floor.' I was right.

Chloe greeted us and offered us a cup of tea before we passed through the front door. She showed us into the lounge where her flatmate Tien was waiting. Tien was the one moving out; she was moving back home to South Korea.

'Beth should be back soon. She stayed at her boyfriend's last night,' Chloe said as she brought in our tea.

The girls told us about the rent and how the bills work, how the transport links were great and that Lordship Lane—the main road in East Dulwich—had a variety of shops and bars and was currently the place to be in London. I had never heard of East Dulwich before the viewing. The girls didn't know each other before moving and had moved in at different times, but they had become friends as well as flatmates. They had all lived there for over a year. Chloe was a textile designer originally from Surrey, Tien was an art student, and Beth was Australian working in finance.

'But don't let her profession put you off,' Chloe joked about Beth. 'She's friendly and lots of fun.' As she said that, Beth arrived back at the flat. She was warm and bubbly, just as Chloe had described her.

Tien showed me around the flat. Wooden floorboards and shutters gave the flat a French feel. The furniture wasn't French shabby chic, more of a mishmash of slightly worn items. There was a separate toilet as well as the one in the bathroom—which had a morning rota. There was a double divan bed, a rickety wardrobe, cheap-looking shelves and a tired mirror in Tien's room, but it was homely enough. There was a knack for using the gas hob in the kitchen, and the front door didn't seem as secure as it should but I loved the flat and was delighted when the girls asked me if I wanted to move in. I had found my London home, my London family.

The following day, I called my parents to tell them about the flat.

'It's a safe area,' I reassured them. 'Girls were jogging on their own, and the area is known for its "yummy mummies", and there's a lovely high street.'

'What's a "yummy mummy"?' Dad asked.

'You know, young, hip mums with babies who frequent bars and coffee shops with other yummy and hip mums.'

'When do you move in?' Mum asked.

'Friday evening, straight after work.'

'But that's your first week in your new job. Won't it be a bit much?' Mum said.

'It'll be fine, Mum. That's how London works; it's fast. I can't wait.'

We spoke more about the job, and they told me that Daisy had popped around for dinner earlier in the week. Mum started gossiping about one of the neighbours when Dad interrupted.

'Hang on, Alice…I'm just browsing the internet about East Dulwich. There was an armed mugging yesterday. Are you sure it's a safe area?'

'That's awful, Dad.' I hesitated. Anything can happen anywhere at any time. I thought I was safe living in Devon. I was physically; I had never been mugged, but I had lived in fear for almost half of my adult life. I was scared of the loneliness I felt, fearful about how my life would move forward and petrified of my judgement. London was my chance to push through all of that. 'I'm still going to move in.'

CHAPTER 15

Then

After Daisy's call about Tobias, I stared out of the window. It had been a cold and dry winter so far. It was overcast and as still as a painting. No birds were flying, no leaves flickered. Maxwell's key turned in the door just as it started raining. It was the type of rain that fell heavily, vertically. Birds suddenly zipped from nowhere, trying to find shelter. Tree branches moved around, trying to take cover from the wet. The still picture was disappearing with every drop of rain, like the chalk sketch from Mary Poppins. I wanted to jump into the image and return to the past—to Cornwall. This time, Tobias would propose, and I would say yes, and everything would be different.

Maxwell shouted from the kitchen. I heard his voice but not the words.

He walked into the lounge. 'I said, do you want any soup?'

I didn't turn to look at him. I carried on staring out of the window, looking at everything and nothing. 'Tobias has died.'

'Oh,' he said and fluffed a cushion. He walked back out. 'Did you want some soup?'

I didn't have any soup. I didn't leave Maxwell. I didn't cry. I curled up on the sofa and drifted in and out of a zombie-like sleep for the rest of the day.

Daisy called a week later to say that Tobias's body had been flown down from Scotland, and the date for his funeral had been set. I still hadn't cried. Nothing seemed real: Tobias's death, my plan to leave Maxwell. I didn't feel anything. When Maxwell returned home that evening, after a day of meetings with new candidates, he was in a good mood and suggested going out for dinner. I was still in my pyjamas. I dragged myself upstairs and showered. The thought of going out for dinner rather than staying indoors with Maxwell was more appealing. Maxwell bounded upstairs like a prancing goat and jumped in the shower afterwards.

He walked into the bedroom with a towel wrapped around his waist. He came up behind me and started kissing my neck. I stared at the dirty washing basket; my body didn't react, not even with disgust.

'I need to take next Thursday off for Tobias's funeral.'

'You're joking!' He stopped kissing my neck.

Still staring at the bin, I replied, 'Why would I joke about something like that?'

'I've finally managed to arrange a meeting with that client I've been after for ages.' He grabbed my arms and spun me around to face him.

'And?' I said.

'And I need you at the meeting.'

My voice increased in volume. 'But you don't normally ask me to go to these meetings with you.'

'Do I have to explain to you that this business is your priority!' he shouted.

'You can't tell me what my priority is,' I shouted back.

He shouted so loud that it hurt my ears. 'I know what's best for you.'

I laughed. 'How is that possible? I don't even know what's good for me anymore!'

He glared. 'Don't you dare laugh at me.'

'I am going to the funeral!' I screamed.

Maxwell was rigid. He lowered his voice and pointed at me. 'If you love me, Alice, you'll go to the meeting.'

'I don't love you, not anymore.' I stared into his eyes. 'I haven't for a long time.' I rushed over to the wardrobe, dragged my suitcase off from the top of it, and started throwing everything I could into it.

Maxwell sat on the bed, his voice weaker. 'But what about our future?' I continued packing. 'The business, our first home together, marriage?'

I stopped ripping clothes from hangers and turned to face him. 'Marriage? I would be embarrassed to have your name,' I spat and carried on packing.

He watched as I paced around the room, looking for what little items belonged to me. He eventually broke the silence. 'But I love you.'

'How is any of this love?' I said whilst zipping up the suitcase.

Then I left.

Daisy picked me up from my parents' house on the morning of Tobias's funeral and drove to his parents' house afterwards for the wake. We sat in silence on both journeys. My gaze was fixed outside the window. The familiarity of turning onto the road where he used to live suddenly made it real. The last time I had been down this road was with him. Nothing had changed on the wide tree-lined avenue. It was like time stopped. I almost expected to see Tobias and me walking down the road, hand in hand.

We drove past the bus shelter where Tobias told me he loved me for the first time. My heart ached at the thought that we would never sit there together ever again. 'I can't go in,' I said. 'Can you make my apologies to his mum and dad for me?' Daisy nodded. 'Can you give them this?' I handed Daisy a letter which I had written that morning. It included some photos of Tobias that I had taken from my memorabilia box. I got out of the car and walked back to the bus shelter. And for the first time since Daisy's phone about his death, I cried.

Dear Mr and Mrs Greenwood,

First of all, I want to tell you how sorry I am for your loss. Tobias often spoke about you and I know he loved you very much.

I managed to find some photos of Tobias from our time together and thought you may like to keep them. My favourite one is the black and white photo of him in his wetsuit, carrying his surfboard from the sea. Even though Tobias and I lost touch during his time out of the country, I often thought of him. I am grateful that we got to see each other one last time in Scotland and rekindle our friendship.

I also want you to know that Tobias will always have a special place in my heart, and I promise I will never forget him, my first love.

Alice x

Maxwell called me that evening. He had called a few times since I walked out. Our conversations didn't last long. They weren't about anything significant. He asked me about my days or told me about his day. I only spoke when I needed to. This time, I didn't answer. He left a voice message saying the meeting was a success. The was no mention of the funeral. I decided that I would no longer take his calls.

A few weeks passed when I bumped into Tobias's mum, Mrs Greenwood, in Plymouth. I had just been for an interview for an administrator role. She said she was doing well, considering everything, and thanked me for the letter and photos. She asked if I had time to go for tea and cake with her. I had plenty of time. I had no job. No boyfriend. No hobbies. No interest in doing anything.

She chose a café that overlooked the sea. It was a comfort for her to be close to the place that Tobias loved. She picked up her cup and saucer and stared out the window.

'I always hoped you two would get back together.' I took a sip of my tea. She turned to look at me. 'Tobias always felt guilty for what he did.'

'It's what he wanted to do.' I wanted to save her feelings but bury mine. At times, my grief had turned to anger—if Tobias hadn't been selfish, thinking only about himself, then he wouldn't have gone to Hawaii, I wouldn't have looked at Maxwell, I'd have a career, and he would be alive.

She leaned forward and placed her hand over mine. 'He didn't mean what he did. He loved you. His guilt over the kiss with Daisy never meant a thing.' She patted my hand and sat back in her chair.

'Kiss?'

'At your twenty-first birthday party?' she said. 'He mentioned it a few times on his calls from Hawaii, but I told him not to feel guilty. His feelings were all over the place at the time. He had so much going on.'

I felt sick. The long, blonde hair I found on him in the shed. My heartbeat raced in my chest. I had to lie to her. 'Of course,' I swallowed hard, 'I've forgotten all about that.' I finished my tea and wrapped the rest of my cake because I was *too full* to eat it all now. I needed to get away from her as quickly as possible.

By early summer, and after many more interviews, I finally got a job. It was an unfulfilling role as an insurance administrator. I was earning money, but I could only afford part payment to buy a second-hand car and the rest was money borrowed from my parents. I had been on holiday to Greece with one of the girls from the office, Kirsten—my rebound friend from Daisy. There had been a tearful night when I confronted Daisy about the kiss, which she didn't deny but tried to excuse as a mistake. She said Tobias felt pushed away because he could see Maxwell and me inevitability getting together. Daisy and I hadn't seen each other or spoken since. She sent a handful of text messages, but I ignored them all. I deleted the messages without reading them.

I was happy enough. The past was shut behind me, and all I wanted to do was move on. My salary wasn't great, but I got by. It was mine. I went out a lot, to the extent that Mum said I was burning the candle at both ends. I was having fun. My colleagues, my new friends, were a sociable bunch. On nights out, I would snog a random guy on the dancefloor and even kissed my colleague, Daniel, one night. The following day at work, we carried on as though nothing happened. It was a drunken kiss; it didn't mean anything. I even had a holiday romance when I went to Greece. Kirsten and I dated fire-breathing barmen. We partied with them until the sun rose and stayed in bed until late in the afternoon. I was doing fine without Max. I had healed from Tobias. I had forgotten about Daisy. Or so I thought.

Then I met Blake.

We met on a Thursday night in a crowded bar in early July. Blake was Australian. He had spent a year travelling around Asia and then Europe. His final leg was the U.K. By the time he reached Devon, he had been to London, Edinburgh and Cardiff. As a hobby surfer, he wanted to spend the rest of the summer surfing in Devon before he had to return home when his visa expired. We met during his first week in the county. There was an instant connection. Not love, but something deeper than lust.

'Squeeze in beside me,' I shouted and pointed to the tiny space between me and the next person waiting to be served at the busy bar.

'Thanks,' he said and moved closer. He accidentally trod on my foot.

'Ouch,' I joked, but I also meant it. He was over six feet tall and broad-chested.

'Sorry about that,' he said. He placed his hand on my lower back, and a surge of energy travelled through my body. He bought me a drink as an apology for his clumsiness. We ended up chatting for most of the evening. When they called the last orders, we swapped numbers, and he said he would call.

Dad asked me to check the mailbox the following morning. I was tired and hungover, and I rolled my eyes before scuffing my slippers from the kitchen to the hallway to check. I yanked the post from the mailbox and threw the pile of white envelopes onto the kitchen worktop before slumping onto the sofa.

'There's some post here for you,' Dad shouted from the kitchen.

I grunted and curled up into a tighter ball. It was Sunday morning, and I still hadn't heard from Blake. I thought he was going to message me when he got in last night.

'I said there's some post for you, a postcard from Tenerife,' Dad said as he walked into the lounge. He threw it at me like a Frisbee. The postcard fell on the carpet in front of me. The picture of a Persian blue sea enticed me to reach down and read it. I flipped it over and sighed when I read who it was from.

Hey, hope all's well. I'm having an amazing lads' holiday in Tenerife. I've pretty much tried every water sport going and we're regulars in several bars. The crew in one of the bars calls me "Max the Mover." Hope the weather's not too cold in Blighty.

I tore up the postcard and threw it on the floor. A fire raged in my belly, which drove me to call Maxwell. Postcards took days, even weeks, to arrive after the holiday has finished and people returned to their normal lives. He must be back. The ringtone confirmed he was in the UK.

'I knew you'd call,' he said, answering the phone.

He tried to make conversation, but I interrupted him. 'I need the rest of my belongings.'

'Sure, when do you want to come round?'

'I don't. Bag it up, and let's meet somewhere neutral.'

We arranged to meet the following day at a park in the centre of Plymouth, not far from the recruitment agency where we met. I arrived first and found a bench near the entrance, which was slightly hidden from the road by a conifer tree, like a protective buxom older lady. The entrance was visible from the bench, and within minutes of arriving, Maxwell drove past and parked further up the road. I could see him, but he couldn't see me. He climbed out of his car and checked his appearance in the rear window. It had been months since we last saw each other. It felt strange seeing him. He looked familiar but shorter and older. It took a moment to compose myself, and I was pleased about having this advantage because he greeted me with ease.

He made small talk about how his business was doing and the recent James Bond movie that he had seen at the cinema. I told him about my job and my new second-hand car, which he playfully mocked because it had manual opening windows and not automatic like his. He made me laugh a couple of times. It was confusing chatting civilly on a bench with birds singing and children laughing as the sun beat down on us.

A squirrel darted past the bench carrying a nut of some kind in its mouth. We sat quietly and watched as it made its way towards the conifer tree. Maxwell interrupted the moment. 'Did you get my postcard?'

I don't know why, but I lied. 'What postcard?'

'I sent you one from my holiday in Tenerife last month.'

'That explains your suntan.'

'It's odd that you didn't get it.'

'They take ages to arrive. Perhaps it'll arrive by the end of the year.' I laughed at my joke. 'What did it say?'

He held my hand and turned to face me. 'How much I love you and how sorry I am.' He squeezed my hand. 'That I really want us to make another go of our relationship.' He looked into my eyes. 'I miss you.' He started crying. I released my hand from his and reached into my bag to give him a tissue.

For the first time in so long, I knew the truth about something. He was lying. I couldn't doubt myself because I knew what the card read, and that was different from what he said, and that was enough. I didn't tell him that I had lied or correct him about his recollections, and that gave me strength. His tears quickly turned into a sob. He was snotty, so I handed him another tissue and watched him. I had never seen a man cry like that before; I almost felt sorry for him. He wasn't crying for me, or us, even. He was crying for himself. When his tears and snot started drying up, he leaned forward and hugged me. I allowed it.

'I miss the smell of your perfume,' he said as he pulled away.

I forced a smile. I wasn't wearing perfume. I didn't confess that either.

Blake called that afternoon and offered to buy me dinner in exchange for a personalised tour around Plymouth. We met outside the train station and went on a pub crawl, where we formed the beginning of a bubble of friendship, happiness and lust. We were blissfully ignorant of the limited time we had together. We were magnetic.

Some days, we would sit at the beach without saying a word, taking in the moment and other times, we stayed up late, not wanting the morning to arrive. He stroked my hand when we chatted, I ran my hand across his back whenever I walked past him, he snuck up to tickle me with his beard, and I tugged at his hair to get him off. His marble green eyes were constantly fixed on me and mine on him. His skin turned darker each day he spent in the sun, and soon, his chocolate brown hair and beard sparkled gold. After everything that had happened, I felt joy, excitement, happiness. I was alive. How was I going to let him go?

By the end of July, two-thirds into our time together, I realised I had fallen in love with him. It wasn't something I thought was going to happen. My barriers were up because we had a limit on our time before he had to go. It happened at the most unexpected moment. Blake invited me to his flat on an overcast Sunday afternoon. I stopped at a shop on the way to pick up popcorn for a movie marathon. Just as I got back into my car, he messaged to say he was walking to his local shop to pick up something for dinner. I drove to his flat but he still wasn't in, so I walked towards the local shop to meet him.

As I approached the shop, I saw Blake through the window. He was standing at the back of a long queue. A basket full of shopping dangled from his hand as he perused items on the shelf next to him. He was wearing a pair of creased jean shorts and flip-flops and looked as though he had woken from an afternoon snooze. He was also wearing his olive-green jumper. The colour complimented his eyes, and cuddling him in it made me want to hold onto him forever. I loved him in it.

It looked so normal, him buying last-minute bits at the local shop. For the first time since being together, I thought of us as a proper couple. That was the moment I knew I was in love with Blake. Except this wasn't his local shop; it was a nearby shop on a temporary basis. We weren't going to have the chance to see where our relationship could go because our circumstances wouldn't allow for that. He had to leave in less than six weeks. The happiness I felt walking to the shop was suddenly replaced by an anxious feeling: how was my life going to be without him in it?

The last sunny day of summer barely reached twenty degrees. It felt like the end of heat and so much more. Autumn was coming too soon. I told Blake I loved him a couple of weeks before he had to leave, but he didn't say it back, and I didn't doubt his feelings. The nearer we got to his final day, the longer our hugs lasted and the deeper our gazes. How were we going to be able to let go of each other?

I woke before Blake on the morning of his flight. He was lying on his back with his arms raised above his head. I watched him until he woke naturally. He smiled before opening his eyes. I leaned in close and kissed him. The taxi arrived at midday and tooted to let us know we had minutes of precious time remaining. I started crying as I followed Blake out of the building. Neither of us spoke from the moment he picked up his backpack until we reached the taxi.

'Don't cry,' he said and pulled me into him. We hugged quietly, taking in each other one last time.

I squeezed him harder. 'I love you,' I said with my head resting against his heart.

He squeezed me tighter. 'I love you too.' I knew it!

He rested a kiss on top of my head before pulling away and climbing into the taxi. It slowly pulled away and Blake mouthed the words that he loved me through the window. I sobbed as I watched the taxi drive off until it was out of sight.

He called me after he checked in at Heathrow Airport that evening. The following day, a text pinged through from him when I was on my lunch break. He had landed in Singapore. As I was falling asleep that night, he messaged me that he had safely landed in Sydney. He said he loved me. I cried myself to sleep. How had I gotten myself into this position again?

Blake and I naturally fell into a routine of emailing and texting every day. On Sundays, evenings for him and mornings for me, we chatted for two or three hours at a time. Hearing his voice was the highlight of my week. We continued this pattern for a month, and as the nights started to draw in in the northern hemisphere, spring was waiting to welcome summer for him.

'It's not fair,' I said. 'You've had summer here and now you're going to have another one soon.'

'It won't be as good as the one I spent with you.'

'I miss you,' I clung to the phone.

'I miss you so much.'

'I wish you were still here.'

He took a deep breath. 'Why don't you come out here and live with me?'

CHAPTER 16

Now

The morning commute to work on Monday was simple. I even managed to get a seat on the Tube from Bethnal Green to Chancery Lane. That gave me the space to read through my job description once more: answer the phone, greet visitors, open and distribute the post, raise invoices for both professional and residential rents, chase payments, issue parking permits, organise the annual dog show and ad-hoc duties. The role wasn't taxing, but I got distracted reading the list and missed my stop. I knew to change at the next stop and head back one station, just like I had to on the day I arrived in London—that felt longer than a month ago.

After the manager introduced me to the small team, we sat in his office, and he gave me an overview of the role and the history of the Inner Temple. A large sepia map hung on the back wall of his office, exposing secret passages to find ancient hidden treasure. He pointed out key areas on it to help me get my bearings: Inner Temple Gardens, the Peony Garden, Middle Temple Lane, Crown Office Row, Victoria Embankment, Temple Tube Station, the Thames and Temple Church.

The afternoon passed much quicker than the morning. I was left alone to get on with simple work, emailing monthly invoices to barrister chambers or residents living in the apartments within the Inner Temple. After that, my manager began the handover for the planning of the residents' dog show that was being held on the first bank holiday weekend of May. That was less than four months away.

'Sorry to interrupt, Alice,' the friendliest colleague interrupted, 'but the clerk from William Rose Chambers is on the phone for you.' He handed me a cordless phone.

Before I finished saying hello, an angry voice cut me off. 'I refuse to pay this month's invoice until you repair the unstable paving stone outside our office.'

I blushed, fully aware that the team were watching and listening.

'Could you repeat the name of the chamber you work in, please?' I asked, braced with pen and paper. He sighed before slowly and sarcastically confirming his name and the chamber he was calling from. 'Could I have your telephone number, please?'

'It's already on your system. Call me when you can confirm the work is being done.' He hung up. Dogs were much more pleasant to deal with than humans.

I met Kate back at her flat after work. She helped me take most of my belongings to the flat in East Dulwich in preparation for moving in straight after work on Friday. There were several ways to get to East Dulwich from Bethnal Green, but we decided to take a short walk to Whitechapel to pick up the number seventy-eight bus. It took the longest time, but at least it was direct.

We had a quick cup of tea with my new housemates before Kate and I walked to Lordship Lane for dinner. There was plenty of choice on where to eat, but Beth had recommended The Green Parrot pub because it did the best macaroni cheese in London, and it did table service. Kate and I were starving by the time we reached the pub, so we decided on a starter as well as a main meal and ordered battered halloumi sticks to share. The pub was steady rather than busy, and most people were drinking, not eating. It was gone eight so the mad rush must have passed, which was good for us because the manager brought out our starter straight away.

'That's not halloumi,' Kate said after her first bite, 'it's feta.' I was ravenous and hadn't noticed despite being a halloumi superfan.

The manager walked past our table on the way to the kitchen. 'Excuse me, but these halloumi sticks aren't halloumi,' I said after getting his attention. 'We think they're feta.'

'They're definitely halloumi,' he said. 'I'm the manager, and I source all the ingredients myself. The cheese is from the deli down the road.'

He was so adamant that I almost believed him. 'But halloumi is my favourite cheese, and this isn't halloumi.'

'Fine, let's agree to disagree,' he said, standing with his hands on his hips. 'Choose something else from the menu, not the specials board, and I'll give it to you for half price.'

Kate and I looked at each other and then at the menu again. It was tempting to disagree on agreeing to disagree, but at least he was willing to compromise, even though he still thought he was right. We opted for a half-price glass of wine each instead of another starter, and when the manager brought our drinks over, he also had three shots of sambuca on the tray.

'I have an apology to make,' he said as he moved the drinks from the tray to the table. 'I've spoken to the chef, and he informed me that we have run out of halloumi. You were right, it was feta.' As tempting as it was to say, "we-told-you-so", we thanked him for checking with the chef and for being honest. *How refreshing for a man to take responsibility for his actions.*

'Why are there three shots?' Kate asked.

The manager sat down with us. 'One's for me.' We chinked our glasses and downed our shots. 'These are on the house,' he said, 'and next time you come, halloumi sticks are on me.'

Tuesday and Wednesday flew by at work, and on the Thursday, I met up with Sholina and Nikki near their office. The bar looked as though it was a bank in its previous life, with its high ceiling and marble pillars at either end of the bar. There was even the disused vault downstairs on the way to the toilet. We managed to find a U-shaped booth and ordered a bottle of Prosecco.

The booth next to us was livelier, with a mixture of men and women crammed in. Their table was covered with champagne coolers, empty champagne bottles, spilt drinks and an array of other alcoholic concoctions. In comparison, our booth looked like we were holding a secret meeting about gold bullion.

We shared the bottle of Prosecco, and when we started livening up, we were still nowhere near as jovial as the adjacent booth. They looked like city workers who had attended a daylong meeting that had leaked into social drinks. They probably started drinking late afternoon, judging by how loud they were being—it was only seven o'clock. The men were dressed in tailored suits, but as the night progressed, they removed their ties, rolled up their sleeves and loosened off their buttoned shirts. The women wore smart, figure-hugging dresses. None of the women wore an engagement or wedding ring, but all but one of the men did. They became more and more flirtatious, and at one point, one of the women sat on the lap of one of the married men. The two of them disappeared downstairs in the direction of the vault. They didn't return to their booth by the time we left twenty minutes later. I was pleased I no longer felt that lonely or needed that type of attention to feel better about myself or my life.

We were in the mood for dancing, and Nikki knew of a place off Fleet Street where they made good cocktails. We jumped on a bus and made our way in the direction of where I worked. Nikki guided us down a cobbled alley that led onto a narrower alleyway. We crossed an empty back road, and as we passed through a small opening, I tripped over a cannon strategically cemented in the centre of Gunpowder Square—I was half expecting to stumble across Guy Fawkes himself. London had a modern heart, but it was magical delving deeper and discovering its ancient soul.

In the dimly lit, pedestrianised area, the sound of music tiptoed amongst the sleeping office buildings. There was no way I would be able to find this place again. Every direction looked the same: glass and concrete, concrete and glass. The only thing that hinted that we were outside a bar, apart from the music, was the potted palm trees and Easter Island statues on either side of the door. As we stepped inside and passed through a black velvet curtain, we were transported from a historical winter in London to the tropical South Pacific. There were wicker tables and chairs, bamboo-lined walls and palm leaves hung above the bar. Sholina's cocktail came in a tiki mask, Nikki's arrived in a ceramic parrot and mine was served in a coconut.

We ordered a second round of cocktails and drank them before making our way to the busy dance floor. We recreated moves from our favourite R 'n' B music videos, sang along to nineties indie tunes, and wore ourselves out jumping around to sing-along eighties rock music. It didn't take long for the cocktails to shake up with the Prosecco. I started feeling slightly tipsy; drinking on an empty stomach was never a good plan. I was hot, so I squeezed my way through the crowded dancefloor to get to the bathroom. I cooled down by splashing water on my face; it sobered me up slightly too. It was time to go home. I had work in the morning, and it was still only my first week. Plus, I was moving into the flat properly after work tomorrow. And I was hungry.

'I'm going home,' I shouted to Nikki and Sholina across the dance floor, pointing to the exit.

'Me too,' Nikki shouted back. She and Sholina pushed their way towards me.

'I need the toilet before we go,' Sholina said. Nikki did too. I headed to the cloakroom to collect our coats.

It was too hot to put my coat on whilst I waited for the girls, and I was even hotter with three winter coats draped in my arms. I moved towards the velvet curtain by the entrance to cool down. The music seemed to get louder, I felt hotter and hungrier, and the coats felt heavier. I needed to adjust them like a parent carrying a toddler. A small crowd of men appeared from behind the curtain at the same time I was adjusting the coats. They were followed in by someone rushing to catch up with them. He accidentally knocked one of the coats from my arms and it fell onto the floor. But he didn't notice what he did.

'Thanks for waiting for me,' he said as he joined the group.

I bent down to pick up the coat, but as I did, another one slipped off my arm and landed on top of the other coat. A hand reached down and picked up both coats. 'I'm so sorry for knocking your coat on the floor.'

The stranger's face looked familiar. Someone looking familiar in London was not familiar. 'You're the delivery guy,' I blurted out as he handed the coats back to me. 'From the Inner Temple?'

He smiled and raised his eyebrows.

'Come on, let's go. I'm starving.' Nikki said. She took her coat from me and walked outside; Sholina followed. I turned back before following them behind the curtain. The delivery guy was still looking at me.

'What's your name?' he shouted.

'Jess,' I replied and disappeared behind the curtain.

'Did you say your name was Jess?' Sholina asked.

'I did. I don't know why I do it, but if a guy asks my name on a night out, Jess always comes out. It's not intentional but it's a habit I've gotten into over the last few years. It must be a defence mechanism, I guess.'

'But you only spoke to that guy for a few seconds.'

'Perhaps I'm on alert because I'm still new to London.' Or had I detected something about him that I had to remain on guard?

We found a late-night fast-food shop before going our separate ways on the Tube. My journey was less than ten minutes, but within that time, I fell asleep and woke up at the end of the Central line in Epping, Essex. Fortunately, there was one more train before the service finished for the night, and to ensure I didn't miss the stop a second time, I stood up for the half-hour journey back to Bethnal Green.

I woke during the night with my top lip stuck to my teeth. I stumbled to the kitchen for a glass of water and shivered as I drank it in one go before crawling back into bed and snuggling into the lingering warmth beneath the duvet. It felt good knowing I could fall back to sleep, but just as I was dropping off my alarm startled me like a military drill instructor bursting into the room. I dragged myself out of bed and marched to the bathroom.

Once dressed, I packed the remainder of my belongings into a carry-on suitcase that Fabrizio lent me to transport my belongings to my new home after work. Kate offered to make me breakfast, but I refused and grabbed a takeaway coffee before getting on a bus to work. The thought of the heat and dry air on the Tube was too much, and the bus seemed a safer option if I needed to swiftly disembark. It was strange how alcohol affected the body. Sometimes, I could drink a substantial amount and feel fine in the morning, yet on another occasion, I could drink the same amount and feel terrible the following day. Like today. I put my alcoholic effect down to being tired from having a new job, new home excitement, busy social life and a delivery man on my mind. It was going to be a long day.

My manager asked me to hand-deliver dog show flyers to

residents and chambers of the Inner Temple. He thought it was a great opportunity for me to get my bearings and for people to put a face to my name when they contacted the office. I was more than happy to do that, even though it was cold outside. It had been a battle to stay awake at my desk in the warm office. George, the old boy who looked as though he should have retired twenty years ago, warned me that it might take some time to deliver the flyers because chamber clerks liked to gossip, especially about each other. I was happy to spend as long as possible out of the office.

It took over almost two hours to hand out the first batch of flyers before the cold set in. I decided to head back to the office to grab another bundle and warm up with a hot drink. As the office came into view across the courtyard, I spotted the delivery driver walking towards the office empty-handed. My heart quickened, and my legs felt weak. I darted back around the corner and waited for him to leave. Ten minutes passed, and he still hadn't left. What was taking him so long to collect something? I couldn't wait much longer. I was desperate for the toilet like a child playing hide and seek. The toilet was just inside the front door, so I decided to dash inside. I'd spotted the delivery guy standing in my manager's office as I hurried in.

The round mirror above the sink reflected how tired I looked: my bun looked messy, my eyes were puffy, and my complexion was pale. Last night's leftover makeup, which I tidied up instead of removing and reapplying this morning, brightened my face slightly. I heard footsteps pass by the toilet door, followed by the front door opening and closing. It must have been him, so I guessed it was safe to go into the office. I let out a long sigh and relaxed my shoulders before walking back in.

'Alice,' my manager called me into his office before I had the chance to make a hot drink. 'Close the door,' he said but didn't offer me a seat. 'Did you see the gentleman in my office earlier?'

My heart started thumping. I felt weak again at the thought of this crush that I had developed overnight and cemented this morning on seeing him unexpectedly. My mind raced at what my manager was going to say next; had I forgotten to wrap a parcel? Was *he* putting in a complaint about me? Perhaps he asked my manager about me?

I finally spoke. 'The delivery guy?'

My manager looked at me and laughed. 'He's not a delivery man, Alice.' He took a sip of his coffee and sat forward in his chair. 'That's Mr Hartington.'

Harry Hartington was one of a few non-barrister residents who lived and worked in the Inner Temple. His father was a senior QC, as was his grandfather and so on. Harry hadn't followed in their footsteps and instead ran a few successful businesses, one of which was property investment. He owned several properties on Temple Avenue, just outside the Inner Temple, which he rented to barristers when the Inner Temple ran out of accommodation. For the privilege of being allowed to live in the privacy of the Inner Temple, and when he had time, he volunteered at their social events.

'He's keen to get involved with the dog show, so I told him you would visit his office at three o'clock today.'

I walked into the kitchen and stared at the boiling kettle.

'Make sure you deliver the rest of those flyers before your meeting, Alice,' my manager said as he passed the kitchen. There was a three-hour window for the universe, if it actually does work in mysterious ways, to find a way of getting me out of the meeting with Mr Hartington.

CHAPTER 17

Then

Blake's invite to live with him in Australia was a surprise but it made sense. We wanted, needed, to be together. We had to give our love a chance to see where it could go. I loved my family and Devon, but my love for Blake overpowered all of that. Apart from my parents, there wasn't much to leave behind.

Mum cried when I told her about my plan. Dad was supportive. Blake and I wanted to be back together as soon as possible, so I opted for a two-year working holiday visa because it was quicker to obtain than a partner visa. We could sort out that paperwork once we were back together. I booked a flight on my credit card for early December because I had to work a month's notice. During that time, I sold my car and Mum and Dad let me keep their half of the money.

Blake and I carried on emailing and texting daily. We also made our weekly Sunday phone calls, but on one of those days, Blake had plans to go out afterwards. I was hungover and stayed over at a friend's house after a late night. I got back late to Mum's to call Blake from the landline. Instead of our normal three-hour conversation, we only had time to chat for twenty minutes.

Mum cried every time something came up in a conversation about Australia. I understood it was sad for her, but I started to feel irritated by her for making the situation harder than it already was. I just wanted to go.

With over a week to go, my suitcase was packed, the money from my car had been exchanged for Australian dollars, and the plan was for Mum and Dad to pick me up after my last day at work and drive me straight to Heathrow Airport. Blake and I had our final Sunday call pencilled in. I was looking forward to confirming our plans on what time he would leave his house to get to Sydney Airport, what time we were visiting his parents on my first day, and where we would eat out to celebrate our first meal back together.

During the call, Blake was excited about our reunion, but there was something different about him. It wasn't obvious, but I felt something. He told me about his night out with his colleagues the night before and how they all ended up at a house party and sleeping over. Perhaps it was my nerves, but the following day, he didn't reply to my message, so I spoke to Dad about my concerns.

'I'm sure everything is fine, Alice,' Dad said.

'I can't work out what it is, but something is different.'

'He loves you, and he's asked you to move to the other side of the world to be with him. He's probably nervous about making sure everything is ready for when you get there.'

Blake eventually replied, and it woke me in the middle of the night. His reason for taking so long to reply was that he had a long day at work and fell asleep as soon as he got home. He was trying to get on top of work ready for the few days he had booked off for my arrival.

'You're right,' I said to Dad in the kitchen in the morning, 'Blake messaged last night. I'm nervous, too, and excited to see him again. I just want to be there and not have to say goodbye to you and Mum.'

'See, I told you.' Dad cleared his throat. 'We're going to miss you, sweetheart, but we're so happy that you're happy. You deserve it.'

I finished breakfast and skipped upstairs to the bathroom. After showering, I returned to my bedroom, where I saw another text notification from Blake—he said he had sent me an email. I smiled and hugged the phone to my heart. Since he landed back in Australia, Blake and I had created an email thread called 'Hey you'. It was so long that it could probably wrap itself around the planet. I switched on my laptop and quickly got dressed. I pulled my woollen jumper over my head, and before I had time to poke my arms through, Blake's email flashed up, and I swallowed hard. It was titled 'I'm sorry'. My heart rate and body temperature increased, and my breathing became shallow. I opened the email.

Alice,

I'm not sure how to write this email. I've typed, retyped and deleted it so many times, but there doesn't seem to be an easy way to say that I can't do this. The bizarre thing is, I don't know why. You're the most wonderful person I've ever met, and I don't think I'll ever be as happy as I was with you for those three months in Devon, but things just won't be the same for us over here. I work long days, and I can be grumpy when I'm tired, and that wouldn't be fair on you leaving everything behind to move to the other side of the world to spend your time with somebody who doesn't have much free time. It just won't be the same.

As hard as it is to admit it, I think it will be best for both of us to keep the memory of our incredible summer together like that. I will treasure that forever.

I'm so sorry.

Blake xx

My body started shivering as I reread the email. I replied, asking if I could call. I texted him the same thing, but there was no response. I ran to the toilet to be sick. I emailed and texted him again on my lunch break and again in the evening, but there was still nothing. I woke in the middle of the night to a blank phone screen. I sent him a text message telling him how much I hated him.

I woke the following morning, curled into the foetal position and started sobbing. I still hadn't told Mum and Dad. I was hoping Blake would change his mind, but he didn't. Dad's expression of pain on his face was as heart-wrenching as the devastation I was already feeling. Mum cried and I cried again.

Blake finally sent an email later that day. It was another apology. He was sorry for his decision and sorry he couldn't talk to me. I replied, but there was no response. I bombarded him with emails for weeks; sometimes, they contained one or two swear words, and others contained an outburst of my broken heart. My emotions constantly switched around, like the sound of music panning from earphone to earphone: anger, frustration, pain, hopelessness, rejection, sadness, loss. As the New Year delved into darker months, my thoughts did the same.

It was midwinter in England—Australia's summer. Jealousy cut through me at the thought of Blake's tanned body in the Australian sun whilst I was scraping ice off my old, high-mileage, second-hand car at the end of a late shift at a hotel on a zero-hour contract. I imagined him sipping an ice-cold beer as a warm breeze tickled his curly hair as I sat rubbing my hands together, waiting for the engine to warm up. Blake would be walking around in shorts and flip flops, or thongs as he called them, but even with my scarf wrapped around my neck and face, I was struggling to keep warm. He would be diving into the sea as gale-force winds and rain slapped me in the face. In the warm evenings, he would be sitting in the garden watching beautiful sunsets, whereas I would be wrapped up in fleece pyjamas and would sleep for hours.

On a sunny wintery morning, fields were sprinkled with snow, so I decided to go for a walk to get out of the house. I needed to breathe. The heat from the low sun was surprisingly warm. I closed my eyes on the edge of a field, pretending I was in Australia with Blake. It was comforting for a moment, but then the temperature abruptly dropped. I opened my eyes to see wintry clouds creeping over the sky. I was shocked back to reality. Life before I met Blake felt warm enough, but my life became tropical meeting him. When he disappeared, I felt colder than I had ever been. I was freezing to death.

On nights out, I drank myself into an alcoholic blur, often fantasising about bumping into Blake again in a bar. One night, Mum and Dad came home and found me slumped behind the front door. Mum screamed because she thought I was dead, and Dad had to wake his neighbour to help him push open the front door.

'Why don't you go see a counsellor?' Dad said the following morning. 'You've been through a lot over the past few years, and it might do you good to talk about how you feel.'

I snapped, 'I know how I feel, Dad. Tobias abandoned me and died. Maxwell made me miserable, and Blake broke my heart. I don't need a counsellor to tell me what's wrong. I already know that.'

The thought of Blake being happy without me was torture. How was he able to live without me? With him, my life had been full of happiness like a baby rabbit bouncing around naïve to the dangers of the world. I jumped and hopped and skipped around fields dotted with daisies and dandelions, but my contentment left me vulnerable and unprepared for the falcon looming high above, its shadow moving silently across the earth, waiting patiently for its prey. Suddenly, and as swiftly as an email being sent from the other side of the world, I was snatched into its firm grip—its talons tightening and draining the life out of me.

I functioned on autopilot: I got out of bed, sometimes showered, sometimes not, threw on clothes, gulped down breakfast, and quickly brushed my teeth before rushing out of the house. Most nights, I got more than the recommended dose of sleep, but I was still tired. After work, I drove home, ate a meal and snacked whilst watching mindless television. I often soaked in the bath for hours, trying to replicate the body heat from Blake onto my skin. Loneliness made me restless, and it was impossible to escape. And unlike an illness or the physical pain of a headache or period cramps, nothing could soothe it. The overwhelming feeling was like sorrow being drawn out by a large syringe from my stomach and pierced back into my heart.

My life was slipping into an emotional sinkhole.

'Alice, look at the state of your room,' Mum said, carrying in a clean pile of washing.

I dodged left to right to keep my eyes on the television screen. 'Shush.'

Mum tutted as she picked up a mouldy plate from underneath my bed. 'Look at this.'

I pulled my eyes away from the screen to look at the plate, and then at Mum, and back to the television. Mum left the room.

I felt claustrophobic living with my parents, but I couldn't afford to move out. I couldn't afford to move forward with my life. I didn't have the desire to do that anyway. Where was I going? I hardly left the house, only for work and for the occasional night out, forcing myself to go to escape Mum and Dad. Summer came and went, and the following winter, I obsessed about Blake in the Australian sun again. That empty year passed quickly, considering I waited every day to hear from him, desperately wanting him to admit he had made a mistake, but that email never came.

The following Easter, my cousin Kate visited from London for her thirtieth birthday. Her mum arranged a surprise party at a bar in town. I often wondered why Kate and I weren't closer, but with a three-year age gap between us, she seemed much older when we were growing up, and by the time I started university, she had moved to London. I got ready at my auntie's house with Kate, and we made our way to the venue from there. Mum and Dad arrived later on for the surprise, and by that time, I was already drunk. Alcohol helped numb the emptiness I felt. Distant relatives chatted about Great Auntie

Norma or their second cousin Robert and other family members I didn't know. I smiled and nodded in the right places. I escaped to the toilet to get away from all the boring small talk.

When I returned from the toilet, I overheard Mum and her sister talking about me. 'We don't know what we can do to help her,' Mum said.

My auntie agreed. 'She's not the same girl I knew.'

Mum started crying. 'It's so hard that at times I sometimes wish she would move out.'

I ran back to the toilet because my throat tightened, and air couldn't get to my lungs. I hated Mum for saying that. She knew what I had been through, and now she was rejecting me. As anger rose above the loneliness, my breathing eased. I needed another drink.

I watched the tattooed barman shake and flip cocktail mixers for a group of giggling women. He was handsome, but he knew it.

'How's your night going?' he shouted over whilst shaking a mixer of his left shoulder like a maraca.

'Fine,' I said.

'What's your name?'

I didn't want to tell him my real name. I didn't want anyone to know anything about me anymore. 'Jess.'

'I'll be with you in a moment, Jess.' One of the women leant onto the bar, which emphasised her cleavage. The barman smirked at her before walking over to me. 'So, you're just fine, are you, Jess? I reckon I could make your night better than just fine.' He winked at me.

I rolled my eyes and muttered, 'Idiot.'

He stopped shaking the mixer. 'What did you say?'

I stared at him. 'I said, how about you get on with what you're paid to do and hurry up making those drinks so I can order mine and get on with my night.'

Before he had the chance to respond, I felt Kate wrap her arm around my shoulders, and she ushered me away from the bar. 'Come on, let's get you home.'

I stayed in bed most of the following day, nursing a hangover whilst watching back-to-back movies and drifting in and out of sleep. The final movie was *Grease*. I knew the words to every song and a lot of the dialogue—I had watched the movie countless times since I was a young girl—but for the first time, I cried for Sandy at the end. She changed so much of who she was for Danny: smoking, curling her hair, changing her clothes. I realised I had done the same for Maxwell, Blake, and even Tobias. Each relationship bled into the next, draining me of who I was.

I climbed out of bed and stood in front of the mirror to take a look at myself. The skin on my face was pale and puffy, my hair was greasy, there was extra weight on my hips and stomach, and my eyes looked empty. I needed to get out of my room and out of the house. I needed fresh air. My jeans from last night lay in a screwed-up mess on the floor. Mum started calling my room the floordrobe. But it was my space, so If I wanted to leave clothes on the floor, then I would. I scraped up my jeans and threw a hoodie over the top of my pyjama top. My hair was a mess. I didn't bother brushing it. I grabbed a bobble and tied it into the messiest of messy buns.

I didn't have a plan for where I was going to walk, but I ended up walking past the dream house that I could see from my bedroom window. The driveway was boarded up, and a notification from the council said something about a new estate being built there. Could anything else go wrong in my life! I suddenly hated my dream house and was pleased it was being knocked down! A sob tugged deep from my solar plexus, but it couldn't fully escape because the pain was stitched into my flesh. I continued walking and ended up alongside the river. The wind was strong and blew messy waves across the water. Metal pulleys from halyards clinked and chinked against the masts of moored-up sailboats. It sounded like a warning. The boats on the water thrashed around as though trying to escape their anchors. The air howled like wolves—something was coming.

Further along the shoreline, a pair of swans were facing the wind together. One swam in the shallows and the other waddled alongside the mud bank. They mated for life—I remembered that from university. The swan in the water began flapping its wings, and the other copied. They were making their escape to safer ground. They started sprinting, ready for take-off. The one in the shallows was running on water and then made its gradual ascent. The second slipped on the mud bank, lost its balance, and fell into the mud.

That was Blake and me. He was the swan that flew away, and I was the swan that landed face-first in the mud. 'Come back,' I called out, 'please come back.' Unlike Blake, the swan returned for its mate. I cried again. I was jealous of their loyalty.

Crying felt different since Blake. Unlike sad tears that fell from my eyes on hearing sad news or falling over and grazing a knee, it was deeper, like wringing out a cloth; my entire body twisted in agony from my thoughts and feelings.

My P.M.S. had changed too. Since the age of eleven, my periods had been regular, arriving in twenty-eight-day cycles, give or take a day. There were the predictable symptoms of irritability, clumsiness and the munchies in the days leading up to the main event, but things now were more intense. I cried a lot, felt low, and occasionally wondered what the point in life was. I ate a lot too, to the extent that I worried if I would ever stop wanting to eat. The emotional pressure that built up inside of me each month seemed to intensify, making me angrier, like the pressure build-up of a volcano waiting to erupt.

Colds and flu were more frequent, and headaches had become a reoccurring problem. They had also changed. Instead of the discomfort aching around the eyes or in my forehead, it felt as though someone was reaching inside my head and gripping and squeezing onto my brain, causing my face to feel so heavy that it might slide off of my skull.

Further along the river, a white egret flew overhead and then swooped into the water and dragged out a fish. It spat the fish onto the rust-coloured mud. The fish flapped around as its life was slowly being pecked away. I wanted to run over and save it but knew the kindest thing to do was to allow it to be eaten. It was already injured, and I hoped it had gone into shock to lessen the pain. Why was the egret's life more important than the fish's? Was it down to strength and being overpowered? If so, then my life was worthless.

It started raining, so I turned around and walked home. My clothes were soaking wet by the time I got in. I stripped off and took a long soak in the bath. When the water started to cool, I raised my foot to nudge on the tap with my toes. The heat from the new water pulsed through the cooling water, and it gradually soothed me. When the bath temperature reached the hottest temperature that my skin could bear, I raised my foot again to turn the tap off. This time, I noticed the hairs on my leg. It had been ages since they were shaved. I leaned forward to take a closer look. It was mainly fine hair that covered my legs, but there was one hair that was thicker and darker than the rest. It reminded me of an unkempt grave at the older end of the cemetery where Tobias was buried. That grave was unloved, forgotten and overgrown with ivy and spikey thorns. The headstone was no longer visible. I grabbed my razor and shaved the hair off.

One evening, during summer, after a busy shift at the hotel making reservations and dealing with guest queries and complaints, I headed to the beach to watch the sunset. It had been a while since I had been there, and summer was almost over. The beach reminded me too much of Blake. The sea was calm and still. I took off my shoes, rolled my trousers halfway up my calf, and stepped into the sea. The water was cold at first, but it became bearable once my feet numbed. The swell increased, which caused small yet strong waves to break on the shoreline. Each time a wave broke and the sea dragged back out, loose sand retracted with it. My feet sunk a little deeper into the seabed as the waves tugged at my legs. I felt as though I could fall at any time and drown. But I didn't try escaping.

Mum and Dad had friends over one evening for pre-Christmas drinks, so I stayed upstairs in my room to keep out of their way. I was bored after two movies and decided to have a well-overdue sort-out, starting with the floordrobe. There was a pile of magazines scattered under my bed. I dragged some of them out and took a quick scan to see if any were worth keeping. They were mainly filled with pictures of bronze-bodied celebrities in tiny bikinis and scandalous infidelity stories. The trim, size-zero bodies didn't inspire me to lose weight, but they did make me realise I hadn't been taking care of myself. The nearest I came to having five-a-day was five biscuits dunked into my tea after dinner each night.

I threw all of the magazines into a recycling pile in the corner of my room. The one that landed on the top caught my eye. It was different from the rest. I remembered it was one that Daisy gave to me. That was a long time ago. I hadn't read it. The front page listed what was inside the lifestyle magazine: personality tests, healthy recipes, horoscopes, the latest exercise trend and a pull-out section on relationships. The special section had articles on the ideal partner, a compatibility test, the latest dating apps and a section titled, *Are You in a Mentally Abusive Relationship?* I turned to read that article.

It wasn't something I had considered when I was with Maxwell; he could be bossy and moody and generally wanted things his way, but he was caring and generous at the same time. We ran our course, wanted different things, and I fell out of love with him. But a fifteen-point checklist intrigued me, as well as the tagline: *it can happen to anyone…abusive relationships aren't always physical…don't let him think you're crazy.*

I suddenly realised that my relationship with Maxwell may have been abusive. I closed the magazine before reading any further. I wasn't ready to face that truth just now. It would have to keep for another day before I could face reading the checklist.

CHAPTER 18

Now

The universe didn't come up with any plausible plan to get me out of the meeting with Mr Hartington. As much as I didn't want to go, I didn't want to be late either. His office was visible on the walk over, on the far side of Inner Temple Gardens. It looked like a gated fortress. Five unevenly worn concrete steps in the doorway where I first saw him lead up to a locked door, barricaded from the rest of the world. No one answered the buzzer; just a clicking sound indicated the door was now unlocked.

The sound of my timid footsteps echoed off the silent marble floor and walls. I peered up the spiral staircase. Warm light cascaded down from a grand chandelier hanging from the very top. The stairs curled like a snail's shell, and the longer I stared up at them, the more difficult it became to tell if they curled up or down. It made me feel slightly giddy, so I took hold of the wooden banister to steady myself before making the ascent.

My breathing became heavy halfway up to the final floor, and my nerves exaggerated the difficulty of the climb. My legs felt weak too, from fatigue and my emotions. I stopped on the windowless staircase to calm my breathing before carrying on to the top. There was a different chamber on each floor, and located on the fourth floor was the chamber housing the abrupt clerk from my first day. I quickened my pace to pass his floor but slowed again as I got near the top. My mouth went dry, and it was difficult to swallow. I forced my throat to do what it normally did subconsciously. I walked slowly to the door, and as I raised my hand to press the bell, my arm froze, my fingertip brushing against the bell. My throat tightened. I stepped away from the door.

'Come on, Alice,' I whispered. 'He's only a man, a human, just you like you.' I took a deep breath and returned to the door.

I pressed the bell, and the door instantly opened. 'Hi…I mean, hello.' I swallowed hard. 'My name is…' *What is my name?* 'Miss Berry and I'm here to see Mr Hartington about the dog show.' I said to the expressionless man who answered the door. 'I'm from the main office.'

'Come in.' He gestured for me to enter, even though it sounded as though he didn't mean it. He asked me to wait whilst he informed Mr Hartington of my arrival.

It was also as quiet in the waiting area. Hands from a clock on the wall above my head counted down to three o'clock, and as it softly chimed three times, the door to Mr Hartington's office opened.

I followed the non-emotional man into the office. Mr Hartington was sitting behind his desk and already facing the doorway, looking at us. I was pleased with the formality when my guide explained my reasons for being there. I made no eye contact whilst I stood there silently, but I did have a discreet look around the room. Mr Hartington's desk was sat in front of the middle three windows out of five in a curved wall. A bouquet of unusual purple and green flowers perched on the end of his desk. *He must be able to see along the Thames in both directions from any of his windows*, I thought. I guessed the Peony Garden must be visible from the furthest window to the left. I wondered how he did any work with such amazing views. The far-right window had built-in seating with a thick blue mattress-like base, firm tartan cushions and a woollen throw. I wanted to climb onto the seat, curl up under the blanket and close my eyes. That was partly because I was still tired from the night before but mainly because I wanted to hide away from what was happening.

The expressionless man left the room.

On the few occasions that my and Mr Hartington's paths had crossed, it was apparent that he was a man of few words, which was the case now. He stared at me as though he was frozen under a spell. I looked down and read from my notes.

'The dog show is being held on the first bank holiday in May and starting at eleven a.m. I believe that you have some information that you'll be sending to me from previous events?'

'Jess?' he said.

I stopped reading, but my eyes remained focused on my notepad. I squeezed my pen before looking up at him.

'Yes, Mr Hartington?'

He smirked. 'Please, call me Harry.'

I winced. 'My name is actually Alice.'

'So it seems. Your manager must have thought I was going crazy when I asked if Jess was coming to see me about the dog show. He looked confused and then informed me that nobody called Jess worked there and that it was someone called Alice who was arranging the dog show.' The muscles in his forehead tightened. 'Why did you lie last night?'

I was surprised that the heat from my body didn't cause the bouquet to wilt. I was slightly embarrassed, and I was tired and hungover, but it was the fire in my belly that made me flash red. I had slipped into survival mode.

'I'm not the only one who lied.' I felt under attack. 'You didn't deny you weren't a delivery man?' His jaw clenched like a boxer flexing his muscles before a fight. He didn't say anything and just stared again.

The winter sun flashed through the window and highlighted his hair; it was dark blonde rather than what I first thought, light brown. His golden-hazel eyes squinted as the sun reflected off his desk. Harry took a sip of water before pulling up his sleeves and talking about the dog show. He clicked the top of his pen with his thumb throughout the time he spoke: *click, click, click, click.* I didn't register anything he said. He reclined in his chair and dropped the pen on the floor. He picked it up and then asked if he could get back to me about the information he needed to provide.

Yep, just let me of here, I thought. I wrote down my email address and left.

The entire scenario, from walking up the stairs to leaving his office, replayed over again in my mind on the walk back and several more times whilst sitting at my desk. I hoped he couldn't tell that I liked him. I thought I was finally ready to be in a relationship, but the doubt from my judgements of past relationships flared up. My defence mechanism had resurfaced. Besides, nothing could happen between us; he probably earned in a month what I earned in a year, and that would make it impossible for me to live his lifestyle and remain independent. Since my healing process, I have been adamant to be financially independent.

Chloe and Beth were home when I arrived at the flat. As a welcome gift, they treated me to a Chinese takeaway that we washed down with a bottle of wine whilst watching *Dirty Dancing.* I was busy Saturday with unpacking, organising my bedroom, and doing a food shop. It was a twenty-minute walk back to the flat with my arms laden with bags. The handles left red indentations on my arms. I missed having a car today.

After unpacking the food, I made the short walk to Peckham Rye to buy toiletries from a discount store. The vibe in Peckham Rye was tropical in comparison to East Dulwich, even though they were next-door neighbours. The scent of exotic fruit and vegetables swirled in the air from market stalls, reggae music played from a mobile phone booth, and flashing lights from a hardware store lit up the street as balls of what looked like black tumbleweed danced outside a hair salon. After shopping, fairy lights on a side road tempted me into a railway arch bar for pizza and a rest before heading back to the flat.

Beth and Chloe went out separately that evening, and I was surprised at how lonely and homesick I felt being on my own. I had a job and somewhere to live, plus I had made some London friends. I no longer had to push to make things happen in London. The city had been gradually becoming familiar, but it suddenly felt like a stranger. Reaching this point, I was expecting to feel proud, excited, relieved, or independent, but I didn't. I burst into tears.

I spent the evening in the lounge with the television for company but kept the volume lower than necessary to listen out for unexpected noises. I didn't know what to do about locking up when it was time for bed. Did I leave a light on for when the girls arrived back? I wanted to double-lock the front door but was unsure if the girls had keys for the extra lock—I didn't. Did I have the right to text them and ask if they were coming home that night?

I pushed my bedside table in front of my bedroom door—it wouldn't stop an intruder, but hopefully, it would make a noise and wake me if someone did try breaking in. I pottered around in my room for as long as possible in an attempt to stay awake until one of the girls hopefully returned, but neither did. I climbed into bed but sat up until I couldn't keep my eyes open any longer. Every creak, rattle or thud in the darkness slapped me awake. The sound of the front door being delicately opened pinned me to my bed. I held my breath to prevent the sound from interfering with my hearing, but all that did was emphasise the sound of my heartbeat pulsating in my ears. I heard a male voice, and then the front door closed. I pulled my duvet up higher. A floorboard creaked outside my room, and my eyes darted towards the door handle, but nothing happened. Beth's bedroom door squeaked shut before the sound of her laughter allowed me to take a breath. I rolled over onto my side, tucked into a ball, pulled the duvet over my head and fell asleep.

Monday morning was the start of my new routine: a short walk to Peckham Rye Station to catch the train to Blackfriars Station, a walk along Tudor Street—passing by Harry's office—and arriving at work. Lunch was at one o'clock every day, but it could be flexible, with prior notice. That day, I walked along Fleet Street to buy lunch from one of a multitude of delis, sandwich shops and cafés whose wares ranged from salads to dim sum. That evening, I ventured to an art exhibition at Somerset House on my own. On Tuesday, I met Kate for dinner in Soho and on Wednesday, I watched a comedy at a pop-up theatre off Shaftsbury Avenue with Teagan.

It was sunny on Thursday, so instead of walking back to the office to eat lunch, I sat on St Paul's steps in the winter sun. It was unseasonably warm for February, but I still needed to wrap up. After I finished eating, I walked down to Victoria Embankment and along the north bank of the River Thames, parallel to Inner Temple Gardens. It was busy with tourists stopping to take photos. Four lanes of traffic passed by slowly, and in between each vehicle, the red bricks of Harry's office were visible through the railings and trees.

The road was too busy to cross over, so I walked further along to a set of traffic lights. A guided walking tour was already waiting to cross over too. The guide stood at the front of the group, holding a Union Jack umbrella in the air. I stood to the side of them and listened to the variety of languages and accents within the group: American, Spanish, Japanese, Chinese, Irish and English.

One person was waiting to cross over from the opposite side of the road; it was Harry. As soon as I saw him, I ducked behind the group, but as I moved, Harry did a double-take in my direction. The lights changed from red to green, and Harry and I got closer. My mind raced. *What should I do*? Pretend I hadn't seen him? Smile? Say hello? When we reached each other in the middle of the road, I smiled and said 'hi', but it sounded more like a sheep bleating. He nodded his head and carried on by. Brilliant!

The following day, my manager gave me the key to Inner Temple Garden and asked me to take photos and measurements for the planning of the dog show. I had never seen anyone in the main garden, even though it was surrounded by apartments and offices. It was as though I had discovered a secret garden in the middle of London, and I felt like an intruder as I stepped inside. I walked down some steps, walked around a sundial and passed by an empty cordoned-off flower bed—a chalkboard noting it was reserved for bulbs and wildflowers—and down some more steps towards the main area of the garden where a variety of trees were rooted around the expansive area as though the seeds had been planted with a shot from a bow with a cluster of arrows.

It took a leisurely hour to walk around the garden, taking photos and measurements, and I purposely left the best bit to last: the Peony Garden. A bronze statue of a man holding the dial above his head sat nestled amongst a circular flowerbed of dead and dying flowers. No peonies were in bloom. I didn't know much about flowers, but it was winter, so I assumed that's why there weren't any yet. A pathway snaked past mulched flower beds and evergreen bushes. At the far end, bare wisteria branches entangled themselves in front of a brick wall and amongst black railings that sat on top of the wall, hiding the garden from the street above.

In front of the wall was a bush with dangling buds like gold drop earrings. I moved nearer to take a closer look. As I did that, I noticed an entrance hidden within the wall behind. I crept in. It looked like a U-shaped trench, sunken from the street above. Spindly wisteria branches loomed overhead like gigantic arthritic fingers trying to warn me off. Cracked and uneven paving stones were covered in brown, decaying leaves as though the wind was too scared to blow them away. Black identical doors stood regimentally along the curved wall on the lookout for the enemy. My curiosity outweighed my fear that I might get lost and never be seen again, so I followed the walkway.

I peered ahead of the never-ending, never-changing, rounded walkway. The adventure was soon over after I reached the end of the tunnel to steps that reached the road above, but a locked gate stood in the way of the two spaces. It was time to head back to the office anyway. I started retracing my steps, but before I reached the entrance, a noise crept out from behind one of the doors. I froze—trapped between here and a locked gate behind. I crept up to the door and gently pressed my ear against the peeling black paint. There was another sound, much fainter than before, like metal on metal. I peered down to look through the keyhole, but only a hazy light was visible.

'Ouch!' someone cursed behind the door.

I jumped back. The sound of falling metal silenced whoever was inside.

'Are you okay?' I shouted and opened the door into a small storeroom filled with tins of paint, wonky cardboard boxes and a running machine.

'I'm fine,' a voice travelled from the darkness behind a pile of boxes. 'I dropped something on my leg, but there's no damage.' The person appeared from behind the boxes. They were hunched over, rubbing their leg. They moved into the light and stood up.

'Hi,' Harry said when he saw me. Before I could reply, he carried on sifting through the pile of paint pots, seemingly on a mission to find a particular colour. He lifted one tin at a time, examined it, and placed it back on the pile before repeating the process.

'I'm glad you're okay,' I eventually said. 'I'll leave you to it.' I turned to leave the room but remembered that he still hadn't emailed me the information he promised. I stopped and asked him for an update.

'Pardon?' His focus remained on the paint tins.

'The information for the dog show; it's just that I need it for next week.'

His voice got louder with each word with irritation. 'I'll get it to you when I can, Alice.' He still didn't look at me.

'Thanks,' I huffed and turned on my heel, slamming the door behind me. I marched back to the office.

It took longer to type up my notes than it should have. Every keystroke was exaggerated on the keyboard. There was only an hour left at work, but it felt like a Monday morning. I couldn't concentrate, so I offered to make everyone in the office a drink. When I returned to my desk, there were a dozen emails in my inbox. Most were invoice queries, one was a weekly newsletter, another was a not-so-funny joke from one of the guys in my office, there was a maintenance request from a resident, and an email from Harry Hartington. My stomach flipped even though the subject was simply titled, 'Dog Show'.

Alice,

Please accept my apology for the way I spoke to you earlier. I'm not always a guppy git. I've got a lot on at the moment.

Anyway, attached is the information you require. If you have any questions, please do not hesitate to contact me. As an apology and another update on the dog show, could I take you out for lunch next week? The second half of the week works best for me as I'm away for work during the start of the week, and I don't return until Wednesday morning.

Have a good weekend,
Harry

I read the email a handful of times before pressing the reply button. My fingers managed a couple of sentences before pressing the backspace button to delete every word. He could wait until after the weekend for my response.

CHAPTER 19

Then

It was only a couple days before the curiosity of the checklist got to me. The magazine article explained how complex abusive relationships are and how they are a mix of fear, hope and confusion. Abusers are victims, according to the words I was reading. They cope by rejecting your feelings and dreams, which is not good for the abusee's mental health. Some victims can suffer from Post-Traumatic Stress Disorder. It isn't easy to recognise the behaviour of an abusive partner because they are manipulative. They can be overly keen one moment but often shift their behaviour and put the blame onto the victim—this is the confusing part. At school, we stayed away from the bully and remained close to our friends, but a mentally abusive relationship blurs these two dynamics together. But the abusive partner is a bully in disguise pretending to know what's best for you.

Surely it was obvious to anyone if they were in a mentally abusive relationship? Most people have encountered a bully in their life, be it at school, work, or a social setting, whether they were the victim or a witness to the act. It didn't seem possible that someone wouldn't see that their partner was a bully. Maxwell never hit me, so I was confident the checklist was irrelevant, but something made me want to read on.

Fifteen points were listed. I didn't bother to get a pen to mark anything down, but after skim-reading the first few points off, I scrambled from my bed and grabbed one. I read through all of the points thoroughly before rereading and adding ticks. I then counted them up. Most of them were ticked. Surely not. Maxwell was unreasonable at times, but he was also affectionate and generous. He did the majority of cooking—not many men did that—and he often treated us to weekends away or meals out. He would surprise me with random gifts for no reason. I re-read the list.

1. Coming on strong at the beginning of your relationship – Maxwell had come on strong, but I was flattered by that. It was a welcomed distraction from Tobias. Was that abusive?

2. Jealousy – Surely everyone felt jealous at some point? I had.

3. Controlling finances – Maxwell did control my finances, but that was because he was my boss. We lived off his commission, but he paid all of the bills and the majority of our food, including meals. I thought he was being generous, especially for all the weekend trips he treated us to. But I guess we ate a lot of the food he liked and dined at the restaurants he chose. He often had money to buy designer clothes, whereas I could hardly afford to buy high-street clothing. He had a company car, and I relied on him for lifts. He got angry with me about the cost of my Scotland trip, but then he booked himself a skiing trip that cost five times as much. Tick.

4. Isolation – Maxwell thought Daisy was jealous of what we had—perhaps he was right. After all, there was the Tobias kiss. He often said Mum and Dad were interfering. When I left him, Mum told me that she and Dad weren't keen on him but felt I had to make my own mistakes. She was worried that if she did say anything to me about their concerns, Maxwell would drive a deep wedge between us. There was an occasion when Mum asked me to go shopping with her to help buy a new outfit, but Maxwell asked me not to go because I couldn't afford to go shopping. I reassured him I wasn't going to buy anything and that Mum was treating me to lunch. As our food was served, Maxwell rang to say he had an awful migraine and desperately needed painkillers—he said he couldn't move from the pain. I snapped at Mum when she suggested we should eat first before leaving to get his tablets. I felt anxious to get back to him. When she dropped me back, Maxwell was sunbathing in the garden—he found some tablets in a drawer, and they worked straight away. He forgot to call me back because he felt drowsy, but I was relieved he felt better. Tick.

Maxwell went on a business trip to Cardiff and was staying overnight so Daisy offered to sleep over to keep me company and have an overdue catch-up. We made dinner and afterwards started watching a movie, but partway through, Maxwell returned home unexpectedly. He wanted to surprise me, so he came home early. He sat in the lounge with Daisy whilst I made him something to eat, and before I finished in the kitchen, Daisy and Maxwell had heated words, and Daisy made her apologies to me and left. I took Maxwell's dinner into him. He was upset and apologised for upsetting Daisy. He said he only wanted to watch a programme of his choice on his television. I comforted him. Daisy sent a text shortly after apologising again for leaving, but she felt Maxwell didn't want her there. I thought she was being oversensitive.

5. Blames others for his mistakes – The handbrake incident at the wedding came to mind. Tick.

Maxwell wasn't good at laughing at himself. We did a food shop one evening and he needed a coin for the trolley but didn't have any change. I rooted around in my purse for my pink trolley token and handed it to him, but it fell to the floor. Either I released it too soon, or he didn't place his hand near enough to mine. I laughed at the silliness of it, but Maxwell didn't find it funny. He snapped at me under his breath and told me I was embarrassing.

6. Verbal abuse – We often teased each other. I can be clumsy at times, and he made fun of that. I mocked him with flexed bicep poses whenever I caught him admiring himself in the mirror. But sometimes, the comments got personal, albeit in a joking manner. He said my hairline was receding—I do have a high forehead—and that I have lizard skin (I never understood what he meant by that). Occasionally, he did take things personally and would say hurtful things. I once joked that I may have had a high forehead but at least it could keep wrinkles away because my skin stretched over my forehead and my skin was greasy in the T-zone. I was fortunate not to get many spots. I forgot that Maxwell suffered from acne as a teenager; he had faded scars—proof of that time. He had the occasional flare-up as an adult. He thought I was being spiteful about his spots, and he retaliated by saying that my breasts were small and that my bottom could do with losing a few inches. I felt guilty that I had hurt his feelings. Tick.

7. Mood swings – I couldn't think of anything specific, but I regularly joked with him that he suffered from P.M.S.

8. Threats of violence – There was the time he threatened to break my finger when I pointed at him in an argument and when he said he wanted to strangle Daisy for offering to pay for my flight to Scotland. I never believed he meant those things. I've never heard my dad say that he would break my mum's finger or strangle her friend. Tick.

9. Aggression – I thought about my bruised hip and the freezing water from the time I was sick on myself. Also, when he over-tightened my dress at the wedding. Tick.

10. Competitiveness – Perhaps Maxwell was being competitive at that time with the chilli flake. We played a board game in a pub one evening, and I had to name a movie that began with the letter 'T'. My answer was *The Lord of the Rings,* but Maxwell was certain it was wrong. He said it was *Lord of the Rings* and disallowed the point. The following day, I found his *The Lord of the Rings* DVD and showed him that there was a 'The' at the start. He got annoyed and accused me of never letting things drop. Tick.

11. Control – Maxwell often got frustrated with my eating habits and didn't understand why I chose to eat meat substitutes like vegetarian sausages or mince. He said that I should either eat meat or not. I smiled at the memory of Mum and Dad's barbecue held for Maxwell's 27th birthday—one of the rare occasions he visited them. They cooked vegetarian burgers but didn't mention that, and when we left, Maxwell thanked them for hosting the barbecue and said that he especially liked the burgers. Nobody pointed out they weren't meat.

Did I postpone university because I wanted to help Maxwell, or did I do it because that's what he wanted?

12. Humiliation – There was a time he told me, in front of Daisy, that I couldn't afford to go on a night out. We visited Oxford for a romantic weekend away, and Maxwell wanted to go punting on the river. It was a warm and sunny day, and it seemed like an ideal thing to try. We passed under a bridge, and when we came out the other side, a group of Japanese tourists waved down to us from the bridge. I waved back. Maxwell hissed at me loudly enough for the punter to hear him call me childish. The punter smiled awkwardly and looked away. Tick.

13. Lies – The words on his postcard were lies. Tick. The time he made out he had been to New York but hadn't. Perhaps he was trying to impress me? It was still a lie. Tick.

14. Cheating – I don't know if he cheated on me. It wasn't something I believed he would do. But there was that time he had scratches on his back after the stag do, and there was the earring under his bed. I went to my triennial smear test, and the nurse asked if I was willing to participate in a chlamydia study. All I needed to do was wee in a tube, and then I was sent a twenty-pound gift voucher as a *thank you*. I told the nurse there wasn't much point in me being included because I was in a committed relationship, but she tempted me to do it anyway. When I returned home and told Maxwell what happened, he was interested in it and asked me to let him know when the results came back. He chased me up a number of times for the results—they were negative, of course they were. We both got tested before having unprotected sex. Did he put me in a sexual health risk by sleeping with other people? I'm certain he and Sara-Ann were more than acquaintances. Tick

15. Promotes self-doubt – Mum has regularly said that I have a photographic memory. It's not that accurate, but it is fairly good, and I can often pinpoint past dates and locations with ease. Maxwell often doubted my recollections, though. There was even a time when we tried something a little adventurous in the bedroom—something neither of us had tried before, or at least that's what I believed at the time—and when I reminded him of that experience a few months later, he denied it was with him and said that it was something I must have done with another partner, but I know I hadn't. Tick.

Maxwell hated smoking as much as I did, and neither of us had ever smoked or dated a smoker. He asked me to pick him up after a night out—one of the few times he allowed me to drive his car—and he kissed me on the cheek as he climbed in. He smelled of nicotine.

'Have you been smoking?' I asked.

'No.'

'Are you sure? I can smell smoke.'

He shouted so loud that it hurt my ears. 'So, what if I have? What are you, the smoke police?' He continued to accuse me of always trying to pick a fight. Tick.

After the checklist, there was a list of websites and contact numbers that offered help and support for people affected by abusive relationships. I went online and viewed some of the websites. The statistics were shocking. So many people had encountered this type of relationship, and some had bravely written about their experiences of mental abuse. I was shocked that I was able to relate to many of their experiences but comforted to know I wasn't the only one to go through it. I now understood that people can hurt the ones they pretend to love. I didn't ever want to fall back into that trap.

Mum and Dad had prompted me on several occasions to see a counsellor, and each time I had refused. Even though I felt low, I was sure I could shake everything off. But now I knew what type of relationship I was in, I felt empowered to do something about it because I understood that what I went through with Maxwell wasn't normal, and I realised I needed help to move forward from everything.

There were website listings for domestic violence charities and services. I looked on a national website for counsellors and psychotherapists and found a therapist directory. It noted the code of conduct that all counsellors followed and emphasised that sessions were confidential. I thought it was odd that they stated that. Everyone knows medical appointments are confidential even though your name flashes up in the reception area of doctor surgeries, announcing to everyone there that you have a medical issue. *Alice Berry, please go to room four for Dr. So-and-So*. Why was a visit to see a mental health professional so explicitly secretive? It was an illness like other aches and pains of the body. One counsellor stated they wouldn't acknowledge you if you bumped into them in a supermarket or the street, only if you said hello first. GPs don't need to reassure patients of their confidentiality.

There were a few options and after whittling down the profiles, based on the friendliest profile photo, I chose Vera. She looked like the oldest therapist in the directory, but her eyes looked at me like those of a supportive grandmother. I fidgeted on my bed, took a deep breath, and called her number.

CHAPTER 20

Now

I waited until late morning before replying to Harry's email. I thought about it a lot over the weekend, and him. Was Monday morning too soon to reply? He may not have access to his work emails until he returned later this week, but if I waited until Wednesday to reply, that may look as if I waited for him to return. I sent the email. I agreed to meet to discuss the dog show in more detail. I awaited his response.

I offered to cook dinner for Chloe and Beth later that week to thank them for helping me settle in, and to get to know each other better. On my Tuesday lunch break, I popped to a local supermarket to buy the ingredients for a vegetarian curry and a couple of bottles of red wine, but when I returned to the office, I realised I had forgotten to buy poppadoms. I had worked late most evenings since starting the job, so I asked my manager if I could leave five minutes early to dash to the shop before heading home to cook dinner.

My computer screen was off, my drawers were locked, and with five minutes and twenty seconds before the end of the working day, I scooped up my shopping bags and rushed out of the office. I hurried up and down the aisles of a small grocery store near work and scanned the shelves for poppadoms. I wasn't even sure they would sell them. If not, I would have to go to a supermarket in East Dulwich, but that was a lot more effort than buying them here. The weight of the shopping bags was draining my energy. I couldn't see any. My train was in less than ten minutes, so I ran over to a young male assistant for help.

'Excuse me, do you sell poppadoms?'

He nodded once. 'Yep.' He stopped stacking the bottom shelf, stood up and told me to follow him.

I struggled to keep up with him as he raced passed the aisles before making a sharp bend into one that I hadn't looked at. He halted. 'There you go.' He pointed to a shelf. I moved to the side of him to look at where he was pointing. I quickly realised why I hadn't been down that aisle.

'Thank you for your help, but I'm looking for poppadoms, not condoms.'

His complexion turned the same colour as it would if you ate a Vindaloo curry. 'We sell those too, aisle three,' he said and hurried off.

'That's an interesting ingredient for a curry.' A male voice surprised me from behind. I spun around and in front of me was Harry. He was standing so close that I could smell the mix of fresh air and his wood-scented aftershave. 'I wonder if they'll have that on the menu when we go for lunch on Thursday,' he smiled. It was my turn to blush.

'Thursday?'

'Yes, is that okay with you?'

'I guess so,' I said whilst trying to act as though I wasn't aware that my face was on fire.

He carried on talking and pretended not to notice how red I had gone. I was grateful for that. There was nothing more guaranteed to make me go redder than someone pointing out the blush. He asked me to inform my manager that the meeting should last between two to three hours and that he would meet me outside his office at midday.

'What does "guppy git" mean?' I asked. Harry looked at me blankly. 'You wrote it in your email when you apologised for being…busy.'

'That must have been a typo,' he said, and a hint of pink appeared on his cheeks. 'See you Thursday,' he said and walked away.

I missed my train, and the next one wasn't for another twenty minutes, so I decided to get a bus home instead. It took a whole six minutes for one to arrive. My impatience amused me. I was becoming a Londoner.

Before leaving the office on Thursday, I reapplied a little bit of makeup and put on a tiny dash of perfume. Harry was already waiting outside the building when I arrived.

'Come on, I'm driving,' he said and walked over to a black four-by-four vehicle. He opened the passenger door.

'Where are we going? I asked as I climbed in.

'To my favourite restaurant,' he said and closed my door. He jumped into the driver's side and pulled away. 'It's in Knightsbridge. It'll be quicker to drive than to jump on the Tube.'

The minimal exterior décor disguised the fact there was a restaurant inside; the brickwork and blacked-out windows made it seem invisible, and only a small, grey sign dangling high above indicated there was something behind the windowless door. The maître d' welcomed us in and informed us he had reserved "Mr Hartington's favourite table". We weaved our way past individually decorated booths. The interior décor made up for the minimalist exterior: one booth was covered with white padded walls; black velvet drapes with gold fringing hung from another; a smaller booth was smeared in animal print; and a booth tucked in the corner was fitted out with mirrored walls and silver seating. It was a relief to see Harry's favourite booth was plain in comparison with wooden beams and plants dotted around the edge. It looked far less claustrophobic than the others.

We discussed the dog show initially, but gradually, the conversation turned personal. Harry asked if I had moved to London because of a boyfriend. He didn't mention a girlfriend or wife. I got the impression that his work was his life. He loved animals, and I told him I loved them too but felt embarrassed to tell him about my unfinished degree. That was another lifetime ago, and I didn't want to discuss my past, not yet. He was chatty and open and even made me laugh a few times. He was so different from what I first thought. On the drive back to work, he asked to take me out for a non-work-related dinner, and I agreed to go. I was ready to be brave, even though my protective wall was still high like a dam. During our lunch, I felt a few bricks fall away, weakening my defence and allowing a tiny amount of pressure to release. I knew that if things continued to improve with him, more and more bricks would disappear, and water would start flowing faster and stronger and eventually breach the dam, and nothing would be able to stop the flow. I was okay with that. He was easy to talk to, sensible, reliable and exciting. I trusted myself more than I did in the past. My judgement had to be better than it was, surely.

Harry picked me up in a taxi at seven o'clock on Saturday evening. He took me to a vegetarian restaurant in Battersea, which he chose based on the fact I had told him I was a flexitarian.

'I've never heard of flexitarianism before,' he said as we were seated in the restaurant. 'I gave it some thought after our lunch meeting, and as an animal lover myself, I realised I'm a bit of a hypocrite.'

'I think we all get brainwashed into social norms, but it's only when you take time out to think about things differently that you realise you could be living your life better for the sake of yourself, others and the planet.'

'I don't think I could ever be able to be a vegetarian, but I'll give being a flexitarian ago.' He smiled. 'I'm glad there isn't steak on the menu to tempt me.'

It was refreshing to be understood instead of being told what I should and shouldn't eat. Unlike Maxwell, Harry listened to my views and made an effort to understand. A warm feeling trickled over my body.

We visited a couple of bars after our meal, and then I called it a night, not that I wanted to. I could have stayed out all night talking to Harry; he was so easy to be around, but Beth had given me some advice before the date: leave earlier than you want to. End the date on a high—that will leave him wanting more. She made it sound easy, and as it turned out, it was. My dating skills were on the up.

Harry offered to drop me home in a taxi. It was generous and thoughtful, but I was happy to get a night bus. He insisted on waiting at the bus stop with me, and I agreed to that. I felt genuine pleasure being in good male company, something that had been missing from my life for so long. It had been years since I had been in a relationship. Yes, there had been dates to the cinema or dinners and the occasional drunken snog on a night out, but that was it. I hadn't been ready to give anything of myself. The thought of allowing someone in and seeing the real me, my fears, thoughts, and feelings—after everything, it was too much. It was risky.

It might have been the timing, or the move to London stretching my confidence out of its comfort zone, or because of Harry's openness, but something was helping me find the strength to want to take a risk. There had been times when I thought I would be too fearful to be open to love ever again, but something was flowing inside of me that made me realise I could make that leap.

When Harry gently placed his lips against mine, a ripple of warmth travelled over my body like a gentle raindrop disturbing the dryness of the desert. When he pulled away, I involuntarily held my breath as though paralysed by the sting of a scorpion's tail before striking for the kill. He placed one hand on my lower back and pulled me nearer. His other hand cupped my neck, and he kissed me again. I smiled the whole way home, and it took me ages to fall asleep. I couldn't stop thinking about his kiss.

I was greeted with an email from Harry on Monday morning telling me how much he enjoyed Saturday, and he asked to see me again that week. We went to a late opening of The National Gallery on Tuesday evening, where we browsed famous paintings. Art wasn't something I was interested in or understood, but I was happy to be there with him and learn something. We went to a fringe theatre on Thursday evening to watch a play about a play, and on Friday, we went for a meal near St Paul's and ended up in the tropical bar, where we bumped into each other.

The bar was even busier than before, but we managed to

squeeze in side by side at a table near the dance floor. The music was loud, so we had to shout in each other's ears to be heard. After a while, we started playing games. We played Thumb War, which turned into an arm wrestle. He let me win, and we high-fived to celebrate, but instead of pulling away, our hands held on. Harry gently stroked his thumb against mine, and then our fingers interlaced. Our eyes locked, and my breathing quickened to a shallow rhythm. The music and people dancing disappeared into a blur, and the only sensation I was aware of was his presence.

'Why did you tell me your name was Jess?'

'I don't know,' I said. I pulled the back of his hand to my face and brushed my cheek along it as we maintained eye contact. 'Why didn't you deny being a delivery man?'

'I don't know,' he said, still looking at me. He pulled me towards him, and we kissed. 'Shall we go?' he asked, and I nodded.

It took a moment to realise where I was when I woke the following morning. I laid still with my back to Harry. The evidence around the room confirmed the closeness we felt last night: my black blouse was draped over a chair, and Harry's white shirt was on top of it. His jeans were crumpled in a corner of the room whilst mine were doing the splits in the middle of the room, and our underwear was in an entangled pile in the middle of the room.

Harry soon reminded me of where I was and why I was there. He cupped my waist, kissed the top of my spine, and then pulled me onto my back. His legs entwined mine like ivy around a tree, and he tucked his arm around my shoulders, and I snuggled into him. I kissed his chest, and we both fell back to sleep in the warmth of each other's bodies.

I woke a couple of hours later to a kiss on my forehead. 'What would you like for brunch?' he whispered.

'Anything.' I smiled and opened my eyes. He smiled back, kissed me, and then jumped out of bed to get dressed.

'Stay there. I won't be long,' he said and popped out to the shop.

His pillow was still warm, and it smelt of his woody aftershave. I cuddled it into me and squeezed it even tighter than he squeezed me. Happiness filled my stomach: the warmth of his skin, his attention, the romance, and the overall feeling of being wanted and chosen. I realised I wanted more than I had allowed myself to admit. Harry had given me that gift. Tears filled my eyes from a mix of gratitude for the incredible moment of joy but also tears of sadness for the years that had slipped by from hiding my vulnerability. I allowed myself to believe I was protecting myself from further hurt, but what I had done was punish myself by denying any hope.

Harry asked me to stay a second night, and he drove me home after brunch to pick up clean clothes and an overnight bag. We stayed in that evening, and he cooked us dinner before we attempted to watch a movie—we managed to watch the opening scenes before being distracted by each other.

Before Harry drove me home on Sunday morning, he wanted to show me his favourite place in London. We jumped in his car and headed east, parallel to the River Thames, passing by London Bridge before turning inland down a deserted main road.

'I love the city at the weekend,' Harry said as he turned right down a cobbled side road. 'It's so peaceful, and hard to imagine this place will be rammed again tomorrow.' He bumped up onto the kerb, straddling a yellow line, to park.

'I could never drive in London,' I said. 'There are too many yellow lines and restrictions, let alone turning left with bus lanes in the way.' Harry laughed and took hold of my hand.

Tall buildings dominated the road, but up on the far right, and set back from the road and other buildings, was a church. A tall steeple with a pointy spire stood at the far end, and black railings protected the area. Harry hadn't mentioned that he was religious. There was a lot we didn't know about each other, even though his friendship felt as though it had been in my life for years.

We stopped outside a doorless archway. 'Close your eyes,' Harry said and placed his hands over my eyes before guiding me up some steps. Birdsong sounded as loud as it did outside the church as we reached the top of the steps, and after a few small footsteps, the hard ground turned soft, grass-like. *Perhaps it was a rug.* I didn't know much about churches. 'I visit this place when I need time to think or reflect,' Harry said. 'On the count of three, you can open your eyes: one, two, three—ta-dah.'

I was surprised at what I saw. There were gothic-style windows, but they were glassless. There were walls, but it was roofless. There were headstones and a church tower, but this wasn't a place of worship. There was no rug.

'This church was bombed during the Second World War and, miraculously, most of it survived.'

It was eerily peaceful in contrast to the devastation it had endured. History stood still, showcasing its force of destruction, yet nature thrived and continued to grow. It did not allow the pain of the past to stop it from living. This was now me. Three pigeons flew in formation overhead, walls surrendered to tall climbers, green moss camouflaged patches of grey bricks, grass invaded the floor, trees stood to attention, and shrubs had been planted uniformly along the walkway. It felt more like a secluded monastery hidden in the depths of a lush rainforest rather than a bombed-out church in Central London.

Delicate raindrops started to fall, and we took shelter under a tree.

'Thank you for showing me this.' I rested my head against Harry's arm.

'Thank you for coming with me. I wanted to show you this because I like you a lot, Alice.'

We stood in silence until a guided group of tourists disturbed the peace.

On the drive back to my flat, Harry told me he had to go away for a week. He was going to France for a couple of meetings, and afterwards, he was meeting friends in Switzerland for a long skiing weekend. He asked to see me as soon as he returned from his trip.

I missed Harry whilst he was away but that didn't stop me from carrying on my city adventures and discovering more of *my* London. When he returned from his trip, he took me to dinner at a rooftop restaurant with impressive views over St Paul's Cathedral. On the road below, it wasn't possible to see the intricate detail of the statues looking down on the world below from high above, protecting the city. I loved how Harry was showing me parts of London I hadn't yet found on my own.

He ordered a bottle of champagne. 'So, what have you been up to?' he asked whilst pouring champagne into our glasses.

'I went to a silent disco at the Natural History Museum the other night, did a tour of the Globe Theatre on Saturday and on Sunday, I met up with my friend Teagan and went to a pop-up photography exhibition on 1950s New York Street Gangs, at Somerset House.'

'Not much, then.' He smiled.

'Don't worry, I did miss you a little bit.' I was surprised at my honesty.

After our meal, the waitress handed us dessert menus. 'I have to go away again at the end of the month. I do travel quite a bit for work, but not normally this much.'

I took a sip of champagne. I felt disappointed, but I was unsure as to whether that was due to him going away again or because it was a reality check of his jet-set lifestyle compared to mine.

'Would you like dessert?' the waitress asked after giving us time to peruse the dessert menu.

'Shall we share something?' Harry suggested.

'Yes, you choose.' I hadn't looked at the menu properly whilst contemplating our different lifestyles.

'We'll go for the New York cheesecake, please,' Harry said to the waitress before looking at me. 'It'll get me in the mood for my business trip.'

'Are you going to New York?'

'I am.'

'Have you been before?'

He smiled. 'Once or twice.'

I blushed. Of course, he had. 'I've always wanted to go,' I said. 'Is it similar to London?'

'It's different.'

'In what way?'

'You tell me?'

'What do you mean?'

'Would you like to join me and make up your own mind?'

CHAPTER 21

Then

I woke in the dark before my alarm on the morning of my first counselling session. It was the middle of January. I rarely woke before my alarm, especially in winter. In my dream before waking, I was an old-fashioned deep sea diver wearing copper hat gear, weighted to the seabed. As I was waking, I had to break free from the dive gear and scramble to the surface before gasping for breath. I opened my eyes and felt as though I had the bends.

In the bathroom, my reflection stared back at me in the mirror, expressionless. Was it necessary to go through with it today? I felt a bit better, and if today's appointment was to see a doctor for a physical symptom that had started to clear up, I would cancel the appointment. My thoughts and emotions felt stable at that moment, but experience had taught me it wouldn't last. I needed the appointment.

My mind raced in the shower about how the session would work: how would we know what to discuss? Who would start the conversation? What if I got upset? Would Vera think I was wasting her time? What if we ran out of things to talk about? What was I doing?

Smoke coughed from the chimney nestled amongst the thatched roof of Vera's cottage. Ivy clung to the brick walls, rows of shivering lavender lined the pathway to the front door, and sunlight poked and prodded pastel-coloured windmills twirling around in the cold breeze. They were enticing me in like someone pulling at my arm. At the end of the path, the top half of the stable door was open. I was unsure whether to ring the doorbell or call out. A dark and short hallway was all that was visible. I rang the bell. According to my phone, it was two minutes to ten, and Vera took what seemed like ages to come to the door. My finger hovered over the bell, poised to ring again, but when a cuckoo clock in the hallway chimed on the hour, I jumped in the air in fright when Vera appeared at the front door as though waiting for her cue.

Her appearance hinted that she was probably in her late seventies—she looked around the same age as my nan when she died. Vera's wiry, grey hair was pulled back into a bun, and her clean fingernails looked years younger than the dotted papery skin on the back of her hands. She smiled. Her dentures beamed bright white as she gently shook my hand with her soft hand over the stable door. She opened the bottom half, allowing me into her home. Apart from her name, address and telephone number, Vera was a stranger, and I was about to expose my inner world to her.

In the hallway, a dozing black cat was snuggled on a well-used cushion on top of a stool; its tail flicked in the air as we passed by, but it didn't bother opening its eyes. We turned a corner and a vintage display unit, neatly organised with bric-a-brac, stood next to the only open door. Sunlight seeped into this part of the cool hallway exposing floating dust particles in the air. She asked me to step inside the room, followed me and then closed the door behind us.

Cream walls dripped into a worn, cream carpet, a tall plant sat cheerily in the corner, and a clock hung silently on the wall behind an eighties corned beef hash-patterned sofa. Vera gestured for me to sit there. She sat on a brown Chesterfield chair opposite. Scratch marks on the front of the arms were probably from the cat, but I wondered if they were marks left by clients trying to escape the room or themselves. More bric-a-brac sat in a row on a high shelf behind Vera. Some of the ornaments had faces, and they glared down as though waiting to be entertained or to judge.

Four faded photos of the same hefty-trunked tree were displayed in a diamond shape on the wall near the window. Each photo represented a season. The photo at the top was summer, its leaves in full bloom like a green Mr Whippy ice cream; clockwise below was autumn, the green now mixed with red and gold leaves—the chorus from 'Karma Chameleon' repeated in my mind as I considered it: red, gold and green, red, gold and green; below that photo the tree's branches were bare. That was me, but I wanted to be the last photo, spring. The tree was coated in white and pink buds of new beginnings. A glass of water sat next to a box of strategically placed tissues on the table next to the sofa. Vera pointed them out before informing me about how the sessions worked.

'Today's session will last an hour, and it's important we stick to the allocated time slot,' she said with her hands resting flat on the notepad sitting on her lap. I nodded. 'Everything we discuss is in confidence, and this is a safe place to express yourself.'

I nodded again.

She picked up a pen and opened her notepad before proceeding to ask questions that I already knew about myself: name, address, age.

'So, tell me more about what brings you here today, Alice.'

I breathed in and paused. 'My first love died the day I planned to leave a mentally abusive relationship—I didn't know it was abusive at the time—and later that year, my Australian boyfriend asked me to move out there to be with him, and after buying a flight ticket, selling my car and handing in my notice, he emailed days before I was due to fly to say he couldn't go through with it.'

Vera's eyes remained focused on the pad as she continued making notes. 'Okay.' She carried on writing. 'And what do you hope to achieve from these sessions?'

My foot twitched as I picked at the skin around my thumbnail, making it bleed. I stared at the blood that seeped from the cuticle, like half-hearted removed red nail varnish.

'To stop crying and to stop feeling angry?'

'Anything else?' She continued writing.

'I want to be happy again, within.'

'Good.' She dragged out the word.

She finished writing, placed the notepad on the arm of her chair, and repositioned herself to mirror me: legs crossed at the ankles, hands tucked in between her legs. We agreed to book ten weekly sessions on the same day, at the same time. There could be some flexibility, but only for illness or emergencies. It was important to set these boundaries, which she emphasised numerous times.

Now that I understood what my relationship was with Maxwell, I felt better knowing why it was hard—it was abusive—but I still agonised over Blake and wanted to explore the reasons why he may have done what he did. Perhaps Vera would tell me she thought we might get back together. Were counsellors also psychic? She focused on Maxwell. I didn't want to talk about him, not that I told her that. I wanted to scream. *I know Maxwell treated me badly. I don't need you to tell me that. I need you to tell me if Blake will come back to me.* But she didn't. I let out a heavy sigh and fidgeted my way into another position: legs crossed, arms crossed. Vera mirrored me again.

'Right, that rounds up our hour,' she said after I told her how Maxwell and I met. *But there's more I want to say*, I thought as we both stood up. My shoulders were slumped forward. 'See you at the same time next week.'

I nodded.

The session stirred up stale feelings and triggered an unwelcome sensation, as though waking in a deep bath and choking with water-filled lungs. These sessions were supposed to help, not make me feel worse than I already did. Now that I had gained a clearer insight into my relationship with Maxwell, he was controlling and emotionally abusive, why wasn't this knowledge enough to move forward? Why didn't she focus on Blake? Walking out of her garden, I noticed a red winter shrub protruding from the soil as though it had been hung, drawn and quartered. I didn't want to return next week.

A memory from university popped into my mind as I left. I couldn't remember the animal, the snake, or the plant, but somewhere in the world that animal simply smells that plant as a cure from that snake's venom. I needed a plant to cure the poison stuck in my mind and body.

I had a nightmare that night about tornadoes.

'Tell me about Maxwell's relationship with his parents,' Vera asked during the second session. I met his parents a few times. We occasionally met his dad, mainly at his favourite wine bar or briefly at his gated property when he wasn't working away—the conversations generally focused on what he had been up to and which celebrities he met during his engineering job in the racing world. Maxwell tried to impress his dad with his work. I often felt sorry for him because his dad never gave him any praise. We saw more of his mum, but those meetings were uncomfortable, and there was normally a reason why Maxwell arranged to see his mum: to pick up his ironed shirts, have dinner, or anything where Maxwell gained something from it. His mum was quiet, and Maxwell often got frustrated with her.

'Does he have any siblings?'

'Yes, an older sister, but I never met her. She lives in Germany and, apparently, is a renowned scientist, something to do with malaria research. She's married to her job and was always back and forth between Africa or South America or somewhere else in the world. That's what Maxwell told me.'

Vera frowned as she made notes.

'Do you know why his parents separated?'

'His dad had an affair. Maxwell was around nine or ten at the time, and I know little of what happened. Neither of his parents spoke about it and whenever Maxwell did, he gave snippets of what happened.'

'Did Mum leave his dad at that point?'

I shook my head. 'Not straight away—she supposedly stayed for the children. Once they grew up and left home, she left.'

Vera sipped from her glass of water. 'Do you think Maxwell understands consequence?'

'In what way?'

She tilted her head to one side, 'Dad had an affair, and Mum stayed.'

'I hadn't thought of that, perhaps not.'

'Was Maxwell unfaithful?'

'Not that I know for sure, but there were behaviours that made me think he might have been. I found an earring under his bed when I first moved in with him; he had scratch marks on his back after a stag do, and I overheard an overly flirtatious telephone conversation with another woman.'

'How did those incidents make you feel?'

'They didn't seem real—not at the time.'

'Did he ever hit you?'

'No'

'How do you feel knowing that he may have been unfaithful?'

'Like he never loved me. Why did he stay in a relationship with me if he wanted to go elsewhere? He obviously wasn't happy with me; otherwise, he wouldn't have behaved the way he did, any of it. I wish I had left much sooner.'

After that session, I thought about another university lecture. I realised I was Maxwell's ant, and he was zombie ant fungus. The fungus tempts the wandering ant onto its lush leaf, grows through the ant's body, drains the nutrients, and then takes over the body and mind.

I dreamt about tornadoes that night.

I never came away feeling noticeably cured from any session. There was something more subtle about the process. Like a plaster for a graze or crutches for a sprained ankle, the supportive treatment slowly helped to heal my emotional wounds. There were days when I still cried and got angry, but the tears were less frequent, and my patience started slowly increasing.

'I wonder,' Vera said during another session, 'do you think you were a victim of a victim?'

'How do you mean?'

'Of all the things we've discussed during our sessions about Maxwell and his family and your relationship, do you think he was a victim in his upbringing, which he then passed on to you?'

'Possibly,' I said. Tears brimmed in my eyes. 'That makes me feel sad for him.'

'Why does that make you feel sad for him?'

'If that's the case, then he'll never be happy. If he can't see how he's behaving, he'll never change, and he'll never know why he's doing what he's doing.'

'But that's not your responsibility, Alice, it's his. Do you think that's the reason why you stayed, to show him love? To heal him?'

'There were times I felt sorry for him for the lack of love and support from his family. I guess there were times that I thought I could fill a void.'

'Do you think it's somebody's responsibility to heal another in a relationship?'

'Not now.' I shook my head and lowered my eyes.

'You've recognised your unhappiness, and you're doing something about it, Alice, and it's his responsibility to do the same.'

'I hope he does, for his sake and his future relationships.'

Vera smiled at me.

'Sometimes I sense things around some people,' Vera said as she walked me to the front door. 'Be mindful of signs from the universal signs, Alice.' Was she going to tell me that she could see Blake returning to my life? I crossed my fingers in my coat pocket. She smiled whilst staring past me. I turned around. There was nothing there just a plain wall in the hallway. 'I can see candy floss. You've had signs, and there will be more.'

I thanked her and left. I wasn't into woo-woo, but I told her that I would keep an eye out for these signs.

During our final session, I mentioned a recurring dream that I had been having since the first counselling session.

'Do you want to draw it?' Vera asked.

'I can't draw.'

'Everyone can draw,' she said and stood up and walked behind her chair. She returned to her seat with a plastic box. Inside was a pad and a pencil. 'Here you go,' she passed them to me. 'Draw it.'

I started by drawing a squiggly line across the bottom of the page; this represented the shoreline. Clouds at the top of the page looked more like legless and headless sheep. I added a splash of lazy lowercase w's across the bottom half of the page to show there were waves. The finishing touch and the main theme in the drawing and my dreams, the tornadoes. They varied in number in each dream, but they always started at sea on the horizon. I started panicking in my sleep when the tornadoes spun faster and moved erratically the closer they got to the shore. I would run and hide in a tiny house and wait, crouch down until they passed over. The power and force of them shook the building, uprooting it slightly like a nineteen-eighties Wendy house on a breezy day.

Vera took the pad and stared at the drawing.

'What's going on in this picture?'

'They're waterspouts, the tornadoes in my dreams, well, they're more like nightmares.' I sniggered at my ridiculous attempt at drawing them—they looked more like coiled bedsprings.

'What else?'

'They're clouds, and that's the sea.'

'What do you *really* see?' she said, looking at the drawing perched on the edge of her seat. I shuffled forward and mirrored her.

'Well, they're waves,' I said, pointing at the drawing. Vera's eyes remained on the drawing. She didn't acknowledge the waves.

There was a long pause. 'Why are there three tornadoes?'

I looked at her and then back at the drawing. 'I don't know.' I was surprised there were only three on the paper. In my dreams, there were normally more.

'What could three possibly mean?' She finally looked up at me.

I stared at the picture. 'I suppose,' I cleared my throat, 'perhaps they represent the three times I've been in love: Tobias, Maxwell and Blake?'

She stared at the drawing again and then pointed at the first one, 'Why doesn't this one touch the sea or the sky like the other two?'

I gasped when I realised what I'd drawn. 'Tobias is no longer alive.' His tornado floated on the paper like a ghost.

For the first time throughout our time together, Vera hugged me. 'Remember, people treat you the way they feel about themselves.' We pulled apart, and she took hold of my hand and tucked a card inside. 'Keep this with you.' It read:

Self-Worth
You can't always feel the warmth of the sun when clouds block it from your view, but it is always there, and when it disappears into the night, be patient for it to return in the morning because it always will.

I walked along the lavender-lined path for the final time. It was early spring, and the lavender waved me off with its beautiful scent. When I reached the end of the path, I turned to wave. Vera was leaning on the lower half of the stable door. She waved back and then closed the top half of the door.

I thought about buffalos from another lecture after Vera closed the door. I needed to be more buffalo. When Tobias went to Hawaii, I didn't want to feel the loneliness he left behind, so I sheltered under Maxwell. I thought I was free when I left Maxwell, but I dodged my trauma during the summer with Blake. Buffalos don't like water. Instead of running away from the storm to avoid it, they charge towards it to get it over with quicker.

I never dreamed of tornadoes again.

Summer arrived with a punch not long after the counselling sessions ended. When I wasn't working, I spent long days at the beach reading books, listening to music, and relaxing in the sun, but I still felt lost and unfulfilled. The hotel didn't pay much, even as a senior receptionist, and my social life was near non-existent due to irregular and unsociable hours. With many early morning starts or midnight finishes, friendships were more acquaintance-based. I had been single for a few years, through choice at first, because I needed time to heal and figure out where my life was going, but I still hadn't worked that out. My life was boring. My confidence was low, and I was fearful about the future. I was stuck. I didn't know how to make a change for the better. Counselling helped me to start healing, and from that, I felt less hurt, less angry, less frustrated and less lonely but I wasn't yet fully healed.

The following year, I turned thirty, and not much had changed. There is something about a milestone birthday that forces you to reflect. I thought about Daisy. With the support from counselling, I realised that not only had I pushed Tobias away, but I had pushed her away too when I got together with

Maxwell. She was always there for me even when I didn't see that. No wonder she and Tobias took comfort in each other on my birthday seven years ago. I was the one that changed first, not them.

One warm mid-summer evening, I stayed at the beach to watch another sunset. It was the only time and place I felt a sense of happiness; it helped me escape the monotony of my life. But this time, it was spoilt by a noise which was impossible to tell if it was the sound of a squawking seagull or the cackle of a woman's laugh. The sea was calm, but the gentle waves bubbled along the shoreline as though a pressure pot was waiting to explode. There was a gentle breeze, and clouds floated across the sky. One passed over faster than the rest, like a flying carpet—I wanted to jump on it and let it take me away. That's the moment I realised I needed to get away from Devon, from my life. With views stretching far out to sea and a clear blue sky, I felt claustrophobic. I needed to escape. The only available option I had was Kate's open offer in London. She was the only person I knew outside the county, and with little funds to make a move without a job lined up, I needed her help. But first, I needed to see Daisy.

Daisy opened her front door, and a familiar citrus scent hugged me before my friend did. Neither of us said a word, but she gestured me in. I sat in the lounge whilst Daisy made us tea. A photo of the two of us posing in our prom dresses was still sitting beside the television, and the Scorpio horoscope mug I bought for her sixteenth birthday was on the coffee table. It was chipped, and there was a crack around the handle, but I was grateful that she was still using it.

We laughed and cried and laughed again and spent a couple of hours catching up about the past few years and reminiscing about times before that. She eventually showed me an email Tobias had sent her when he first arrived in Hawaii. It was an apology for kissing her and for putting Daisy in an awkward situation. The kiss was an impulsive reaction to him moving away and because I had called off our relationship. It was foolish, he said and asked Daisy to take care of me. I cried again.

'But you're coming back?' Daisy said when I told her about my move to London.

'I don't know. I'm not sure what I want. All I know is that I need to get away from here.'

'At least we have a few months together before you go.'

I was happy that Daisy and I had time to make up before I left. I was surprised that I still wasn't tempted to stay even though someone so important was back in my life. She had to get up early for an important meeting and was going out for a meal later that day with her fiancé's parents, so couldn't stay up late.

'Look at you. You're all grown up and sensible,' I said as we hugged again.

'I know, who would have thought?' she said.

'I did,' I said and squeezed her harder.

After telling my parents of my impending plan and checking with Kate that her offer was still open, I pre-booked a one-way ticket to London.

CHAPTER 22

Now

Harry's invite to New York was as unexpected as it was generous. He offered to pay for my flight, and because he already had a hotel booked as a business expense, that wouldn't cost me anything either. He didn't know that I had longed to visit New York. I was hesitant. The thought of flying on my own from Heathrow to JFK Airport made my body shiver from the rush of adrenaline because the last time somebody asked me to fly and meet them in another country, my life broke apart. Back then I was naively in love, but now I was much more cautious. My internal body armour made sure of that. Was I ready to fulfil a dream with someone who I hardly knew? I told Harry I would have to think about it.

Anxiety prevented me from getting to sleep that night. I had already stretched myself making the move to London less than three months ago, and now an opportunity had arisen to push me even further. Perhaps it was too much too soon. London was still new, and there was plenty of time to visit New York. I was only thirty. New York could wait. I fell asleep.

When I woke in the morning, my thoughts had changed. I dreamt about my nan, as though she was speaking to me in my sleep. When Grandad died a few years before I met Tobias, I grieved not only for him but also for her life for being left alone in the world. I couldn't imagine the feelings of loss she must have experienced for someone she loved so deeply and for so long. I often wondered how she was going to cope without him for the rest of her time on this planet. I naively thought she would live forever, but her death was just as inevitable as it is for us all, and she died just twelve months later.

After she died, I thought about what she did with her life between Grandad's death and her own. That unknown time of years, months, or even days she had left and not knowing how long her life would be without her beloved husband. Did she ever stop to realise she too wouldn't last forever, or was she too consumed by the void in her life to carry on living? I never thought to ask her.

Time, that was the answer. It is so precious. We never know when it will end, but it will, and I had wasted so much of my time holding back from life. I wanted to make up for that. I needed to live again, take more risks and not just survive. Moving to London had helped to get my life moving again, and now Harry was allowing me an opportunity to spread my wings even further. I said yes to New York City.

Harry flew there on the last Wednesday in March, and my fight—which I insisted on paying for—was booked for Friday after work. That meant travelling in economy and not business class, as Harry had offered, but I did agree that I would accept a free upgrade if the airline offered us that when we checked in together for our return flight. Harry had to work Monday and Tuesday, which meant we would cram in as much as possible over the weekend, and then I would have to discover the streets of New York City on my own for those two days. If I could get around London on my own, I reasoned, I could do the same in the city that never sleeps.

Heathrow Airport was easy enough to get to by Tube and straightforward to navigate around. Like the underground, it was well signposted. After check-in, passport control, security checks, a quick phone call to Harry, and two Cosmopolitan cocktails to get me in the mood and to help me sleep on the flight, I boarded the plane. The flight departed on schedule, and in no time, we descended into JFK Airport.

It was eleven p.m. East Coast time when we landed. I could see below that New York was still busy despite the hour. There weren't any visible skyscrapers, but streetlights and vehicle lights lit up the land as far as I could see. The ground was covered in snow, and snowploughs the size of tanks passed by as we taxied to the gate. Airport trucks and fire engines made their equivalents back home look like toys. *Were Americans giants?*

The queue for immigration was long and slow. It was midnight, or five in the morning back in London, by the time I neared the front. Harry sent a text to say he would wait up for me and estimated that I should arrive at the hotel in Manhattan at around one in the morning. The queue moved quicker the nearer I got to border control. The faces of the customs and immigration officers were intimidatingly expressionless and made me feel as though I was guilty of something. An older gentleman with white hair and a matching moustache summoned me to his booth. He didn't look at me; his eyes remained fixed on his screen when he asked me to place my passport on the counter.

'Your reason for travel?' he asked, still not looking in my direction. It was like my arrival in London all over again.

'I'm visiting my boyfriend for a few days. He's already here for work,' I said, twisting my hands around each other.

He looked at me. 'Place your right hand on the scanner, please, ma'am.' He looked back at his screen before instructing me to repeat the process with my left hand. My eyes were scanned next.

As all of this was going on, I practised my answers to questions I assumed he would ask: where I was staying, when I was departing, the name of Harry's business, how long had we been together, Harry's full name… I panicked. I didn't know his middle name or if he even had one. Harry had told me his age; he was thirty-three, three years older than me, and his birthday was on New Year's Day. He had three older brothers, the eldest two being half-brothers. His parents were still together and divided their time between London and their country home in a Gloucestershire village. But I didn't know his middle name.

He looked at me again, at my passport, and then at me again. There was an uncomfortable pause. 'Enjoy your trip, ma'am,' he said and handed my passport back to me. 'Tell your boyfriend not to work too hard,' he smiled.

'Thank you, I will, and I'll try not to shop too hard,' I laughed and instantly regretted saying that. Was that too familiar? Did that make me sound suspicious? But he laughed, and I continued into the baggage hall.

A smartly dressed man was waiting in arrivals, holding a sign with my name on it. He looked about my age and had a coolness about him that made him look like he could be in a hip-hop music video.

'Good evening, ma'am. I'm Brandon, your driver for this evening,' he said and took hold of my suitcase. 'Welcome to New York City.'

'Thank you,' I said and followed him to the car park. He was a chauffeur from the hotel which Harry had organised because he didn't want me to get a taxi on my own at that time of night, and unlike the flight, I accepted his generous offer.

During the first three-quarters of the journey, travelling through Queens towards Manhattan, the buildings were standard height, from shops and houses to high-rise buildings, but there were no skyscrapers. It was only when we drove around a large bend and entered the Ed Koch Queensboro Bridge that the Manhattan skyline revealed itself. Skyscrapers stood proudly across the river like the Terracotta Army, and as we crept over the bridge, they grew taller. I felt like a passenger in a toy car driving amongst the soldiers' feet.

Brandon must have seen the awe on my face. 'It's easy enough to get around,' he laughed. 'Avenues run north to south, and the streets are numbered and run east to west. Much easier than London, I guess?'

I already knew about the grid system, but I didn't want to admit that to Brandon. 'Yes, it looks much easier than London.' He was proud to show off *his* city. 'Have you ever been to London?'

'Nope, not yet, ma'am, but I hope to go someday.'

Brandon pointed out Central Park, but it was too dark to make out anything. In contrast, Times Square shone so brightly that it could have been daytime. Piccadilly Circus looked dull in comparison. We travelled south along Seventh Avenue; it was long and straight, and it seemed as though it would go on forever, like a mirage in the desert. Eventually, the one-way avenue narrowed, and side roads started jutting off at angles here and there, diluting the sense of the grid system. We waited at a set of traffic lights. Vehicles passed by in both directions. A sign was hanging from the traffic lights, which indicated we were now on West Broadway. We turned right at the lights and travelled a few blocks along Chambers Street before I noticed a dark mass up ahead.

'What's that in the darkness?' I asked Brandon.

'Oh, that's the Hudson, ma'am.'

'So that must be New Jersey on the other side of the river.'

'So, you *do* know your way around!' Brendon clapped his hands once and smiled at me through his interior mirror.

'A little,' I said.

'That's Jersey City, in the state of New Jersey,' he explained. 'But if you plan on adventuring outside Manhattan, I'd recommend Brooklyn.'

'Is that where you live?'

'No, ma'am. It became the trendy borough; way too expensive for me. I live on Staten Island. That's home for me and always will be.'

We pulled up outside the boutique hotel in Battery Park City, in the lower south-westerly tip of Manhattan. Brandon collected my suitcase from the trunk and placed it outside the front door of the hotel. He stood, smiling at me. It took me a moment to remember I needed to tip him. Afterwards, he jumped back in the vehicle, and I watched as he drove away. I suddenly felt all alone in New York. I hoped he had dropped me off at the right place because I had forgotten to text Harry when we reached Manhattan, and it was too late to do it now. He was probably asleep.

The receptionist was expecting me and gave me a key to Harry's room. I declined their concierge service and dragged my suitcase into the lift and up to the penthouse suite. Harry was asleep in bed. I crept around the room and changed into my pyjamas, it was cold, and jumped into bed. I cuddled up behind Harry and fell asleep instantly.

I woke before Harry in the morning. I gently peeled off the duvet and tiptoed over to the window to peek behind the curtain. Remnants of snow remained on the ground, but a bright-blue sky shone above, welcoming me to my first day in New York City. Harry stirred and, without saying a word, held out his hand, summoning me back to bed. Within an hour, we were dressed and ready to explore the city. The sun was shining, but we needed plenty of layers to keep off the chill. Within a few blocks, we stopped to buy hot takeaway drinks to help us warm up against the crisp air that stung our faces and the tops of our legs.

'I can't believe I'm here,' I said as we left the coffee shop. 'Thank you for this opportunity.'

Harry kissed me on the lips. 'Thank you for coming. I've missed you and the way your eyes light up when you're excited about something, which is most of the time.' His words touched me deeper than his kiss. He noticed me; he saw me. I had been invisible to the world for years, and now, after all this time, I was no longer hidden. I felt alive and not just because I was in the city I had always wanted to visit.

Like London, the financial district was quiet on a Saturday morning. We passed through it to reach Brooklyn Bridge, and once we were on the bridge, we decided to walk only halfway because it was even colder. Icicles clung from the cables. We quickly nestled ourselves back amongst the buildings and walked south to Battery Park past Wall Street, where we passed a yellow school bus and more taxis of the same colour. By that point, I was certain I had seen every yellow cab in the city—they were everywhere.

Lower Manhattan was tricky to navigate. The numbered avenues and streets didn't reach that far, but luckily, Harry knew his way around. From Battery Park, we could see the Statue of Liberty, Ellis Island, and Staten Island, which looked further away than the state of New Jersey. From there, we jumped on the subway and headed north to Grand Central Station. Even though I was still fairly new to the Tube in London, seeing signs for Westminster, Leicester Square, or Baker Street had become normal to me, but seeing signs for Uptown, Coney Island and The Bronx was surreal. New York was as I expected it to be: the sights—steam rising from underground; the sounds—taxi horns constantly wrestling with each; and even the smells—fast food and roasted chestnut aromas sizzled in the air.

Grand Central Station was grander than the name suggested; it looked more like a gallery than a train station. Rectangular pillars rose from the ground reaching up high to support a zodiac mural ceiling. Light shone through its gigantic windows, lighting up the concourse like stage spotlights. We stopped for a hot lunch in the huge food court on the lower level before heading off again for more sightseeing. We walked south along Madison Avenue as far as Thirty-Fourth Street and crossed over a block to find the Empire State Building on Fifth Avenue. From there, we continued south until we reached the Flat Iron Building before jumping back on the subway to return to the hotel.

We had an hour to relax at the hotel before we had to get ready to go back out. Harry had bought tickets to watch a basketball match at Madison Square Gardens, something he had always wanted to experience but had never found the time to do. I knew nothing about the game, but I was more than happy to go along for him even though jetlag was starting to settle in. I fell asleep on Harry's shoulder during the shouting, cheering and music, and when the match finished, he had to shake me to wake me.

We were up and out early again Sunday morning. We walked along the Highline, an elevated disused railway line between Eleventh and Thirty-Fourth Street, where a public garden weaved its way amongst buildings and showcased pieces of art dotted along the route. Most of the plants remained buried under snow. After the Highline, we made our way north towards Central Park. It was slightly warmer than the previous day, but we still needed to wrap up. Most of the snow had melted on the streets, but Central Park was still covered. The temperature plummeted as we made our way deeper into the park. Harry bought some hot sugar-coated peanuts to help warm us up, but we didn't venture too far because it was too cold there.

The sun came out as soon as we left Central Park. It was surprisingly warm. I removed my hat and gloves and wished I had brought my sunglasses. Sunlight reflected off skyscraper glass windows and shone up from puddles on the ground as melted snow, and ice cascaded down from the same buildings. We had planned to have lunch at the Rockefeller Centre overlooking the famous ice rink, but Harry decided we should go to a rooftop bar on Fifth Avenue to make the most of the sunshine. With amazing views towards the Statue of Liberty and the Empire State Building within touching distance, we stayed for a few drinks until the sun dropped lower in the sky, transforming it from blue to bright-orange, lightening to a soft-pink before turning grey as it disappeared behind skyscrapers. We wanted to stay longer; we were warm enough with the complimentary red blankets, but Harry had an early meeting in the morning, so we headed back to the hotel for an early night.

The hotel phone startled me in the morning. It was still dark, but a trickle of light from underneath the bathroom door indicated Harry was already in the shower. The phone continued ringing. Harry wouldn't be able to hear it, and by the time I got out of bed to walk over to the bathroom to let him know it was ringing, it probably would have stopped. I rolled over to his side of the bed and answered it.

'Hello?' I managed to say, clearing my throat.

'I'm so sorry to disturb you,' a female's voice replied. 'I think I have the wrong room. The receptionist was supposed to put me through to the penthouse.'

I rubbed my eyes. 'This is the penthouse.'

'Where is Mr Hartington? And who are you?' Her English accent sounded sharper with each word.

I had to think for a moment, who was I to him? 'Erm, his girlfriend.' I quickly concluded that we must be official because he had invited me to New York to see him.

'How can you be, you stupid girl?' she snapped, 'I'm his girlfriend!'

My mind whirled, struggling to work out what was going on.

Her tone changed. She sounded unsettlingly composed. 'Tell him Sophie Chawley wants to speak to him. Now!'

I put the call on hold and stared at the phone for answers, but nothing came, only the slow dread of realising what was happening. I slid out of bed, threw on yesterday's clothes and coat, and grabbed my toiletry bag and handbag before walking over to the bathroom door. I hesitated before knocking.

'You don't need to knock,' Harry shouted from the shower. He greeted me with the most adorable smile. It melted me and winded me all at the same time. My throat tightened. His smile quickly vanished, 'What's wrong?'

'There's a phone call for you.'

He stopped washing his hair and stood frozen as though the water had turned him to ice. Shampoo suds slid down his wet body. His reaction confirmed Sophie Chawley was telling the truth.

I shook my head from side to side. 'No, not again,' I wailed and ran out.

There wasn't time to wait for the lift. I needed to get out of there fast. I pushed through the fire door and started running down six flights of spiralling stairs. I started to feel dizzy and sick. As I neared the bottom, I heard my name. I stopped and looked up. Harry was leaning over the bannister, his hair dripping wet. A droplet landed next to my feet. We stared at each other for a moment, but before he could say anything, I continued running and barged into the hotel lobby.

Tears filled my eyes, so I ran outside before a sob left my body. I was breathless from running down the stairs, and with the emotions and tears, I started to hyperventilate. Each time I tried to breathe in, a high-pitched gasp stung my throat. I crossed over the road towards the Hudson River, walking slowly and taking calmer, smaller breaths. As my heart rate slowed, my throat relaxed, and my breathing began to stabilise.

My mobile rang, it was Harry. I didn't answer it. I needed to get away from the hotel. I walked towards Chambers Street to flag down a yellow cab.

'Where to?' the driver asked.

'Anywhere.'

CHAPTER 23

Now

The taxi journey lasted long enough to absorb me into Lower Manhattan so that Harry wouldn't find me. The driver crisscrossed his way along two-way roads and up and down one-way streets until I asked him to stop alongside an open space. He told me we were at Washington Square Park, but that meant nothing to me. I thought I knew a lot of places before my visit, but now that I was here, NYC made me realise that I didn't know as much as I thought. A tree-lined pathway led to a circular fountain and I stood on the edge and closed my eyes, listening to the water explode into the air and pitter-patter as it fell back to where it started from. The sun warmed the side of my face as it rose in the east, and a cold and gentle breeze blew soft water droplets onto it.

A brief moment of peace shielded my thoughts and

emotions from the mayhem of what had just happened. And then my phone screamed. Once it stopped ringing, I retrieved it from my bag. There were four missed calls and three voice messages. I dropped the phone back into the bag, and I closed my eyes again, allowing the soft droplets from the fountain to dilute my salty tears. I stayed like that until I was ready to listen to Harry's messages.

'Alice, please call me back,' said the first message. His voice sounded familiar, and that's what hurt. He wasn't my Harry anymore. I hit the pause button, cradled my arms around my waist, and rocked back and forth. As tears fell faster from my face, mucus dripped down my throat like glue, making me retch. I had to wait for the tears to stop before I could listen to the second message. 'Alice, I'm really worried about you. Please, call me back.'

Hearing Harry's voice made me want to jump in a taxi and rush back to the hotel and hug him and for him to tell me it was all a misunderstanding. But it wasn't. The third and final message confirmed that. 'I wanted to tell you about my situation.' He let out a long sigh. 'But I haven't found the right time to tell you.' Adrenaline started pumping around my body, and I shook as though I was going to freeze to death. 'Sophie is my girlfriend, but after five years together, we're more like brother and sister. The relationship has been over for a while, but it's just, well, neither of us wants to be the person that finally ends it.'

My head buzzed like a cloud of gnats on a humid summer's evening. What was I going to do? Where could I go? The surrounding buildings looked like they were sporadically pushing up from the ground like a booby-trapped fortress. I needed space. I needed a friendly face. Brandon. Staten Island. It was a long shot, but it was the only thing I could come up with.

I didn't want to use my mobile too much as the battery was only fifty per cent. I did manage to remember my charger in the mayhem, but I needed to find somewhere to use it. Plus, I didn't want to see Harry's name flash up on the screen. I used logic instead. The Empire State Building was visible from the park through the archway up Fifth Avenue, so that was north. Battery Park was at the southern tip, so I turned around and walked in the opposite direction.

Tourists swamped the upper deck of the Staten Island Ferry. It looked more like a yellow cruise liner due to its size. Their accents and languages blurred into one as Lower Manhattan got smaller and smaller. Seeing the city at a distance felt like an out-of-body experience. It still didn't seem real that this was New York City. It didn't seem real that Harry had another girlfriend. Up until this morning, I had been skipping along in life—in London and on the streets of New York. But suddenly, somebody pushed open a revolving door which sucked me, spun me around like a cartoon character and spat me out, lying flat on my back on the sidewalk.

As the tourists shuffled into positions, taking photos and selfies, I stood amongst them motionless and in tears again. Why didn't anyone choose me? Why couldn't my relationships be normal like everyone else? Was I cursed when it came to romance? What was I doing wrong?

The boat sailed closely past the Statue of Liberty but not close enough to take in her full beauty. She stood tall and proud with one arm raised in the air, like a suffragette. I stopped crying and reminded myself that I had gotten through much worse. No more tears. I had wasted too many on unrequited love. But it still hurt.

The ferry was returning to Manhattan from Staten Island half an hour after docking, but they ran frequently enough so I could return whenever I was ready. A map of the island showed a public swimming pool nearby. I needed a shower. I needed to clean my teeth. A shop in the terminal sold toothbrushes and toothpaste—presumably for commuters running late on their journey over to Manhattan and not for a broken tourist.

I paid for a swim solely to use the showers and used their liquid soap to clean my hair and body. After washing, I stayed in the shower, taking comfort from the heat. I didn't want to feel unwanted again or lonely and not to feel the warmth of skin on my skin. They didn't have complimentary towels, so I dried off using my t-shirt and blew a hairdryer up my jumper and down my jeans to help me dry off. I cleaned my teeth and applied some light makeup. Showers were magical. They could wash away heartbreak, if only temporarily.

I wandered around, unsure of where to go. Staten Island was a lot bigger than I assumed, which meant there was little chance of bumping into Brandon. I came across a row of shops on Victory Boulevard. It looked like a wild-west movie set with wooden three-storey buildings draped with canopies, but instead of a sheriff's office, general store or saloon bar, there was a laundrette, nail bar and pizza restaurant. The road forked, and I headed right towards a residential area. A chain link fence surrounded a play area—it was the Hollywood-style fence where baddies scramble over the top to escape from cops but where they always got caught. That wasn't going to be me. Wooden, clapboard houses painted in creams, greens and blues lined the avenue with the occasional taller red-brick building with external horizontal fire escapes mixed in between.

The vibe of the neighbourhood changed further along the avenue where wooden exteriors looked tired and in need of a fresh coat of paint, wooden fences with holes, others were covered in graffiti. Litter was tangled in bushes, grass verges were overgrown, and a mattress had been abandoned in a parking space. I quickened my pace.

The esplanade at the end of the avenue was a welcome sight. My phone remained in my bag, so I used logic again and turned right to head back to where the ferry terminal probably was. I wasn't ready to go back. I didn't know what to do. Park benches were dotted along a promenade. There was no rush to return to Manhattan, so I sat down in the winter sun.

My feet hurt, and my stomach rumbled with hunger. The last time I ate was a light snack back at the hotel the night before. Manhattan was visible in the distance across the water. It reminded me of Harry, so I closed my eyes and focused my mind on the warmth of the sun on my face. But a cool breeze soon softened the sun's strength, and as it picked up, it pulled low dark clouds from Manhattan towards Staten Island. Within seconds, Manhattan was no longer visible. Like an artist cleaning his paint-soaked paintbrushes into a clear pot of water, it disappeared.

A fat, cold raindrop slapped me on my cheek, and then another on my forehead, and another, until rain fell so hard it bounced off the ground. I stood up and ran. Headlights from passing cars on the parallel road struggled to shine through the darkness. The ferry terminal was still out of sight. A glowing light from a sports bar tempted me out of the rain. I walked straight to the restrooms to dry off, and for the second time that day, I dried off by using hot air, this time from a hand dryer.

The aroma of food tempted me to stay. My stomach rumbled in discomfort. I needed to eat and warm up. Sports memorabilia filled the walls: jerseys, baseballs, American football helmets, and signed photos. An enormous television dominated the wall behind the bar, showing match highlights. Most of the tables were busy, but there were plenty of empty bar stools. I climbed onto one and ordered a glass of white wine, some tap water, a Margarita pizza and chips. The barman handed me a bag of crisps, so I placed a second order, and this time, I asked for fries.

I devoured the crisps and then the first three slices of pizza, but my appetite disappeared when I asked the barman if I could charge my phone. More messages and missed calls from Harry were on display. I gulped down a large mouthful of wine and emptied the glass. The alcohol went to my head, so I thought it would be sensible to force down the final slice of pizza and eat some of the fries. It was still raining. My feet and shoes were wet, but my cheeks glowed from the alcohol as it pulsed through my bloodstream. I ordered a white wine spritzer.

The barman poured the wine and hovered with the tap in hand. 'Soda water, or Sprite?

'Lemonade, please,' I said.

'Sprite, you mean,' he said with a serious expression.

'Yes, sorry, Sprite.'

'Hey! UK!' a guy said as he approached the bar. 'You wannanother after that one?' He pointed at my drink.

'No, I'm fine, thanks. I'm leaving after this one.'

Another guy approached the bar. 'Hey, sorry about him.' My eyes fixed on the stranger. He smiled and my stomach flipped. He nudged the first guy. 'I hope my friend isn't bothering you?' He smiled again.

My eyes stayed on him. His navy-blue sweatshirt complimented his light-brown skin, and his golden eyes sparkled. He could have been a model and quite possibly one of the most handsome men I had ever seen, ever.

'Oh, no, he's fine,' I smiled.

He held out his hand to shake mine. 'I'm Tyler, by the way.'

'I'm Alice.'

'Hey, what about me?' his friend said and nudged Tyler.

'This is Joey,' Tyler said.

Joey shook my hand. With his smile and his blonde hair, he could have been a model too, but his overly confident demeanour made him less attractive.

'So, you're from England?' Tyler asked.

'I am.'

He gestured to a bar stool. 'Would you mind?' I shook my head. Joey bought a round of drinks, handed Tyler's to him and then re-joined a handful of guys at a nearby dining table. 'So what brings you to Staten Island?'

I cleared my throat. 'I'm visiting a friend, and they're here for work. I wanted to see the Statue of Liberty and thought I'd do it for free.'

'How come you didn't head straight back to Manhattan?'

'I was going to but then decided to go for a quick wander before heading back, but then it started raining, and I was hungry…' I didn't know what else to say, so I gulped my drink.

'So, *they're* at work at the moment?'

'Who?'

'Your friend?'

'Oh, yes. I'm having to entertain myself during the day.'

He looked at me. 'I see.'

'How about you? Do you live here?'

'I do, but I work Midtown.'

Tyler was a firefighter, born and raised on Staten Island. He was thirty-four. As soon as he was old enough, he joined the fire service. It was what he had always wanted to do. He and a few of his colleagues had recently finished their shift and stopped off for some birthday drinks and to watch some March Madness basketball matches on their way home.

'Is it obvious?' I asked.

'What's that?' Tyler looked at me.

'That I'm from the U.K.' He laughed. 'What's so funny?' I asked.

'We overheard your accent when you were talking to the barman: the chips and lemonade gave it away.' He laughed again.

'Good, I'm glad I don't stand out.'

'But you do, in a good way.' He winked. 'Are you sure you don't want another drink?'

It was still raining. 'Go on then, I'll have a *lemonade*, please.'

'You mean Sprite?' He nudged me.

'No, I mean lemonade.' I nudged him back.

Tyler invited me to join him and his friends at their table to watch the rest of the basketball highlights. I was jetlagged at the Madison Square Garden game, so I didn't pick up anything about the sport. Tyler and his friends explained the rules, tactics, and terminology.

By the time the highlights had finished, all of Tyler's friends had left.

'What time is it?'

He looked at his watch. 'What time do you think it is?'

'Half past five?'

He laughed. 'You sound so English.'

I laughed. 'How?'

'I would say five-thirty.'

'Well then, Tyler, is it five-thirty?'

'Almost.'

We continued our playful debate on British English and American English: pavement and sidewalk, football and soccer, jumper and sweater.

'Are you hungry?' he asked.

'No, I had a margarita pizza when I first arrived here.'

'I hope you asked for extra oh-reg-an-oh?' he whispered in my ear. 'Their pizzas can be a little bland at times.'

'What's oh-reg-an-oh?'

'The herb that comes with a margarita pizza.'

'Oh, you mean, ori-gar-no.'

'You're making that up,' Tyler said.

'No, I'm not. You're making it up,' I said, and we both laughed.

At seven o'clock, the barman turned down the volume on the television, dimmed the lights and switched on some music.

The bar gradually got busier as more commuters popped in for drinks on their way home. Tyler ordered a range of bar snacks, potato chips, nuts and a bowl of what looked like oversized sweetcorn—everything in New York was bigger. Before I could ask what they all were, he placed the tray of goodies on the table and went to the restroom.

I retrieved my fully charged phone from behind the bar. There were more missed calls, voice messages and text messages from Harry. I couldn't listen to or read the messages, so I created a new message telling him that I had checked into a hotel for the night and that I would see him the following day before I left for the airport. I switched off my phone to avoid Harry's response. I snacked on some crisps before trying the large-looking sweetcorn. It didn't taste like sweetcorn; it was buttery with a firmer chickpea-like texture. Tyler started laughing when he returned to the table.

'What now?' I laughed.

'You're not supposed to eat Lupini like that,' he said.

'What's Lupini?'

'Lupini is Lupini,' he said, pointing at what I thought was sweetcorn. 'You're supposed to pop the bean out of the skin before eating it.' He smiled.

'Oh, will I be okay?'

He laughed. 'You'll be fine.'

After Tyler regained his breath from laughing, his expression altered. 'Look, there's something I gotta tell you.'

'There's something I should tell you, too.'

'I've kinda got a girlfriend, but she's away at the moment,' Tyler said.

'I've kind of got a boyfriend in New York.'

'Kinda?' He looked at me.

'It's a long story, and I don't want to go into details,' I said. 'In fact,' I picked up my glass, 'I don't want to talk about it at all.' I raised my glass. 'Here's to new beginnings and experiences.' I held his gaze as we sipped our drinks. As soon as we finished our drinks, he slapped some dollar bills on the table, and we left the bar arm in arm.

We kissed in the back of the taxi and outside the front door of his home. We stumbled in as he opened it. We laughed again. He switched on a lamp in the hallway, and next to it was a photo of him and his girlfriend laughing. They were eating candy floss, or rather, cotton candy. He pulled me in for another kiss, but I pulled away. Vera and my universal sign were all I could think about. Going home with someone in a relationship is not me; it's the hurt version of me—the rejected and lonely me. But me today also didn't want to be alone. I wanted to feel wanted. I stayed with Tyler in his bed, and we kissed a lot, but I couldn't take it any further. He understood. He didn't get angry or try to convince me otherwise. Thank goodness I found him today.

Tyler woke me the following morning with a delicate kiss on my nose. He started laughing, teasing me about my English accent again.

'Do you want your egg over easy or sunny side up?' he asked as he climbed out of bed.

'Fried?' I said.

He laughed again. 'Do you like your egg cooked well done?'

'Yes.'

'Okay, then, you'll have it over easy.'

I felt guilty for Harry as I ate my well-cooked egg. Despite what he had done to me, allowing me to become the other woman. I didn't feel so good about staying at Tyler's. Harry sounded genuinely sorry. His relationship probably was over with Sophie—I knew how that felt with Maxwell. But he lied. Even Tyler was honest about his situation even though he would never see me again, and yet Harry implied that this was something special between us. How could that be if he wasn't fully committed to me?

After breakfast, Tyler dropped me off at the ferry terminal. It was a strange farewell. It was sad but also happy. I wasn't a fan of goodbyes; I'd had too many sad ones, but Tyler left me with a feeling of hope. For once, a goodbye was going to leave me feeling okay.

After showering and packing back at the hotel, I wrote Harry a note before dropping my suitcase with the concierge. There were a few hours left to explore the city before having to leave for the airport, so I hailed a cab to the Empire State Building. To the south, the Statue of Liberty was visible from the viewing platform, as was Staten Island, and below was the rooftop bar where Harry and I drank cocktails whilst watching the sunset. On the streets below, yellow cabs buzzed like a swarm of busy bees. All the snow had melted. In the east, planes were taking off from JFK Airport, transporting people all around the world. I was ready to be transported home to London, even if that meant travelling in economy and alone.

CHAPTER 24

Now

A month had passed since New York, and Harry and I still hadn't seen each other, not since the morning of the phone call. The note I left him said everything I needed to say; there was no point in him trying to get me to accept his apology and that if he respected me, he would not contact me. Work-related contact only. We were over before we began. What we had wasn't real, and that's what I reminded myself of each time I felt upset. Plenty of work-related emails passed between us about the dog show, but that was it. Most of my emails received out-of-office responses, and I tried hard not to wonder where he was or, more painfully, who he was with.

As well as work, my social life was busier as I continued exploring more and more of London—that left little time to ponder over Harry outside of work. My relationship status may have returned to being single, but I was okay with that. I was alone, but I wasn't lonely, and that felt good. My relationship with Harry had ended and my life moved on. I felt proud of myself.

May Day Bank Holiday crept up, and I suddenly felt nervous about the chance of bumping into Harry at the dog show. He was tasked with handing out the awards for the dog with the waggiest tail, the brightest eyes, and for the dog that most looked like its owner. The complaining chamber clerk from my first day volunteered to coordinate the awards, so apart from setting up in the morning and helping to clear up at the end, there was a good chance I would be able to avoid Harry.

The rumble of the Tube vibrated underneath the lawn—travelling to or from Temple Tube Station—as I stepped into the garden early in the morning. I wished there was some way the grass would open up and allow the Tube to take me away from here. I accepted the situation with Harry, but it didn't mean I felt comfortable seeing him at work. Volunteers and colleagues were due to arrive at half past seven to help hang bunting on the railings around the garden, to register and direct exhibitors to their pitches and to place hidden clues for a treasure hunt. I arrived earlier to get a head start.

'Alice,' one of the volunteers called out once preparations were in full swing, 'I've put most of the clues out, but I'm desperate for the toilet. Could you put these two in the Peony

Garden?' Without a response, she handed over the clues and dashed off.

Bunting glittered in the sun as a warm spring breeze tickled the pastel triangles that hugged the peony garden. Unlike my first visit, the flowerbeds were full like a white carpet dashed with shades of bubble gum pink and raspberry ripple. Protruding high above the peonies was Harry's tower, and heat from the sun reflected off of it, making it feel even hotter than it already was. The wisteria on the wall to the secret passageway had blossomed and hung like bunches of lilac grapes. The secret entrance was disguised even more than before.

A wren perched on a wisteria branch and sang for a mate. When it flew away in the direction of Harry's window, it took all of my willpower not to look up. Bees buzzed from peony to peony, collecting as much pollen as they could. One of them had so much stuck to its legs that it looked like it was wearing yellow Tudor shorts and looked too heavy to fly. The scent of the flowers mixed in the air with freshly cut grass and as the warm breeze stroked my skin, I listened to the hypnotising hum of the bees at work. It wasn't so bad working at the weekend.

I placed the final clue amongst the peonies and accidentally disturbed a bee. It hovered at my eye level and then buzzed around me like the bee I saved with Mr Wigglesworth. I spun around to watch it fly higher and higher until it was too small to see—and that's when I noticed Harry looking down at me from his window. I walked away.

'Alice?' someone asked.

'Yes.' I looked up from the registration desk.

'I'm Mindy from Capital Canines.'

'Hi Mindy, it's so nice to put a face to a name.'

'Thanks for being patient with me. I'm not normally disorganised. My dog walking and grooming business has suddenly gone crazy. It's growing at a pace I can't keep up with.'

I smiled. 'That sounds like a good problem to have. You're over there, pitch number sixteen.'

The day went as planned. The weather stayed warm and sunny, and I managed to avoid bumping into Harry. We caught each other looking from a distance a couple of times, but I pretended not to see him. I missed him more than I realised, but I kept reminding myself he wasn't the person he made out he was. Who I thought he was.

Pollen floated in the fading sunlight like fairy dust sprinkling its magic as the event came to a close.

'You're a natural,' Mindy said.

I was standing on a chair, trying to reach the bunting to pull it off the railings. 'You made me jump,' I said.

'I'm sorry,' Mindy said. 'Are you okay?'

I stepped down from the chair with a trail of bunting hanging from my hand. 'Yes, I'm fine. I was in a daydream.'

'I said you're a natural. I've been watching you with the dogs today. With your organisational skills too, I could do with someone like you.'

'Thanks, I've forgotten how much I enjoy working with animals,' I said as Mindy's black labrador leaned against my legs.

'Have you worked with animals before?' Mindy asked.

'Yes, but it was a long time ago.'

'Well, do you want to change that?'

'Are you offering me a job?'

'I am. Initially, I can offer you a contract until the end of summer, possibly September, but if things continue as they are, then there is a high chance that it could be made into a permanent role.'

Mindy needed support with enquiries, ordering supplies, organising the staff rota, dog walking and managing the diary for the dog grooming service. It sounded ideal. Also, if it meant getting away from moaning chamber clerks and Harry and spending more time around dogs, there was nothing to consider. I accepted. Mindy wanted me to start as soon as possible, and because the dog show was a success, I was able to negotiate my two-week notice period to just one. It felt good to be excited about a job.

My boss asked me to keep quiet about leaving, and I was happy to do so. My colleagues remained colleagues, not friends. On Friday, my last morning, I opened up a new email, but I sat there for twenty minutes before pressing a key. I didn't know what to say to Harry. Eventually, I just typed 'goodbye' and pressed send—to my relief, another out-of-office message replied to my email. Relief washed over me that I could relax for the remainder of the day, knowing I wouldn't bump into him possibly ever again. I was surprised by a sense of sadness, knowing that this was the real goodbye.

It was a hot day, and after my normal routine of buying lunch from Fleet Street, I convinced my boss to give me the key to the garden for one last visit. As Harry was out on business, I decided to sit in the Peony Garden for the remainder of my break.

The naked, bronze sundial from winter was now clothed in roses and lavender and leaves from a sprouting tree. I walked along the circular path, past the secret entrance and towards the bench on the far side of the sundial. As the curve of the path unveiled the bench, it also revealed somebody was already sitting on it. Harry. He stood up when he saw me and stared. I stopped walking and stared back at him. My breathing stopped.

'I thought you were away on business?' I managed to say.

'I was. I've just returned.' He was still staring.

'I've sent you an email.'

'I know, I've read it. You're leaving?' He walked towards me and placed his hands on the tops of my arms. 'I'm so sorry for keeping the truth from you.'

I looked at him and felt sorry for him because I knew he meant that. I could feel it. 'I know you are.'

His head lowered, but his eyes remained fixed on mine. 'Does this mean you're willing to give me a second chance? Sophie and I have separated.'

I shook my head. 'No, Harry, there isn't a second chance.

I'm tired of lies and people making decisions about me and my life. That's not the type of relationship I can be in anymore.'

Harry's hold tightened. 'But why did you send me an email if you didn't want me to win you back?'

'I sent it because it was the right thing to do. I couldn't disappear without saying goodbye. I thought it was fair for you to know I wasn't here anymore.'

He sighed and released his hold. 'Okay.'

'I want to spend my final lunch hour here in the Peony Garden,' I said. Harry went to sit back down. 'On my own.'

He stood back up and walked away. 'Goodbye, Alice.'

At the end of the day, I washed up my cup, switched off my computer, and wished everyone a lovely weekend. Instead of having a leaving party, I hopped on the bus and met Chloe in Peckham Rye for celebratory drinks. We met at the top of a multi-storey car park at a summer pop-up cocktail bar with views that stretched from east to west London. The sun reflected off the glass buildings of Canary Wharf, and the distinctive curves of the Gherkin and the dome roof of St Paul's stood prominent in the city skyline. Planes flew over as they made their descent into Heathrow Airport. They were so low that if I stood on my tiptoes and stretched my arm as high as possible, I was almost able to stroke their bellies.

Chloe returned with another round of cocktails, 'Here's to your new job,' she raised her glass, 'and for being a fabulous housemate.'

'Cheers and thank you for being a fabulous housemate too.'

'Friends for life,' she added.

I smiled. 'Yes, friends for life.'

Daisy arrived at Paddington Station the following morning. I had a mild hangover and hoped Daisy would be okay to make her way from Paddington to the flat—she was more equipped to get around London on her own after her European travels, but she insisted she needed me to meet her. We screamed and hugged, and hugged and screamed on the platform.

From Paddington, we jumped on the Tube and made our way to Peckham Rye.

'Wait for me,' Daisy shouted as we left Peckham Rye Station. 'I can't keep up with you.'

'Sorry,' I stopped and waited for her to catch up. 'Everyone walks fast here. I'm used to this speed now.' We crossed the main road, and as we approached the bus stop, the number twelve pulled up. 'Perfect timing.'

'How do you know that's our bus?' Daisy asked. I laughed.

There was a large crowd of people waiting to get on the bus, and most of them surged forward when the driver opened the door.

'Come on,' I said to Daisy. I held onto her hand.

Daisy held my hand tight. 'Don't people queue for buses in London?'

'Kind of.' We shuffled nearer to the door.

We dropped Daisy's holdall off at the flat before walking to Lordship Lane to show her around my neighbourhood. We soon worked up an appetite, so I took her to The Green Parrot for lunch.

'Excuse me,' I said to the manager as he passed by. 'I've got a complaint to make.' We had been sat down for less than five minutes and were still perusing the menu. Daisy looked at me. The manager looked at me. 'It's to do with your halloumi.'

He laughed. 'Oh yes,' he said, 'halloumi on the house coming up.'

'Do you know him?' Daisy whispered.

'Not really.' I told her what happened with cheesegate.

'I can't believe he remembered you. I thought London was way too big and busy for that.'

'It's not as big as it first seems.'

The manager returned with the free halloumi. 'No free shots today?' I said.

'Don't push it,' the manager laughed and left us to it.

'So, what are your housemates like?' Daisy asked as we waited for our main meal to arrive. 'Are they around this weekend?'

'Yes, they're both around. They might even come out with us tonight.'

'What are their names again?'

'Chloe and Beth. Chloe's the designer, and Beth's the Australian; they're both lovely.'

'I'm pleased you've found somewhere lovely to live and with nice people too,' Daisy said.

'Don't worry,' I nudged her, 'they haven't replaced you.'

Daisy took a sip of her wine. 'When are you going to come and visit us back in Devon?'

I choked on my wine. 'Not yet! I've only just arrived here.'

'It's almost five months.'

I changed the subject.

That evening, we caught the bus to Shoreditch and planned to meet Chloe and Beth later on. Daisy and I started at a sports bar filled with pool tables, arcade machines, table football and an old-school air hockey table. We managed to get on the last free pool table, and whilst Daisy set it up, I went to the bar to buy the first round of drinks. When I returned to the pool table, two guys were chatting with her.

'Come on, one game,' one of them said to Daisy as I handed a drink to her. 'Boys against girls?'

'Thanks for the offer,' I said, 'but we haven't seen each other in ages, and we've got lots to catch up on.'

'Come on, one game,' the taller one repeated himself. 'Are you scared we'll beat you?' his mate said.

Daisy smiled at me, 'Okay, one game,' she said. My pool skills were passable, but Daisy played for a pub team whilst we were at university; one of her boyfriends introduced her to the sport.

The taller guy picked up a pool cue and chalked the end. 'Winner buys the drinks,' he said and blew the blue chalk residue.

Both of the guys were handsome, metrosexual-looking, and around the same age as us. They were friendly, perhaps cocky at times, but they seemed good sports. It was a close match, but we won, and without asking, the taller guy went to the bar and bought a round of drinks.

'Same rules again?' the other one asked before sipping on his fresh pint.

'No, thanks, we're going to leave after these drinks,' I said, 'but you're welcome to have the pool table.'

'So, you've got a free drink out of us, and now you're off,' the taller one said.

'But you…' Daisy said but stopped talking when I placed my arm across her.

'Here's twenty pounds to cover our half of the drinks,' I said and placed it on the pool table. 'You can keep the change.' We placed our half-drunk cocktail glasses on the pool table and left.

Chloe and Beth met us in a packed piano bar where two guys, wearing flat caps, provided the entertainment for an old-fashioned cockney knees-up. One was on the piano while the other was singing. Nearly everyone was singing along to songs like 'Any Old Iron' and 'My Old Man's a Dustman', and as the night progressed, more and more people got up to dance to livelier songs like 'Knees Up Mother Brown'. It felt as though we were in a musical or that we had been transported back in time. It was one of the best nights of my life. I looked at Daisy, Chloe and Beth and felt so much love.

The following morning, the four of us went for brunch at a local café. It smelled of coffee and fresh orange whilst chilled

Sunday music softly played from speakers.

Chloe started laughing.

'What are you laughing at?' Beth asked.

'Alice and that Swiss guy.' Chloe leaned forward and hugged her stomach.

'Don't,' I said and started laughing, and so did Daisy.

'What happened?' Beth asked and started laughing at us laughing.

Daisy just about managed to speak. 'It was typical Alice.'

'A handsome Swiss guy started talking to me at the bar last night. His English was really good, but because the music was so loud, he had to speak close in my ear,' I said.

'And?' Beth said.

'Chloe asked me if I wanted another drink, which I did, so I tried to finish off what was left in my glass so she could take the empty glass with her,' I managed to say before tears filled my eyes.

All four of us sat at the table laughing for ages—some of the other customers started laughing too, and some gave disapproving looks. Once we calmed down and caught our breath, I was able to continue telling the story.

'I took a sip through the straw. Well, I tried to, but I couldn't find it with my mouth, so I pulled the glass away to check where the straw was, but it wasn't in the glass. I looked on the floor, and it wasn't there either, and that's when I caught the end of it poking out of my face. It was sticking out of my nose.'

'It got stuck up your nose?' Beth asked.

A squeaky sound left my mouth. 'Yes!'

Beth looked in disbelief. 'What did you do?'

'She yanked it out of her nose and clung onto me.' Chloe said, struggling to breathe.

'She could hardly stand up from laughing.' Chloe wiped tears from her eyes.

'Where was I when this happened?' Beth asked.

'It happened just after you left,' I added.

We all burst into laughter again: Chloe held onto her stomach again, tears filled Daisy's eyes, Beth could hardly catch her breath, and I sat with my hands over my face.

'Did he see?' Beth said and roared with laughter again when I nodded.

'I think we scared him off with our laughter.'

After breakfast, Daisy and I collected her belongings from the flat and made our way back to Paddington. Daisy filled me in on people from school and university: A guy in our year at senior school had gone to prison for burglary; Jonny was getting married, and Tristan was his best man—we both agreed how sad it was that Tobias wouldn't be there. Catherine, who we both knew from primary school, now called herself Kitty since marrying a professional footballer, had just given birth to her fourth child.

'I bet she still looks immaculate.'

Daisy moved the conversation onto Harry and asked me to tell her everything about New York and the firefighter. She wanted to know if Harry had tried to make contact and if I missed him.

'Have you got a photo of him? What's his full name? I'll see if I can Facebook stalk him.'

I hesitated. 'Harry Hartington.'

'He asked for some planning permission a few years ago to add an extension to a property in Wandsworth,' Daisy said whilst staring at her phone.

'How do you know that?' I asked. 'You should have been a detective, not an accountant.'

'This type of stuff is all online,' Daisy said and shrugged her shoulders. 'Sophie looks stuck up, and you're much prettier than her.'

Daisy turned her phone to face me. A pretty woman with strawberry blonde hair and a friendly smile beamed from Daisy's phone. Harry was sat next to her with his arm around her shoulders. They looked happy.

'It's unfair to judge her,' I said. 'She's not the dishonest one. Yes, she was rude, but wouldn't you be if another girl answered your boyfriend's phone?'

Daisy didn't answer. She was too engrossed in the photo. 'This photo was taken late last year, so not long before you met,' she said, poking and prodding the screen. She laughed. 'Can you believe some of the comments on here: gorgeous couple, love you guys, stunning Soph, come and visit us again soon.'

'That's enough,' I said.

Daisy put her phone away. 'Sorry.'

'I'm proud of myself for walking away from something being so close to what I've wanted for so long. As much as Harry represents some of that, he only represents part of it, and I want all of it.'

Daisy hugged me. 'I'm so happy to see you've finally been able to let the past go.'

'Me too.'

We arrived at Paddington, and I waited behind the barriers and watched Daisy make her way along the long platform to board the train. She looked back three times and waved before reaching her carriage. As she stepped into the carriage, she waved a final time and blew a kiss before disappearing inside. She was gone. Suddenly, a pang of homesickness hit me.

CHAPTER 25

Now

I loved my new job. It was jam-packed with everything Mindy said it would be and more, and the best part about it was being around dogs. The majority of owners appreciated the work we did. Naturally, there was the occasional person who liked to complain, but generally, it was a pleasure—it didn't feel like work. The environment made me feel so much more like myself than I had in so long. It was nice working at Mindy's home, a beautiful, red-bricked terraced house on a quiet one-way street not far from Buckingham Palace. The commute to work was straightforward—a direct bus or train to Victoria. The early morning starts, occasional late finishes, and the occasional Saturday morning shift didn't seem a chore. Plus, many of the regular clients started to feel like friends.

One early morning, one of the dog walkers called in sick because her child was unwell. Mindy called me and asked if I minded starting work earlier to pick up two dogs on the way in. I didn't hesitate and jumped out of bed—another thing I loved about the job was the dress code: I could throw on a pair of jeans and a T-shirt, shove my hair up in a messy bun and be ready for work in minutes. Frankie, a wiry Bedlington terrier, and Beano, a medium-sized, mixed-breed dog, greeted me with excitement.

'They're happy to see you, Alice,' said the owner, Laura, as her dogs ran around us in circles.

'I'm happy to see them too.' I stroked Beano and Frankie nudged me for some attention too.

It was a short walk from Laura's home in Pimlico to Green Park. The dogs knew where they were going. Sunlight dappled through the trees, and the birdsong got louder the further we ventured into the natural space, replacing the noise from passing traffic on the outer edges of the park. Behind us stood Buckingham Palace, and to the right was St James's Palace. I had to pinch myself that I was being paid to do this.

As I threw balls for Frankie and Beano to fetch, I thought about my fast-approaching thirty-first birthday. So far, it seemed my thirties were going to be happier than my twenties. They were busier, too. The night before last, I went on a date with a guy called James, a city banker who I had bumped into several times around Victoria on our respective commutes. He surprised me with a picnic in Regent's Park whilst watching a

Pride and Prejudice play at the outdoor theatre. He was sweet and handsome too, but I wasn't looking for anything serious—I had only just started making myself happy.

He asked to see me again, and, at first, because I was tempted, I said yes, but on the Tube journey home, I was annoyed with myself for not being honest with him or myself. When I arrived home, I messaged him to thank him for a lovely evening, but I had to decline his kind offer to take me out for dinner. I explained why. He thanked me for my honesty. Last night, I signed up for an intensive ten-week dog grooming course starting in September. I messaged Mindy and asked if I could volunteer extra hours to gain more hands-on dog grooming experience. Tonight, I was meeting up with Nikki and Priya in Clapham for an outdoor cinema experience, and tomorrow night, I was meeting up with Teagan and some of her friends to watch live music straight after work.

'Have you heard of London burnout?' Mindy asked when I arrived at work after dropping off Frankie and Beano. 'In London, you work hard and play even harder, but you sometimes need a break from it.'

'I haven't heard of it,' I said, tickling the belly of a playful golden retriever that had just arrived.

'It happened to me when I first arrived here, many moons ago, and still does now and then. Lots of my friends have experienced it too. Make sure you take some time out from the city.'

'I did. I went to New York a few months back. This is the

best that I have felt in a long time. Years.'

'That's the risk; there is so much to do and see, and when you're floating along in the city's energy, it's easy to overlook that you've had no downtime. It's healthy to have a proper break from London life. Perhaps you should take a visit back to Devon in the summer?'

It was two weeks short of six months since I moved to London, and pangs of home surfaced when Daisy left, but it wasn't enough to tempt me to visit. Mum and Dad were planning a visit soon enough, so there was no urgency for me to return. But Mindy was right. I couldn't stay away forever.

I developed a mild headache in the afternoon before meeting up with Teagan. I didn't bother taking any tablets because it was probably hunger or dehydration or both, so I took an early lunch break, and that helped me feel a bit better. I volunteered to work later as it was convenient to meet Teagan and her friends straight from work at the art centre near Buckingham Palace. I grabbed a panini from a food stall in Victoria Station en route to meet them. The sun still had a lot of strength, and the heat bounced off concrete and glass buildings like an alien infrared ray trying to zap humans into dust.

The music was loud and flashing lights triggered the return of my headache. My eyes felt sensitive, and with each flash of light, my head pounded. I needed some fresh air. Outside, it was muggy, and the heaviness of the air indicated a storm was brewing. Dark clouds preyed above—my headache was getting worse. I texted Teagan to let her know that I had to go home.

The clouds released a tirade of rain just as I reached Victoria. My head was throbbing. I managed to avoid getting wet. I needed to be in bed. The departure board showed that all trains were delayed until further notice, and an announcement confirmed this was due to signalling problems from a lightning strike. I went back outside to catch a bus instead.

The bus stop was only a twenty-meter dash from the train station, but I got drenched. My umbrella did little to stop the rain from beating me. My feet were soaked in my open-toed sandals. Fortunately, waiting at the first stop of its route was the bus I needed. The doors were wide open, but inside, the bus was already overflowing with passengers. All of the seats were taken, and the remaining space was crammed with standing passengers. Two more people squeezed on after me before the driver closed the doors. We waited for a few more minutes for lift-off. Each second waiting for it to move seemed too long.

The bus was sticky and humid. A mix of wet clothes and body heat caused the windows to steam up. It was impossible to see out of any of them apart from the driver's window. A man standing nearby had a damp patch on the back of his white shirt; it was hard to tell if it was wet from the rain or sweat from the heat!

The bus made its way south of the River Thames and past the Oval Cricket Ground before an announcement rang out telling us that the bus was terminating at Country Grove, just short of the main interchange at Camberwell Green. I was halfway home. Groans and sighs filled the bus as it pulled into the stop. Instead of hesitating to step off the bus and into the rain, everyone charged off of the bus—we were London's buffaloes, desperate to get away from the cramped conditions and determined to get onto another bus to get out of the pouring rain. Another bus pulled up behind us, and a lot of the disembarked passengers managed to transfer over to it, but there wasn't room for everyone—including me. There were two choices: wait at the bus stop, which wasn't big enough to shelter all of the abandoned crowd and with no guarantee of getting on the next bus or walk half a mile to the Camberwell interchange, where there would be many buses arriving from lots of directions. I chose to walk.

Even though my feet were already soaked, they somehow got wetter as the rain continued falling. The worst part was the rainwater flicking in between my sandals and the underside of my feet and the soggy cold water seeping in between my toes. The only break from the wet was a brief moment underneath the railway bridge. A train passed overhead. They must have sorted out the signalling problem. The next train station wasn't too far away—if it was a dry and sunny day and I didn't have a throbbing headache and my shoes weren't soaked. The interchange was now in sight. The train rumbled overhead like a loud clap of roaring thunder, interspersed with flashes of light. It was so bright that, for a moment, it looked like daylight.

Car headlights whizzed past. There was no respite from the discomfort from my head to my toes. At the cross junction, the traffic lights changed from amber to red as I approached, forcing me and a small group of people to wait in the rain to cross. A long queue of traffic was waiting for its turn to go. The car in the front of the traffic queue looked familiar: it was Harry's car. As the light turned amber, it shone onto his car, and I could see him chatting with the passenger sitting next to him. A woman. It was too dark to tell if it was Sophie; I had only seen her image briefly on Daisy's phone or somebody new. I slid to the far side of the crowd to reduce the chances of him seeing me. The lights turned to green, and I watched them drive off in the warmth and comfort of his car. For the briefest moment, I wished it was me sitting next to him.

I closed my eyes and rubbed my hands over my face to ease the pain, which didn't help with anything. The lights changed from green back to amber, and instead of the last car slowing down, it sped up and whizzed through as the light turned red. It made a sharp left and sped through the large puddle that had gathered on the corner kerb. It felt as though someone had thrown a bucket of ice-cold water over me. It also splashed some of the others who were standing nearest to the corner. A few of us screamed as the car raced through the puddle. A few people swore, me included.

When I got home, I rushed through the front door, swallowed two painkillers, peeled off everything and climbed into bed, but I couldn't get comfortable. The discomfort made me restless. I switched on my meditation app to soothe my mind, but it was interrupted by the whooshing sound of an email entering my inbox. My focus easily disappeared from the meditation, and I picked up my phone to see who the email was from so late.

My heart raced. It was from Blake. I instantly fantasised that this was it, that we would be together again. For years, I had desperately waited to read an email with these words, an email where he admitted he made a mistake. I fantasised about an airport reunion, one of us waiting in the arrivals lounge and the other walking through the arrivals door. We would run up to each other and Blake would scoop me into his arms and kiss me.

It wasn't good for my headache, but I couldn't help but re-read his email.

Hey Miss Berry,

I hope things are good and that you and your parents are well.

It's been pretty cold here and I already can't wait for summer to arrive.

I saw on the news that the U.K. is having a hot spell… I bet it's still not as hot as we get here! Haha.

I've been thinking about you a lot lately and wondering how you're getting on. Knowing you, I'm sure you're doing well.

Look, I know it was my fault that things ended the way they did, and I never meant to hurt you. The summer we spent together was amazing, and I often think about that time in the car when we couldn't stop looking at and touching each other, not in a sexual way, but in a connected way.

Everyone I've met since you I've compared to you. I was the happiest I have ever been when I was with you, and I realise now that I was an idiot for throwing it away.

Work is making redundancies, which I volunteered for and I've been lucky enough to get accepted. I want to go travelling again, and I want you to come with me. I know it's a big ask, but I'd like us to pick up from where we left and try again.

I hope you're enjoying your Friday night and that I haven't disturbed you.

I hope to hear back from you soon.

Blake xx

Images of Blake in his olive-green jumper flashed in my mind. I loved that jumper on him; he was wearing it the time that we couldn't stop looking at and holding each other and when I knew that I loved him. I smiled. The connection between us at that moment was so strong. I started crying. The overpowering memories of our time together brought back the intense love and happiness I felt that summer. That was the last time I felt happy. His words made him real again. He was there. I was there. We were there together. It was real. My memories are his memories. Six years had passed, and, at times, I doubted myself that what I felt was real. Had I imagined it? Did I really feel the way I thought I did? If I did, and he felt the same, how was he able to call it off and walk away from what we had?

I wanted to reply straight away and say yes, but something stopped me. Perhaps it was my headache or maybe something else. I needed to sleep before giving him an answer. As soon as I woke in the morning, I read his email again. I had slept well and my headache had disappeared, but I was tired and full of a cold. I realised that last night, I had reverted to the broken version of me, but that wasn't who I was anymore. I had spent years glueing myself back together. *And travelling*? Where was his apology for the responsibility of the financial strain that was all my burden? If he was genuinely sorry and felt the way he was making out in his email, then he should be coming here instead of travelling and offering to pay me back at least half of my flight ticket. He has no idea how much he let me down because he never agreed to a phone call or hear my side of things. I started crying as I typed my response. It was emotional, but they were tears of relief. I finally had closure—not because he declared his feelings years on but because I finally saw that he wasn't as shiny as I had always believed. I kicked him off the pedestal.

Hi Blake,

All is good, thanks. Mum and Dad are too. I'm living in London and have made some amazing friends. The only downside to living here is that there aren't enough hours in the day to do everything!

I finally made it to New York, by the way. I went in March. They had snow and I saw lots of touristy spots and even watched a basketball match. I want to go in the summer next time.

Your email was a surprise, and it brought back so many lovely memories. It upset me too. Our time together was bittersweet: it was amazing to find such happiness even for a small amount of time, but it was cruel the way it ended so suddenly.

It gives me peace of mind that you have finally acknowledged your poor decision in calling off our plans prematurely and for not allowing me to decide whether I was happy or not to leave everything behind. I'll never have the chance to know if going to Australia to be with you was the right decision or not.

Looking back and holding onto the past is tiring, and I no longer have the energy or desire to do that. I am happy in London, and after all this time, I finally have some direction in my life. Please allow me to fully move on by not contacting me again.

I wish you all the best, and I hope you have fun on your travels. Our summer together will always have a special place in my heart, but it's time to let go.

Goodbye, Blake.

Tears fell from my eyes and onto the phone screen. I got up from my bed and went to the toilet to blow my nose and splash water over my face. When I returned to my bedroom, I opened the blinds and felt instantly lifted. It was a glorious sunny day, and I was going to spend it sunbathing and relaxing on the common across the road. I threw on some shorts and a

T-shirt and packed a bag with a blanket, book, sun lotion, croissant and apple. I made a lemon and ginger tea to take away and left the flat.

The drink was too hot to drink, so I removed the lid and swirled it around to cool down quicker. I lay on the blanket and stared at the yellow, brown and grey tea leaves as they swam within the teabag. They reminded me of grains of sand being mixed up by ocean waves on the shoreline. Perhaps Mindy was right. Some timeout from London may be a good thing. I picked up my phone and booked a return train journey to Devon in August. A long weekend before starting the intense dog grooming course in September was a sensible idea.

CHAPTER 26

Now

As the train pulled away from Waterloo, familiar landmarks passed by like food on a conveyor belt: the London Eye, Big Ben, the Houses of Parliament and Battersea Power Station. After Clapham Junction, the train sped up and everything turned into a blur. The train reached Woking half an hour after leaving Central London, and as the train left the station, it felt like an elastic band was attached to me and it started to pull and stretch the further the train travelled away from London and then it snapped. It retracted back to London and catapulted me to unfamiliar territory, the countryside.

Everywhere was green. Humans were replaced by cows, sheep, horses, and the occasional darting deer. Roads and traffic were outgrown by trees and fields, and the sky dominated the view instead of a swamp of concrete and glass, allowing more sunlight to brighten the earth. It felt like a different country.

The train arrived in Exeter three hours later, but it felt more like an overnight journey. It felt so different being back in Devon. The station was quiet compared to Victoria and Waterloo. There were more pigeons nestled in the rafters than people standing on the platform. The air was warm and fresh, lighter, even.

'Sorry, me lover,' an elderly lady said when her suitcase clipped my leg. I had forgotten that people acknowledged you outside of London.

'Alice!' Mum's voice shrieked from the far side of the ticket barrier. Mum and Dad were waving, and I rushed towards them. We embraced in a group hug before I passed through the ticket barrier properly.

'We've missed you,' Dad said.

'I've missed you, too.'

Dad had a brief meeting in the city, so Mum and I caught up over tea and cake before we all ventured back to Plymouth. Dad drove, and Mum allowed me to sit in the front of the car to allow him to hear my stories better. It felt strange being in their car. It was lower than I remembered—I was used to trains and buses. We stopped off at a supermarket on the outskirts of the city to pick up some bits for a barbecue, but the stench of manure in the car park put me off the idea of eating anything.

We split up inside: Dad was in charge of getting charcoal and alcohol, Mum picked up salad bits and veggie meat alternatives, and I was tasked with bread rolls, crisps and dips. It was a challenge deciding what crisps to get—salt and vinegar, cheese and onion, or something a bit spicier. I wondered which rolls Mum would prefer from the vast selection. I was used to buying for one. Somebody called my name, but I ignored it, it must be for another Alice. They called again, louder this time. I turned around and saw Tobias's mum walking towards me.

'Alice,' she called again.

'Mrs Greenwood,' I said.

'Oh, please, call me Sandra.' She hugged me. The hug lasted longer than the group hug at the train station. 'It's been so long.'

'I know.'

'What have you been up to?'

'I live in London now.'

'That sounds exciting. Did you meet someone from there?'

'No, I just decided that I wanted a change of scenery.'

'How long are you home for?'

'A long weekend. I go back on Monday.'

'It would be lovely to have a proper catch-up with you before you go back. Who knows when we'll bump into each other again. Please come round for Sunday tea if you're free. Richard would love to see you too.'

I agreed to go.

Mum and Dad were already at the checkout by the time I

found them. They were chatting with the checkout lady.

'Have you got anything planned for the bank holiday?' the checkout lady asked. 'The weather's supposed to be glorious.'

'Our daughter's home from London. We're having a barbecue this evening to celebrate,' Mum said.

'How lovely.' The woman smiled.

'Here she is now,' Dad said. The four of us continued with small talk until Dad paid. In London, checkout staff barely make eye contact, let alone strike up a conversation.

Daisy picked me up the following morning and drove us to the beach. As we got nearer, the scent of the salty sea air mixed with wildflowers and freshly cut grass drifted in through the windows like a natural unisex fragrance. It smelt familiar. I closed my eyes and breathed it in. The beach was already busy by the time we arrived mid-morning. A mixture of families, surfers and groups of friends covered the beach with towels, surfboards, pop-up tents and ball games. We managed to find a spot between two large families.

As soon as we laid our towels down, I undressed down to my bikini and immediately jogged towards the sea. Hot sand massaged the soles of my feet as the sun warmed my skin. Instead of diving straight in like I used to do, I stopped in the water at ankle height and watched as the sand glistened gold in the turquoise sea like a shimmering sand globe—and then I dived in. The water was invigoratingly cold, and my body tingled from head to toe. I took a deep breath as I surfaced and swam fast, like a sped-up Victorian black and white movie, to acclimatise to the Atlantic Ocean. Once my body temperature regulated, I turned onto my back and floated, allowing the sea to take the weight of my body and mind—rocking me to the rhythm of the tide.

Daisy called from the shoreline, snapping me out of my daydream. 'Do you want to go out into Plymouth tonight? One of the girls I work with has messaged to say there's a few of them going out.'

'Yes, sounds good,' I said and started swimming back to shore.

We stopped off at Daisy's on the way home to pick up her outfit and makeup and then popped into an off-licence to buy a bottle of wine to get ready with. My skin had a golden glow spending the day at the beach, and it was rejuvenating, washing away sand and salt from my hair and body. After drying off, I opened the blinds and window to allow steam to escape from the bathroom. The steam was replaced by evening bird song, lavender and more freshly cut grass. The sun had dipped in the sky and turned the colour of egg yolk. Its orange glow filled the bathroom. Nights out in London normally consisted of a quick touch-up of makeup and a spritz of perfume in the toilet before heading straight from work. It felt nice to experience the build-up to a night out with company: chatting in between blasts of the hairdryer, popping into the bathroom to brush our teeth, shouting over the music whilst sipping on wine and dancing as we did our makeup. The enjoyment flowed into the bars.

We went on a pub crawl, and it was strange recognising

faces in the bars and bumping into people we knew, which had never happened in London. Unfortunately, we bumped into Catherine Hurleston.

'Alice!' Catherine screamed with fake excitement when she saw me at the bar. 'How long has it been since we last saw each other?' She hugged me.

'Hi, Catherine,' I said and pulled away from her embrace, 'I don't know, but it has been a long time.' *Not long enough.*

'I'm called Kitty these days since I got married,' she said and held out her left hand to show off her rings. I was tempted to comment that it was normally only the surname that changed from marriage but I resisted biting.

'Daisy mentioned you've got children as well.'

'I do, four of them. But you know what these modern husbands are like,' she slapped my arm, 'they're willing to do their bit. All I had to do tonight was express my milk and he did the rest.' She sipped on her glass of Prosecco.

'That's great,' I said and disguised a yawn. I didn't want to be rude, but we weren't keen on each other at university, and we didn't have anything in common now.

'So, what have you been up to since you dropped out of uni?' She smirked.

'Not much, really.'

She flicked her long, blonde hair over her shoulder. 'We live in a huge house in Salcombe overlooking the estuary.'

'That sounds lovely,' I said and meant it.

She smiled. 'It is.' Her expression changed to a look of pity. 'I hear you're living in a flatshare in London?'

'Yes, I moved there earlier this year.'

'I see you haven't got a ring on your finger. Have you got a boyfriend or any children?'

I gulped my cocktail. 'No, and no.'

Catherine snorted. 'Come on, Alice, when are you going to catch up with the rest of us?' She snorted again and looked at me as though waiting for a funny punchline.

'You know us Londoners—we're too busy for that,' was all I could think to say. 'Well, I'm going to head off soon. I'm tired.'

'Tired?' she laughed. 'Until you have children, you don't know the meaning.'

How dare she be so opinionated about my life? I thought as I leaned against the cubicle door. She knows hardly anything of what I've been through, and, for all she knows, I may not be able to have children. I don't know if I can or can't; my life had never reached that milestone, but that wasn't the point. It was a bad idea to come back to Devon. I should've just visited Mum and Dad and Daisy and then snuck back to London without anyone else knowing.

'There you are,' Daisy said as she walked into the toilets. 'Come on, let's get you another drink.' She pulled my arm, and we returned to the bar.

Daisy and I went for a country walk the following morning. Strangers said good morning as they passed by, and when we stopped off for brunch at the village pub, other customers made small talk about the weather. On the walk back through the village, we passed a garden with clean washing blowing in the breeze; the scent of it danced along the street. There was a noise and a scent that indicated somebody was cutting their lawn, the smell of a roast dinner cooking drifted from a cottage kitchen, the musical tune of an ice cream van played out as children laughed in the park, bees hovered around the village flowers, the hum of tractors ploughing fields was in the distance, and neighbours chatted over garden fences making friendly small talk.

Mum lent me her car that afternoon to visit Tobias's parents; it was the first time I had driven in eight months, but it all came back quickly enough. With the music turned up loud, the windows down, and the sun shining in the clear sky as I wound my way along clear country lanes, I realised I missed driving. I switched off the music when I reached Tobias's road and came to a jolting stop on the gravelled driveway; my heart did the same.

His basketball hoop still hung above the garage door, his green curtains still hugged the windows in his bedroom, but the porch where we regularly kissed goodbye had been recently decorated. Fresh paint lingered in the air from the white walls; I couldn't remember what colour they used to be. The knocker on the front door sounded the same, and as Mrs Greenwood opened it, a familiar aroma of baking and pot-pourri stirred up the past.

I returned to an empty house a couple of hours later, Mum and Dad left a note saying they wouldn't be long. It felt strange, like the first night on my own in East Dulwich. I sat on the sofa but quickly moved to the garden for some fresh air and to contemplate the past and the future. Mr and Mrs Greenwood offered me the most unexpected opportunity. I needed to think. But I needed space, so I walked down to the river.

New houses were being built on the land where my dream home used to stand. Apart from that, the walk looked the same as it always did. Swans glided along the river's edge, and boats sailed in both directions. I walked along the river up to the point where it opened up towards the English Channel. A lone tree stump sat near the water's edge, offering a seat. It was getting dark, and the night sky started glowing. Stars were hardly noticeable in London; they were outshone by artificial light. There weren't any clouds, which allowed the stars to twinkle on the river, lighting it up like dancing fireflies. I stared into the water, looking for answers.

'Where have you been?' Mum asked when I returned home. 'Surely you haven't been round at the Greenwood's all this time?'

'I've been for a walk and lost track of time,' I said and kicked off my shoes. I started walking upstairs.

'I've been calling you,' Mum said.

'Sorry, my phone was on silent,' I said and took it from my pocket.

Mum stood at the bottom of the stairs. 'I don't mean to fuss, love, but I know it must have been emotional for you today.'

I stopped halfway up the stairs but didn't turn around. 'Sorry, I should have told you I was going for a walk. I'm not used to telling someone where I'm going anymore.'

'Is everything okay?'

'Yes, it was lovely seeing Tobias's mum and dad. They showed me family albums from when Tobias was a boy. We shared stories about him.'

Mum held onto the bannister and took one step up. 'So what's wrong, sweetheart?'

I turned around to face her. 'They've offered me their holiday cottage.'

'But you're going back to London tomorrow?'

I sat down on a step. 'To live in.' I told them about my job and course. I realised that I wanted to set up a dog walking and grooming company. They told me they could help—it's what Tobias would have wanted, they said. Their holiday cottage was handed down to them in the family so any income they received from it was a bonus. They didn't have any bookings from November, and the diary was clear so far for next year. They never advertised; it got booked by word of mouth. They said I would be doing them a favour by giving it life.'

'But you live in London now.'

I sighed. 'I know.'

Mum walked up the stairs and sat beside me. 'Please don't take this the wrong way,' Mum said and placed her hand on my knee, 'but please don't feel you have to take it because of Tobias.'

Feelings from the past were being disturbed. They had been buried deep for a long time and now it felt like they were being exhumed by a gravedigger. Dig. Dig. Dig.

'I know, Mum.' I stood up and walked up the rest of the stairs.

'What are you going to do?' Mum turned to look at me.

'I don't know; they said not to rush my decision.'

'But—'

'Leave it...please. I'm going to bed.' Mum went to speak, but she was interrupted by a text message on my phone. It was from Chloe. I walked into my room to read it.

Hey, hope you're having a nice time back home. What time are you back tomorrow? Fancy takeaway and movie? Missed you ☺ xx

CHAPTER 27

Now

Mindy arranged a little get-together to celebrate her business's fifth birthday. She invited employees, friends, family and some of her long-term clients like Laura, who came along with her husband, Alistair.

'Frankie and Beano were jealous when I told them I was going out with you tonight, Alice,' Laura joked as we waited to get served at the sleepy suburban Pimlico bar. One person was serving who was too busy chatting with the regulars rather than pouring drinks.

'I've missed them,' I said. 'I've just got back from a long weekend in Devon.'

'A romantic getaway with the boyfriend?'

I laughed. 'No, it's where I'm from. I went back to visit my parents.'

Laura looked at me for a moment as though she had asked me what two plus two was and I answered seven. 'What are you doing here?'

'I'm here for Mindy's party.'

Laura laughed. 'No, I mean, why are you in London? I love Devon, and ever since our best man, Smithy, moved there, I've been begging Alistair to move there too.'

I changed the subject back to Frankie and Beano.

After the gathering came to a natural end, a few of us decided to go on for more drinks, but Laura and Alistair couldn't come because they needed to get back for the dogs.

'You should come round for dinner one night. The dogs would love that,' Laura said as she was leaving. 'Take my number and call me so I've got yours, and then we'll get a date in the diary.'

The evening moved onto a busy cocktail bar in Covent Garden. It was full of tourists and city workers, and we managed to get the last table. Mindy offered to buy the first round of drinks, and I offered to help her carry them back from the bar.

'I love your lip colour,' a German girl standing next to me at the bar said. 'I have been looking for a nice pink-orange lipstick for ages. Do you mind me asking where it is from?

'I can't remember; I've had it for a few years now. It's vegan.'

'What is it called? I will look for it online.'

I retrieved the lipstick from my bag. 'It's called Candy Floss,' I said and passed it to her to take a photo of the brand. She handed it back, and I dropped it on the floor. As I picked it up, a sense of déjà vu filled me. I had dropped this lipstick before.

'I hope I can find it before I return to Germany; it's for my sister back home.'

'Are you on holiday?' I asked.

'No, I have been studying for an arts degree here for three years.'

'Are you excited to go home?'

The girl hesitated before answering, 'I wasn't at first. It felt odd to think that everyone's lives would be the same as they were when I left. I have met so many new people in London and experienced so much. Then I realised that if everyone back home had done the same thing as me, then there wouldn't be anyone to go home to.'

'That's a good way of looking at it.'

'And I am now looking forward to starting my career and, how do you say in English…putting down roots.'

September, my favourite month, with its fresh, sunny days and a sense of nostalgia mixed with a feeling of change, flew past. I was well into my course, and my initial contract at Capital Canines was also due to expire. Mindy wanted to keep me on a monthly rolling contract until she had compiled her three-year business plan, after which there was a good chance she would be able to offer me a permanent role. With six months of hands-on experience, the dog grooming course, my volunteering time back in Devon and two years of a degree completed, I felt I was in a good position with my career, whatever Mindy's decision. I was almost certain I was going to stay in London, but the thought of the cottage niggled.

Mindy took me by surprise and completed her business plan much quicker than she thought and asked me to stay late one evening to discuss my position. She offered me a full-time permanent position with study support and a small pay rise.

'So, what do you think?' Mindy asked. I was surprised by my reaction—I didn't know what to say. I hadn't given the cottage much thought, but suddenly it was screaming out. I had been offered a permanent job in London with career prospects and the kindest offer to live rent-free to start up a dog grooming and walking business in Devon. I needed to be honest with Mindy—she had been good to me.

Mindy stared at me when I told her. 'You're a lucky lady. When do you need to let them know?'

'It is a fortunate position to be in, but I'm torn,' I sighed. 'They said there's no rush as the cottage will remain empty until Easter.'

'I wish I could be that flexible, Alice, but I'm afraid I can't. This is a tight business plan with little room for manoeuvre.' She closed her laptop. 'I'm sorry to push you for an answer, but I'll need to know by Monday. Have a good think over the weekend, and we'll catch up Monday morning.'

I went to Laura's straight after the meeting. 'Sorry I'm late,' I said when Laura opened her front door.

'Don't be silly. Come on in.'

Frankie and Beano danced around my legs. 'Sorry guys,' I said, 'I'm not here to see you; I'm going out for dinner with your mummy.'

London was enjoying an Indian summer, and the weather was too good not to be outside. Instead of taking a fifteen-minute Tube journey, we walked to the South Bank. We chose a small restaurant with alfresco dining on a quaint wharf where brightly painted shop and restaurant fascias adorned a long, brick wall, like a fake movie scene in Paris's Old Artist Quarter.

'I'm in a dilemma,' I said whilst perusing the menu.

'Is everything okay?' Laura asked.

'Everything's fine; it's a good dilemma, really,' I said and drifted off into a daydream, watching a police helicopter flying overhead.

'Alice,' Laura called to regain my attention. 'Well, what is it?' I told her about the two offers. She started pouring sparkling water into our glasses. 'The good thing is that whatever you decide to do, we will still get to meet up, and Frankie and Beano will still get to see you. You can't get away from them two easily.'

I took a sip of water. 'How's that?'

'If you stay in London, well, that's self-explanatory, but if you decide on Devon, we'll still see each other because Alistair and I visit our best mate, Smithy, as often as possible. Any excuse of getting out of London, even though Alistair and Smithy act like naughty schoolboys when they get together.' She rolled her eyes and smiled. 'And, if you do move back to Devon, you're more than welcome to stay with us anytime you visit London.'

'This is good news, but it doesn't help my decision.'

Laura leaned over the table and grabbed my arm. 'I know, but let's celebrate your positive dilemma with cocktails. They do an amazing one here called Fizzy Floss,' she suggested.

'What's a Fizzy Floss cocktail?'

'It's Prosecco and something else alcoholic, but the pièce de résistance is candy floss.'

'I like the sound of that.' A sign from the universe, but that didn't help me either with what to do.

After the waiter brought over the cocktails, Laura raised her glass. 'Here's to friendship and making the right decision.'

The first weekend of October remained unseasonably hot. Kate recommended spending Saturday at London Fields Lido. I stayed at hers Friday after dinner and drinks with Laura so that we could leave the flat early in the morning and make the short walk north of Bethnal Green to reach the lido before it opened at nine o'clock.

'They operate a one-in-one-out policy when it's full. I hope we've made it in time,' Kate said when we saw the crowd of people queuing outside. We joined the back of the queue, and Kate stood up on her tiptoes to do a rough head count. 'It's going to be tight, but we should get in.'

Devon's sandy beaches popped into my mind's eye, the never-ending sea and the sneaky shortcuts to the beach that only the locals knew about and not the tourists. There weren't any shortcuts for getting into the lido. 'How big is this place?'

'Fifty metres and it's heated,' Kate said.

We managed to squeeze in, and a couple behind us in the queue were the last ones allowed in before they adopted the one-out-one-in system—around twenty people were left queuing. We found a tight space to lay our towels underneath a tree overhanging the brick wall. Sunlight and shade battled between the leaves in the breeze.

Sunbathing on concrete slabs wasn't the same as lying on sand; they didn't mould to the shape of your body. Even pebble beaches allowed a little comfort compared to this. The pool was busy with people splashing around, and loud music blasted out from speakers. It wasn't relaxing enough to float, but the pool was refreshing enough for a swim, even if it meant weaving around people standing around chatting and dodging dive-bombing children.

We stayed in the lido until it was too cool to sunbathe under the tree, by which time we were hungry for some lunch. Kate suggested a walk over to Hackney's leafy village, Victoria Park. The area looked similar to Lordship Lane with its trendy pubs and trendier canopied eateries on the tree-lined street. We briefly browsed the shop window of a contemporary furniture shop and a few estate agents before heading to the chip shop—even that had a canopied front. We decided to do takeaway and sat on a nearby park bench.

'It's peaceful here,' I said before biting into my battered halloumi burger.

'This is my favourite part of London,' Kate said. 'Last summer, Fabrizio and I were going to buy that flat over there.' She pointed to a flat above a newsagent.

'How come you didn't?'

'We had a mortgage approved and put in an offer for the asking price, but the owners were on holiday and by the time they returned, they refused the offer because house values had gone up. We were already at our maximum budget and were outpriced and gazumped overnight.'

That was the moment I realised what I needed to do. There was only one realistic financial option for fulfilling my plans of starting my own business, and that was in Devon.

'If I were you,' Mindy said in our next meeting, 'I would take up that offer.'

My emotions burned in my throat. 'Would you?' Mindy nodded. 'I know it is the right decision, but it doesn't feel like it. I'm going to miss London.'

'I'll miss you. You've done a great job here, and you have helped set me up for the future. You will be brilliant at running your own business. How long have I got you for?'

'How much time do you think you'll need to find someone?'

Mindy sighed. 'Taking into account finding someone and then training them up, ideally at least six weeks.'

'That works for me. It gives me time to complete my qualification, and it would be nice to do a full year in London before returning to Devon for good.'

'That sounds like a plan to me,' Mindy said.

'I've got an idea; my friend Teagan is looking for a new job. She hasn't worked with animals before, but she loves them. She's organised and friendly. I worked with her when I first moved to London.'

'Great, can you ask her to send her C.V., and we can take it from there.'

With less than three months left in London, I intended to squeeze in as much as possible with my new friends: shows, galleries, sightseeing, historical talks and tours, pub crawls, dinner, outdoor ice skating and anything else the city had to offer.

Teagan invited me over for lunch to see her new flat in Stoke Newington, which she was renting with some friends. I wanted to tell her my news and about the job. She wanted to fill me in on work and Sean Richard—he had finally been suspended for inappropriate behaviour after a complaint by another female colleague. There was a lot to celebrate.

Stoke Newington was in North London and an area I hadn't yet explored. I needed to pre-plan the journey before making my way to Central London to catch a midday train to Teagan's from Liverpool Street. On the way to Liverpool

Street, the driver announced that due to security concerns, we wouldn't be stopping at Shoreditch High Street—which is where I planned to change. I adapted my plan to get to Liverpool Street. When the Tube train pulled into the station, I realised I wasn't concerned about the security issue or that there may be danger. I was just trying to catch the train on time. I had come a long way since first arriving in the city, and I was proud of that. My confidence was soaring. I had become a Londoner.

The train left Liverpool Street Station as scheduled and was due to arrive at Stoke Newington at quarter past twelve. Teagan was going to meet me there, but there was another delay. This time, there was a trespasser on the track.

I called Teagan. 'We're being held between stations. We've just left Hackney Downs.'

'Get off at the next station,' she said, 'and I'll walk down and meet you there.'

'Okay, what's the next station called?'

'Rectory Road,' Teagan said as the train started to move. 'Once you get there, start walking up Rectory Road, and we'll bump into each other somewhere along there.'

I disembarked at the station and checked on my phone to find Rectory Road. It wasn't easy to tell amongst the flats and houses if I was already on that road. It was easy enough to find on the screen: exit right from the station and turn right at the crossroad junction. I zoomed out to get an idea of how long Rectory Road was, but as I did that, someone dressed all in black with their hood pulled up and a scarf wrapped around their face with only their eyes on view rode up from behind and tried snatching my phone from my hand. It all happened quickly, but it seemed to happen in slow motion, like a dream where you try running away but get nowhere fast. I watched as the gloved hand lifted my phone from my left hand, but somehow, it fell back down into place, and then everything sped back up as though pressing a fast-forward button. The mugger rode away on their BMX. They stopped and looked back but then rode off down a narrow alleyway. I continued walking towards Rectory Road and chuckled to myself that I had survived a mugging.

'You're probably in shock,' Teagan said after I told her what happened. 'My flat isn't far from here. As soon as we get in, you should call the police.'

Within minutes of arriving at Teagan's flat, two plain-clothed officers knocked on the door. First, they asked questions about the incident, and then they asked if I was willing to ride in the back of their unmarked police car to help find and identify the mugger. I agreed. Whilst driving around, the officer in the passenger seat took my details. After twenty minutes, and with no success in locating the mugger, they returned me to Teagan's flat before disappearing as quickly as the mugger. I left Teagan's flat earlier than planned. I wanted to get home before it was dark, and instead of getting the train, I took buses—for the first time in a long time, I ensured my bag was zipped up, and I kept a watchful eye on everyone as they boarded.

I started feeling unwell by the middle of the following week. Lethargy and an achy body made me think that the flu was on its way to get me. But nothing came, and yet the symptoms remained. Chloe and Beth took turns making me dinner whilst I rested in bed the following weekend.

'I don't think you've got the flu,' Chloe said as she handed me a plate of dinner. 'Mum's a nurse and she said that in stressful or dangerous situations, your body releases fight or flight chemicals, and if you don't release them from your body—by crying, getting angry, or shouting, they fester in your system and can make you ill.'

'So your mum thinks I'm feeling like this because I didn't react after the mugging?'

Chloe sat down on the bed. 'She does and she said you need to keep resting.'

I smiled. 'Thank you. I already feel better by knowing what this is.'

Chloe hugged me. I felt emotional for feeling unwell. I was going to miss her, and because my life was torn in two whilst waiting for my time in London to come to a close.

By the time December arrived, my twelfth and final month in London felt too soon. It had been the best year of my life in such a long time.

Before leaving for good, I booked a coach ticket back to Plymouth for New Year's Day. I hired a fancy dress costume for Laura and Alistair's New Year's Eve party, where they planned to introduce me to their best man, Smithy. They disguised their obvious matchmaking under the guise of him being a vet—he would be a great contact for my business back in Devon, they said. I had to sift through numerous online applicants for my room, move back in with Kate and Fabrizio on Christmas Eve, arrange leaving drinks at work, arrange leaving drinks with my London friends, complete coursework and sit the final exam on my course. There was also final sightseeing of the year to squeeze in: the changing of the guards at Buckingham Palace, visit Hampton Court Palace and go to a silent disco at the Natural History Museum.

It was an emotional morning on Christmas Eve, my last hours living in the flat. All three of us were up early. Chloe was getting ready to travel back to her parents for Christmas, Beth had to go to work, and I had to pack. Beth left the flat first, and the three of us had a group hug but instead of feeling emotional, I felt hopeful for the future. When Chloe left, we chose not to say goodbye because we would see each other soon. She wanted to visit Devon as soon as I was settled in.

Kate arrived mid-morning to help me with my belongings. I packed up everything from my bedroom, but when I checked the lounge and kitchen for my items, it was a blur remembering what was mine and what belonged to the flat: a teapot, a gold cushion in the lounge, and a London mug. It was hard to see where my life began and the flat finished. I packed the mug and left the other bits.

The flat felt empty and instantly no longer felt like home by the time I was ready to leave. We piled up all my belongings on the path, and then I closed the front door for the final time.

CHAPTER 28

Now

I left Kate and Fabrizio's flat for the final time. It was New Year's Eve, and I was dressed in my fancy dress costume as a scrubs doctor. Kate offered to help me with my bags, but I declined. I could do it on my own just as I did when I arrived in London a year ago tomorrow. I was the first to arrive at Laura and Alistair's house, and I left my belongings in the spare room that I was staying in that night. I'm not sure who was more excited to see each other, Frankie and Beano or me.

Laura introduced the other guests as they arrived.

'That's Suzie and Matt.' Laura pointed to a blonde-haired couple dressed as a caveman and woman. 'The three of us went to uni together.' Alistair came over and topped up our glasses with Prosecco. 'The couple over there dressed as a vampire and a witch are our neighbours, Diane and Rupert, and those girls there, the Spice Girls minus Posh and Ginger, are from work. Come on, I'll introduce you.'

The party got busy quickly. Mindy and her partner came but only stayed for one drink because they had another party to go to. We waved them off from the front door and then Laura grabbed my arm in excitement. 'He should be here anytime now!'

Laura had mentioned Smithy a few times once she knew I was returning to Devon. He was single. A vet was a good contact to have, but my focus was establishing my business, and I couldn't risk anything or anyone jeopardising that.

'It will be nice to meet him,' I said.

Alistair passed by, and Laura linked her arm to his. 'Have you heard from Smithy? He should be here by now.'

'He texted me about ten minutes ago to say he can't make it. He's got man flu, and even though he's dosed up, he still feels awful.'

'Why didn't you say before, darling?' Laura sounded more disappointed than I was. 'When is he going back to Devon?'

'On the second. I said we'll pop over to see him at his parents' place tomorrow if he's feeling up to it.'

'I'm sure we'll get to meet each other when you guys visit Devon,' I said.

'Exactly, which means we'll have to visit Devon sooner rather than later.' Laura squeezed my arm again.

My alarm woke me at quarter past six, after only four hours of sleep. I crept around the house trying not to wake anyone, and then made the short walk to Victoria Coach Station. The coach departed on time, and as it left, it stopped at a red light. I looked out of the window and noticed a single snowflake falling from the sky. What a difference a year made. This time last year, I left Devon searching for something, and today, I was returning back to my future. When I arrived in the capital three hundred and sixty-five days ago, I was like a deep wound roughly sewn together after reoccurring infections. The stitches tore and unravelled several times during this year, but I had managed to stitch myself back together and now I was fully repaired. The lights turned green, and the coach continued onwards. I pulled my coat over me like a blanket, and I fell asleep before the coach crossed over the Thames. I didn't wake up until the driver announced our arrival at Plymouth Bus Station.

Winter soon passed and as the birds sang louder, enticing buds from their dormant winter state to burst into colour and welcome the bees, my business, Scrub and Stroll, already had regular clients. Nita welcomed me as a volunteer at the rescue centre every other Sunday morning. I registered to take in foster pets for women escaping abusive relationships. I signed up to complete the final year of my degree on a part-time basis starting in September.

Chloe had visited in February and at the start of April and was coming back for a week in the summer. Teagan and I had plans to meet halfway in Bristol for a day, Nikki had been in contact regularly, and Mindy became my unofficial business mentor. Daisy and I caught up at least once a week.

'I'm so glad you're in today, Alice,' Nita said as I arrived for a Sunday morning shift. 'One of the kennel assistants will be in late because their car has broken down, and the duty vet had to dash off because his wife has gone into labour ten days early.'

'Is anyone coming in to cover the vet?' I asked, but before Nita could reply, the cordless phone hanging from her belt rang.

She removed the phone from her belt. 'We've got a locum vet coming in,' she squeezed in before answering the phone. She covered the receiver with her hand and whispered, 'He should be here in ten minutes.'

The vet arrived by the time I returned from the first dog walk—there was a car parked in the allocated vet's space. I didn't see him when I collected the next dog for their morning walk. The final dog to go out was a retired greyhound called Jazz, who had the sweetest temperament. I had to keep reminding myself that I didn't have a favourite, but there was something about her. If my business was established and my life more settled, I would have adopted her the first time I saw her.

'Is the vet still doing the rounds?' I asked Nita when Jazz and I returned from her walk. 'She started limping on the way back.'

'I think he's finishing up,' Nita said, and the phone rang again.

I returned Jazz to her kennel and hurried around the centre to find the vet before he left.

I knocked on the men's changing rooms, but there was no answer. I checked the office, but it was empty, as was the staffroom. I hurried past the kennels, but there was still no sign of him. I eventually caught up with him in the medication room. He was filling out a form when I walked in.

'Excuse me, I assume you're the vet?' He looked up and nodded. 'Could you take a look at Jazz, I mean the blue brindle greyhound in kennel four? She started limping during her walk.'

'Sure,' he said and carried on with the form. I didn't leave the medical room because I was unsure if he needed me to show him to the kennel. 'Thank you,' he said, glancing back up. 'I'll be able to find kennel four.' He smiled and carried on with the form. I left the room and collected my belongings before heading to reception to sign out.

'What are you staring at?' Nita asked as I looked at a name in the visitor book.

'That name looks familiar.'

Nita walked over and looked at the name I was pointing to. 'Tom Appleshaw,' she read it aloud. 'He's the vet.'

'I can't think where I know that name from.' His face wasn't familiar, but after seeing so many faces in London, that was no surprise.

Nita winked at me. 'Surely you'd remember a handsome face like that.'

I blushed. 'I'm off. Can you call me to let me know how Jazz is?'

'Of course,' she said, smiling.

I pushed the door open. 'Don't forget!'

Nita called later that day to inform me that Jazz was fine. She had torn her dewclaw, and the vet clipped it and bandaged her up.

'Thanks for letting me know,' I said.

'You *do* know him,' Nita teased.

'Who?'

She laughed. 'Tom, the vet.'

'Do I? How do you know that?'

'We were chatting when he signed out, and he asked if you still worked at that recruitment agency in Plymouth. He said he registered there when he first moved to the area.'

'That's a time in my life I try not to think about.'

'He said he hoped you hadn't recognised him earlier.'

'Why?'

'He sent you flowers, but you never acknowledged them. He assumed you didn't like him in that way. I think he was embarrassed.'

'Flowers?' I racked my brain, trying to piece together the information. 'We are talking a long time ago, Nita. Are you sure he means me?'

'Oh, yes. He blushed when I asked what he thought of you now. I think you've still got an admirer.'

I woke up during the night thinking about flowers. *The shoebox*, I thought and jumped out of bed. I hurried into the spare room in the dark and switched on the light before jumping up onto the bed to reach the top of the wardrobe. The shoebox contained memorabilia from my past: school photos, birthday cards, a champagne cork from a bottle my grandparents gave to me on my eighteenth birthday, a flower lei Tobias sent me from Hawaii, the tornado drawing from my counselling session, and silly letters between Daisy and I from university. I picked up the lei and held it to my heart for a moment before looking through the box.

I kept searching and eventually tipped the box upside down, and everything left inside fell onto the bed. Some of the photos and cards landed face up and others face down. I spread the pile out like a deck of cards and scanned over it all, but I still couldn't find what I was looking for. I picked up one card at a time, opened it and shook it to check if anything was caught inside. The more I searched, the less convinced I was that I was going to find it but then something fell out of a twenty-first birthday card from my colleagues at the recruitment agency. It landed on the floor.

The back of a message card stared up at me. I stared back at the image of a pink bouquet before reaching down to pick it up to read the other side.

Happy 21st birthday.

Thanks for your help this week and for taking the time to return the passport x

I slid off the bed and sat on the floor. I assumed Max had sent the flowers; he took credit for them, but they weren't from him. They were from Tom. Tom had sent them.

'We've got the same birthday,' I said to Nita before she had the chance to say hello when I called her.

Nita smiled. 'I know. He told me.'

'He remembers that?'

'Yep. He said he felt foolish because he didn't realise you and Maxwell were together at the time.'

'We weren't, not at the time he sent the flowers.'

'He said he bumped into Maxwell at the bar the night you were out celebrating your birthday, and he told him you were together.'

'He must think I'm rude for not thanking him for the flowers and for not recognising him the other day.'

'He's going to the village fete on Bank Holiday Monday. I could ask if he has a spare hour to volunteer on the stall at the same time as you.'

I blushed. 'No, please don't—that will look obvious.'

After the phone call, I burst into tears at the frustration of knowing Maxwell had been manipulating my life before we even got together.

A text message interrupted my tears; it was from Laura.

Good news! We've managed to get a last-minute booking for the first weekend in May. Will forward details by email so you can find the cottage. We're having a BBQ Saturday evening so just bring yourself and perhaps a bottle… or two. Can't wait to see you xx.
P.S. Alistair has invited Smithy… so make sure you've got some animal questions up your sleeve ;-)

I went for a sea swim after my final appointment on Saturday morning and then made my way over to Laura and Alistair's cottage. It was hot and felt more like mid-summer than early May. Feathery clouds sat delicately in the sky, and a warm breeze carried the scent of the sweet freshness of late spring. It was the ideal weather for a barbecue, and the forecast predicted the same weather all weekend, which was great news for the village fete. Laura and I had spoken a handful of times since I left London and sent regular text messages too, but I didn't tell her about Tom. She was so excited about setting me up with Smithy that it had to be something I told her about in person. Today would have been the ideal time to speak to her. I would like her advice on what to say to Tom, but with Smithy there, it wouldn't feel right asking.

Frankie and Beano greeted me first at the cottage, followed by Alistair. 'You're looking well,' Alistair said when he answered the door. 'Devon suits you.'

'Thanks, Alistair. It was the right decision to move back,' I said as Frankie and Beano danced around my legs. I followed Alistair to the kitchen, where we found Laura chopping up cucumber and mint for her homemade cocktails.

We hugged and squealed with excitement.

Alistair got a couple of beers from the fridge. 'I'll leave you two to it.' He went into the garden.

Laura handed me a cocktail. 'Smithy's here.'

I smiled. 'So, are you going to give me the grand tour?'

Laura showed me around the cottage with its wonky staircase and low ceilings, and then we returned to the kitchen.

I decided that I needed to tell her about Tom after all, but then her mobile rang. 'It's Mum, I've just got to take this.'

I topped up our glasses and waited for Laura to return. Outside, barbecue smoke blanketed the far side of the garden, denying me the opportunity to take a sneaky look at their best man. Tom popped into my thoughts, and my stomach flipped with eager anticipation of seeing him in less than forty-eight hours. Memories of the day we met sprung to my mind. It was the day he registered at the agency. He was polite and slightly shy, but there was a connection between us. I wish I had taken notice of that and not been fooled by Maxwell. I felt impatient, wanting to explain myself to him. But then it dawned on me that I knew nothing about his situation. Did he have a girlfriend? Was he married? He didn't wear a wedding ring, but most people working with animals didn't wear jewellery. Surely he would have mentioned something to Nita?

Laura returned to the kitchen. 'Everything's fine.'

'With who?'

'With Mum; that's who I was just talking to.'

I shook my head. 'Oh, yes, sorry.'

'Are you okay?'

'Yes, I'm fine, just a little bit tired from work,' I said. My courage to tell her about Tom disappeared. I couldn't say something right before she introduced me to the man she had been trying to set me up with for months. 'Come on, this cocktail will perk you up,' she said and squeezed my arm. 'Let's go into the garden so you can finally meet Smithy.'

The BBQ smoke was thick, like a stage curtain offering anticipation of what was hidden behind it. Laura burst through the smoke, and I followed. It caught the back of my throat, making me cough and squint. My eyes started stinging. *What an entrance*, I thought as two figures became clearer upwind of the smoke.

'Smithy,' Laura managed to say in between coughing, 'this is Alice and Alice, this is…'

'Tom!' I blurted out.

'You know each other?' Laura and Alistair said at the same time.

'Kind of,' Tom said.

I smiled at Tom. 'We bumped into each other the other day. I'm sorry for not recognising you from the recruitment agency.'

Tom took a swig of his beer. 'That was a long time ago.' It was hard to tell if he was pooh-poohing the acquaintance or if he was saying that because it really was such a long time ago.

'It was ten years next month, in fact,' I said.

He asked how I ended up in London, and Laura slowly backed away. Tom (I couldn't get used to Smithy) already knew how Laura became friends with Frankie and Beano's dog walker. He told me how well his veterinary practice was going.

'Why are you called Smithy?'

'Alistair came up with it when we first met at uni; it's something to do with apples and my surname, I think.' He smiled, and my heart danced. 'We called him Winger, but no one can remember why, and luckily for him, it hasn't stuck.'

After eating, Tom and I cleared the table. He loaded the dishwasher whilst I made a pot of tea.

'Are you still in touch with Maxwell?' Tom asked.

'No, not for a long time.' *Not long enough*, I wanted to say.

'I've heard from him a few times over the years trying to get business. I think he's on his third attempt at running a recruitment agency. I don't trust him, and I would never do business with him,' Tom said. 'There's a bad vibe about him,' he added as he turned on the dishwasher. He turned and looked at me. 'Sorry, I hope I haven't offended you?'

'Not at all,' I said. 'I wish I was observant like you.' Tom looked at me. 'It's me that owes you an apology,' I said, twiddling the teabag string around my finger, 'a long overdue apology.'

Tom walked towards me. He was close enough that the heat of his body penetrated mine. 'What for?'

I looked down. 'For not thanking you for the flowers.'

'Nita told you?'

I nodded and blushed before explaining what happened. 'So, after all this time, *thank you* for the flowers,' I smiled at him. 'Can we start afresh?'

'That sounds good to me,' Tom said and raised an empty mug to toast to new beginnings.

'There's one more thing,' I said. My hands were clammy, my mouth dry, and my heart was beating so hard that strands of my hair resting close to my chest pulsated with each beat. We had lost out on ten years of opportunity, and I didn't want to waste any more time. 'Would you like to go for a drink sometime for a proper catch-up?'

'I'd love to,' he paused, 'but I've got a new female in my life, so I can't commit to too many plans at the moment. She's recently moved in with me, and we're still adapting to living together.'

My heart fell from my chest. *Why didn't Laura or Alistair know about this female? I thought they were all best friends?* I swallowed hard. 'Ignore what I said.'

Tom looked happy. 'I was thinking of bringing her along to the village fete tomorrow.'

'That's…that's a nice idea.'

'I'm sure she'd love to see you.'

'Thank you. It's always nice to meet someone new.'

Tom laughed. 'You already know her.'

'Do I?'

'Yes, you introduced us recently.'

'Nita?'

He laughed again. 'No, not Nita, but you're getting warmer.' He held onto my arms.

I looked up at him. 'I can't think who it could be.'

'I think you're as fond of her as I am.'

'Am I?'

He nodded. 'Yes, you are. Jazz will be excited to see you.'

Relief and happiness danced around my soul. I smiled, 'You're right, I am very fond of Jazz. When did you adopt her?

'I fell in love with her the day I looked at her paw.'

My heart swelled. 'Well then, I'd love to see you both tomorrow. Where shall I meet you?'

Tom smiled. 'How about by the candy floss stand?'

ACKNOWLEDGEMENTS

Firstly, thank you to my friends and families who read and listened to snippets of my work and for your patience, belief and encouragement that my imagination made some sense to others. A special thank you to Keen for your support and for sense-checking my work.

Also, I am grateful for the courses, tutors, free online material and books available for people like me with minimal writing experience. Thank goodness for these services that helped begin to educate this late-comer. A special thank you to the City Lit tutor for your generosity in reading a poorly written first chapter in your free time. Also, for making me aware of needing a higher perspective to help show my story.

This section would not be complete without a shout-out to my fellow 2019 Writing Retr-eaters. Thank you to Kath and Jane for arranging the writing residential. It was a memorable week, not to mention the delicious food!

Finally, to Estelle and the team at TAUK Publishing, your service was just what I needed. I don't know how I would have gotten over the final hurdle without your hand-holding. Thank you for your knowledge, advice and for helping me get my novel over the finishing line.

Thank you to everyone else who has helped me to reach this point.

AUTHOR BIO

Erika Kyles started to learn to write while drafting her debut novel. It took her over thirteen years, from jotting down ideas on sticky notes, attending numerous courses, applying new skills and editing multiple drafts to self-publish her work. Her determination comes from the hope of helping others with their self-worth.

Social Media

Instagram: @for_fates_sake

This is how my writing journey began: one Sticky Note step at a time.

CHARITIES

Victim Support:

We are dedicated to supporting people affected by crime and traumatic incidents in England and Wales.

"Controlling or coercive behaviour is now a criminal offence under the Serious Crime Act 2015."

www.victimsupport.org.uk

Call on 08 08 16 89 111

Refuge:

Refuge is the largest domestic abuse organisation in the UK.

www.nationaldahelpline.org.uk

www.refuge.org.uk

Call free, 24/7 on 0808 2000 247

Women's Aid:

Women's Aid is the national charity working to end domestic abuse against women and children.

www.womensaid.org.uk

helpline@womensaid.org.uk

Online chat

Samaritans:

We're here to listen, no judgement, no pressure, and help you work through what's on your mind. We'll never tell you what to do.

www.samaritans.org

jo@samaritans.org

Call any time, day or night, 365 days a year - 116 123

British Association for Counselling and Psychotherapy:

…we champion the counselling professions

as a viable, and increasingly evidence-based choice for people. We know counselling works.

www.bacp.co.uk/search/Therapists

bacp@bacp.co.uk

Call Monday-Friday, 10am to 4pm - 01455 883300

Printed in Great Britain
by Amazon

38615413R00227